FORTY YEARS IN A DAY

a novel

FORTY YEARS IN A DAY

Mona Rodriguez and Dianne Vigorito

Second Edition
ISBN-13: 978-1-54303-405-9
ISBN-10: 1543034055

1. Fiction / Historical
2. Fiction / Sagas
3. Fiction

www.FORTYYEARSINADAY.com

DEDICATION

This book is dedicated to our family and the millions they mirror.

ACKNOWLEDGMENTS

Many thanks to the Ellis Island Immigration Museum and the Lower East Side Tenement Museum for their wealth of information. We are forever grateful to our family for having the prudence to share their stories. Our love and appreciation to our husbands and sons for their encouragement and support, and to all of those who gave us constructive feedback throughout our journey.

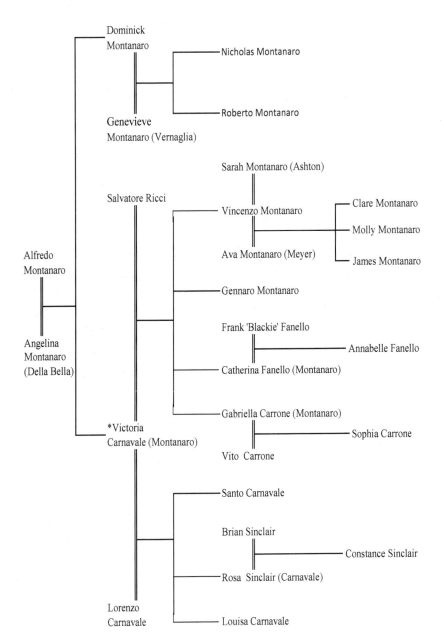

* Victoria Montanaro used her maiden name when she came to America in 1906.
When she married Lorenzo Carnavale in America, she took his surname.

———◆●◆———

Every person has a unique recollection
of his or her childhood.

Distinct visions pop into your head
when you remember events or hear stories
about growing up.

A smell, a taste, or a sound can trigger a glimpse
of the past that flutters through your mind.

The littlest things can prompt vivid
memories that can escort you on a personal
journey back in time.

———◆●◆———

PROLOGUE
New York, 1991

For me, it has always been a challenge to give a gift of distinction, a gift whose relevance and usefulness far outlasts the occasion, but today was different. Today I had wrapped my gift with ribbons I hoped would be forever tied to my father's heart. He had reached a major milestone in his life that deserved to be commemorated— it was his ninetieth birthday. My thoughts danced with anticipation, knowing that I would be sharing this experience with him. I planned to take him on a special outing—one I imagined would be a passage through time for both of us.

We sat in silence as the ferry glided across the Hudson River. Memories flooded my mind of this man who lived every day of his life with such passion. I allowed myself the opportunity to appreciate his presence, to reflect on my father, to see life through his eyes. I was filled with admiration for all he had accomplished and for all the wisdom he possessed; not the wisdom attained by academics, but the wisdom that can only be acquired by living a lifetime.

We arrived early that October morning—I wanted to spend the whole day. Ellis Island had recently reopened its doors to visitors after many years of eerie silence. A tribute to generations of human spirit had been memorialized, and its interior exploded with thousands of personal stories of hardship and hope. Slowly, we wandered through each room, absorbing all that was presented. As I scanned the multitude of haunting faces that lined the walls, I realized my father's could have been any one of the forlorn expressions that mirrored the disquietude of an era. I tried to comprehend the magnitude of their struggle and courage, so unlike the life I had been living, but it must have been too real for my father, his silence was unsettling. Maybe the memories were too painful for him; maybe too many years had passed and he could not remember; maybe he did not want to remember.

The morning drifted by, awakening a plethora of emotions within me, but my father looked weary, and I suggested we take a break. Outside, in the crisp autumn air, we rested on a bench overlooking the river—the welcomed warmth of the sun somewhat melting the chilling reality we had just beheld.

To ease the silence, I commented on the weather, saying, "It's a beautiful day."

My father simply replied, "Clare, every day you're alive is a beautiful day."

Throughout his life, the phrase "it's a beautiful day" had become his mantra. I had always thought of it as cordial chitchat used to fill the uncomfortable gaps of silence in conversations, but only now did I comprehend the depth of his penetrating words. As if I had been sleepwalking through my years, my eyes opened wider, and I sat up straighter. His profound statement made me realize I do not respect the fragility of each day, the simplest pleasures in life, every precious moment. Life is a gift, and every day is an opportunity to revel in its glory.

As though seeing it for the first time, my father, Vincenzo Montanaro, stared transfixed at the Statue of

Liberty that stood magnificently before us, her presence so significant, his expression just as compelling. Witnessing the depth of emotion so apparent on his face, my curiosity had piqued. I wished I could snuggle inside his thoughts and mimeograph his memories. There were many questions about his journey to America and our family, but I wondered if he was willing or able to fill in the pieces of the puzzle that made up their lives. He was the sole surviving member and the only one who could escort me across the bridge to their past. Tenderly, I gazed into his eyes and asked him what he remembered.

Suddenly, on this still day, a gust of wind swirled around us, rustling the leaves on the trees, and an unexpected chill permeated the air. Had I not known better, I would have thought that the ghosts of the past had just descended upon him to refuel his mind. Gently, he took my hand in his—its size dwarfed mine. Shaking his head insistently, he chuckled and said he remembered it all as if it were yesterday. He exclaimed it was befitting to start his story at the very beginning—the one he had read in his mother's journal revealing the circumstances that forced her to escape from Italy and come to America. When he said his mother's name, Victoria, it was as if he were uttering a synonym for a saint. His eyes stared mysteriously into the distance; his mind focused on the past; his words echoed another time, another place, as he recalled the details with colorful lucidity, and I unconsciously slipped into an unfamiliar world and envisioned I was there.

CHAPTER 1

Caivano, Italy, 1906

Dusk refused to abate the heat of the day filtering in with Alfredo as he lumbered through the door. The usual carafe of wine on the table would allay his aches for the night, but as Angelina added ingredients to the simmering pot, she wished there was one that could numb the wound she was about to inflict.

She waited for her husband to drain his glass and pour himself another. He smiled weakly at her from his chair at the table. Tonight he seemed especially tired. By now he was usually sharing the events of his day.

Removing his spectacles, he sluggishly rubbed his eyes with the tips of his fingers. "Dinner smells good," he said.

Angelina turned her head to look at him and forced a smile. "It'll be a few more minutes," she said, wondering whether she should tell him now or wait until after they ate. Pulling the handkerchief from the sleeve of her blouse, she blotted the beads of sweat from her forehead. Her nerves were getting the best of her, and she felt the spoon in her hand shaking. It had to be done now, she decided. "How was your day?" she asked. At least it was a start.

He frowned. "One of our mares fell ill, and I had to put her down. She was one of our best, too," he said, scratching the bald spot on the top of his head.

Angelina instantly regretted she had asked, knowing she was about to make his bad day worse. Hopefully, the wine had soothed him somewhat. Walking over to the table, she wiped her palms on her apron. "Alfredo, I have something very difficult to tell you. I want you to know that I thought long and hard about this, and I believe it was the right thing to do."

"Then why do you sound so unconvinced?" He lifted his eyebrows and raised his hand along with the question.

She held on to the back of a chair for support and looked down at the table to avert his gaze. Her heart was pounding hard inside her chest, and she took a few deep breaths, trying to calm down. "There's no easy way to tell you this," she finally said.

"What is it, Angelina?" he said, heaving a sigh of slight impatience.

"I gave Victoria our savings so she could go to America and be with Dominick. She'll be safe with her brother. He'll take care of them." As she spoke she saw her husband's face twist into a knot of disbelief and rage, and panic descended upon her like darkness on a moonless night. "She was miserable. She was so unhappy…and the children. Believe me, Alfredo, it's the only way they could get away from him."

Slamming his hand to his chest, he demanded, "Where are they?"

"They left before dawn."

"Tell me this isn't true!" His voice grew louder, and his skin flushed crimson. "What were you thinking? You should've come to me!" His bulging eyes bore into her. "Damn it, Angelina! Didn't you think how this would affect all of us?"

Overwhelmed by her own guilt and loss, Angelina had no reply and looked away.

Jumping to his feet, Alfredo bounded over to the mattress and threw up its corner, exposing the empty spot where their coins had been hidden. Spinning around, he shoved her with both hands, and she caught the bottom of her skirt with the heel of her boot as she stumbled backward. Regaining her footing, she stood rigid and took a slow, ragged breath. She realized her betrayal had warranted his harsh reaction, but the words that followed struck her harder.

"How could you have disrespected me this way? What's wrong with you? I've lost my family! I've lost everything!" Glaring down at the floor, he brusquely paced back and forth. "My God, there's nothing left," he added with an abandon Angelina had never heard before.

"Please, don't say that," she pleaded, her body quivering along with her voice. "Someday they'll come back, or maybe we'll go there."

"What are the chances of that? Don't you understand, woman, we'll never see them again! How can I ever forgive you for this?"

Angelina clasped her hands over her ears, attempting to shut out his irrefutable words, his consummate anger.

Alfredo collapsed onto the edge of their bed. He sat hunched over and covered his face with his hands, catching the tears that poured from his heart, and his agony mercilessly pierced Angelina to the core.

CHAPTER 2

Six years earlier, 1900

The sweet nectar of ripened grapes drifted through the air as Victoria walked through the vineyards toward the river with a basket of clothes balanced upon her head. A disarming inquisitiveness stirred inside her when she caught a glimpse of Salvatore's thick, dark hair and smooth, olive skin glistening in the afternoon sun. The muscles on his arms and back flexed as he heaved the heavy logs onto a cart.

Victoria knew little about the boy she was admiring and found herself wondering why words had never passed between them. Salvatore lived on the outskirts of the village, and she was aware his family worked the lumber mill. It was rumored that his mother had taken her own life many years ago, but Victoria did not pay it much heed until now. Watching him, she suddenly felt a twinge of compassion and decided to question her father that evening.

———◆◆◆———

Relaxing at the end of the day, Papa and her brother, Dominick, sat at the table sipping wine, while Mama juggled the well-worn pots and utensils that hung like a frame around the hearth's perimeter. Victoria and her sister-in-law, Genevieve, watched Angelina tend to the blackened cauldron suspended above the flames. The fragrant aroma of its contents mingled with the air, tantalizing Victoria with an assortment of the earth's finest treasures. She could feel the golden warmth sautéing in her stomach—a fusion of flavors garnished with her mother's tenderness.

Placing bowls on the table, Victoria nonchalantly asked, "Papa, what happened to Salvatore Ricci's mother?"

Alfredo looked up at her. The autumn air was warm and still, and he swiped the sweat from his brow with the back of his hand. "Life is more difficult for some than for others, my child," he finally said.

His abbreviated explanation did not appease Victoria. "What do you mean? Tell me, I want to know."

"It's complicated. Let's just say a good woman left us before the Lord was ready for her."

"Wasn't she married to your cousin Francis?" she asked.

"Francis is my second cousin, but we no longer speak of him in this house."

Angelina turned from the hearth to face her husband. "Alfredo, maybe it's time you told them what happened with Francis."

Victoria glanced at her brother curiously, and he shrugged his shoulders, looking just as confused.

Alfredo bent over and struck a match on the wood floor and lit his pipe. "Francis and I haven't spoken for years. He thought his personal life was none of my concern, and he reacted with fists rather than words." He took a drag on his pipe and watched the smoke as he exhaled. "You have to understand, Francis is as hard as the wood he mills. With a heavy hand, he sends his children home each evening covered in sawdust and craving a sliver of praise or affection." He paused. "The sad truth is that Josephina took her own life to escape the severity of the husband who broke her spirit, leaving behind her six children." His voice was soft, and he shook his head as he spoke. "It was a sad day indeed, not only for her family, but for much of the village. There are some that still look down upon her for what she did. I say only God can judge us."

Genevieve walked over to Dominick. He slipped his arm around her waist and pulled her close as Victoria muttered grimly, "How awful."

Eyeing Victoria, Alfredo asked, "Why this sudden interest?"

"I saw Salvatore working at the mill today, and I was just wondering…"

In a firm tone, Alfredo insisted, "Victoria, I want you to stay away from him."

She was taken aback by his curt reply. "Why?"

With his elbow resting on the arm of his chair, he pointed his finger in the air as he spoke. "Although I have pity for him, his childhood has been filled with the kind of grief that stirs the soul and torments the mind."

Standing at the opposite end of the table, Victoria opined, "But, Papa, maybe he could use a friend."

"Then let him look elsewhere for his friends."

She straightened her back. "That's unkind. I'm fourteen and—"

"And nothing! Salvatore is a man at eighteen, and you're merely a child."

Unnerved to think her father still considered her a child, Victoria's eyes grew wide as she swallowed the judgment.

Turning to his son, Alfredo asked, "Did you finish loading the barrels so everything's ready for the morning?"

"It's all done," Dominick said.

Victoria slumped into her chair with her eyes still wide on her father and her frustration festering inside, and dinner began in an awkward silence.

Now it made sense to Victoria why Salvatore's family kept to themselves. She thought that it was unfair the children had been left without a mother and were living with a father who was so cruel. She was surprised her father was so insensitive. His disagreement with Francis should have no reflection on his children. Her father claimed that God was the only judge, but Alfredo had already judged Salvatore without even giving him a chance.

Victoria had lost her appetite but forced herself to eat. Her stomach felt queasy, and she declined the ladleful of stewed pears her mother offered for dessert. She wondered if Salvatore was having dessert, she wondered who cooked him his meals.

When everyone had finished, she and Genevieve cleared the plates while Angelina filled the basin with the kettle of warm water that was hanging above the hearth. It was Victoria's turn to wash, and Genevieve picked up the towel to dry.

"That's so sad what Papa just told us," Victoria said to Genevieve, keeping her voice low.

"Francis must be a horrible man. I feel sorry for his children," Genevieve said.

Victoria turned around to look at her mother. "Did you know Josephine?" she asked.

"Not that well. She was a quiet woman...kept to herself. It was heartbreaking what happened." Angelina sighed. "I'll never forget the look on her children's faces when she was laid to rest. It was all so sad." She took the dried pot from Genevieve, hung it on a hook by the fire, and turned back around. "Papa didn't want to go to her funeral because of Francis, but I told him that he should out of respect for Josephine." They worked together in silence until Angelina put the last of the cleaned dishes on the shelf and broke the lull. "Let's sit down now," she said.

Alfredo removed the Bible from the sideboard near the cottage's entrance. It was their most treasured possession. It guided their family with lessons of faith, and he taught Victoria and Dominick how to read and write its sacred words. Gently carrying it in the palms of his hands, he placed it on the table and sat down. He carefully opened the book—its edges frayed and pages brittle—and started his story in an animated flare. "The sun beat down on the thousands upon thousands of people in the desert who were starving, and they begged Jesus for help. He told his disciples to gather food, and he took the five loaves of bread and two fish and asked God for a miracle. He ordered his disciples to feed the masses, and everyone sat and ate their meal in awe until their stomachs were filled and..." As Alfredo spoke, he twisted the stiff hairs of his arched mustache with his fingers as if conjuring the scene. In the glow of the candlelight, his weathered skin was thick and creased, and his round, blue eyes were encircled with wisdom.

Normally, Victoria absorbed his every word, the conviction of his tone, and the resoluteness of his expression. Tonight, however, she was having trouble concentrating on her father's voice. For the first time, she was listening to the beat of her own heart.

When Alfredo ended the parable, he made the sign of the cross before closing the book. "Tomorrow's going to be a long day, and we should all get our rest."

Victoria was the one to always pout a protest and plead for more, but this evening she was relieved to be alone with her thoughts.

"Genevieve and I will be back at sun up," Dominick said to his father as he rose from the table. "Good night, Mama. Dinner was delicious." Angelina held out her cheek, and Dominick affectionately planted a kiss next to the smile on her face. "Good night, sis," he called out.

"See you in the morning," Genevieve said. Following her husband out the door, she gave Victoria a sympathetic smile and her eyes flashed concern.

Victoria felt a sudden rush of gratitude. Genevieve had sensed her interest in Salvatore was more than a passing breeze; of that she was certain. Her sister-in-law had grown up just over the hill, and she was Victoria's best friend prior to becoming Dominick's wife. Over the years, she and Genevieve had developed a silent language only they had the power to discern.

Yawning, Victoria blew a kiss in her parents' direction and mumbled a weak, "Good night." She climbed the ladder to the loft and quickly changed into her nightdress. Lying down on the feathered mattress, she haphazardly covered herself with a quilt—so worn, the designs of her great-grandmother had long since faded—and turned on her side. Alfredo blew out the last of the candles dotting the cottage's interior, causing darkness to descend. Below, her parents' bed rested on a timbered frame as intricately molded as the people it lulled, while Victoria lay wide-eyed above them, eager for the morning to come, eager to see Salvatore again.

CHAPTER 3

When the leaves changed shade and sprinkled the ground with their multicolored brilliance, it signified the end of the harvest season and the beginning of a well-deserved celebration. The Grape Feast was an annual tradition that dated back further than anyone could remember. It was a reprieve from the toil of the last six months, cultivating and harvesting the fields and vineyards. The custom brought with it the entire village, everyone ready to participate in the merriment.

While her mother buttoned the back of Victoria's blouse, they heard the clanging of the church bells in the distance, signaling the commencement of the feast and the highlight of their year. Victoria felt the excitement thickening in the air and quickened her pace as she whisked a brush through her unruly hair, the taut of the red ringlets bouncing back into curls.

"Hurry, dear," Angelina urged. "Dominick and Genevieve are waiting outside with your father. The procession is approaching."

"I hear it, Mama!" Victoria said with breathless enthusiasm, turning to face her mother. Angelina's auburn hair was sprinkled with gray and twisted into a bun at the nape of her neck to keep her curls tame. She wore a kerchief tied under her double chin and an apron firmly secured around her rotund waist. The folds in her serene, sweet countenance rendered a semblance beyond her years; however, her ample body brimmed with youth. Using a cloth, she effortlessly lifted the cast-iron pot that was filled with rabbit stew. Dropping the brush on the table, Victoria rushed out the door and caught sight of the assembly descending the path. Led by a life-size statue of the Virgin Mary balanced upon a handcrafted wooden base and hoisted onto the shoulders of the lucky, the group paraded between homesteads and fields, accumulating en masse with faithful followers along the way.

Victoria and her family settled into the revelry, and they traversed up the hillside to the church. Carts overflowing with grapes were left at the entrance, and several baskets filled with the fruit were brought inside and offered at the altar.

As Victoria scanned the pews for Salvatore, she thought she had never seen the tiny church so full. Spotting him sitting across the room with his family, she smiled to herself, thinking that today she would make sure they had a chance to finally speak.

Preaching a compelling homily of plentitude and gratefulness, Father Pietro praised everyone for their hard work. Victoria thought about the days she spent laboring in the fields with the summer sun baking her back. Looking down at her hands, she noticed that bits of soil were still embedded under her fingernails.

At the conclusion of the service, the humble congregation solemnly bowed their heads for a blessing and filed out the door just as eager as they had come.

The crowd converged on the village center, a courtyard of stone set centuries ago in front of the church. Bushel after bushel of grapes were dumped into wooden tubs big enough to fit several people. After rinsing her feet in a pail of water, Victoria climbed over the edge of a vat and joined in the ceremonious custom of stomping the grapes to the tempo of flutes and fiddles. She delighted in the sensation of the ripened grapes tickling her toes and the texture and moisture of the pulp bursting through its skin beneath her beat. The froth rose like purple clouds above her ankles as she held up the ends of her skirt and nimbly maintained her footing on the slippery surface. She became lost in the rhythmic movement until she was euphorically exhausted.

Catching her breath, Victoria held on to the edge of the vat and wiped her feet with a towel. She noticed Salvatore was approaching, and she stood upright as he stopped by her side.

"I saw you walking past the lumber yard yesterday," he commented.

A flutter of nervous pleasure warmed her face. "I pass the lumber yard almost every day," she said.

"But yesterday you stopped." He paused as if waiting for her to respond. "Was it something you saw?"

"Actually, I stopped to rest. My basket was quite heavy," Victoria replied without hesitation.

"Oh, my mistake," he said. "I was sure you were looking at me."

His comment caught her off guard, and she tried to keep her face expressionless. "Well, it seems to me like it was the other way around," she said. She could tell by his smile he was pleased with her answer, and she walked away before the smile in her chest transposed onto her lips.

———— ◆•◆ ————

Victoria watched with casual regard as Salvatore helped the men pour the trampled grapes and their juices into the empty barrels then load them onto the wagons to later be brought to the cool, musty cellars to ferment.

The carts were filled by the time everyone had a turn buoyantly dancing in the vats.

The women had covered the tables with a collective contribution of their hearty fare, and when everyone was seated, Father Pietro led them in a prayer of thanksgiving. Zealously, they indulged in the bountiful meal and drank glasses of past years' vintages with gratification, savoring its body and character. Every bottle told a different story, its composition a mixture of pride and commitment. Victoria listened to the conversation peppered with laughter, which became more spirited with every sip of homemade wine.

Pushing his chair back, Leo, who was known as the village drunk, stood up and swayed. Flailing his glass, droplets of wine splattered onto his already soiled shirt. "Alfredo, tell us one of your regal tales," he loudly slurred.

Victoria turned her head to look at her father. Chuckling slightly, he rose from the table, holding his glass up in his hand. He was just a tinge taller than her mother and a mere fraction of her girth; nonetheless, he had a towering presence.

"The king and queen held the grandest ball. Elegant carriages pulled by magnificent horses came from near and far, carrying the noblest of men and women," he began.

Victoria rolled her eyes and shook her head while smiling to herself. Every ear was tuned in his direction as if cuing to the breezy tones of a golden flute as he amused his audience with his lavish account of pampered royalty. His stories had a way of becoming more imaginative with each rendition, more magical with each narration.

A year before Victoria was born, Alfredo had been summoned to work beyond the village for King Umberto I, the proclaimed ruler of Italy. It was an honor to be a servant of the monarchy they trusted, and Alfredo was admired by many for his unique occupation. Growing up, Victoria had witnessed her father tame even the most feral horse. His admiring respect for God's creatures cultivated his ability, and he treated the submissive beasts with both authority and consideration. His laudable reputation preceded him, and he was appointed to care for the horses and prepare the mounts and carriages for the king and his court. Several men worked under his direction, following his skillful techniques.

As Victoria listened, she could picture the grand palace with its ivy-covered walls rising majestically amidst the hills cloaked in olive groves and vineyards. She and Dominick had a broadened opportunity for learning not only because of the many yarns of royalty and privilege their father told, but they also had the advantage of occasionally accompanying him to the stables. She saw firsthand there was more to life than the one they were living, a far grander world than she could have otherwise perceived.

When Alfredo finished his story, the elders began clapping, and a medley of voices burst into song. Standing, Victoria gleefully joined in the swelling circle of prancing feet. She watched Salvatore from the corners of her eyes as he edged closer until he was dancing by her side.

He unexpectedly grabbed her hand at the end of the song and backed away from the others.

"What are you doing?" she asked.

He smiled a crooked smile, and his voice was crisp. "I want to show you something."

She shook her hand free. "Maybe later."

Now both sides of his mouth curled upward, and his face flashed amusement. "Are you afraid of me?"

"I'm not afraid of anything."

"Prove it," he said with narrowed brows, "and come with me."

She turned around and saw her parents heading toward their table. Looking back at Salvatore, she nodded agreeably.

"Follow me," he said, ducking under the low branches.

When they reached the clearing, they briskly walked side by side down the winding path. The soft moss creeping through the ground created a pattern of contrasting textures that tickled their bare feet. Homes of stone surrounded by trellises woven with vines, dotted the slope of the hillside. Avalanches of vibrant flowers tumbled forth from their window boxes, enhancing the weathered façades.

Breaking stride, Salvatore leaned over and nimbly picked a daisy from the side of the lane and handed it to Victoria with a chivalrous bow. Genuinely touched by his gesture, she kept her eyes poised on the delicate flower, aware of every breath he took.

Victoria looked up as they cut through a cluster of timbered pines. "I didn't know this was here," she said, gazing at a pond bedecked with lily pads and marbled by the sunlight shining sideways through the brush. The air was turning crisp as dusk drew near, and she rubbed her arms to ward off the chill.

"It's part of my family's land. It's my favorite place," he said.

"It's beautiful."

Turning toward her, their eyes locked. "That's why I brought you here." He gently parted the curls from her face.

She stepped back, and the earth felt unsteady under her feet. She hoped he could not see her trembling.

"I'll be here at dusk tomorrow. Can you meet me?" he asked.

"I don't think that's possible," she said. Immediately regretting she had answered so quickly, she tried to push aside her father's words of warning and added, "I'll think about it."

"Then I'll wait for as long as it takes," he said.

As they walked back to the feast, Victoria thought about the touch of Salvatore's hand and could not wait for tomorrow to come.

CHAPTER 4

When Alfredo finished his eggs, he leaned over and kissed Angelina on the cheek. "I already plucked the chicken I killed this morning for dinner. I know how much you hate doing that. Do you want me to get it?" he asked, getting up from the table.

"Thank you," Angelina said, "but I'll bring it in later." She handed him a satchel containing a hunk of bread, cheese, and several slices of smoked ham.

Alfredo kissed Victoria on the top of her head. "Bye, sweetheart."

She smiled weakly. "Bye, Papa."

Opening the door, he glanced up at the sky. "It looks like we might get some rain. We could certainly use it, the river's running low."

Angelina turned to Victoria just as the door closed behind him. "You seem a little preoccupied. Is there something troubling you?"

She sighed. "Salvatore wants me to meet him later."

"You remember what your father said about him," Angelina said firmly.

"I know, but I talked to him yesterday, and he seems nothing like Papa said. I think I'm old enough to choose my friends. I'm almost a grown woman."

"That's exactly the point—you're *almost* a grown woman. When the time comes for you to court, Papa and I will make the decision, and I'm sure it won't be Salvatore."

"Mama, I'm not talking about courting. I'm talking about friendship."

"Enough now," she said dismissively. "We must respect your father's wishes."

Victoria's body tensed, but she tried to sound unperturbed. "I think I'll go for a walk." She stood up from the table, removing her empty plate.

"We have mending to do," Angelina countered, making her point clear.

"Yes, Mama," she said, and for the remainder of the day, few words passed between mother and daughter.

———◆◆———

Victoria waited for her mother's suspicions to subside; consequently, it was several nights before she decided it was safe to slip away. Now, as she quickened her pace toward the pond, she hoped Salvatore would be there, yet she knew she should not be going there at all. Hearing her approaching from behind, Salvatore turned around, and a broad smile lit up his angular face.

Victoria looked down both to step over the brambles and to contend with the rush of exhilaration that swept over her.

"You came," he said brightly.

She nodded modestly as he moved over, giving her room to sit down next to him on the large rock. "I wasn't sure you'd be here."

"I told you I'd wait for as long as it takes," he said. He turned his attention to the water, and she followed his gaze. "I used to come here when I was younger with my brother, Franco, to catch frogs and minnows. I still spend a lot of time here. I like the peace and quiet."

Victoria thought again about what her father had said. "Papa told me what happened between him and your father…that they don't speak anymore," she said, immediately deciding she sounded too abrupt. She slowly turned toward him, and she could see a look of sorrow settle upon his face. Sighing wearily, he ran his hand through his wavy hair, and she also noticed a small scar underneath his chin.

"Truthfully, I don't know the whole story and I don't care, but knowing my father, I guess I can understand. He doesn't talk to anyone really…just when he has to." Salvatore looked despondent. "He's not an easy man to get along with. I suppose you know what happened to my mother."

"Yes," she said, suddenly feeling awkward.

He furrowed his brow and frowned. "Victoria, I'm not my father. He's a difficult man and keeps to himself. He treated my mother as he treats us, like mud on his shoe. It doesn't make sense that he even had a family. When I have children, things will be different. And one day, as the oldest child, I'll take over the mill, and it'll prosper through hard work and respect." He looked down and shook his head. "Sometimes he makes me so angry, I wish he were…" He stopped as if he had already said too much.

"It must be hard for you," she said.

They sat quietly for several minutes staring in the distance and listening to the breeze rustling through the leaves. The sun was descending behind the hills, and the moon was full and hung low in the sky. Victoria turned to look at Salvatore and decided, unequivocally, that he deserved a chance.

———◆•◆———

In the weeks that followed, Victoria created excuses to secretly meet Salvatore and kept her visits brief. She had deluded herself into believing they were just friends, but she soon realized it had become much more. The guilt she harbored for defying her parents was not as strong as the feelings she was developing for Salvatore. When he kissed her for the first time, her body quivered, and she thought she felt the titillation of what it was like to be in love.

They took walks through the hillside, and she savored every minute she could pilfer—the time she spent away from him felt like crystallized moments of infinitude. Her days passed in a haze of activity as she helped her mother with the daily chores, imagining Salvatore working at the mill, picturing his face, the outline of his strong jaw, and the lore of his penetrating eyes. She even pictured herself walking down the aisle on their wedding day.

Dominick was stoking the fire when Victoria tapped on the door and let herself in. Looking up, he said, "What are you doing here? It's dreadful out there. I think snow is coming. You can feel it in the air."

Using the force of her body, she pushed the door closed against the gusting wind. "I came to tell you something," she said. Peeling off her cape, she hung it by the door and straightened her skirt.

Her brother looked at her curiously and stood up from his knees.

Taking a chair from the table, Victoria dragged it close to the hearth and sat down next to Genevieve. The fire felt warm on her face, and she held her hands and feet closer, relishing the heat.

Genevieve squeezed Victoria's forearm reassuringly. "I'm glad you decided to tell him," she said.

Victoria shrugged her shoulders and turned back to Dominick. "It's just that Salvatore and I have become friends." She kept her voice as matter-of-fact as possible.

He looked confused. "When did this happen?"

"It started at the feast...I've been seeing him ever since."

"That was months ago. Do Mama and Papa know?"

"I knew they wouldn't approve, that's why I didn't tell them...but I hope they'll change their mind when I do," she said. "I'm sorry, I should've told you from the beginning."

"I'm not sure about this, Victoria." He thought for a moment. "I don't know much about Salvatore, only what Papa told us—"

"He's really nice. You should get to know him."

"Regardless, you have to tell Papa and Mama."

"That's what Genevieve keeps reminding me," she said, glancing sideways at her.

Dominick rolled his eyes and looked at his wife. "You knew about this all along?"

She chuckled nervously and put the knitting needles down on her lap. "I was sworn to secrecy."

"I will tell them," Victoria said, but there was a slight hesitation in her voice.

<hr>

Victoria became absorbed in an isolated world of desire and disillusion. She promised herself that tomorrow she would explain everything to her parents, but the tomorrows came and went with the nagging possibility her bliss could come to an end.

Salvatore serenaded Victoria with words of adoration, making her heart dance, and every stolen kiss aroused her senses with exaggerated emotion. The couple's passion for one another unfurled itself in stages of seclusion, and they ultimately succumbed to the urge of their unexplored yearnings.

Young and frivolous, Victoria failed to give credence to consequence until she missed her monthly flow, but the queasiness in her stomach refused to abate. Unnerved and humiliated, she shuddered at the thought of her parents' indignation and the disgrace she would bring upon her family. She shuddered at the thought that her innocent child would be born to bear the shame of her sin.

CHAPTER 5

Victoria cowered in the dirt, hugging her legs amongst the terraced rows of grapevines. Her breath was heavy and labored as sweat and tears drained her dress of form. She willed herself to bleed. She willed it not to be so. Guilt and responsibility were shattering her sweet world. She wished she could spread wings and fly far above the blue, leaving no trail, no disappointment, and no broken hearts. Closing her eyes, she prayed out loud, "Dear God, please, I beg of you, let this be over. Let this be a dream." She started to negotiate, "I'll do anything—" but suddenly stopped, for she realized she had nothing to offer in return except to give up the one person she did not want to live without. The chill of the spring morning hovered in the air, but her chest was filled with a dread as stifling as a midsummer's heat as she stared at the flawless, azure sky—God's perfection perfectly poised to illustrate the degree of her imprudence. *How does one atone for an offense considered a mortal sin?* she gravely wondered. *How does one resurrect oneself from a spiritual death?*

———◆•◆———

As the night sky was closing in, Victoria was still nowhere to be found. Salvatore frantically scoured the maze of rows before he stumbled upon her rocking back and forth in a brooding trance. Tempering his relief, he whispered, "Victoria."

She looked up at him, a pensive disquietude covering her dirt-smudged face. Even in her disheveled condition, she took his breath away. He thought her eyes matched the color of water, a glistening of greens and blues that brought forth fire and light underneath the waning sun. Eyes, Salvatore decided, that could tell a story with just one look.

Dropping to his knees, he cradled her into his arms, and at that moment, he thought he could hold onto her forever. "What happened? Are you hurt?" he asked, although he had already surmised the answer.

She burrowed her face into his chest and shook her head back and forth.

"Tell me," he said, needing to hear it from her lips.

She looked up at him. "I'm pregnant." Her voice was faint and dismal.

They locked eyes, absorbing the unspoken words pressing between them.

"It'll be okay...I'll be the one to tell your parents," he said, feeling his heart pumping harder inside his chest. "Hopefully, they'll understand we're in love." He tried to sound reassuring.

She pushed him away. "How can we expect acceptance or forgiveness for our sins?"

"It's not a sin when two people love one another," he said. "Don't be afraid, Victoria." Pulling her to her feet, he lightly brushed the earth from her dress and tried to kiss away the darkness muddling her features.

As they walked hand in hand, the beat of their hearts could be heard above the din of their steps as they traversed the hillside descending toward her home.

Victoria stood in front of the arched, wooden door and looked at Salvatore with eyes fraught with fear.

"It'll be all right," he encouraged. "Remember, I love you."

Her hand was shaking as she slowly took hold of the handle and pushed the door open.

Alfredo and Angelina immediately looked up from the table.

"Victoria, where've you been?" Angelina asked. "We were about to start dinner without you."

Victoria stepped aside, and Salvatore cautiously entered the room.

Looking squarely at him, Alfredo exclaimed, "What are you doing here?"

Taking a deep breath, Salvatore summoned his courage. "Signore and Signora Montanaro...I must tell you, I'm in love with your daughter." Despite their glaring stares, he continued, "I've come to ask you for her hand in marriage."

"Marriage?" Alfredo snapped. "Who are you to ask for her hand in marriage? You don't even know her." His expression was one of pure disdain.

"With all due respect, we've become very close," Salvatore admitted.

Alfredo rose from his chair and stormed across the room, his hardened gait pounding out his fury. His outrage was so palpable that the four walls of the cottage seemed to tremble with a foreboding terror. Deliberately turning in Victoria's direction, he glared into her rueful eyes.

"Signore, Victoria is with child," Salvatore said. The words caught like a knife in his throat.

Angelina covered her mouth with her hands. "God help us."

Alfredo spun around and lunged at Salvatore with the vengeance of a wounded animal. Grabbing him by the neck with one hand, he scorned, "I'll kill you if you ever come near this house again." His breath sputtered hot in Salvatore's face.

"Alfredo, stop!" Angelina screamed.

Choking, Salvatore pushed him away.

Alfredo scowled at him. "Get out and never return," he demanded, holding him tight in his gaze. Turning to Victoria, he spat, "And you—you're nothing more than a whore!"

"But, Papa—" Victoria cried. Her voice was filled with defeat.

"Don't call me Papa! You're a disgrace to this family—I can't even look at you!"

Victoria stood frozen in the doorway. Her tear-filled eyes were as wide as the sky, and Salvatore swore she had stopped breathing. Swallowing the bile rising in his throat, he grabbed her hand on his way out, and they fled from her home. He was convinced in his need for Victoria, but he had underestimated the emotional upheaval of unveiling their secret.

———◆◆◆———

Angelina was just as stunned by the couple's confession, but she was equally frightened by her husband's reaction—his temper had never reached such an alarming extreme. At that moment, her disappointment in Victoria paled in comparison to the anger she felt toward Alfredo. Blurting her disbelief, she said, "How could you speak to our daughter that way? How could you be so cruel?"

Alfredo turned away so abruptly that Angelina could feel the resentment rush from his body. His face flushed a vibrant red and contorted in anguish as he clutched his chest and collapsed into a chair, and she suddenly feared for his health. A sheath of emptiness fell upon her, further fracturing her world, and her agitation gave way to compassion. Rising from the table, she wrapped her arms around him from behind. She bent over and rested her chin on the top of his head. His skin was damp and sticky, and she could feel him trembling. "Alfredo, please calm down, you're scaring me," she said softly. "You're not as young as you used to be."

"I told her to stay away from him!" he shouted. Breaking free from her arms, he jumped to his feet and spun around. "How was it possible that Victoria was with Salvatore? Why weren't you watching her?"

"She's not a little girl and at my side every minute! We can't blame each other. What's done is done." She paused, carefully choosing her words. "Alfredo, please, I'm hurting too, but you must understand the marriage is unavoidable. She's with child, and her reputation, as well as that of our family, is at stake. She's our daughter, and to disown her would destroy our lives. We must accept the inevitable." As she spoke, tears rippled down her cheeks.

"I didn't want this for Victoria," he said. His eyes were cloaked in bitter sadness.

Angelina sighed heavily. "I didn't either."

"That boy will bring more turmoil into our lives, I tell you, and the relationship will wither like a dying vine." His face fell flat, and his shoulders drooped, and Angelina imagined his heart breaking like pieces of china shattering upon impact.

CHAPTER 6

Victoria and Salvatore walked aimlessly through the fields as the sun went down, causing more darkness to fall upon her day.

Salvatore abruptly stopped and turned toward her. Holding her by her arms, he pleaded, "Let's go away. Let's go to America. We could raise our child in a land where nobody knows us, where nobody will judge us."

Shaking her head, she said, "That won't solve our problems...it'll only create more. Our child would never know its family, and we'll wind up living a life of regret."

"My father wouldn't miss me if I were gone," Salvatore said. "He would miss the sweat of my brow. And your parents—you heard your father."

She thought about what her father had said and wondered how a few words could ravage a lifetime of loyalty. Its vileness had drained the air of depth so no other words could fit, no other words could negate its meaning.

Still holding her arms, he shook her slightly. "What's left for us here—shame and gossip?"

Victoria swallowed hard and looked at him despondently. Her breath felt as dense as the earth, and she wished she was standing in the midst of another's dread. "I have to go back," she said. "I have to try to talk to them. I can't just leave it like this."

He released his grasp, and she solemnly turned back down the path, leaving him standing alone in the throes of his plan.

Opening the door to their home, Victoria's gaze met her parents' and she scanned their faces for a trace of forgiveness. Her mother looked at her with utter sadness, yet her father glowered at her with a brew of scorn and consternation. Their three sets of eyes spoke volumes, but they all stood in dead silence for what seemed like an eternity rooting itself in Victoria's mind. She felt as if she were being split by the blade of an axe and falling into disagreeable directions. Racing past them, she scaled the ladder to the loft. Huddled in a fetal position, she spent the rest of the night shivering in the heat.

———◆•◆———

Victoria rose before dawn and shimmied down the rungs of the ladder, keeping her eyes fixated on her sleeping parents. As a child she had memorized every squeak in the floorboards, and she floated over them like a wisp of a feather without making a sound. In sync to her father's grating snores, she opened the heavy door just wide enough to slip through. Daylight had yet to come, and the moon was in a vacant cycle; however, Victoria ran through the inky paths as if they were illuminated.

Bursting into her brother's home, she called out, "Dominick, Genevieve!" Her voice cracked between gasps for air.

Dominick sat up with a jolt. "What's the matter?"

Plopping down on the side of their bed, Victoria dropped her head into her hands to conceal her humiliation and bleated her confession. "I've done something terrible. I don't know what to do."

"What could you have possibly done that could be that horrible?" Genevieve asked.

The heat rose from inside Victoria, and she could feel her face flush. Placing her hands on her stomach, she said, "I'm carrying Salvatore's child." She had trouble believing it herself when she said it out loud. An unsettling void entered the space where she had hoped would be a word of comfort or direction, and she began to weep uncontrollably. "I've shamed our family," she heaved between sobs. "I've shamed myself." Genevieve gently rubbed Victoria's back as she continued. "Dominick, I'm begging you to speak to Papa for me. It's awful. They looked at me like I was a stranger." She took a deep breath and wiped her eyes with her sleeve. "They hate me."

"Does Salvatore plan on marrying you?" he asked.

"When he asked for my hand, Papa threatened his life." She omitted the part where their father decried her a whore.

"What about Mama?"

"She didn't say anything. She just stood there stunned."

Dominick sat quiet for a long moment. He swung his legs over the side of the bed and stood up. Grabbing his pants off the back of the chair, he pulled them on and tucked in his nightshirt. He looked at Victoria and said, "Stay here with Genevieve. Let me see if there's anything I can do." Any sympathy in his voice was coiled in frustration. Taking his sweater off the hook by the door, he somberly left.

———— ◆•◆ ————

Carefully planning his words, Dominick reluctantly walked to his parents' home as the sun started its ascent. When Victoria had first told him about Salvatore, he surmised that they were more than friends. He avoided upsetting his sister by suppressing his misgivings toward Salvatore; unfortunately, her admission was something he had failed to foresee. Now he realized he should have intervened, but he had been caught in the middle of a precarious predicament.

Angelina was pouring Alfredo his morning coffee when Dominick walked in. She rested the pot on the table and looked up at him, her forlorn face revealing her pain. "You know, don't you?"

Dominick nodded his head and slumped into a chair across from his father.

"We thought she'd go to you," she said.

Again he nodded, this time, rolling his eyes slightly. Leaning his elbows on the table, he clasped his hands together and began his appeal. "I've just spoken to her and she's very upset. She's asked me to—"

Alfredo firmly dismissed him with a severe wave of his hand. "Did you have any idea what was going on between your sister and Salvatore?"

Studying his father, Dominick decided there was nothing to hide. "I didn't know how close they'd become. She told me this morning about the baby. Believe me, I'm as shocked as you are."

"Why've you kept this from us?" His voice surged in exasperation.

"I admit I've made a foolish mistake. Victoria said she'd tell you." He sighed. "The fact is she's having a baby, and that can't be changed. Now, what she needs is your forgiveness."

"I can't forgive her." Alfredo's brows narrowed along with his mind. "I won't forgive her."

"You know how much she loves you and Mama. She knows she's made a huge mistake. She knows she's dishonored you, but she also knows she's in love with Salvatore, and they want to be married."

Alfredo banged his fist on the table. "I don't care what they want, damn it."

Angelina grabbed him by his arm. Her swollen eyes were rimmed with red, and her body was trembling. "This is not about what you want, Alfredo. This is about Victoria. How could we abandon the daughter we gave life? How could we shun the unborn child who shares our blood? They must wed whether you agree or not," she insisted.

Dominick's attention veered to the door as Victoria walked through, and the tension in the room grew awkwardly still.

She stopped. The sound of her whimpering now filled the room. "I love him," she said. "I know you're disappointed in me. I know you hate me."

"That's not true, Victoria," Angelina sputtered.

Tears streamed down her cheeks. "I can't blame you. I lied to all of you. I didn't plan for all this to happen. I didn't know…I didn't know I'd fall in love…" Her voice trailed off.

"You gave yourself to a man outside of marriage!" Alfredo's tone was filled with condemnation. "My daughter would know better."

"I can only ask God to forgive the sins I've committed." Victoria held herself as if trying to keep from falling apart. "Papa, we love each other and want to be married. We want to raise our child together. Don't blame this on Salvatore. It was my fault too. He isn't like Francis. Please, give him a chance." She hesitated. "If not for us, but for your grandchild."

Angelina came from behind the table and took Victoria's face in her hands. "We love you," she said. "We'll always love you, no matter what happens." She stepped back and turned to Dominick and Alfredo. "No one needs to know about the baby, not even Father

Pietro. We'll have a wedding, and after they marry, we'll make the announcement at the right time." She sounded desperate. "Make sure Genevieve keeps this to herself."

"Of course," Dominick said grimly.

All eyes turned to Alfredo, and he sat silent for a few moments without looking up. "So be it," he murmured. Rising from the table, he somberly strode past Victoria and out the door.

———◆•◆———

Hastily, a simple wedding was organized, and Victoria and Salvatore were to be married in the small community church.

Victoria entered the vestibule, wearing the same gown Genevieve had donned a year before—a sheath of pure white embroidered with details of the future, and a childhood pact fittingly fulfilled. The flowing gown was conceived by the girls through a childhood of spirited conversations and creativity. They had agreed to wear the same magnificent dress on their special day—a budding promise made years before they ever mused of a man.

The sheerness of the long veil billowed like a soft cloud around her from beneath a wreath of delicate flowers resting like a halo upon her head. She clutched a bouquet, which gracefully spilled forward from her waist, camouflaging the mystery growing inside, although she felt it every minute of every day, and it frightened and amazed her at the same time.

It was customary for the entire village to attend a wedding celebration, and today was no exception. The congregation rose in unison as Victoria walked down the aisle, holding on to her father's arm. She immediately sensed an undertone of suspicion circulating the room, but she believed she had made her amends with God by promising him that she would love her child and her husband more than herself. Straightening her back, she held her head high and focused on Salvatore's reassuring smile.

Approaching the altar, Alfredo stopped and turned to Victoria. The look of distress on his face was unmistakable as he lifted her veil and kissed her faintly on both cheeks. Before taking his seat, he glared at Salvatore with eyes afire, and Victoria could feel the heat of their warning.

Father Pietro cleared his throat and smiled at them. "In the name of the Father, and of the Son, and of the Holy Spirit, amen. Let us pray," he said, bowing his head. "Father, hear our prayers for Salvatore and Victoria through your Son, Jesus Christ, our Lord who lives and reigns with you and the Holy Ghost, one God forever and ever, amen." He looked up. "Salvatore Ricci and Victoria Montanaro, you have come to this church so that the Lord may bless your love in the company of this community. The Lord has already consecrated you in baptism, and now he will enrich you in the sacrament of marriage so that you may be joined in mutual and lasting fidelity. And so, in the presence of the church, your family, and your friends, I ask you to state your intentions."

Salvatore took Victoria's hands in his, and they locked eyes. Her voice quivered, but his remained resolute as they exchanged vows of unconditional love and rings as symbols of their loyalty.

Father Pietro blessed the couple and joined them in marriage, seemingly unaware that their union violated the sanctity of the sacrament.

Alfredo and Angelina hosted a reception, which took her and Victoria days to prepare, and none of the guests eluded it was anything other than a joyous occasion. As Victoria danced with Salvatore under the stars, she contemplated all that had happened in the previous weeks and was astonished her dream had come true. A current of contentment eased through her, and she relaxed under its charm. The devotion of the man that held her in his arms would never allow her to imagine a future less than perfect.

———•••———

The newlyweds took up residence in a cottage at the foot of the village once occupied by Salvatore's grandparents. Salvatore's behavior was that of a responsible, doting husband, and Victoria felt fortunate to have married such a strong, loving man. His genuine portrayal of an honorable mate was the antithesis of what her father had anticipated.

During the months of her pregnancy, Victoria appreciated that her parents made an effort to be more accepting of Salvatore, and she thought the underlying tension between them was lessening with time. The day she placed her father's hand on her stomach to feel the baby kick, he looked at her, and she swore she saw the tenderness return to his eyes. She was relieved the open wound between them was slowly mending. The burgeoning life inside her was inciting immeasurable excitement as it prepared to make its entrance—a tiny thread that was stitching generations back together.

The birth of their baby boy, Vincenzo, brought incredible happiness to the entire family. He possessed Victoria's curly hair—auburn, not red—toned down by the genes of his father. Unmistakably, his eyes came from her—big and round and hazel—and every time she looked into them, she thought her heart would burst.

CHAPTER 7

Since he could remember, Dominick had longed to go to America. The idea alone had him reeling with expectations. The prospect of achieving anything he aspired to had given him the incentive, and the allure of owning land of his own had sealed his decision. He dreamed of the opportunities awaiting him; however, the nightmares about leaving his loved ones behind harassed his mind.

After the spring planting had been completed, Dominick decided to break the news to the family one night after dinner. Watching Alfredo, Angelina, Victoria, and Salvatore around the table and glancing at his nephew asleep on the bed, he felt a pang of grave loss and wondered how long it would be before he would see them again. Taking hold of his wife's hand, he took a deep breath and exhaled slowly. "Genevieve and I have something we want to tell you," he announced. "After much thought and consideration, we've agreed it's time to go to America. We know this may seem sudden, but you all know we've been discussing it for months. We've decided to take the ship that leaves next Saturday." He said it with a pride that comes from a definitive decision, although he still looked at his father for approval. "Papa, there're many people leaving for America. I, too, want to lay claim to a fraction of its fortunes. I want to own my own land. I know you hold the king in high regard, unfortunately there are many who don't recognize him as their ruler."

"We'll soon see better times now that King Emmanuel's in power. He's the one who will unify Italy," Alfredo countered. "We have to give him a chance."

"I feel the same way, but Italy faces many serious problems as well as political unrest—famine and pestilence are said to be kingdom-wide. We all thought things would be better after the turn of the century, yet they're getting worse."

"We live a good life. We have food, shelter, and our health."

"I know, Father, but I'm young and strong, and I want to do this. I'm eighteen and ready to start a family. There're schools in America, and I want my children to have an education, and Genevieve feels the same way. Her parents were also reluctant, but in the end, they gave us their blessing." Dominick glanced over at his wife, who gave him an encouraging look, and he continued his reasoning. "The opportunities are too much to resist. This is something I need to do."

Alfredo sighed as he looked at Angelina, and their eyes met in concern. "How do you feel about this?"

———◆◆———

Angelina struggled to appear calm for the sake of her son, but her nerves were rattling every bone in her body. She did not want her despondency to discourage Dominick's ambition, although composing herself took every ounce of stamina she could muster. "If that's what you both want, then I also give you my blessing. You *are* young and strong," she agreed. "It's better to go now before you have children, and then, if you're not happy there, you could always come back."

Angelina knew this day was coming. Many dinner conversations had centered on the lures of America, and she knew her son was entranced. Still, the impending separation tugged at her heartstrings, and inside, she felt as if she was unraveling. She wanted him to go to America, to make something of his life, to give more to his children, but it was a double-edged sword—its blade slicing away pieces of her very being. When she was alone that evening, she allowed her grief to take over, wrenching her sorrow with torrents of tears.

In the days leading up to their departure, it tormented Victoria to look at Dominick, knowing the next time might be her last. Perhaps they would never see each other again. Perhaps the memory of him would have to last a lifetime, and she wanted to remember the boy of her childhood, not the man leaving for another world.

Victoria and Dominick had been brought up working side by side with their parents. Strong and capable, the siblings had spent their days walking in an adult's shoes and spent late afternoons running, like the children they were, barefoot through the fields. Despite being two years younger than Dominick, Victoria matched his height. He constantly wore a cap too big for his head that shadowed his full facial features except for his smile, which was as bright as the sunrise. Every spare moment she wanted to be by her brother's side. She had learned to run as fast as him and climb a tree with parallel dexterity; she even taught herself to pick up a snake without flinching. They played as equals, yet Victoria preferred to use her imagination and would convince Dominick to go along. In an instant, she would conceive a kingdom out of a summer's afternoon where she regularly whisked him behind the gated walls of the palace, and they donned the elegant vestments of the king and queen. They attended grand galas and danced ceremoniously to the awe of their subjects, and able servants catered to their every fancy. They whimsically ruled a unified land brimming with prosperity and were hailed for the triumph. In the evenings when the sun went down, dreams sustained Victoria's fantasies on even grander scales.

The night before they left, friends and family gathered to bid Dominick and Genevieve farewell. They sat under the trellises lined with tables laden with food, reminiscing, sipping wine, and toasting to their future. The couple intermittently locked eyes, glances of reassurance in the midst of their uncertainty. Dominick was besotted by Genevieve's freckled cheeks, the natural wave of her cinnamon-colored hair, and the confident stature she wore on her petite frame. When he first told her that he wanted to go to America, she readily agreed, and he was forever thankful such a woman was willing to forego her life and her family to stand by his side.

Dominick stood up from the table and held his glass high. "Thank you all for coming this evening. It's the people who make leaving so difficult, but it won't be long before we'll return, and by then, we'll have stories and children to share." He chuckled at the thought. "We'll miss our home, and we'll miss all of you. I know the memory of this gathering will carry us through."

Alfredo took a knife and cut a piece of the grapevine. Handing it to Dominick, he said, "Take this and plant it in America as a reminder of your roots, and may your lives be as fruitful as the vine."

Dominick dripped tears as he and his father embraced. "I love you, Papa," he whispered as he kissed him on both cheeks.

"I love you too, son. May God protect you on your journey to America." Stepping back, he looked at Dominick with a pride that swelled his chest. "The opportunities awaiting you are boundless...I even hear the streets are paved with gold."

Dominick and Alfredo began to laugh, and the applause that followed muddled the sound of the hearts that were breaking.

———◆◆◆———

When the new dawn emerged, many of the villagers escorted Dominick and Genevieve to the edge of its border, expressing their good wishes and hugging their farewells. Dominick saw the trepidation in their eyes, as they were losing two more to an unknown land—one that cultivated mixed impressions of awe and skepticism. He was bringing with him the hopes and prayers of a village, and it helped to kindle his spirits.

As he took one last look, he etched every feature of their faces in his mind, creating a portrait that could never be erased.

CHAPTER 8

Between caring for their new baby and their home and missing her brother and best friend, Victoria's days flew by in a whirlwind of elation and despair. She cherished the walks she and Salvatore took after dinner. They were just like the walks they had taken before Vincenzo was born, but now she had the added pleasure of watching Salvatore carry their son in his arms. She knew how much he wanted to be a devoted father, so unlike his own. Many times their conversations revolved around his animosity toward Francis and why he blamed him for his mother's death. He had told Victoria that when it happened, he felt an overwhelming responsibility to look after his siblings at a time when he barely felt old enough to care for himself. He admitted he longed for the day of his father's passing so there would be an end to the paternal indifference. He also reminded her that she was the one who showed him how to love.

———◆•◆———

It was shortly after Victoria gave birth to their second child, Gennaro, when Francis suddenly died. Salvatore had sworn his father's heart had given out because there was none left to spare. As the eldest sibling, he took over the family's mill, and his aspirations came to fruition, but Victoria observed a steady decline in her husband. It was as if the light in his eyes gradually faded, and the very reasons for which she married him—the caring, the attention, the love—seemed to slowly disappear. He worked countless hours, and she tried to understand the pressure he felt, but he was coming home exhausted and sullen and with the potent smell of alcohol on his breath.

Victoria gave birth to Catherina and, lastly, Gabriella. It had been four long years and four children, and Salvatore's presence in their lives simultaneously ebbed as their family expanded, taking a toll on the marriage. His sole interest in Victoria was confined to the middle of the night when the children were asleep, and he took what he wanted, replacing gentleness with selfishness. Any objections she voiced instantly provoked him into escalating persistence. She quickly realized her silent submissions allowed the children to remain in their innocent slumber. Disavowing the present, she would squeeze her eyes tight and escape to a secret place deep in her soul which no one else could touch.

Salvatore's flagrant disregard for his children was tearing away any shred of attachment Victoria had left for him. She worked just as hard as he did from dawn till dusk, caring for their land and four children, but it did not create the same bitterness within her that reeked from his pores. She drifted through her days under a haze of discontent, wondering what would ever soften his fight.

One night, while the children were protected under the canopy of sleep, Victoria strode outside to where Salvatore sat slumped against the trunk of a tree. Watching him fill his glass and toss the empty bottle on the ground, she decided to confront him again. She had to make him understand the damage he was inflicting on their lives. Walking over to where he was sitting, she stood in front of him and looked down. "What are you doing?" she snapped. "Are you drowning your sorrow or swallowing your guilt?" She had intended to start the discussion without accusations, but it was impossible to restrain herself.

His face was expressionless, and he continued to drink as if she were not there.

"You're just like your father. He was a stern man when he was sober, but he turned on the world when he drank, and you've become exactly like him. Why are you perpetuating a childhood you grew up despising? " She waited for his response; however, he stared at his glass as though it held the answer.

Victoria stood with her hands on her hips and stamped her foot on the ground. "Think of the beautiful family we've created together." Her voice boomed with frustration. "Doesn't that mean anything to you? What's become of you? What's become of us?"

Salvatore seemed unfazed and took another gulp of the numbing libation, further blurring the line between them.

"Answer me! Damn you, answer me!" With all the strength she could muster, she knocked the glass from his hand and stomped inside, leaving him to wallow in his self-pity.

As time went on, melancholy continued to cast a dismal cloud over Salvatore and he unenthusiastically managed the mill, which was also faltering from the bane of his neglect. Drinking occupied most of his time and energy, and Victoria had learned to stop longing for his sober return. When he entered the cottage, inebriated and demanding, the stench of his sour breath filled her with utter disgust, and the sight of him had become revolting. She needed him to be a man, yet he was acting like a child, and she had no energy left to coddle another. The friendship and love they had once shared had been irreparably tarnished by his escalating affliction. It was as if his hardened heart had sculpted his feelings into a mound of stone and offered no remorse.

She discreetly tried to keep her troubles to herself to shield the turbulence within her marriage from her parents and made excuses for Salvatore's absences. She also attempted to keep her private agony from the children by overly compensating for their father's shortcomings. The essence of her being was wrapped up in the four little lives she nurtured. Everything she could teach them, every tale she could tell, and her undying devotion were her contributions.

Trying to fill the void in their lives caused by Salvatore's indifference was not enough, and Victoria contemplated leaving, but she was hounded by conflicting thoughts. *He'll never change. If I leave, I could never come back. I'd be scorned, and my parents would be left to bear the consequence. If only he were dead.* She shook herself out of the insanity; nevertheless, her hunger for a better life for both she and her children remained an inherent desire.

As the days melded one into the next, Angelina's frustration mounted as she watched her daughter silently suffer and her grandchildren withdraw from the bleeding disquietude. While Victoria was busy doing her numerous chores, Angelina was able to alleviate some of her burden by helping with the children, but she wanted so much more for her family. In the past, she had never uttered a malicious word concerning Salvatore. *What good would it have done?* However, his presence in their lives left her to contend with a continuous inner ache.

The day Vincenzo came to her and asked, "Why do Mama and Papa fight so much. Is it because of us?" was the day that Angelina realized Salvatore's malaise was destroying their home.

"Of course not, sweetheart," she protested, hugging him tightly. "Sometimes grownups disagree...it doesn't mean they don't love their families. I know it's difficult to understand, but it's not your fault, nor your brother or sisters'." She bent down and gently cupped his face in her hands. "You're a good boy, Vincenzo."

He furrowed his brows. "Does Grandpa make you cry too?"

Folding Vincenzo into her arms, she said, "I promise you everything will be all right. I promise you this will end."

Angelina knew the intolerable situation needed a miracle to mend, and that night, she begged the Almighty to deliver.

The next morning she offered Victoria what she believed to be the only solution. Slipping her a weighty sac filled with the coins she and Alfredo had been tucking away, she pleaded, "Victoria, I want you to listen to me. I know what's going on—I'd be a fool not to notice. Your father has had his talks with Salvatore, but I know it hasn't made a difference. I want you to take this money and the children and go to America to be with Dominick and Genevieve."

Victoria narrowed her brows and gave her a tragic look. "Mama, I can't take your savings. You'll need it one day! What would happen to you and Papa?"

"That's not important. We'll be fine. What's important is that you get away from Salvatore. He's a sick man, Victoria. He's stolen away your smile, and he's robbing the children of theirs too. Don't you see how it's affecting them? Don't deny them their innocence." Tears streamed down her face. "I'm so sorry your life has turned out like this, but you're still a young woman. You can start over. Trust me, this is your only alternative."

"What did Papa say?"

"He doesn't know, and I won't tell him until you're gone. There's no way he'll ever let the one child he has left leave without a fight." She watched her daughter's face contort in disbelief. "Salvatore is his father's son, and he'll never change. His mother took her life to escape Francis, leaving her children in his heartless care. It was so bad, she saw no other way out, but this..." She pointed to the sac clutched in her daughter's hands. "This is your way out."

Placing the pouch on the table, Victoria said, "I can't take this or leave you and Papa to bear the scandal of my disappearance. I appreciate your offer, but somehow I'll find a way to make things better between us." She smiled reassuringly, yet her voice sounded thin and unconvincing.

"Please think about it...if not for yourself than for the children. They shouldn't have to grow up witnessing this insanity." Her words were harsh, yet honest. "They shouldn't have to grow up suffering because of their parents' mistake."

Angelina prayed her persistence convinced Victoria to at least consider the liberating but bittersweet means to an end.

———◆●◆———

Victoria deeply missed Dominick and Genevieve now that they were living a world away. The words she put on paper did not disclose the constant hell she endured. Why disrupt their lives with her hardships when they were facing their own? Why share sentiments that would be diluted by thousands of miles—sentiments she would keep to herself until the day they hopefully would reunite.

Over the years Genevieve's letters were filled with stories of their lives in America and the births of their two sons, while Dominick's letters were filled with stories of America's opportunities and obstacles— opportunities everyone wanted to seize and obstacles he tried to explain.

"New York is a melting pot of strangers from all over the world, and sadly, many are suspicious of each other's appearances and each other's strengths. Each nationality follows a different set of rules, a different way of life. Some are able in particular trades, while others are searching for a worthwhile skill," he had written. He also wrote that there were more people than jobs, and he felt fortunate to have found work at a slaughterhouse. Victoria tried to imagine the many people and the way they lived, and more and more, she tried to imagine herself there.

———◆●◆———

Salvatore's continued neglect for their children and Victoria's own degradation made her so overwrought that she dwelled on it until it became an obsession. She felt as if she were lying in the bed of a grave waiting for the dirt to be tossed upon her, and she was suffocating from the illusion.

Desperate, and with no other recourse, she decided to embrace the life-altering decision to accept her mother's generous gift and follow in her brother's footsteps; however, the possibility of never seeing her parents again was a ghastly compromise. Saying good-bye to her mother would be heart-wrenching, but Victoria was tortured by the prospect of leaving her father without a farewell. The look of disappointment in his eyes would have mirrored her shame, though he was not privy to the degree of cruelty that was threatening her sanity. Once she had made the choice, Victoria was consumed with apprehension and the details of her departure. Unbeknownst to her, she was taking along another gift from her mother—determination. She was about to leave the security of a familiar life in Italy to discover a new one without any guarantees. Only the auspicious visions she conjured in her mind gave her the fortitude to leave her husband and make the daunting journey with four small children. It meant breaking the sacred vows she shared with Salvatore, although he had already desecrated them.

CHAPTER 9

It was the summer of 1906. Vincenzo was a few months shy of his fifth birthday and too young to understand the impact of what was about to unfold. His normal routine consisted of chores, playing with his siblings, and exploring the alluring countryside. One of his favorite times of the day was when his mother tucked them in at night and captivated their imaginations with her amazing tales.

The night before their departure was no exception. Vincenzo was spellbound as he listened to Victoria's thrilling account of a magical place called America.

"Big ships from all over the world take the best children and their mothers to the enchanted land that overflows with milk and honey." Her eyes grew wide as she spoke.

"Is that all they eat?" Gennaro asked.

"Don't they have other food in America?" Vincenzo chimed in.

Victoria chuckled. "Of course they do. Foods you've never even tasted."

"Tell us more about America, Mama," Vincenzo said.

She tickled his belly. "That's enough for tonight. Tomorrow I'll tell you more." She kissed each of her children with an "I love you" on her lips, leaving them full of wonder and unaware that tomorrow they would be embarking on a journey that would make her story their reality.

Vincenzo and his brother, Gennaro, shared a mattress in the loft. When the weather was cold and the winds blew, he welcomed the warmth of his sibling. Tonight, however, the sweltering summer heat made it excessively uncomfortable, and Vincenzo slept restlessly on the cool floor. Despite his father's drunken snores, he subconsciously heard his mother rustling around the cottage throughout the night.

———◆◆◆———

Never changing into her bedclothes, Victoria packed away their usual breakfast, bread and milk, along with other staples needed for their travels, and nervously paced away the rest of the seemingly endless hours. In the eerie black essence of the night, she nudged the children awake before the village stirred and dawn could shed light on her scheme.

Opening his droopy eyes, Vincenzo sat up and looked at the large sack and basket by the door. When he started to speak, Victoria shushed him with a finger to her lips and handed him his clothes. "Don't wake Papa, and dress quickly."

Vincenzo fumbled with sleepiness as he put on his knickers. He tied his shoes and helped Gennaro while Victoria swiftly dressed Catherina and Gabriella.

With Gabriella dozing in her arms, she quietly ushered the children out of the house, maneuvering them around the squeaky boards that led to the front door. Stepping out into the early-morning fog, they were enveloped in a cloud of heat and humidity.

As she gently closed the door behind them, Vincenzo asked, "Isn't Papa coming with us?"

"I'll explain later. We're going on an adventure." Victoria kept her voice low and calm.

"Where?"

"America, Vincenzo, to America."

His jaw dropped. "The place for the best children?"

"Only the best children," she said.

His eyes lit up. "That means us."

"Yes, that means you," she assured him.

Victoria haphazardly placed their belongings and her younger children onto the wobbly, wooden cart. Remembering their treasured Bible, the one her parents had passed onto them as a wedding gift, she cracked the door open and snatched it from the table.

Holding on to the handle, Vincenzo helped her push the cart down the stone path that led to freedom.

———◆●◆———

They walked briskly in the calm, misty morning air, Victoria's clothes clinging to her sweaty body and her thoughts clinging to hope.

Vincenzo sporadically continued to ask her questions. "How long does it take to get to America? Are we almost there?"

"Not yet, Vincenzo, we still have to go on the big ship. Remember the story I told you last night?" Victoria felt tired and distracted.

As the sun rose, the fog slowly lifted. They rested intermittently throughout the day, and at dusk, Victoria spread a blanket in a clearing on the edge of the forest not far from the dirt road on which they traveled. She was bone weary. Her feet were blistered and throbbed unmercifully, her sensibility spent. The ground was hard and unforgiving against the weight of her uneasiness.

She nestled the children close to her and managed to softly sing, camouflaging the intimidating noises that pricked the night. They drifted off to sleep, and the moon cast a protective glow upon their resting place as if keeping vigil.

CHAPTER 10

Salvatore had woken that fateful day to discover his wife and children were nowhere in sight. Groggy and confused, he tumbled out of bed. Straining to focus his bloodshot eyes against the light pouring through the windows, he could not begin to fathom where his family could be. The notion that Victoria had left him never crossed his muddled mind. Annoyed and hungry, he stepped outside. Looking up, he realized the sun was already leaning west in the sky, and his anger spiked. "Victoria! Victoria! Why didn't you wake me?" he yelled. Traipsing up the hillside toward his in-laws' home, he assumed he would find them there.

Opening the door, Salvatore came face-to-face with Angelina.

"You're not welcome in our home ever again," she said, blocking his way. Her eyes seared through him like a hot poker. "Your contemptible conduct has caused your family unbearable misery. You could've changed, you could've been different from your father, but you chose to do nothing, and now…now it's too late." Tears unleashed her grief along with her words.

"What are you talking about? I want to see my wife," he insisted.

"She and the children are on their way to America." Her voice was filled with conviction and disdain. She spat at his feet and slammed the door in his mortified face.

Salvatore's knees buckled under the weight of the consequences, and he banged the door with his fist in retaliation. "You haven't seen the last of me," he roared.

Bolting back to his deserted cottage, Salvatore kicked the door open. Storming over to the cupboard, he salvaged a bottle of grappa before knocking the cabinet over with one venomous thrust. He ripped out the cork and threw back his head. Pouring the contents into his mouth, he gulped down his woes, and the overflow trickled down his chin, mimicking tears. He thought about how hard he had tried and how miserable he had failed at being a good father to his children. As he swallowed, the heat of the liquid burned his throat but was beginning to temper his insides. It was the method he used to drown the self-hatred that lurked within him—mindful he was not the person he always had imagined himself to be, mindful he did not know how to love his own children.

Salvatore continued to vehemently drink, and his repulsive descent into intoxication fueled his anger, while images of Victoria and the children tortured his mind. He knew the effect his habits had on his wife, and it was he who had chased her away, but he refused to accept this humiliation. "What the hell does she think she's doing? She's a fool to believe she can live without me. I won't tolerate my children being taken away," he furiously bellowed in the empty room. Spiraling deeper into a tunnel of rage, the thought of Victoria executing her preposterous scheme swirled through his mind. "She'll never get away with this."

On his way out, he smashed the bottle on the table that once held their Bible. The bottle shattered, and the table toppled under the force of his self-loathing.

Intent on putting a stop to her insidious plan, Salvatore impetuously concocted a scheme of his own. The effects of the alcohol had inhibited his common sense and his coordination as he stumbled out to the pasture and made several unsuccessful attempts to mount his horse, clumsily falling to the ground each time. Yanking the animal over to the woodpile to use as a platform, he feebly managed to heave himself into the crux of its spine—his slumping body draped parallel over its bare back. He painstakingly pulled himself erect and charged up the hillside, obliviously crushing everything in his path as he made his way to his in-laws' home to boast of his intention to retrieve what was rightfully his.

Alfredo's hands covered his face as he sat slumped over on the edge of the bed, trying to make sense of what Angelina had just told him. The thought that he may never see his daughter and grandchildren again was inconceivable, and his pain bled through his tears. The void he felt when his son had left was soothed by feelings of pride for his ambition, yet his daughter's abrupt disappearance triggered a staggering emptiness.

Breaking the debilitating silence enveloping the cottage, Alfredo heard a commotion outside. He feebly rose from the bed and pushed the door open to discover his son-in-law on horseback, unintelligibly weaving in and out of arrogance. Fury surged through his body, and he ran out of the house in a fiery frenzy. His arms flailing with animosity, he bolted toward Salvatore. "Mark my words—you'll pay for your sins!"

Startling the horse, it reared up and hurled Salvatore backward into the jagged edges of the stonewall. The impact was so severe that Alfredo could hear the sound of bones breaking.

Unable to move, Salvatore looked at Alfredo with eyes that conveyed the vulnerability of a child, begging without words to help him.

Nausea coursed through Alfredo's body as he looked past Salvatore's physical injuries and peered into the darkness of his blemished soul. He wanted to turn his back on the grotesque display that was crumbled before him, but unfortunately, the blood of this swine flowed through his grandchildren.

"Angelina, help me," Alfredo summoned.

She stood rooted in the doorway, and her face was drenched in horror.

"Angelina!" he repeated with amplified urgency.

Snapping out of her morbid stupor, she hesitantly walked toward him. Joining hands, they stabilized Salvatore's limp neck and carried him inside, awkwardly placing him on the mattress—his body so broken the pain did not register. Angelina wet a cloth and placed the cool compress on Salvatore's bleeding head. Using a handkerchief, she blotted the froth oozing from the corners of his mouth.

Alfredo bitterly swallowed the scene in silence, thinking that they would never be able to cleanse the repugnance from their hearts. "I'll be back," he simply said. Lugging his own weighty woes, he trudged to the mill and through the village, somberly notifying Salvatore's family.

———◆◆◆———

Many congregated at his bedside, and the cottage soon brimmed with people. Solemn and confused, they questioned Victoria's whereabouts.

"She and the children left for America." As Angelina spoke, the sea of eyes grew wider.

"That can't be!" an elderly woman yelled.

"This is an outrage! What kind of woman would abandon her husband and take his children away?" another shouted.

Salvatore's oldest aunt puffed out her cheeks. "She's no good, that one, I tell you."

Angelina swiftly turned toward her. "Everyone here knows Salvatore had problems! How can you blame Victoria when it was his neglect that chased her away?"

"If it wasn't for her—he wouldn't have fallen—he wouldn't be dying," she insisted.

Genevieve's mother came to her aid. "Tell them, Angelina. Tell them what happened."

"He was drunk!" Angelina shrieked through clenched teeth in a room roiling with restless emotions.

Alfredo's blood was boiling as the accusations hurled, making a mockery of the situation. Violently smashing a chair against the wall, he exclaimed over the bits of broken wood scattered on the floor, "This is exactly what Salvatore did to our daughter's life, and it was his selfishness that sent her a world away."

In the stunned silence, Salvatore whimpered, "It's true...forgive me." His admission immediately cleared the air of any lingering misconceptions.

Silent tears were shed for Salvatore as well as for all of the lives that had been destroyed. The group winced each time he mumbled Victoria's name as he teetered on the brink of death. They prayed to God to take him, but he suffered throughout the long, torturous night. Undeniably, Alfredo knew that Angelina's and his suffering had just begun. When the sun peeked over the horizon, Salvatore took his last breath and closed his eyes forever. Just as his penitent words had meant nothing to Alfredo, neither did his passing.

As bursts of sorrow infused the room, Alfredo made a rash decision. "I'm going to stop Victoria," he firmly whispered to his wife.

"Don't be a fool. Even if you could find her, she doesn't need to come back and have the guilt of her husband's death hanging over her head." Angelina sounded desperate even though she kept her voice low. "Please let her go." She put her hands together as if praying and looked at him gravely. "Think of how Salvatore's passing would affect the children. It would be horrible for them to know their father died. In America, there's hope for a better future for our family. Leave them be, Alfredo." She grasped his forearm with urgency. "Leave them be." She wept.

Alfredo's thoughts vacillated as his wife's words reverberated through his mind with sound reason. Hesitantly nodding in agreement, he begrudgingly conceded to the dreadful consequences and a brooding disquietude swept over him—its magnitude made him shudder. The love he felt as a father was all consuming, but the wonder he felt for his grandchildren was almost overwhelming. He silently prayed their lives would be blessed with health and happiness—it was the same prayer he had regularly recited for his children in the solitude of the night. In his overburdened mind, he loosely clung to the belief that someday they would be reunited, but at that moment it barely assuaged his grief.

Deliberately omitting the details of what had transpired, the telegram Alfredo sent to Dominick later that day simply stated his sister and the children were on their way.

CHAPTER 11

At the break of dawn, Victoria and the children continued their laborious trek, and they arrived at the seaport in Naples by early afternoon. The children's eyes grew wide at the sight of the massive steamships that lined the harbor. Even the images Victoria had evoked in her imagination did not grasp the enormity these mighty ships commanded.

"Mama, are we really going on one of those?" Vincenzo asked.

"Yes, dear," she said.

"How do they float?"

Engrossed in her own uncertainties, she responded brusquely, "They just do."

"Why's smoke coming out of the top?"

"It's from their engines."

"Are they on fire?"

Victoria was having trouble keeping pace with her son's unbridled enthusiasm. "No, Vincenzo. That's enough for now."

Swarms of people loaded down with their baskets, sacks, and suitcases filled the piers. When Victoria finally reached the head of a queue, a thin doctor with sparse, white hair abruptly told her, "Madam, I have to check you and your children for diseases and disabilities."

Victoria squared her shoulders. "We're all healthy."

"That'll be for me to determine. You can't board until I complete my examination. You must understand we're responsible for your return if you fail the physical inspection at Ellis Island. Now, please, open your mouth wide."

Victoria did as the man instructed, and he looked down her throat with the help of a flat, wooden stick. He used the other end of the same object to tug at her eyelids and came so close that she could smell the residue of tobacco on his breath. As he repeated the procedure on the children, her heart anxiously pounded inside her chest and did not ebb until he told her, "You may proceed to the next line and pay your fare."

Victoria gathered the children and wanted to run, but she walked away quickly before he had a change of mind. She proudly handed a cashier the coins that had been passed onto her by her mother, and in return, he handed her tin plates and spoons, motioning her forward with a wave of indifference.

Leaving her parents behind consumed Victoria with guilt and sadness; however, she had to trust her instincts that she was making the right decision. "Thank you, Mama. I love you," she whispered to herself as tears of gratitude stained her face. With Gabriella straddled on her hip and the bulky basket clutched in her other hand, she filled her lungs with the last scents of her homeland, waiting to board.

Catherina held on to the folds of Victoria's skirt, and Vincenzo and Gennaro dragged the large, heavy sack behind them as they were herded up the wooden gangplank toward the enormous steamship on this blistering summer's day, breathless.

———◆•◆———

Victoria and her children were directed down a ladder to the cramped, windowless, steerage dormitories.

Metal-framed, triple-tiered bunks lined the confining compartments that extended the length of the ship. They were entitled to three bunks for the five of them, and Victoria piled their belongings at the base. A wall of woolen blankets draped over a rope and narrow tables lined with benches, separated the men from the women and children.

Acclimating to the creaking, compartmentalized quarters, Victoria thought it was eerily quiet for the number of passengers who were crammed into the small area. She knew some were fortunate to be joining family in America, while others had no guarantee there would be a bed or a roof over their heads. Exhausted and bewildered, she sat with her children on the bottom bunk, absorbing what was happening around them. Her mind twisted apprehensively as she reflected on all that she had just left behind. She was suddenly struck with amazement how she had come this far, but simultaneously, she felt alarmingly alone in a room full of people. Hugging her children, she tried to draw strength from their naiveté.

The engines vibrated, and the ship lurched forward, signaling the beginning of their lengthy passage across the Atlantic Ocean.

—◆•◆—

Several crewmen entered the quarters carrying huge pots, and the shuffling of bodies and the clanging of plates snapped Victoria out of her pensive mood. Reaching into their baggage, she pulled out their tin plates and spoons, and they joined the end of the line. A crewman ladled an unidentifiable mass of food onto their plates and added a slice of bread. Victoria settled them at the end of a long table and sat down between her daughters. She smiled politely at the strangers sitting near her, but she purposefully kept her focus on her children.

A crewman ordered everyone's attention and read the captain's regulations out loud. Vincenzo's face lit up when he heard the man say they were permitted to get air on a deck separate from travelers in first- and second-class, but Gennaro's face grimaced as he tasted a mouthful of food. Victoria was suddenly grateful she had a stash of salami and cheese in the basket to share with her children later.

———◆•◆———

The next morning Vincenzo was up and ready. "Mama, can I take Gennaro outside? We're allowed to go as long as we don't go past the rope—you heard the man." He looked at his mother with pleading eyes and with the smile she could not resist. Hesitantly, she nodded her consent, though her expression conveyed her concern.

Grabbing Gennaro's hand, Vincenzo bounded toward the wooden ladder, barely hearing his mother call out, "Stay away from the railing."

Vincenzo's strength contrasted Gennaro's frailness as he effortlessly pulled his younger brother into the brilliant daylight.

Temporarily blinded by the sun's radiance, Vincenzo was not prepared for the view that lay before him. Disregarding his mother's warning, he gravitated to the railing. Taking hold of the bars, he slid to his knees and stared in disbelief. As far as he could see was a churning, massive force that beckoned his admiration. "Gennaro, look!"

Specs of light danced above the water's imposing surface as powerful swells defined the compelling energy that stirred beneath, thrusting them into a starry-eyed trance.

Vincenzo was jarred by the taunting voices of several children gathered around the corner of the deck.

"What's in the box?"

"Let's have a look."

"Hand it over, or we'll take it from you."

Rising to his feet, Vincenzo tugged at Gennaro's sleeve, and they edged closer to investigate the object of the scorn. A small boy was backed up against the railing. Clutching a wooden box to his chest, he meekly refused to unveil its contents to the prying eyes and poking fingers. Impulsively, Vincenzo edged his way past two of the children and grabbed the rattled boy by his collar. Shoving him ahead, they fled down the stairs and hid in the crevices of the steerage compartment.

"Thanks," he said out of breath, "I'm Antonio."

"I'm Vincenzo." Tilting his head sideways in his brother's direction, he said, "This is my brother, Gennaro."

Huddled between the bunks, Antonio carefully unlatched the hook of the carved box resting on his lap and exposed his secret. A silver pocket watch reflected in the blur of the mirror framing the inside lid. Picking up the precious timepiece, Antonio said, "My grandpa gave this to me."

"Wow." Gennaro put his hand to his mouth.

"It looks like it could belong to a king," Vincenzo said.

"You can hold it," Antonio said modestly, handing it to him.

Awestruck by its polished brilliance, Vincenzo smiled broadly at the treasure cupped in his hands.

Vincenzo and Antonio became inseparable, and their younger brothers, Gennaro and Giuseppe, contentedly tagged along. The four boys inquisitively searched the labyrinth of the dingy steerage compartments, looking for obscure passages that would lead them to adventure.

During one of their expeditions, they followed the savory smells wafting through the corridors and stumbled upon the place where meals were prepared.

"Let's go in." Vincenzo brazenly nudged open the door of the galley and peeked around its edge. He watched the many men bustling about the room. Some were tending to the large pots that covered the cast-iron stoves simmering the day's rations, while others were removing produce from an enormous, metal box in the corner.

"I don't think we should," Antonio said.

Ignoring his advice, Vincenzo took a step forward, but in the split of a second, Antonio jerked him back. "Let's get out of here," he said in a more convincing voice. Spinning around, he led Gennaro and Giuseppe in a frantic dash down the hall, while Vincenzo dawdled behind as the wheels in his head continued to churn.

That night, Vincenzo wrestled with sleep, tossing and turning on the lumpy, straw mattress, as he envisioned the assortment of food in the galley. Unable to restrain himself, he slithered down from his bunk and quietly maneuvered toward Antonio.

Gently rousing his friend, he leaned over and whispered in Antonio's ear, "Let's go back to that room. Everyone's sleeping."

With slumberous movement, Antonio carefully rolled out of bed without waking his brother. The duo tiptoed through the hallways, retracing their steps to the now deserted galley. Easing open its bulky door, they cringed as it creaked. A cat hissed its surprise as it crisscrossed their path, and their hands flew to their mouths to stifle their startled squeals.

Heeding every second, they zigzagged their way en route to the icebox. Vincenzo forcefully tugged on the stubborn handle, struggling to open the latch of its heavy door. "Stand behind me, and we'll pull together," he told Antonio.

Bracing their feet, they gave it a mighty yank and disengaged its tethered hook. The door swung open, knocking them both to the ground with Vincenzo landing directly on top of Antonio. Giggling, they simultaneously gaped at the display of food shelved before them and jumped to their feet, each grabbing a bottle of milk.

Without hesitation, Antonio said, "What else should we take?"

"What are you two doing in here?" a man's voice demanded from the doorway.

Vincenzo peered over his shoulder, and the corners of his eyes widened at the sight of a shadowy figure of a man holding a lantern. Cautiously returning the milk to the icebox, his knees were quivering and his chest was thumping as he felt his back being penetrated by the angry eyes of their finder. He looked at Antonio, and together they slowly turned around to brave the acrid tongue of reprimand.

"This room is off limits to passengers," the crewman said harshly.

The boys stood in stunned silence.

The man shook his head. "Humph," he grumbled with the gush of a breath, walking toward them. Vincenzo and Antonio jumped out of his way as he reached into the icebox and retrieved the two bottles of milk. Brusquely handing them back, he said, "Don't tell anyone I gave these to you, and I don't want to see you in here ever again." He dismissed them with a gruff rush of his arm. "Now get out."

Apprehensively accepting the charitable offering, the boys' weak whispers of gratitude faded as they sprinted from the room.

———————◆•◆———————

Victoria's many uncertainties deprived her of the luxury of a restful sleep. Standing to check on the children, she saw the empty spot next to Gennaro, and alarm and annoyance assailed her with equal blows. She scanned the narrow compass of the room, noticing Antonio's bed solely held his brother. While deciding whether or not to wake his mother, she caught sight of Antonio and Vincenzo creeping through the doorway and conspicuously concealing something under their shirts. Her uneasiness abated, but her displeasure rallied as she watched her son slink closer.

"Where've you been?" she scolded him in a hushed tone.

Glancing around the room, Vincenzo looked back at her sheepishly and pulled out a bottle from under his shirt. "A man gave it to us. A man in the other room just gave it to us."

"Why were you in another room? You know it's dangerous to wander the ship in the middle of the night."

"We were hungry," he replied meekly.

His words pulled taut at her heartstrings. Stooping down, she embraced him with arms laden with guilt. "You mustn't ever go in there again."

———◆•◆———

Despite Victoria's adamant warning, the boys continued to roam the ship as if it was their playground—the mundane hours prodding them to unearth its mysteries. Marveling at the brilliance of the light bulbs illuminating the gritty ceilings, they devised a plot to locate the source. One night, when Vincenzo was confident he heard the steady breath of his mother's sleep, he crept over to Antonio's bunk again. As they had planned, they snaked their way toward the bathroom, retrieving the crate they had hidden earlier.

"Stand it on its side. It'll be higher," Antonio suggested, closing the door behind them.

Vincenzo braced the crate between his knees. "Step into my hands," he said. Merging his fingers into a sling, he boosted him upward.

Balancing himself on the edge of the box, Antonio reached for the strange glow from above. "It's hot," he yelped. He removed a grimy handkerchief from his pocket to shield his hand from the heat. With furrowed brows, he twisted and pulled, finally freeing the hot object from its socket. The fire that had been contained in the fragile casing had vanished, and he inserted his finger into the vacant hole, searching for the flame. An involuntary twitch shot up his arm, and he flinched backward, plummeting from the unstable platform. In the midst of his spill, the delicate glass bulb crashed to the floor and splintered into sequins of jagged pieces.

Their bulging eyes momentarily locked, and in one swift motion, Vincenzo jerked Antonio to his feet, and they tore from the room. Diving into the refuge of their bunks, Vincenzo pondered the peculiarity until his mind begged for rest.

———◆◆———

Boredom and loneliness broke down barriers, and it seemed that everyone weakened to conversation, either needing an ear to listen or a word of encouragement. Traveling without a husband, Victoria discreetly avoided befriending the men, but she had developed cordial relationships with some of the women.

"Why are you traveling alone? Where's your husband?" they would inevitably ask.

Disguising the details of her departure, Victoria embellished her tale with plausible lies. "My husband left for America last year to find work and a home for us. He misses us terribly and can't wait for our arrival." Every time she said it, she privately wished her fictitious account were true.

Breaking up the monotony of their endless days at sea, some of the men brought along musical instruments and entertained delighted listeners with songs of their homeland. Engaging in the merriment, Victoria bounced Catherina and Gabriella on her lap in tempo to the familiar melodies, while Vincenzo and Gennaro nestled themselves within the circle of dancing children.

In the evenings, everyone gathered to listen to the stories of the country Victoria would never forget and the many possibilities awaiting them in America. The more animated men could keep the captive audience occupied for hours. Spending so much time together, no longer did Victoria feel she was amongst strangers—a kinship had seeped through the air, swirling with similar hopes and dreams. Several women even met their mates aboard the ship and planned to marry once they reached Ellis Island. Victoria understood how much easier it would be to enter a foreign land with a man reassuringly holding her hand.

The wind built steadily, and the ocean's frothing current rocked the ship more and more. There was no reprieve from the confinement and infirmity. Lingering from one to the next, the days dragged on almost vindictively. The air in steerage had become rank with the noxious odors of spoiled food, vomit, unwashed bodies, and tobacco. The majority of the passengers were seasick, dehydrated, and bedridden, and Victoria and the children had not been spared. The ginger water they sipped gave them little relief from the symptoms. Trying to contend with her own debilitating nausea, Victoria feebly cared for her listless children. Dry heaves regularly pummeled their empty stomachs, and the dizziness made it impossible to reach the fetid restroom. Buckets filled with bodily fluids toppled from the jarring of the ferocious seas, while trunks and baskets slid around the grungy floor. Lanterns, swinging on nails from above, lit the grotesquely sad scene that was tragically consuming their lives.

The weather continued to deteriorate, and gale force winds slammed the sides of the ship. Water from the swollen waves bombarded the decks and streamed through the cracks of the closed steerage hatch. Mixing with debris and oil, the mucky liquid slowly accumulated at first and then surged in a portent of drowning doom.

"Abandon ship! Abandon ship!" a crewman bellowed down to steerage. "She's taken on too much water—the captain says she won't hold up much longer!"

Wading ankle deep in the sloshing bilge, Victoria carried Catherina and Gabriella with the strength of a desperate parent while propelling Gennaro and Vincenzo behind the others toward the ladder. Her adrenaline battled the rushing waters as she hoisted her children one at a time into the grasping arms of two crewmen. The rain came down in torrents, obscuring her vision as she forged her way skyward.

When she stood on the deck, wind and water hurled through the air, further chilling Victoria's sodden skin. She squinted against the pandemonium as waves pounded the ship, dropping it like a toy into the bowels of the foaming sea and thrusting it up to repeat the endless badger. Her arms laden with the girls, she had left their possessions behind except for a satchel tied to her waist containing their most treasured belongings. Vincenzo and Gennaro gripped tightly onto her saturated dress, banding together to navigate the menacing motion of the floundering ship as it listed to starboard. One by one, they were hoisted onto a careening lifeboat with the might of several sailors.

Clinging to each other, they were lowered into the raging waters and brutally swept away by giant crests into the shrieking darkness. Mountains of water converged and diverged from every direction around their tiny vessel—a vulnerable speck in the vastness of the violent sea. Using buckets, the men vigorously bailed, waning against the deluge as savage streaks of lightning struck the water relentlessly; the thunderous cracks terrified the children—their screams muted by the clamor of the unforgiving storm.

When the sun rose, Victoria awoke to an eerie silence and returned to the world with assaulting awareness. Rhythmically, the boat rolled over giant swells and wallowed in the depths of its hollows—Victoria expected the walls on either side to collapse and swallow them whole. She hunched over to bind the queasiness in her stomach and hugged the children closely to shield their eyes from the fiery, unyielding sun as her imagination filled her with blind fear.

Traumatized by the experience of drifting in a lifeboat in a turbulent sea without food or water, Victoria floated in and out of consciousness. Her hallucinations fluctuated between cherished glimpses of the past and frightening fragments of what she thought were their final hours. Her prayers were no longer offered to God for their safety but to the mighty sea for its temperance and mercy.

Time was an interminable nemesis as Victoria waited for an uncertain end, and their destiny dangled on the cusp of survival. They were dehydrated, hungry, battered, and exhausted; however, a faint glimmer of a steamship heading their way infused life back into their fate.

Rescuers roped in the last of the survivors as the sun set into the belly of the ocean. The ship brimmed with bodies well beyond its capacity, and the decks were transformed into dormitories of disconcerted dreams. Victoria felt blessed to have been saved, knowing many had perished in the wrath of the ruthless storm, and the cruel injustice enveloped her in a blanket of despair.

It was eight more tortuous days before they sighted the silhouette of land.

CHAPTER 12

The steamship coasted calmly toward the Hudson River, and the unfamiliar vistas grew larger and larger. Structures dominated the landscape—buildings taller than the trees and higher than the hills.

"Is this America?" Vincenzo questioned.

"Yes, this is America," Victoria exclaimed, scanning the horizon and studying its outline. Its magnificence was indescribable, and its magnitude was inconceivable. She felt overwhelmed in the presence of its greatness.

Victoria and the children were crammed shoulder to shoulder with the multitude of passengers now silently staring in reverence at the Statue of Liberty—a gift from those to those intent on freedom. Her towering torch illuminated the path to the land of new beginnings and symbolized a beacon of promise. Her welcoming gesture eased the strain of leaving the sheltered shores of their homelands and signaled shouts of joy, which reverberated throughout the ship. As she loomed majestically before them, everyone waved hats and handkerchiefs and cried in jubilation as if the Lady understood, and Victoria was sure she did.

The harbor was choked with steamships jammed with immigrants waiting for their turn to be ferried to Ellis Island. First- and second-class passengers were permitted to disembark directly onto the Hudson River piers, and Victoria longingly watched the emotional reunions as she searched the crowd for her brother. Word had spread that Ellis Island was full; therefore, steerage passengers were restricted from leaving the dormant vessel for many hours, prolonging her anxieties.

Finally stepping onto the piers, they were hastily corralled onto a swelling ferry to shuttle them to the island. Detained once again, Victoria nestled the children closer while waiting for their turn to go ashore. Handed paper bags containing sandwiches and bananas, Victoria skeptically examined the contents and discerned it was merely a prelude to the many peculiarities they would encounter in this strange land.

———◆•◆———

The delays continued once they were granted entrance into Ellis Island, and Victoria felt like it was a day without end. With Gabriella saddled on her hip and Catherina and the boys tagging behind, they inched toward the stairway of the registry room. Nurses, using hooked instruments, were checking for trachoma before allowing them to ascend. Victoria looked squarely at a nurse, and as the cold metal pulled at her lid, she instinctively tried to shut her eyes. When the woman approached Gabriella, she burrowed into Victoria's chest and began to whimper. She cupped her daughter's tiny chin as the nurse nimbly examined her with the intrusive instrument. One by one, she steadied the equally frightened faces of Vincenzo, Gennaro, and Catherina.

Disoriented and confused, they shuffled up the steps to the registry room. As she stood in line, Victoria's body swayed—it had become involuntarily accustomed to the rocking of the ships and craved stability. Exhausted and weak, she felt even the weight of her clothes was a burden. She gazed around at the astounding parade of people—a trill of voices spouting a profusion of languages echoed throughout the vast registry room. There were more people than she had ever seen in one place, more people than she had ever imagined could inhabit a city—men covered with straggly beards, some in long robes, women in odd outfits, farmers whose skin was baked in folds and embedded with the dirt of the land they had tilled. Some had slanted eyes, and others had dark complexions. With every bewildered breath, Victoria inhaled her new world as the old world lay far behind.

Listening intently to the sporadic commands, she waited for guidance as she scanned the thousands of foreboding faces wearing the same mixture of fear offset by dashes of dignity and hope.

She approached a podium where a man in a navy blue uniform gruffly asked, "France? Portugal? Greece? Italy?—"

"Italia," she said.

He waved over an interpreter. The grim-faced man with a mustache and thick glasses said, "State your full name and the names of your children."

"My name's Victoria Montanaro," she answered, using her maiden name. She did not want to spend the rest of her life labeled with the reminder she married the wrong man. As she pointed toward her children, she slowly said their names from oldest to youngest, "Vincenzo, Gennaro, Catherina, Gabriella."

Checking them off on the manifest, he then pinned tags onto their ragged clothing, indicating the page and line on which they were listed.

Victoria and the children were ushered ahead to another queue where they were poked and prodded by a team of doctors and nurses who communicated with nods and gestures. Those who appeared to be suffering from a contagious disease, mental illness, or physical disability were coded with chalk accordingly. The grueling journey had greatly affected Catherina and Gabriella. Their bodies frail and their skin pale, Victoria worried that the inspectors would think their health questionable. Throughout the lengthy examinations, she methodically rubbed each bead of her rosary as she prayed their clothes would not get branded with the discriminatory blue chalk. Marked individuals' fate was put on hold as they waited with heightened trepidation—fretful of being separated from their families, fretful their dreams would be snatched away. There were those who were taken to Ellis Island hospital for further medical examination or treatment, but there were those who were ordered to be returned to their countries—sometimes alone, sometimes accompanied by a family member, and sometimes their lives would be claimed before they could leave the island. The crying and screaming of the rejected passengers that echoed through the hospital windows resounded in Victoria's ears, ominous rumblings of discontent. She now understood why it was dubbed "The Isle of Hope, the Isle of Tears."

Following their assigned group, they were marshaled into one of the smaller rooms where a stoutly woman directed Victoria to take a seat. Under the stranger's scrutiny, she was given an IQ test—a puzzle of a ship she put together with trembling fingers, knowing an error of her hand could change their future. Passing to the next stage, Victoria was pummeled with questions by a male interpreter whose eyes were hollow and tone was mundane. "Where are you staying? Do you have a job? Single women are forbidden to leave Ellis Island unescorted...who's coming to claim you?"

Nervously, Victoria took out a piece of paper showing her brother's name and address, and the impatient man informed her that she would have to wait for him to be notified. Now thousands of miles away from home, she was faced with a litany of unending misgivings.

After progressing through the dubious day, they were given a canvas cot in one of the narrow dormitories that ran along the balconies of the registry room—its capacity was stretched tenfold. Victoria settled the children on the flimsy padding. Their bodies were huddled together and their four small sets of feet were intertwined in the middle, creating a pile of jumbled limbs. The cold, tiled floor was the only spot for Victoria, and she sat down wearily. Her stiff joints ached, and she shifted awkwardly, searching for comfort. Tucking her legs tightly to her chest, she rested her head on the edge of the cot. It had been an endless day of interrogations, examinations, and patient waiting, and her contorted body was grateful for even the slightest reprieve.

———◆•◆———

Behind a roped barrier at the bottom of the stairs, Dominick anxiously paced back and forth, and each time a name was called, his heart skipped a beat. Finally hearing Victoria and the children's names was as soothing to his ears as the notes of a melody. He watched with exuberance as they descended the flight of stairs. An overwhelming wave of relief swept over him, but summarily, he was stunned by their haggard appearance. As they approached, he pushed through the crowd and hurdled over the rope, wrapping his arms around the weary group. All at once the lump in his throat constricted, unleashing a thankful river of sobs, which had been previously stifled with prayer. Savoring the moment, they were tearfully reunited along with many others at the "kissing post."

Too overcome to form words and too drained to form more tears, Victoria's body wilted in the cocoon of her brother's embrace.

"Thank God you're here—I thought you were dead. Where's Salvatore?" Dominick asked. "Papa didn't mention him in his telegram."

"We're here now," Victoria said weakly. Her eyes brushed past her children and rested on her brother. "We'll talk later."

Sweeping Catherina and Gabriella into his arms, Dominick stared at their tiny faces. "I can't believe it, they're the spitting image of you, sis."

Victoria grinned softly at her brother.

Looking down at Vincenzo and Gennaro, he raved, "Look how big you are, and how brave and strong."

The boys looked baffled.

"I'm your Uncle Dominick," he said. "Vincenzo, when I last saw you, you were just a baby, and Gennaro, you and your sisters weren't even born."

Victoria's arms were free for the first time in many onerous days, and she felt the weight of the world had been lifted as all of the conflicting emotions she had repressed on her journey temporarily dissipated.

As the fading sun sprayed its last rays, Victoria thought how wonderful it was to see smiles gracing the faces of passengers as they walked out of Ellis Island toward the ferries shuttling them to the city.

Stepping onto the mainland, she swooned with her first breath of freedom, making her feel lightheaded.

CHAPTER 13

Horse-drawn wagons clopped along, carrying passengers, while others walked briskly, circumventing the manure and litter that scattered the dusty streets. Victoria's preconceptions of America with its streets paved with gold were the antithesis of the decrepit buildings they passed on the way to her brother's home.

"They call this area of the city Hell's Kitchen," Dominick said.

"Why's that?"

"It's not safe here like home, Victoria. There've been fights and bloodshed between nationalities. Can you believe, they say more Italians live in New York than in Rome itself, but I've yet to feel welcome in parts of this city." He was shaking his head. "Unfortunately, discrimination and mistrust are the first lessons we learned on the streets of Hell's Kitchen."

She was shocked by his critique. "If it's so bad, why've you stayed?"

"Genevieve and I have created a life for ourselves here. We have friends who've become like family. Our sons were born here. They're Americans." He looked at her seriously. "This is our home now."

"Speaking of Nicholas and Roberto, I can't wait to meet them." Victoria brightened at the thought.

"At two and three they're a handful. I don't know how you do it with four," he said. "You must be exhausted. We're almost there...Genevieve has dinner waiting for us."

Entering the three-story brick tenement building on 36th Street, Dominick said, "Six families live here."

"Everyone lives together?" Victoria was confused.

"There're six separate apartments. Each family has their own railroad flat."

She looked at him, still befuddled.

"You know how our house was one big room? Well, here we have three narrow rooms lined in a row, like the cars of a train. We live on the top floor in the front apartment," Dominick said, pointing upward as a mouse roamed past freely, seemingly part of the tenement's décor. The walls and ceilings of the dingy hallway blistered with peeling paint and faded wallpaper. Dim light bulbs suspended on thick, black wires snaked up the stairwell and cast phantom shadows over the domain.

While trudging up to the third floor, Victoria caught sight of Nicholas and Roberto peeking through the top railing. She was enthralled by the sight of her brother's two young sons. "It's them," she said excitedly to Dominick as a burst of energy propelled her up the stairs. Embracing them, she gushed, "My goodness, look at you." Affectionate tears poured out her sentiments as the cherub-cheeked boys eyed her quizzically.

<hr />

Stepping into the hallway, Genevieve's emotions surged with a mixture of happiness and concern—Victoria was almost unrecognizable. She had always possessed extraordinary beauty; however, her pasty countenance exemplified the strain of her crossing while her emaciated body revealed the struggle. "Oh, Victoria, thank God," she exclaimed.

Falling into each other's arms, their joyful sobs echoed their relief.

Sniffling, Genevieve stepped back and wiped her face with her hand. "We were so worried. I'm so relieved you're finally here." Her tears gave way to a warm smile when she realized she had just gotten back her best friend. "We've missed you—I've missed you—and the children." She stooped down, absorbing their faces. "They're beautiful." She gasped, making the sign of the cross. "Come in, everyone." She guided Victoria to a chair inside the congested kitchen as Dominick and the children followed.

A wood-burning stove, a tiny table, and a washtub, covered like an enameled casket and doubling as a counter, left little room to move about. A small window, two wooden shelves, and a glass-fronted cabinet cluttered the wall around the sink where a single pipe led to the faucet that dripped its murky contents. The kitchen was flanked on one side by a boxy bedroom and on the other side by a parlor of the same size. Between the rooms, a doorway and a square opening was framed out of the wall to let natural light and ventilation seep through the apartment from a solitary window in the parlor. Minimal furnishings scattered the warped floorboards where several cracks provided glimpses of the apartment below, and unwanted sounds flitted upward, adding to the commotion from outside.

"I know its small, but we'll manage," Genevieve said meekly. "You're here, and that's all that matters."

Dominick came up behind Genevieve. "Don't ask about Salvatore," he whispered.

Alfredo's telegram had said Victoria and the children left for America, but surely it must have been a mistake that Salvatore was not mentioned, and both Genevieve and Dominick assumed he would be accompanying them. Genevieve noticed that Victoria had gradually stopped writing about him in her letters, but she thought it was because the children were foremost on her mind. She had come to America with a husband by her side and could not imagine undertaking such a journey alone with four small children. She wondered what possibly could have compelled Victoria to undertake such an enormous responsibility alone.

"Why don't we all sit down? You must be starving. We'll have plenty of time to catch up later." She gently squeezed Victoria's shoulder.

Victoria looked up at her and smiled appreciatively.

The stove was covered with simmering pots, and their comforting aromas filled the air.

"It smells wonderful in here," Victoria said.

Adjusting to the limited area, the boys shared seats while the girls straddled an adult's lap. Before Genevieve served their ravenous guests, Dominick bowed his head. "Thank you, God, for the safe arrival of my sister and her children. Thank you for the food set before us. Bless this home and our parents. Amen." Words were otherwise scarce until the pots were empty, the plates were bare, and their stomachs were uncomfortably stretched.

Genevieve noticed her nieces' and nephews' eyes were half-closed. "The children look so tired. Let me get them ready for bed," she said, rising from her seat. She removed the board from the top of the washtub and began filling it with hot water from a pot on the stove.

Victoria pushed back from the table, but Genevieve patted her down. "Rest. It's been a long few weeks for you."

Propping her head with her hands, she said weakly, "Thank you. I really don't think I have the strength to move."

Beginning with Gabriella, Genevieve undressed her, and as gently as she could, she scrubbed the grime from her skin with Borax as the others waited their turn. When she was finished, the water in the sink was dense with dirt. Ushering them into the parlor, she dressed them in clean undergarments and brushed their knotted hair, which was so brittle it fell out in clumps. To accommodate for space during the day, two thin mattresses were propped against the wall, and now she placed them side-by-side on the floor. The children fell asleep the moment they laid down their weary heads. Gazing upon their innocent faces, Genevieve hoped they would eventually recuperate from their traumatic experience. She settled herself on the blanket she spread out on the floor alongside her two boys, giving Dominick and Victoria time to talk alone, time to become reacquainted. There was so much they had missed and so much they needed to share.

"Oh, Dominick, I didn't think we'd make it. It was awful. I was so frightened…I thought for sure we were going to die." Victoria drew in a deep breath and hugged herself. "You can't believe what goes through your mind when you think the day might be your last. When we were rescued, I thought I was hallucinating."

Sitting next to his sister, Dominick placed his arm around her shoulder, and she leaned her head into his chest. "There was word that your ship went down days ago and that some had survived. Every night after work I went down to the pier to check for your arrival, but the names of the rescued passengers weren't posted. I didn't receive a telegram that you were alive until today. They didn't know…" His voice trailed off. Haunted by the thought that his family's fate had resided in the ravenous clutches of the infinite sea, he sighed heavily. "I thought we lost you forever. Having you here is a miracle."

Victoria glanced up at him. "I know you're wondering where Salvatore is," she said in a voice choked with distress.

"I am a little curious," he admitted with a hint of sarcasm.

"It was a mistake to marry him, I know that now. It all started when his father died—it was right after Gennaro was born. He took over the mill just like he wanted, but he was miserable. He began drinking day and night."

Dominick was shocked. *Why did she neglect to mention this in her letters?* Realizing it was her time to purge, he refrained from interrupting and let her continue.

"When he came home, it was always after the children were asleep. He deliberately avoided them." She looked at him and shook her head slightly. "I don't think he knew how to love them." Tears streamed down her cheeks, and she nervously rubbed her fingers over her knuckles. "The only thing he wanted from me was in the dark. If I refused, it made him crazy, and I had no choice but to give in. He never hit me or the children… and I was grateful for that."

Jumping to his feet and slamming his fist on the table, Dominick felt the veins in his neck pulsating with rage. "That selfish bastard! I'd like to kill him with my bare hands."

"It's over now," Victoria said, squeezing his arm and settling him back down into the chair.

There was a long silence as Dominick tried to regain his composure. "Where'd you get the money to come?" he finally said.

"You're not going to believe this—Mama gave it to me. She's the one who begged me to leave. Papa knew nothing about it. The night before I left, I wanted to see him, to hug him, to say good-bye, but he would've never understood I had to go. I had to start over…for myself and my children."

"You made the right decision. Maybe someday we can find a way to bring them here."

Victoria nestled her head into her folded arms resting on the table. Her body surrendered to exhaustion, and she fell into an unconscious slumber—her damp dress glued to her back, her hair a cobweb of dirt and oil. Dominick effortlessly carried her slight frame into the bedroom and placed her on the mattress. Unlacing her threadbare shoes, he slid them off her feet and gently kissed her flushed forehead. Her eyelids laden with sleep, she curled into a fetal position, donning the persona of a child rather than a mother of four. Dominick wished he could erase the trials she had suffered and the lines of woe that marred her delicate features. What she had endured was beyond comprehension. How she had survived had to have been an intervention from God.

———•••———

Getting only a few hours rest with his legs uncomfortably dangling off the arm of their small sofa, Dominick readied himself for his job at the slaughterhouse on Tenth Avenue, an occupation that started at five each morning except Sunday. At an early age, he was taught how to slay an animal. It was a skill necessary for survival in Italy, and the trade he used for survival in America. The men he worked with had developed a camaraderie, which eased the tedium of the endless hours, but not the tedium of the backbreaking labor. Each day he returned home exhausted and caked with the rancid remains of dead animals, and each night he went to bed a little less optimistic.

Rubbing his forehead and yawning, he walked into the kitchen and sat down at the table where his steaming cup of coffee awaited. Allowing himself a few minutes off his feet before spending the next twelve hours standing, he savored the last sip and put the tin cup in the sink.

Genevieve handed him a satchel containing a ham sandwich and an apple.

"I overheard what Victoria told you last night, and it made me cry to think she suffered in silence for so long."

Dominick felt weary. "I couldn't sleep. The thought of what happened to her held me prisoner all night. Mama was right to make her leave."

Together they walked down the three flights of stairs and out onto the stoop. The sun had yet to rise, but the street was already awakening. The milkman had made the day's delivery, and Dominick bent over and picked up a bottle, handing it to his wife.

"It'll be all right," she said. "We'll make this work."

He read the worry in her eyes. "I know," he said, realizing how unconvinced he sounded, and he left her with a slight kiss on her lips.

As Dominick walked to work, the enormity of the situation was solemnly sinking in. Although thrilled to have his sister here, it added to his responsibilities and concerns—there were five more mouths to feed.

Genevieve gave Nicholas and Roberto paper and pencils to keep them occupied while she boiled and washed the filth from her nieces' and nephews' clothes and hung them above the stove to dry. The children slept through the morning, and when they awoke, she dressed them in their clean clothes, which hung loosely around their bony frames.

"Sit down at the table, and I'll get you a piece of my special bread and a big glass of milk," she said. "I think I may even have some honey to put on it." Taking the jar off the shelf, she used a spoon to drizzle the gold, sticky liquid onto the bread. As the children watched tentatively, Genevieve realized how confused they must have been—strangers thrown together, discovering they are family. "Isn't this nice to have all the cousins sitting at one table?" she said.

Vincenzo crimped his eyebrows. "How are we cousins, Aunt Genevieve?"

"You're cousins because your mother and Uncle Dominick are brother and sister," she explained. She removed the sole picture she had of their grandparents from the bureau and showed it to them. "You all have the same grandma and grandpa." Pointing her finger at the couple in the photograph, she added, "And if you look closely, you'll see you all have his big eyes and her round face."

The children stared at the picture and back to one another. As the likeness settled over them with a delighted intrigue, their uneasiness began to taper.

When Genevieve and Dominick first came to America, they had taken English lessons at the church, but their command of the language was rudimentary at best. Genevieve picked up objects from the table and carefully pronounced the English version to the children in a deliberate tone. Taking turns, they repeated the strange words and giggled at each other's distorted enunciations, further lightening the mood.

"Why don't we take a walk?" Genevieve suggested, intentionally wanting to give Victoria more time to rest.

"Should I wake Mama?" Vincenzo asked.

She peeked behind the curtain into the bedroom and saw that Victoria was still sound asleep. Turning around, she smiled reassuringly at him. "It's okay, we should let your Mama rest," she said. "We'll see her when we get back."

They strolled past the drab brick and clapboard tenements that lined the cobblestone streets where taverns and shops were interspersed among the squalor. Clotheslines and laundry crisscrossed and draped to adjacent buildings from open windows. Fire escapes were jammed with mattresses and served as outdoor rooms while the summer heat simmered the city to a slow boil. The streets were transformed into bazaars inundated with masses of disenchanted humanity spewing a montage of dialects and languages. Vendors lined both sides of the streets tending their carts that held assorted commodities. Peddlers, craftsman, and musicians touted their wares or expertise, all trying to make a dime while haggling with customers who were desperate to save a penny. Mothers sat on front stoops as their children darted between passersby and frolicked in the water gushing from a fire hydrant to cool their calloused feet from the sunbaked surface. Tenderly watching her nieces and nephews, who were obviously hypnotized by the unconventional sights and sounds, Genevieve remembered when she first had arrived in America and the dramatic contrast to the tranquility of Italy's countryside.

———◆•◆———

Victoria slept with a serenity she had not savored in years, and sleep had claimed her day. Shaking herself out of her disoriented state, she padded into the kitchen. Squinting through the dim light, her face brightened as everyone else's came into focus. The smell of the savory soup sitting on the stove made her stomach growl. "What time is it?" She yawned, covering her mouth.

Vincenzo enthusiastically greeted her, "Good morning, Mama, but it's really night time." He chuckled.

"You've slept away the day. We're about to have dinner," Dominick said.

"We went for a walk with Aunt Genevieve. There're so many people here...and tall buildings!" Gennaro said.

"There're wagons where you can get all kinds of food for a coin," Vincenzo added. "We even saw a train pass over our heads. It was so loud, we covered our ears."

Baffled by their strange narrative, Victoria was both surprised and relieved that her children seemed to be assimilating themselves to their new surroundings. She had prayed they would be able to forget all the grief and horror they had witnessed, and the process seemed to have miraculously begun. She glanced at Genevieve with thankful eyes only another mother could understand.

Victoria lifted Gabriella off of a chair and sat down, placing the child on her lap. She marveled at the people who graced the table—her brother, his wife, their two sons, and her four children. She suddenly felt relaxed and restored. They had weathered the journey, and she was ready for another to begin.

CHAPTER 14

Victoria sincerely appreciated that Dominick and Genevieve had graciously adapted to the overcrowded quarters, the many meals, the added confusion, and the never-ending work, and she had thanked them many times over. Privacy was a nonentity in the small apartment. The winter months were cold and confining, and the children became restless. The winds whipped off the river and barreled through the streets, whirling their way over the island. Trudging through the snow and ice and then sloshing through the mud and slush of early spring, Victoria thought her bones would never thaw and the sun would never warm.

To reconcile the conflicting need to stay home with her children and earn extra money, Genevieve had brought home piecework. Several mornings a week, she and her two boys walked down to the factories and waited on lengthy lines to procure unassembled goods. Required to leave a deposit to ensure the completed projects were returned, she would then be paid accordingly. Since Victoria had arrived, she stayed home with the children, while Genevieve scurried from factory to factory, taking her position behind others looking for morsels of work.

"You'll have enough to keep you busy until I get back," Genevieve told Victoria, who was already sitting at the table, sewing. "There're plenty more buttons that need to be sewn onto cards. Vincenzo and Gennaro can count them out. Boys, there're six buttons to a card." She patted them on the head. "You two are such a big help. We're really proud of you."

In light of her compliment, the boys immediately sat down, eager to help.

When Genevieve returned to the apartment midday, Victoria, Vincenzo, and Gennaro were diligently working while the younger children were playing with a ball on the floor.

"How did it go?" Victoria asked, glancing up at her briefly.

"The lines were the worst I've ever seen." She sighed, shrugging off her coat. "I'm so glad Nicholas and Roberto were here with you." She took a jar of thick, amber liquid from her basket and held it up. "We have to use this to glue the labels for the cigars. I was told to keep it away from our mouths and to wash our hands when we're done. It could make us sick."

Genevieve's constant companionship was an indispensable distraction for Victoria as they labored into the night; however, she still felt unsettled and uncertain about the future. Her sister in-law had introduced her to America's ways, yet they were still learning together. As Victoria was slowly acclimating herself to the strange customs and language of her new world, she tried to forget Salvatore, although thoughts of him viciously harassed her mind like a host to a hornet's nest. She had started writing down her memories soon after arriving in America, beginning the first page with how she felt the day she noticed Salvatore working at the mill. Remembering the good times and the bad, she wrote on the nights when she wrestled with sleep and her mind churned with doubt. She wondered if it were her fault he began drinking and avoiding them. She wondered if she could have been more forgiving. She believed she had given Salvatore her heart, but she knew she gave her children her soul. She thought if she read it on paper, it would help her understand what had happened between them, alleviate some of the guilt and confusion, or at least help her forget. But no matter how much she tried to make sense of it all, it still frightened her that it could all start again. For no matter where she was, every unaccounted for sound and every unseen face held the ominous dread that Salvatore would reappear in her life.

"What's wrong, Victoria? You seem like you're a million miles away," Genevieve said.

"I was just thinking," she said, taking a cigar from the pile and slipping a label over its tip.

"You know you can tell me anything."

Victoria looked up at her and frowned. "The children and I can't stay here forever," she said, shaking her head. "You and Dominick have been so kind, but you need your privacy." She tried to sound casual and confident. "With the money I saved this past year from doing the piecework, I'll have enough to rent an apartment if I take in a boarder—"

"A boarder? Victoria, that's not necessary."

"It'll be fine." She smiled, knowing her sister-in-law was genuinely concerned. "Many people take in boarders, and I'll be careful who I choose. I need to depend on myself. I need to be on my own."

"But who knows who'll come knocking at your door."

"We'll be okay," she added for Genevieve's benefit as well as her own.

A few weeks later, Victoria rented an apartment in an adjacent building. She had the reassurance of knowing her family was next door, and by now, neighbors had become more than friends and looked out for one another like family, making her feel secure within the confines of the tight-knit community.

The first thing she did when she moved into the sparsely furnished rooms was to find a place for her parent's Bible. She placed the heirloom on the bureau by the door as a solid reminder of the home she often pondered. The book had been passed from generation to generation—its pages rippled by the voyage, its contents still a comfort for her future.

It took her most of the afternoon to scour the kitchen and scrub the windows and the floors. The repetitive work numbed her fingers and stiffened her spine, but she was feeling satisfied with the results. Sitting down at the table, she tried to remember the last time she had spent several hours alone. She was glad Genevieve had offered to watch the children, and she felt herself relax into the notion of a place of her own. Spotting Dominick across the alley tying a rope to a pulley jutting from his window's ledge, she called out, "What are you doing over there?"

"I strung a rope to your ledge." He pointed toward her. "I did it while you were busy packing here last night. I wanted it to be a surprise."

"A surprise?"

He leaned out the window and jiggled the line. A bell dangling from his end of the rope clattered. "There's a bell on your side too," he said.

She stood up. "What's this for?" she asked, eyeing the contraption.

"Ring the bell if you need us, and use that to pass things back and forth." He gestured with his hand to the basket suspended on the rope.

"I'm impressed," she said. "Do you think it'll hold a child?"

"I don't think that's a good idea." A devilish grin came over his face, and for a second, it brought her back to their youth. "But I wouldn't put it past any of them to try it," he added as he looked down at the children peering out the window around him.

Together, Victoria and her brother shared a hardy laugh.

———————◆•◆———————

The women continued to assemble piecework; however, their days were spent in Victoria's apartment, while the nights brought her an emptiness she assumed would last the rest of her years. To fill the void in the bedroom and earn extra income, Victoria painted a sign on a piece of wood advertising a room for rent and hung it from the railing of the front stoop. She would sleep on a mattress in the parlor with the children since they slept together most nights anyway.

By week's end, there was a knock at the door.

The man standing before her was tall and strapping with a full head of gray hair interspersed with the brown of his youth.

Victoria felt a surge of uneasiness, but managed a smile. "Can I help you?"

"Good morning, ma'am," he said. "I'm looking for a place to stay while I'm working in the area, and I saw your sign out front. My name's Lorenzo Carnavale."

"I'm Victoria Montanaro," she said, not quite sure what questions to ask. She thought his chiseled features were those of any European, but his name and accent were certainly Italian. "What part of Italy are you from?" she said, using the language of their birthplace.

The lines on Lorenzo's bronzed, weather-beaten face seemed to soften at the sound of her voice. "Rome, originally," he said.

"I'm from Caivano. It's not far from Naples."

"I have relatives in Naples, but I've never been there."

"You spoke good English. When did you come to America?"

"About five years ago." He paused for a moment. "No six," he said, correcting himself.

"What kind of work do you do?"

"I work for the city, laying cobblestone in the streets. I'll be gone all day except Sundays, and then I go to church and usually visit friends, so I really need just a place to sleep. Is the room still available?"

"Yes," she said. "How long would you be staying?"

"It's hard to say. At least a month…maybe longer. It depends on the job." He smiled.

Lorenzo's blue eyes radiated kindness and his gentle nature conveyed the serenity of someone who was at ease with himself and those around him, making Victoria feel more relaxed. "I'll let you have the bedroom for two dollars a week, and your evening meal is included. I have four children…I hope that's not a problem."

"I've none of my own, but I do enjoy them," he answered politely. Taking several coins from his pocket, he handed them to her. "I can pay you two weeks in advance."

Victoria felt it was strange to have only the span of a short conversation to form an opinion about someone with whom she was about to share her home. "That would be fine," she said.

"I'll be back later this evening. May I leave my belongings with you?"

"Certainly...please come in." She led him through the kitchen and into the bedroom. "This is where you'll be staying."

He placed his satchels in a corner on the floor. "Thank you, and have a nice day," he said with a grateful nod as he left.

Victoria felt jittery all day, and she kept herself busy waiting for Lorenzo to return. She washed one of the quilted blankets she and Genevieve had made together and hung it out back to dry. She swept away the cobwebs and fluffed the feathers in a pillow. She prepared a hearty dinner of ham and bean soup and ate with her children. After putting them to bed, she tidied the kitchen, placing a clean napkin and spoon on the table. The summer sun had set, and she pulled the string to the light on the ceiling to brighten the room. It was later than she had expected when there was a tap on the door.

"Is it okay if I let myself in?" Lorenzo asked as he entered.

"It's your home now too," she said, trying to sound casual.

He held up his hands. "Mind if I clean up?"

"Of course not," she said. "There's a bar of soap on the counter."

While he washed his hands and face, she placed a towel on the edge of the sink.

"Thank you," he said as he dried himself.

She ladled the soup into a bowl and put it on the table along with a slice of bread. "Let me know if it's hot enough for you."

He sat down and tucked the napkin into the collar of his shirt. Picking up his spoon, he dipped it into the soup and tasted it. "Mmm, perfect," he said.

Victoria kept herself busy wiping the stovetop with a dishrag while catching glimpses of Lorenzo eating his meal. She noticed that his hands were large and calloused, and the remnants of his labor were permanently embedded under his fingernails. "There's plenty if you'd like some more."

Lorenzo looked up as Dominick unexpectedly strolled through the door, leaving it open behind him.

"Oh, Dominick," Victoria said, surprised to see him. "This is Lorenzo...he's going to be staying here for a while." She looked at Lorenzo. "This is my brother. He lives right across the alley with his wife, Genevieve, and their two sons." She pointed out the window.

Lorenzo stood up and shook hands with Dominick. "How nice to have family so close. Mine are all in Italy."

"Please, eat," Dominick said, prompting Lorenzo to sit back down. "I just stopped by to meet you." He looked at Victoria skeptically. "Genevieve told me that you rented the bedroom."

"This morning," she said, giving him a wary glance.

Dominick turned back to Lorenzo. "What did you do in Italy, Lorenzo?"

"I traveled the countryside, restoring churches, fountains, and piazzas. I loved what I did. It was what I wanted to do, and I learned from some of the best."

"Then why did you come here?" Dominick leaned back against the sink and folded his arms across his chest.

"Hmm..." Lorenzo sighed. "We've all had dreams about America...the ones where anything's possible. When I turned thirty, and having no wife or children, I decided to make the journey to see for myself what all the talk was about." He chuckled and shook his head. "I came here to seek opportunity and challenge my ability. Little did I know I had to prove myself in a land where everyone needs to prove themselves. I learned quickly, as I'm sure you have, that here all Italians are considered peasants."

"I know exactly what you mean," Dominick said. "So what do you do?"

"Now…I lay cobblestones, which anyone can do." He shrugged. "Following the locations of my job and traveling around the city, I've met a lot of nice people." He smiled slightly at Victoria. "I feel fortunate to have work."

Dominick looked at Victoria, this time, approvingly.

Lorenzo dunked his bread in the bowl and took a bite. Wiping his mouth with his napkin, he asked, "What do you do, Dominick?"

"I work at a slaughterhouse. Like you, it's not what I thought I'd be doing here, but it puts food on the table." He glanced at the clock on the wall. "I should be getting back."

"Tell Genevieve I'm almost finished sewing the lace collars we were working on today. She can take them back tomorrow, so she should get here early," Victoria said.

"Nice to meet you," Dominick said to Lorenzo. "I'm sure we'll be seeing more of each other."

"Have a good night," Lorenzo responded.

Looking at Victoria, Dominick raised his eyebrows. "We'll talk tomorrow."

She rolled her eyes at him. "I'm sure we will."

He gave her a wry grin as he strode out the door.

———◆◆———

In the weeks that followed, Lorenzo developed an amiable relationship with Victoria's children, and they delighted in the extra attention he increasingly showed them. Accustomed to having him around, they pleaded with her to delay their bedtime on the nights when he arrived home late. She appreciated his interest in her children; nevertheless, she was concerned they were growing too attached, and in the back of her mind, so was she. After the children had fallen asleep, she resumed the unending pace of piecing together the mounds of work that lie before her as she and Lorenzo talked about their days, their families, and eventually, their dreams.

Despite Victoria's well-intentioned reservations, she had become very comfortable with Lorenzo and found herself thinking more and more about their blossoming friendship. She thought she had closed the door on that part of her life that included a man, but she also shouldered a rallying discontent. When she had left Italy, she severed all physical ties with Salvatore, freeing her from the shackles that would have bound them together for the rest of their lives, although she was still haunted by the reoccurring nightmare that he would someday appear.

Gradually, the entries in Victoria's journal revolved around thoughts of Lorenzo, replacing the nagging images of Salvatore. Each day, she could feel herself emerging from her lonely cocoon as if her body were undergoing a physical as well as an emotional transformation. She began to take extra care with her appearance. Purchasing a lipstick, she felt guilty she had spent money on something so frivolous; however, she wanted to look her best, and the primping became a nightly ritual. Ardently awaiting Lorenzo's return from work, she carefully applied the red tint to her lips and cheeks. Removing the pins from her hair, she loosened it from the day's chignon and it fell in crimson spirals upon her shoulders. It had been many years since she had affectionate feelings for a man, since someone had made her feel attractive. The well of emptiness inside her was now brimming with desire, but unfortunately, Lorenzo could leave on a moment's notice since his work dictated his destinations.

———◆●◆———

One night after the children fell asleep, Victoria sat at her usual place across the table from Lorenzo.

"I have something to tell you," he said. The concern in his voice made Victoria look up from the artificial flower she was assembling and search his eyes.

"I've been assigned to a job on the east side of the island. I'll be leaving tomorrow."

She felt as if she had been punched in the stomach, but she forced herself to speak. "The children will certainly miss you," she said. "Please come back and visit if you're ever in the area. We've enjoyed your company. You've been the perfect guest." She managed to keep her face expressionless, yet sadness pulsated beneath her skin.

"You've made me feel very welcome here. I'll always remember your hospitality."

Hospitality, is that all it was? she thought. "I'm glad you found it comfortable." She struggled to keep her tone light.

"I've never felt more comfortable in my life," he said.

Nevertheless, the next morning Lorenzo was gone from their lives as quickly as he had appeared, and Victoria stoically returned the sign to the front door, refusing to cry over another man. She knew Lorenzo would leave one day, and she talked herself out of falling victim to the inevitable. The next person she allowed into her home would remain a stranger. This time she planned to have more rules. This time she planned to keep her distance.

———◆•◆———

Several nights later, while Victoria was at the table writing a letter to her parents, she heard a knock at the door. She continued what she was doing, assuming it was Genevieve or Dominick and they would let themselves in. The knock became more insistent, causing her body to tense. *Who could it be at this hour? Could Salvatore be standing on the other side?* She stood up and reluctantly cracked the door open, just enough to peek out.

"I understand you have a room for rent," Lorenzo said, holding his satchels and wearing a serious look on his face.

"I'm looking for someone who can promise me a few months," she said dryly.

"What if I can promise you more?"

She heard the longing in his voice and opened the door wider.

Dropping his baggage, he eagerly took her into his arms. "It was impossible for me to stay away," he said. "There's something so right about being with you."

Lorenzo had always kept a respectful distance from Victoria, but now she melted within the warmth of his embrace. Kissing her on the lips, she immediately felt her inhibition release itself from its lonely abyss. When he picked her up and carried her into the bedroom, it seemed like the natural thing to do.

CHAPTER 15

Gennaro was a year younger than his brother, Vincenzo, but still resembled a toddler. Even the robust could not always fight off the germs that ominously lurked throughout the polluted city, and Gennaro was frail and vulnerable and, therefore, often ill. Requiring more and more of Victoria's attention, there was little time for anyone or anything else. Without an ounce of dissension, Vincenzo's nimble fingers produced the bulk of the piecework. When Victoria watched her eldest son labor, she wished he could remain a child rather than do the work of an adult.

As Gennaro's health deteriorated, he spoke less and coughed more, and it seemed that lately it was the only sound Victoria heard. Holding him close to keep him warm, she paced the apartment until her arms and back ached as much as her heart. Under her breath, she continually recited a prayer to Mary, the mother of God, hoping another mother would take pity on her son.

———◆◆◆———

Early one morning, while Victoria was sitting on the edge of Gennaro's mattress and stroking his damp hair, she was feeling utterly helpless. Her son lay with his eyes half closed, and his cheeks were bright red and looked swollen. She pressed her ear to his chest, and she could hear the distinct gurgle of liquid.

Lorenzo walked into the parlor. "I'm leaving," he said. "Is there anything you need before I go?" He bent over to kiss her good-bye.

She looked up at him. "Lorenzo, feel his head. He's burning up." She whispered so as not to wake the other children.

She removed the wet cloth from Gennaro's forehead and Lorenzo rested his hand in its place. "We can't wait any longer," he said, sounding equally frightened as the color drained from his face. "I'm going to get a doctor."

"How will we pay him?" She choked on the words.

"We'll find a way," Lorenzo said from over his shoulder as he headed out the door.

Replacing the wet cloth on Gennaro's head, Victoria felt nauseous, and she could taste the bile in her mouth. *What if it's too late?* she fretted. Unable to rid herself of the horrid notion, she leaned over and held him tightly. He was shivering, yet she could feel the heat from his body penetrating through the layers of cloth between them.

Catherina stirred and opened her eyes.

"Good morning," Victoria said, forcing out the cheer.

Wearily, Catherina stood up, her droopy eyes now level to her mother's. Her tiny face was surrounded by a tangle of dark brown curls, and her nightshirt was bunched up around her waist.

Bending closer, Victoria pulled it down and kissed her daughter on the cheek. "You still look sleepy," she said, thinking that out of all her children, Catherina resembled her the most. "Go inside, breakfast is on the table."

Victoria watched Catherina sluggishly shuffle into the kitchen and climb onto a chair. Kneeling, she tilted the pitcher and carefully poured a glass of milk, and Victoria was impressed she did it without spilling a drop. Looking down at Gennaro, she wondered if he would ever be strong enough to pour himself a glass of milk or sit at the table to eat a meal.

He began to cough again, gagging on the phlegm lodged in his throat.

Immediately, she sat him upright. Supporting him with one hand, she rubbed his back in a circular motion with the other. She knew with each breath his fight was growing weaker.

Vincenzo and Gabriella woke up when they heard the fussing.

"Good morning," Victoria said again, although she felt that this morning was anything but good. She feigned a smile. "Catherina's already in the kitchen, why don't you two go and have something to eat."

Vincenzo stood up, groggy and unsteady on his feet. Taking Gabriella by the hand, he led her over the mattresses and joined Catherina at the table.

——◆•◆——

Two arduous hours had passed before Victoria heard footsteps ascending the stairs. She jumped up from the floor when Lorenzo and a doctor walked through the door. Grabbing the man's gloved hand, she pulled him into the parlor. "Please help my son," she begged.

"Victoria, this is Doctor Stern," Lorenzo said, following behind.

Kneeling down on the floor next to Gennaro, who was curled up beneath a pile of blankets and coats, Doctor Stern placed his worn leather bag beside him and pulled out a stethoscope. Removing his gloves, he pushed the layers aside to expose the child's chest and listened closely in several places. He placed his hand on Gennaro's forehead and felt his neck, but it did not seem to take him long to come to a diagnosis. "I'm afraid he's showing signs of tuberculosis," he said, shaking his head. He looked up at Victoria and Lorenzo with a bleak expression tightening his narrow face.

"I don't know what that means," she said.

Doctor Stern stood up. His hair was thin and wiry, and he peered at them over spectacles that hung low on his nose. "He has a severe infection in his lungs," he said, "and it's very contagious."

Victoria did not fully understand, but the look of distress in the man's eyes confirmed its severity, and she threw up her hands in consummate frustration. "What should we do?" she asked as tears clouded her vision.

In a hurried haze of activity, Victoria and Lorenzo did as Doctor Stern instructed. She removed Gennaro's clothes, while he filled the sink with tepid water. Producing a jar of salve from his bag, the doctor gently massaged it into Gennaro's heaving chest, motioning for Victoria to follow his lead.

"While I'm here, I'd like to check your other children," Doctor Stern offered, holding up his stethoscope and pointing to the sofa where Vincenzo, Catherina, and Gabriella sat silent and scared.

Victoria felt of surge of terror, realizing anyone of them could be next. "Yes," she said with a plea in her voice. Anxiously, she watched as he thoroughly examined each child.

"They're fine for now," he said, sounding relieved. "But keep them away from their brother." He removed the stethoscope from his ears and dropped it onto his neck. Handing her a small, brown bottle from his bag, he took a teaspoon off the counter. "Twice a day." He held up two fingers and looked at Gennaro.

Victoria nodded, hoping the elixir she held in her hand would cure whatever sickness was invading her son's body.

At the height of their dismay, Lorenzo asked Doctor Stern to come to their home once again, and this time, he brought along an elderly woman.

"My name is Philomena," she said in Italian. She looked compassionately at Victoria cradling Gennaro in her arms. "The doctor brought me along to explain the severity of your son's condition and answer your questions." Her voice was soft, and her brown eyes crinkled at the sides when she donned a tempered smile.

Instantly, Victoria felt a tinge of relief that the woman spoke Italian. "We've done everything we were told, but he seems to be getting worse," she said.

"There's nothing more that you or the doctor can do," Philomena said. "The invisible toxins in the air have infected your son's delicate lungs, and you're all at serious risk."

The news was staggering for Victoria, and she began to sway. "What about my other children? Catherina and Gabriella have started to cough. Will they get worse?"

"It's possible. At this point they're not showing any other symptoms of the disease, but they should be watched closely. Let us know if either of them develops a fever." Philomena glanced sideways at Doctor Stern, and he gave her a slight nod. "If Gennaro were to stay in the city, he has little chance of survival," she said. "Doctor Stern's brother-in-law has helped to establish a sanatorium at Saranac Lake in New York State where there are dedicated doctors and nurses who might be able to foster someone in your son's dire condition back to health in the fresh mountain air. He'd be placed on a healthy diet, and as he improves, exercising and attending classes would be part of his rehabilitation." She paused. "The patients at the facility are isolated from their families, but letters would regularly update you on his progress."

Victoria felt like the air had been knocked out of her and glowered at Philomena and Doctor Stern in disbelief. "How could I send my son away alone? How far away is Saranac Lake? How could we possibly afford this treatment?" She tried to stop the barrage of questions reeling in her mind and concentrate; however, the room was spinning, and so were Philomena's words.

"Through charity, a bed has been set aside for Gennaro by Doctor Stern, but we must take him right now, or it'll be given to another." The woman spoke louder so Victoria could grasp the lifeline that was being offered.

Victoria locked tear-filled eyes with Lorenzo, and he nodded his assent. She had no choice but to hand over her son and their trust to the doctor, and Gennaro was too listless to comprehend the transfer.

Wrapping him in a blanket, Philomena cautioned, "Say your good-byes from a distance. He's much too contagious."

Victoria ignored her warning and clasped her son's hand, her tears dripping onto his angelic face, her lips tasting her own pain.

"You must burn anything he has come in contact with and wash the rooms to rid them of his germs," she said firmly.

Slowly, Gennaro's tiny, limp fingers slipped out of Victoria's hands as he was carried out the door in the custody of strangers. She dropped to her knees and brushed away the stray tears from the faces of her frightened children. Needing to hear the words herself, she said, "They're going to make your brother well again. I promise he'll be home soon." She tried to sound optimistic, but her tone was forced and fragile. Overcome by the thought that another might succumb to the mysterious ailment and be taken away, she gathered them into her arms.

Outpacing their anguish, Victoria and Lorenzo combed the apartment, collecting everything Gennaro had come in contact with and tossing it into the belly of the blazing stove. They feverishly scrubbed every surface of the rooms, attempting to prevent the loss of another, yet Victoria could not wipe away the possibility that she may never see her son again.

———————•◦•———————

Victoria became sick with worry. Her son's fate was in the hands of strangers, and she was powerless. *Who would give him the dose of love to help him along? Who would kiss him good night?* She ate almost nothing, and her body rebelled. The months of agony and loss of appetite were destroying her emotional as well as her physical state, and she should have been confined to a bed. Her only motivation to continue were her children, or thoughts of taking her own life would have prevailed.

In the midst of it all, Victoria realized she was pregnant. After she and Lorenzo had consummated their relationship, he comfortably and willingly became an integral part of the family, but she decided to hold off with the announcement, unsure if he, or she, was ready to add another child to the mix.

———————•◦•———————

In what Victoria believed to be the beginning of her third month of pregnancy, she remained in bed later than usual and tried her best not to stir as she listened to Lorenzo dress for work. Last night he had commented that she looked tired, and she almost told him about the baby. The truth was she had been having minor cramping for several days, normal she had thought, but yesterday she was experiencing sharp pains in her stomach and was worried if their baby was all right.

As the severity of the contractions increased, she waited in silent agony for the door to close behind Lorenzo. Sliding her legs over the edge of her bed, she sat up with her arms pressed against her stomach as perspiration oozed from her quaking body. Dropping to her knees, she crawled, one hand in front of the other, into the hallway. When she reached the toilet tucked under the stairwell, the normal stench that oozed from its stagnant interior made her vomit repeatedly into its bowels. Rising on all fours, she sat down on the seat and doubled over. She felt the life drain from her body, beginning with clots and ending in a stream of blood that was released into the bowl.

The physical pain gripped her like a vice, compounding the psychological trauma inflicted by the image of her sequestered son. *I don't feel alive, so how could I give birth to another?* She deemed this her destiny. *Has fate stolen my unborn child because I'm unfit to care for the ones I already have, or is this punishment for taking the children away from Salvatore?* Once again, guilt tore through her ravaged psyche, leaving in its path searing streaks of shame and condemnation.

By the time Lorenzo returned from work that evening, Victoria deftly hid her secret from him behind a semblance of casual words and gestures, cleaving onto the vestiges of normalcy. She did not have the stamina to grieve for a child she never held, when time was running out to hold the one she cherished.

———◆•◆———

The first letters from the sanatorium were optimistic, although the tone slowly shifted and delivered a steady chronicle of decline. Victoria was tormented by the impending loss of a child she loved more than herself. She wished she could change places with Gennaro—it was a request that began every prayer. She wanted to trust in God's reasoning, yet it was beyond her comprehension that he would deliberately compromise the well-being of a child, and she questioned her faith. She was defenseless against the invisible forces that gnawed their way at her son, and it tore her apart physically, emotionally, and tragically. The entries in her journal were testaments to the purgatory of her days, and the puckered pages were reminders of the tears. Sleep was her only reprieve.

———◆•◆———

Each evening, Victoria was drawn to church where the possibility of a miracle was housed. Lorenzo remained home with the children; however, his prayers were with Gennaro, and his heart was with Victoria. He was watching her crumble and strove to pick up the pieces, but he too suffered the pain of a parent without biologically being a father.

Victoria was at church, and the children were asleep when a knock interrupted Lorenzo's solemn mood. Opening the door, he was stung by the defeat in Doctor

Stern's morose eyes as he handed him a small urn and lowered his gaze.

Philomena stepped from behind and put a consoling hand on Lorenzo's arm. "The doctors did all they could," she said, choking back her tears. "I'm sorry, but it was necessary for his body to be cremated for sanitary purposes. You have our sincerest condolences."

Lorenzo was seized with a crippling wave of sorrow and a formidable sense of dread. "How will I tell Victoria that her son is dead?" he muttered.

Walking into the apartment, Victoria was confronted by a look of devastation drenched with sympathy on the faces of Lorenzo, Dominick, and Genevieve, who were sitting at the table. Locking eyes with Lorenzo, she felt the blood drain from her face and the room began to spin.

Unable to utter words, he shook his head and reached out to her, and she fainted into his open arms.

Victoria woke to the sight of Genevieve kneeling beside her and holding the bottle of smelling salts in her hand. Panic swept back over her, and she pushed Genevieve aside. Jumping to her feet, she came face-to-face with Lorenzo. She searched his eyes for an answer, and instantly, they filled with tears.

"Oh, Victoria...I'm so sorry. Philomena said they did everything they could do for him," Lorenzo sobbed.

"Where is he? I want to see him!" She glared at him with penetrating horror.

"I don't know how to tell you this, but there's no body," Dominick said.

Victoria slowly turned to her brother. Grabbing him by the shoulders, she shook him violently. "Where's my son!" she screamed.

Genevieve rocked in sobering silence on the edge of her chair as Dominick picked up the urn from the table and handed it to Victoria. Weeping through his words, he said, "His body was burned so the disease wouldn't spread to others."

Clutching what remained of Gennaro to her aching chest, Victoria's deafening moans echoed throughout their small apartment. She needed to see her son, to touch his flesh, to say good-bye. She wondered what act of penance she must make for her sins to be forgiven. She wondered why her child had to bear the consequence of her immorality.

———◆•◆———

Wakes were held in the home, but Victoria was consumed by insurmountable grief and refused to receive visitors. She believed her son had been denied the rite of resurrection into heaven, as there was nothing left of him to ascend.

At a private mass, the priest prayed over the small wooden box that housed Gennaro's remains, and then he prayed for the shattered family. A horse-drawn carriage transported Gennaro to Potter's Field, the final resting place for those who died alone or indigent, which made up a majority of Hell's Kitchen.

———◆•◆———

Every day for over a year, Victoria dressed in black, mirroring the darkness that had settled deep in her soul. She was plagued by a crisis so traumatizing that Gennaro's memory and struggle would haunt her for the rest of her life.

CHAPTER 16

Vincenzo's siblings were too young, but he was about to turn seven years old and ready to begin school. Victoria took him to the Sunday market in the park, and she bought fabric to make him a pair of knickers and a white, long-sleeved shirt. As his mother cut and sewed, she told him each loving stitch was entwined with threads of promise for his future.

Wearing his new clothes, Vincenzo dragged his feet behind his mother and siblings to the schoolhouse on his first day. He did not want new clothes or an education; he wanted to keep things just the way they were and imagined running away.

When they came to the front of the four-story brick schoolhouse, Victoria stopped and turned around. "You look so grown up," she said as she bent down to straighten his suspenders. "I'm so proud of you. You'll be the first in our family to get an education. This is one of the reasons why we came to America. This is an opportunity."

Vincenzo rolled his eyes, while his mother spouted its advantages for what seemed like the hundredth time.

She hugged him, pressing a kiss on the top of his head. Handing him a coin from the pocket of her skirt, she closed his fist around it. "This is the first nickel I made here. It's my good luck piece. Keep it with you."

Why would I need good luck? he thought. Standing tall, Vincenzo held her gaze and gave it his best effort.

"I don't know anyone. I don't want to go…please…take me home," he grumbled.

Victoria smiled broadly. "It'll be wonderful. You'll see." Turning him around, she scooted him toward the building. "By the end of the day, you'll have so many exciting things to tell us."

Vincenzo knew even before he had opened his mouth that his mother was not going to budge, so he assumed a brave facade and marched up the stairs and through the daunting doors of the unknown.

A rotund man with a gray beard stood alone in the hallway. "Are you a new student?" he asked.

Vincenzo nodded his head.

"I'm Principal Graham. You can go to the top floor," he said, gesturing toward the stairway.

Vincenzo's legs felt heavy and his stomach felt queasy as he plodded up the four flights and joined the back of a line.

One by one, the children held out their hands while a tall woman wearing a white apron examined their fingernails and scraped their scalps with the sharp, pointy teeth of a comb. "You're clear to go in," she said to Vincenzo when she had finished.

Taking stiff, small steps, he moved forward with his arms clamped at his sides as he suspiciously scanned the interior of the classroom. From the sooty window, filtered rays of sun highlighted its dingy contents. A large desk and a chair were centered at the front, and behind it, a blackboard stretched the length of the wall. Evenly spaced hooks lined the back of the room for winter garments, and a potbelly stove in the corner tempered the cold, regimented atmosphere.

The children sat silently in wooden desks lined one behind the other in perfect rows. Vincenzo recognized a few of the boys and girls from the neighborhood, but he broke into a smile from ear to ear when he saw Antonio, the treasured friend he had made on the ship. Quickly, he took an empty seat behind his buddy. "What are you doing here?" he exclaimed.

"I live two blocks that way," Antonio answered, pointing out the window.

"I live on thirty-sixth by the—" Vincenzo was silenced by the jarring crash of the teacher's ruler striking her desk.

"Good morning, class. My name's Miss Patton," the matronly woman said dourly as she wrote it on the blackboard. Turning around, she peered over the rim of her spectacles and eyed the class contemptuously, her thin lips compressed into a line of discontent. "For the benefit of our new students, I'll go over my rules," she said. "First and foremost, bad behavior will not be tolerated in this room. My job is to teach you reading, writing, and arithmetic, and it's not an easy one I might add." She held up the ruler in her hand. "I don't like to use this, but I will if I have to." She smacked it against the edge of her desk.

Vincenzo flinched in his seat. Looking down, he folded his hands on his lap, trying to understand what this unpleasant woman was saying.

"I'll do my best to teach you to be moral and productive human beings." Miss Patton let out a loud sigh and frowned. Pacing back and forth in front of the room, she continued, "No one is to speak in this classroom unless they're spoken to. Raise your hand when I ask a question, and wait to be called upon. I'm going to read the names of the new children. Stand up when yours is called." She looked at the paper in her hand. "Anthony Rubino?"

No one stood up.

"Is there a Rubino in the room?" she coarsely repeated.

Antonio raised his hand timidly.

"Yes," she said, gesturing with the ruler in his direction.

"My last name is Rubino, but my first name is Antonio."

"It reads Anthony on your immigration papers so that's your name in this room," she said in a definitive tone. She continued her routine, branding them with their new identities, before she called, "Vincent Montanaro."

Vincenzo had the routine down by now and jumped up from his chair. *Vincent, I like that name,* he decided. *I like that it sounds American.*

———◆◆———

For Vincenzo going to school definitely had its advantages. The students were given a steaming bowl of soup for lunch; hence, he and Antonio affectionately referred to it as *soup school*. The day before Christmas vacation, the soles of their shoes were mended before their toes poked through, and they were given a new shirt and a full meal, including dessert. Vincenzo made sure he was present that day. Recess was held on the schoolhouse roof where games such as tag or pitching pebbles were refined and nicknames were invented. By their classmates, Vincent and Anthony were given the monikers Vinny and Tony.

There were many aspects of school that Vinny enjoyed—reading, addition, and subtraction, and most of all, showing off to his siblings when he arrived home. What he detested was Miss Patton's righteous lectures and coarse manners. Vinny and Tony would meet on the way to school; however, their attention would occasionally veer elsewhere. There were alleys to discover and a whole waterfront to explore while watching the ships, the fisherman, and the activity that engulfed the piers—an enticing lure that excluded them from being subjected to Miss Patton's wrath.

———◆•◆———

Every day Vinny hoped would be the day she would forget, yet he knew his mother was never going to forget the portent of disease since Gennaro had passed away. Illnesses such as smallpox, dysentery, cholera, typhoid fever, tuberculosis, and malnutrition were claiming so many lives that every other tenement had a crepe draped outside a window, signifying a death. Placing the necklace of garlic cloves over his head like a shield of armor, she tucked it under his shirt and kissed him good-bye.

Vinny puffed out his cheeks and sighed. "Do I have to wear this?" he protested again. "I bet I'm the only one in the school who has to."

"The other children are none of my concern. How many times have I told you, Vincenzo, garlic will keep sickness away," Victoria insisted.

Although his mother's efforts seemed excessive, Vinny indulged her, knowing it was easier than listening to her launch into one of her sermons of irrefutable logic.

———◆•◆———

During the normal course of the school day, Miss Patton strolled through the aisles of the classroom while rhythmically hitting her palm with a pointer, goading the children to recite their times tables out loud. As she was passing Vinny, her nostrils flared and she glared at him with scalding eyes that penetrated his very soul. Cracking her weapon down on his desk, she fumed, "It's you! It's you that's emitting that intolerable stench! Go—go home now and bathe or never return to this classroom."

Vinny felt his face flush and slowly rose from his desk. Turning toward the door, he sprinted from the room before his tears could drip, narrowly deflecting the thrash of the pointer Miss Patton furiously brandished in his wake.

The walls in every Italian household in Hell's Kitchen permeated with the pungent aroma of garlic; therefore, Vinny was unaware of the degree of its distastefulness to others. From that day forward, he wore the garlic out of the apartment, but he hid it in the alley on the way to school to evade Miss Patton's scorn and the snickering of his classmates.

"I'm not going to school today," Vinny announced again to Tony when they met up one balmy spring day. "It's too nice out to sit inside."

"What do you mean? We didn't go yesterday or last Friday, as a matter of fact."

Vinny shrugged his shoulders. "Why ruin a good thing?"

Tony thought for a short moment. "I guess," he conceded, throwing his hands in the air.

They cheerfully walked down to the pier, discussing their options for the day.

"While we're here, let's go for a swim," Tony suggested.

Stripping down, they jumped naked into the cool, clear waters of the Hudson River.

When they surfaced, Tony splashed Vinny in the face. "Race you." Suddenly, Tony stopped and his eyes grew wide. "Vinny, there's a cop coming. Let's hide under the pier before he spots us," he whispered, while quickly wading chest-deep toward the overhang.

"Whose clothes are these?" The patrolman looked over the edge of the pier. "I know you're down there. Come out right now," he demanded.

Knowing the man was prowling for truant children, Vinny prayed he would leave. He held his breath and tried to keep his teeth from chattering so as not to make a sound.

"Damn you, kids," the officer yelled, kicking their clothes and shoes into the water. "Don't let me catch you here again. Next time, they'll be hell to pay."

Vinny enjoyed the challenge of being the first to retrieve his drifting belongings, but not the discomfort of wearing wet garments on his walk home or needing to fabricate a sodden story to mollify his mother.

———◆•◆———

"Vincenzo, do me a favor and take this spaghetti down to Mr. Pachini," Victoria said, handing him a plate of food. "Keep the towel under it, it's very hot. You're a lucky boy to be going to school. Look at Carmen…the poor man. Do you think if he had an education he would be living in the basement with the dirt and the rodents?" Victoria sighed.

"Why doesn't he just eat here?" he asked.

"I think he feels like he's bothering us. I don't know, maybe it's because he doesn't have clean clothes."

Opening the door for him, she said, "Remember, don't leave until he's finished...and bring the plate back."

Balancing it in his hands, Vinny walked down the four flights of steps to the basement. "Mr. Pachini, are you down here?" he called out. He squinted through the darkness toward the light bulb hanging in the corner.

"Yeah, I'm here, Vinny."

Vinny spotted Mr. Pachini's thin silhouette sitting slouched on a chair and walked over. He thought everything about the man looked disheveled. His stubbly, black beard contrasted his pale skin, and his hair was long and greasy. He placed the food on the crate in front of him.

"Have a seat and keep me company," Carmen said, putting the newspaper down on his lap.

Vinny sat down on the edge of his mattress. The air smelled like a brew of body odor and mustiness, and he purposely breathed through his mouth.

"Tell your mother thanks again. She's a kind woman." Using the fork resting on the plate, Carmen twirled the spaghetti into a large ball and shoved it into his mouth. "Vinny, when I look at you, you remind me of my son," he said in between bites. "He's your age now, you know. What are you, eight? Nine?"

Vinny nodded, not bothering to clarify which one it was.

"You see that jar over there? I've been saving. Soon I'll have enough to bring my wife and son to live in America."

Looking at the jar half-filled with coins, Vinny thought it held no more than a few dollars. "Are they going to live down here with you?" he asked.

Carmen chuckled. "I'll have an apartment by then," he said. Taking a flask from the pocket of his worn shirt, he took a few swigs, washing down his food. He wiped his face with his sleeve. "Do you want a sip?"

Vinny put his hand out in front of him and shook his head briskly.

"That's a good boy. You don't want to start a bad habit," he said, slipping the flask back into his pocket.

As they talked, Carmen gratefully devoured his meal and tried to fill Vinny's mind with optimism, yet the melancholy veiling Carmen's eyes revealed his dreams had been dashed long ago. The image of this lonely, unkempt man sitting on a broken chair and eating a plate of pasta left Vinny with a lifelong impression that stirred his sympathy and cultivated his motivation.

———◆●◆———

Vinny would do anything for the chance to garner a coin, and street gambling—pitching pennies, playing dice, basically betting on anything that moved—provided him with the possibility, and the thrill of the win had him yearning for more. In contrast to his mother's preaching, he did not see school as a road to riches. Conspiring with Tony, they would meet up in the mornings and make their decision, missing more days than they went.

As part of the boys' deceit, they kept an extra set of garments hidden under the stairwell of a vacant building. On the days they agreed to play hooky, they would change out of their school clothes, ditch their books, and eagerly set out in search of their fortunes. The neighborhood had numerous prospects for the quick-witted to pursue, and Vinny and Tony took advantage of all of them with an unquenchable thirst.

Men came with their wagons loaded with dandelions, garlic, fruits, and vegetables from the farms in Brooklyn to peddle their goods. They became accustomed to the energetic duo soliciting their strengths and would prudently hire the young boys for a pittance. Aiming to please, Vinny and Tony did everything from pushing the carts, to guarding produce from pilferage, to packing orders. Sometimes they were even permitted to hold the reigns of the overburdened horses used to pull the wagons that transported coal and wood to tenement basements. A day's work would earn them a nickel from their frugal employers, and they cherished the coins they amassed as if they were holding stars in their pockets. With youthful pose, they predicted the moon was well within their grasp. Returning home, redressed in their school clothes and with their books dangling from a strap swung over their shoulders, they surmised their parents were none the wiser.

CHAPTER 17

Victoria and Lorenzo relied on each other more and more, creating a bond that started out as one of convenience but blossomed into love. They had matured into a family built on necessity and friendship—a treasure even the poor could possess. This time when Victoria was sure she was pregnant, she decided to tell Lorenzo right away.

———— •••• ————

Lorenzo was awed by Victoria's miraculous transformation. Her skin glowed with the luster of a ripened apple as her stomach swelled with the blessed consequence of their love. Every time he felt the budding life inside her move, he deliriously anticipated the birth of his first child with the woman he adored, but when Victoria woke him in the middle of a bleak winter night, gasping in pain, his joy gave way to fear.

Snow accumulated on the sills, and a tempestuous wind seeped through the sockets of the windows that shuddered against its mighty gusts. Just as Lorenzo pulled the light string, the power flickered, and their apartment, along with the neighborhood, became drenched in darkness. Instantly, he felt a tremor descend his spine and weaken his knees.

With the jitteriness of a father-to-be, he scurried to light a lantern. Throwing open the window, he vehemently rattled the line and shouted for help, but the noise of the sinister storm muted the clanging of the bell and the alarm rabid in his voice. He snatched the lantern from the table and flew next door. Pounding on the vestibule door, he bellowed, "Genevieve, Dominick, wake up! The baby's on its way!"

Stepping back, he squinted upward, and he could swear his heart did not pulse another beat until Genevieve yelled from their window, "We're coming."

Dressed in their nightclothes, the couple ran behind Lorenzo, slipping and sliding as they tilted into the haze of the gusting white powder. They barreled into the apartment, dusting off the layers of frozen particles to ward off their chill.

Genevieve's movements were as swift and competent as a midwife. She took one look at Victoria, who was huddled on her side in the bed, and told Lorenzo and Dominick, "Lift her onto the kitchen table—it'll be easier for me to deliver the baby." She continued to dictate her instructions to the intimidated men. "Stoke the stove. I'll need boiling water and clean towels."

Victoria's intermittent screams raged louder than the storm outside. The commotion woke Vincenzo, Catherina, and Gabriella, and they padded into the kitchen from the dim of the parlor.

"You're mother's having the baby," Lorenzo said, struggling to keep his voice light. He ushered them into the bedroom, and one by one he picked them up and sat them in a row on the side of the bed. "Wait in here. It'll be over soon." He saw the terror splattered on their faces and took a moment. "She'll be okay," he added. Closing the curtain between the rooms was a futile attempt to muffle the sounds of their mother's mounting agony.

Panting and moaning, Victoria writhed in pain as Lorenzo stroked her matted hair. Her skin beaded with sweat despite the chill that permeated the air. Between contractions, his silent prayers for a blessed end filled the room.

Victoria shook uncontrollably from the pressure building between her straddled legs, and Genevieve ordered her to bear down. The blood vessels in her contorted face threatened to burst as she strained and pushed. Clenching the sides of the table with her hands and curling her toes around its corners, she braced herself. She gave one final push, and Genevieve gently guided a baby boy into the tiny alcove that was their kitchen.

Dipping a knife into a bowl of whisky, Genevieve carefully sliced off the umbilical cord attached to the baby's heaving stomach then doused the severed connection with the amber liquor.

Watching her perform the procedure, Lorenzo felt faint and slid into a chair.

Genevieve wrapped the wailing newborn in a towel and placed the tiny infant into his trembling arms. He stared awestruck at his child—his tiny features shrouded within the cloth, his delicate body snuggled within his father's awkward embrace, his eyes closed to the emotion. "I'm your Papa," Lorenzo whispered. Humbled by the experience, he cried openly along with his son, feeling as if his own life had just begun.

Dominick pushed aside the curtain to the bedroom. "You can come out now," he said to the children.

Their eyes were wide with curiosity as they softly tiptoed into the kitchen. Lying flat on the table and covered with a sheet, Victoria prompted them closer with a weary wave of her hand to be introduced to the miracle cradled in Lorenzo's arms.

They gazed with wonder at the squirming infant.

"Meet your new brother," Victoria said. "His name's Santo. It was his grandfather's name." She looked at Lorenzo and blew him a kiss.

He was genuinely surprised. "Thank you for naming him after my father," he said.

Seeing Lorenzo cradling their newborn, Victoria felt blessed to have given birth to his baby. The child they created together validated their love and loyalty. He had proven to be so much more of a father than Salvatore had ever been, and her children called him Papa, a well-deserved accolade. She felt privileged to have a man of such conviction in their lives, knowing some fathers in the neighborhood spent their nights drinking and begrudgingly staggering home, while many opted not to go home at all.

Still haunted by the premonition Salvatore would show up at the door and her nightmare would begin again, Victoria had periodically inquired about him in her letters home; however, her parents' responses were vague. In the past she was not ready to speak of another man, but Santo's birth gave her the courage to write to them regarding her relationship with Lorenzo.

Several weeks later, Dominick was the one who received the reply that filled in the details they had previously withheld and told the end of Salvatore's story.

Dear Dominick,

We're writing this letter with much guilt. There's something we haven't told Victoria, and she needs to know the truth. We want you to be the one to break the news to her, as she shouldn't be alone when she hears this.

On the day she left for America, Salvatore had a horrible accident. He fell from his horse and broke his neck, barely surviving through the night. It was a terrible time for all, and we were glad Victoria and the children had been spared. We chose not to tell her so she could have a fresh start in America without this tragedy affecting her decisions. We now realize this was a dreadful mistake. We pray she'll understand why we did it and find it in her heart to forgive us.

When we read in her recent letter that she had found someone so special and had given birth to a son, we felt it was time she learned the truth and time she moved on. It seems we've all made mistakes, and we're not in a position to judge her choices, but we hope Lorenzo will do right by her and they'll soon wed.

We're so sorry and long for the day when we can all be together again. We pray our love will lessen the distance between us.

We miss you all,
Papa and Mama

Dominick was dumbfounded by the senselessness of their logic, and it took a while before he digested their sobering words. *Why have they waited this long to tell Victoria? How odd that Salvatore's life ended on the day she left to find a new one.* He cringed at the thought of being the messenger of misery, and a biting chill pricked his core while beads of sweat formed on his skin.

When he entered Victoria's apartment, her welcoming smile wilted at the sight of his grimacing face. In a tempered tone, he suggested, "I think you should sit down. Papa and Mama have something they want me to tell you." He took the letter out of his pocket and unfolded it.

Victoria's drew her brows together and her voice cracked. "Are they sick?"

"No," he said, trying to sound reassuring.

"It must be *something* serious if they didn't want me to read it myself."

"Just give me a chance to explain," he said, settling her into a chair. He drew a deep breath and slowly exhaled to steady his nerves and read their words like an act of contrition. Victoria's wide, unblinking eyes stared right through him, and when he finished, she exhaled a long, anguished moan.

"How could they've done this? Why would they've kept this from me?" She was shaking her head back and forth in exasperation. "I could've dealt with Salvatore's death...I could've avoided years of worry by burying him long ago."

"Thank God the children were spared witnessing his passing," Dominick said. He choked back his tears as Victoria's flowed full, and he drew her into a consoling embrace. "I know this is hard to digest, but think about it...it's finally over now."

———◆•◆———

When Victoria handed Lorenzo the envelope containing her parents' confession, he read and reread the inconceivable words. Their silence had kept their daughter condemned to a sentence of confusion and unresolved issues—a secret that had put many lives on hold. With dogged determination, he swore to himself that he would be the one to salvage the ruin and guide her honorably forward.

Lorenzo came home the next evening, holding a small bouquet of daisies behind his back. While Victoria was frying meatballs in front of the stove, he came up behind her and whispered, "Victoria." His voice was filled with sincerity and desire.

She turned around to find him on bended knee, holding up a ring in one hand and flowers in the other.

"Will you marry me?" He opened his heart and his arms to her. "I never thought I'd find someone to make me want to settle down…to make me want to be a better man. I'm so fortunate to have you in my life," he said. "And how lucky am I?" He jokingly added, "Along with you, I gain an entire family."

Tears pooled in her eyes, and he hoped they were ones of joy. "Of course I'll marry you," she said.

He slipped the ring onto her finger. "This was my grandmother's. My mother gave it to me when I left for America and made me promise to love the woman I gave it to without a doubt…and with you…I have no doubts." He lifted Victoria off the ground and twirled her around the room.

Immersed in their mutual happiness, they savored the joyous mood.

Lorenzo's proposal immediately quelled the raw emotions that had gnawed at Victoria since she had learned of Salvatore's passing. When the priest blessed their union, she felt a surge of happiness she had not felt in years as if her heart had suddenly swelled inside her chest. She was in awe of the man who was willing and able to rescue her from another cycle of regret. In her mind, he was already a wonderful mate and father; however, the marriage certificate legally decreed them husband and wife.

The next time Victoria wrote in her journal, she felt that she was, at last, able to close the book on Salvatore.

As a toddler, Santo was small for his age and had bright-blue eyes. Corkscrews of curls wildly protruded from his head and framed his thin face. His scrawny body pulsated with energy, never allowing an ounce of fat to adhere. Mastering walking before he began talking, he moved with agility and constancy, awakening the respiratory ailment residing in his chest.

Regularly agitated by bouts of labored breathing, Santo was a fussy child. Victoria would cuddle and rock her son while praying out loud for his relief. She was grateful that her older children often kept Santo entertained, distracting him from his discomfort. Sometimes frightened by his disturbing gasps, they would hide from the hurt, leaving her to cope with his distress. Victoria would scramble to boil water, adding camphor and eucalyptus oils to create a steamy antidote. Oblivious to its therapeutic benefits, the medicinal smell of the potion made Santo disagreeable. With maternal coaxing, she would restrain her fidgety child on her lap and drape a cloth over his head so he could inhale the soothing vapors. The fear and empathy she felt for her son's condition was so overpowering that, at times, she found herself struggling to breathe.

Victoria believed God had given her Santo to mend the losses that had snatched away pieces of her heart, yet she felt she was still being tested. She had quickly learned the roads in America were paved with trials and tribulations, and it seemed she had settled in a land without justice. There had been moments when she thought she could conquer the challenges of life and make the best of the worst, but the worst was getting the best of her. Her hair was flecked with gray, and narrow lines defined her eyes, symbolizing the crosses she bore. Her skin had lost its luster, and now, her daily primping was done to remedy the pastiness the strain produced.

Watching Lorenzo leave for work in the mornings, Victoria felt overwhelmed having to face her day alone. When he returned in the evenings, she appreciated that he left the drudgery of his day outside the door and did his best to make it seem like everything was all right with the world. The sight of him made her angst momentarily slip away. Every time he kissed her hello, she caught a faint glimpse of her beauty in his eyes, reminding her that she was still a desirable woman.

After dinner, the children snuggled around Lorenzo while he entertained them with tales of his work and his travels, giving Victoria time to do her chores and iron out the scorching agony of her blistered emotions. *When did I become so despondent, and why does life seem so complicated?* She often tried to pinpoint her decline. *Was it triggered by the death of Gennaro, his sweet face popping up wherever I look? Was it the loss of my unborn child, whose face I didn't have the chance to behold? Is it Santo's illness? Or was it simply America, the disillusion with its possibilities and living with its realities?* It was a daunting challenge to mask the ache—a perpetual ache that had become embedded in her soul.

These were the times Victoria desperately missed the simplicity and fellowship of her homeland. She missed her parents, she missed the lush land and its openness, and most of all she missed the likelihood her children would grow up healthy.

CHAPTER 18

When the sun lasted longer than a twelve-hour workday, the outdoors was a gathering place to dodge the stifling heat of the tenements' sweltering, swollen wombs and catch a faint breeze off the river. As if the street were a stage, Victoria and the other mothers congregated in tiers on the front stoops. Mending clothes, their hands kept pace with their conversations, which shifted between the perversity of their lives and anecdotes about their children. Lorenzo played cards with some of the men at a makeshift table on the sidewalk, while others played bocce in the alley. Sharing their homemade wines, they boasted whose was the tastiest, never revealing their personal ingredients or techniques—a formula they swore they would take to the grave. On unbearably hot nights, families would sleep on the rooftops and fire escapes to avoid the oppressive heat that loomed indoors.

Sundays were sacred. It was a way of life in Italy and a tradition they brought to America. For Victoria, it meant waking up at dawn to begin the routine of preparing Sunday supper.

"The coffee's ready," Victoria said when Genevieve and her boys arrived.

"Dominick brought home some ground meat and pork bones," Genevieve said, placing the brown paper package on the counter. "We're certainly lucky he works at a slaughterhouse."

"Boys, there's warm bread on the stove, and I made strawberry jam," Victoria enticed her nephews. She cut the loaf into thick slices and slathered them with the sweet preserves.

Enough for a week's worth of meals, the woman mixed, rolled, and sliced mounds of dough and draped it over strings crisscrossing the room. The kitchen became a maze of dangling ribbons, and every crevice was coated with a dusting of flour. Maneuvering around the lengths of spaghetti, Victoria and Genevieve gave the children scraps of dough to mold and keep them amused, but more often than not, the two mothers were the ones amused by the little ones' imaginations.

"Look, I made a cat," Gabriella said, looking up from the table and proudly holding up the animal she shaped.

"Mine's a mouse," Catherina said.

"They're both wonderful," Victoria assured her daughters, although Gabriella's creativity clearly stood out from the others.

Victoria brushed the flour from the tip of her son's nose. "What's that, Vincenzo?"

"A big building. It's where I'm going to work one day, and it's filled to the top with everything you could ever want, Mama."

"Like what?" she asked.

"Like clothes and food…lots of food."

"Ahh," she said when she caught on. "That's nice, but I have everything I could ever want…I have you and your brother and sisters." She bent over and kissed the top of his head.

Victoria knew the smell of the fresh baked bread and sauce simmering on the stove were ones the children looked forward to six days to Sunday. The minute she and Genevieve left the kitchen to ready themselves for church, Vincenzo would rip a loaf of the warm bread into pieces, dunk them into the sauce, and dole them out to his cousins and siblings. By the time Victoria returned, washcloth in hand, one of the loaves would have inconspicuously disappeared. Smiling to herself, she would casually wipe away the residue of red that rimmed their lips, pretending she was unaware of their weekly ritual.

Dressed in their Sunday best, they walked to church for noon mass. Even though it was several blocks past Saint Michael's, Saint Raphael's offered a service in Italian, and the familiarity of the language made them feel more at home, more like they belonged.

———◆•◆———

Returning home, Victoria and Genevieve immediately donned their aprons and busied themselves in the kitchen. Randomly setting the steaming bowls of food on the table, they prompted everyone to take a seat.

When they were settled, not a morsel was touched before they joined hands and a prayer of thanksgiving was offered—the grownups adding their own sentiments. The homemade wine was ceremoniously uncorked, freeing their inhibitions and temporarily allowing them to forget the adversity of their *onerous* existence.

After second helpings were consumed and before the dishes were cleared, Dominick and Lorenzo led the chorus of songs that made them happy, the songs that made them dance. Parading in and out of the parlor, the children banged pots with utensils while Victoria and Genevieve twirled about. Their gatherings were simple, but in those moments, their world was filled with a richness that could not be bought.

———◆•◆———

Surviving on the barest of necessities, they had no money for wants or desires. Their primary objective was to have enough food to feed the growing family, and extra pennies were stashed away to pay off their debt to Doctor Stern. Existing day to day and living from hand to mouth, they had little time to look to the future. Victoria's evening prayers were spent on appreciating what they had, and her daily wishes were spent on pleas for good health.

There were intermittent periods when Victoria thought there could be a light at the end of the tunnel only to be thrust back into the drowning pool of poverty.

"Lorenzo, we're going to have a spring baby," she told him one evening when there was no doubt left in her mind.

"I'm going to be a father again!" he shouted, jumping up from his chair and embracing her.

She pushed him away. "Where will we put another child? Look around us." She waved her hand through the air, encompassing the rooms.

"Then maybe we can find a bigger place."

"What are you thinking? We work so hard, and we're barely getting by. How could we afford more?"

"You worry too much—we're having a baby," he said brightly.

Victoria thought it was inconceivable that another body would have to be squeezed into their cramped quarters, and she shook her head in sheer bewilderment.

———◆•◆———

Life had a strange way of adding bumps to the road and jolted them with another shocking surprise six months later when Victoria gave birth to twin girls, Rosa and Louisa.

The twins' arrival caused quite an uproar in their household. Financially and logistically unprepared for a new addition, they were further humbled by two. Catherina and Gabriella were on hand to help their mother with the endless chores and chaos, but for Victoria, sleep came in small spurts as the babies cried their needs day and night. Despite the calamity and constraints, the two pixie-faced girls were delightful to look at, a pleasure to hold, and seemingly inseparable.

As toddlers, Rosa and Louisa followed Victoria around as if they were tied to her apron strings. Their adoring eyes would beam up at her, invariably reminding her that she had reasons to smile. But as time went on, it was apparent that the fraternal twins could not have been more dissimilar. They were the center of a turbulent storm erupting with unnerving frequency, and their appearances were as distinct as their personalities. Although beautiful in her own right, Rosa's jet-black hair and pensive, gray eyes contrasted Louisa's wavy, red hair and dark, exotic eyes. Rosa had a passive nature, whereas Louisa was a whirlwind. Victoria tried her best to be equally attentive to all her children, but Louisa was exhausting. Her energy electrified a room, overshadowing and overwhelming the rest.

CHAPTER 19

When it snowed, Vinny and Tony were out of bed well before the neighborhood stirred to get to the railroad station ahead of others who would vie for a job. Knitted gloves and worn boots where no barriers against winter's frigid temperatures; however, the boys were fueled by the reward. They would make a dime clearing the stairways and platforms that led to the trains and be back in time to solicit work from the vendors.

It was a particularly bitter day, and the snow cleansed the city in a thick blanket of white. After their strenuous morning of shoveling and long day of working alongside the vendors, Tony started pitching snowballs at Vinny in the street.

Vinny retaliated, and their rollicking continued until Tony hit him right in the cheek. "Hey, you cheated. Below the waist, remember," he said, wiping the frost from his face.

Tony laughed. "How about ducking, stupid."

Vinny blew his warm breath into his gloved hands and rubbed them together. "Let's make a fire," he suggested, still feeling a little annoyed at his friend. "My toes and fingers are frozen."

Snatching a few potatoes that had fallen from a peddler's cart and a newspaper from a stand, they ran a few blocks and slipped into a deserted alley.

"There's a barrel back there," Tony said, pointing. "We can burn those broken chairs in the corner."

"I'll get the chairs, and you start the fire," Vinny told him.

While Tony crumpled the paper into the barrel and threw in a match, Vinny smashed the chairs into pieces on the ground. Together, they tossed in the broken bits.

Once the wood ignited, Tony dropped the potatoes into the embers to cook. He placed a long stick on the ground, ready to retrieve their snack.

Standing close to the barrel, Vinny relished the warmth of the blaze and took off his gloves to dry. "I can finally feel my fingers again," he said.

"Do you hear that?" Tony said, patting his grumbling stomach. "I'm starving."

When the flames had receded somewhat, Vinny jabbed a blackened potato with the stick. "They feel soft enough to me," he said. He shook it onto the snow and did the same with the other three.

After letting them cool a few minutes, they feasted on the fruits of their labor.

"I could eat at least another two," Vinny said as he licked the remains from his fingers. "Let's keep the fire going while we get some more."

They scurried around the alley, collecting debris and tossing it into the barrel.

"I think that's enough," Tony warned after throwing in a stack of newspapers.

Vinny marveled at its increasing intensity. "How high do you think we can get it?" he said, eyeing a dilapidated dresser. Using a slat of wood from a broken drawer, he started to pry it apart.

The wind kicked up, and glowing bits of ash had floated skyward, licking the eave of the adjacent building.

"I think we have a big problem," Tony said, looking up.

To Vinny's astonishment, the roof of the vacant tenement was smoldering with a darkening cloud of foreboding disaster. "Jesus Christ! Let's get the hell out of here!" he shouted as they fled from the scene, dodging accountability.

———◆◆———

The boys also became adept at who to know and who to avoid, and their running skills came in handy. Vinny and Tony were forfeiting an education, although they were learning to master the art of survival on the streets. They walked with their eyes wide open and steered clear of grazing bullies looking to demonstrate their superiority, but when their efforts failed, they had devised other ways to cope.

Stepping around the puddles as they walked through the slushy streets late one afternoon, they turned a corner and came face-to-face with several sneering boys who blocked their path. A thick-bodied teenager with squinty, close-set eyes stepped forward. "Hand over your money, punks," he demanded." He turned to his friends and snickered. "I think the little one wet his pants."

Vinny glanced at Tony, who shook his head adamantly in denial.

The cocky youngsters laughed at their seemingly intimidated prey.

Since this was not the first time Vinny and Tony were accosted, they knew the routine. They kept their coins tucked away in their shoes and devised a clever guise of retaliation. Simultaneously, they thrust their hands deep into their pockets as if gathering their hard earned wages. Just as they had practiced, they each pulled out fistfuls of dirt and pebbles and forcefully flung it with a spray of their arms at their unsuspecting antagonists. Spinning around, they darted from the scene, ignoring the shower of obscenities sputtering from the startled hoodlums as they wiped the grime from their eyes and the humiliation from their faces.

———— ◆•◆ ————

Vinny had few complaints about his best friend, but it irritated him to the core that every Saturday he would knock on Tony's door, let himself in, go straight to his bed, and would have to drag him out by his feet.

Today Tony sounded exceptionally cranky. "Cut it out. I want to sleep," he grumbled, turning over.

"No kidding, that's the problem. If it weren't for me, we'd never make a dime."

"Tony, eat your breakfast and remember to wash the kitchen floor before you leave," his mother called from the front bedroom as he reluctantly rolled out of bed. "Vinny, there's plenty for you, help yourself," she added.

"Thanks, Mrs. Rubino," he said.

Sitting at the kitchen table, Vinny enjoyed the steaming bowl of porridge, but he was outwardly miffed at Tony again. "I swear you do this on purpose," he said between mouthfuls.

"I didn't know she was going to make me do it until just now," Tony feebly objected; however, Vinny knew he was lying.

To expedite the task, Vinny picked up the bucket and tossed the water, and it spread with a gush around the perimeter of the room.

"Are you crazy? What are you doing?"

"Get the mop and sop up the dirt, it'll go faster," Vinny told him.

The apartment butted the ceiling of a local tavern, and the overflow seeped between the floorboards, dribbling like a light rain into the room below.

"What the hell's going on up there?" a man bellowed from below, banging the floor above him with the end of a broom.

Hurrying into the kitchen, Tony's mother slid on the soapy water and landed with a thump on her backside. "What'd you two do now?"

"There's water dripping all over my bar," the owner yelled. "Whoever did this get your ass down here and clean up this mess." His voice echoed up through the floor, almost sounding as if he were in the room with them.

Rolling her eyes, Tony's mother let out a sigh of exasperation. "After you finish here, get downstairs. I don't know what's wrong with you boys." She held out both hands. "Now help me up,"

"Sorry, Mom," Tony said, while glowering at Vinny.

"I am too, Mrs. Rubino," Vinny muttered as they pulled her to her feet.

She dried her hands on her apron and rubbed the ache in her back. "This is just what I needed today. Now, get busy."

Sulking, the boys obediently cleaned the kitchen floor and then trudged downstairs to dry the contents of the bar under the watchful eye of its infuriated proprietor.

———◆◆———

Along with the money he was earning, Vinny thought he had earned free reign, but he realized his ruse had been uncovered when he brushed past the stranger, wearing a badge on his shirt pocket and a grimace on his face, descending the dim stairwell. The officer grabbed him by the shirtsleeve and hauled him back in his tracks. "What's your name, kid?" he asked, glaring at him skeptically.

"Joey Pizzaro," Vinny responded, trying hard not to show any expression. Pulling himself free, he soared up the stairs to the next landing and ducked out of sight until he heard the man's footsteps fading away.

Slinking the rest of the way up to his apartment, he opened the door. His mother's face showed no mercy, causing Vinny's throat to close and his stomach to clench. Deciding it was better to confess than deny, he dashed to his drawer and retrieved a pouch filled with coins, hoping it would douse the fire in his mother's eyes. "I've been wanting to give this to you, Mama," he said, relinquishing his savings to her.

She opened the cloth bag, sternly examining the contrite offering, and Vinny quietly breathed a premature sigh of relief.

"Where did you get this money?" she asked.

"I've been working...that's where I've been."

"What do you mean you've been working?" Pulling her brows together, she hesitated for a moment. "You should be in school. There're no alternatives to an education, Vincenzo. There'll be plenty of time for you to work."

"But it's for the family," he said, expecting his mother to soften.

"The money will stay with me," she said, "and tomorrow morning you're going back to school."

"Four years is enough. I can't stand those teachers and their stupid sticks. Look what Miss Dorchester did to me this time." He held out his hand to show her the latest welt across his knuckles.

Eyeing his wound, she frowned. "What'd you do to deserve this?"

"I asked Pete what page we were on. She's so mean. It's not just me. There're plenty of kids that don't go," he said as he continued to argue his case. "I never wanted to go to school. It was your idea. I'd rather spend my time making money. It's not like we don't need it."

"I'll decide what we need," she said. "The truant officer will be back. You'll have to go."

He straightened his back and took a deep breath. "If he does, I can run faster."

"If you choose to work, all your earnings will be used to help support this family."

"I'd rather work around the clock than sit in a classroom for another minute," he said, unflinchingly accepting her ultimatum with a shrug of his shoulders.

Victoria sank into a chair and sighed. "Vincenzo, I can see that you're old enough to do a man's work, and for that, I'm proud. But you're eleven years old and surely not old enough to make this decision."

"School's a waste of time, and I'm not going back."

Clutching the sack to her chest, her eyes welled with tears.

Vincenzo leaned over, hugging her from behind. "It'll be okay, Mama, you'll see."

———◆●◆———

Vinny and Tony's first steady job was for a local barber, shining shoes in front of his business on Tenth Avenue. The shop was a gathering place where men would socialize and enjoy a glass of wine or a shot of whiskey, the smells of cigars and booze continually wafting out the door. The proprietor was known to everyone as

Sal Cigar because of the habitual brown roll of tobacco clenched between his yellowed teeth. His garbled speech was difficult to understand when he gruffly barked orders at the boys. Their puzzled expressions would compel Sal Cigar to repeat himself, but his words were still befuddling. They learned to agreeably nod their heads, pretending to comprehend; yet they continued to perform their duties using their own discretion.

Vinny and Tony ambitiously worked on the street in front of the busy barber shop in most weather conditions and made one dollar a week, polishing shoes that had been shined so many times they were worn from the rub.

The exuberant youngsters had an unmistakable pleasantness. "Good morning, mister. I think your shoes could use a shine today," Vinny would coax.

He always seemed to entice one of the regulars, and their exchange was always the same. Mr. Adams would give him a hearty pat on the back and say, "This is the place for the best shoe shine in the city, kid."

Every time Vinny heard the compliment, he felt as proud as if it were the first and grinned his gratitude.

Vinny sat straddled and slouched on a wooden box with a slanted foot rest, while the impeccably dressed gentleman sat comfortably, leaning back on a chair and reading his newspaper. Noticing the man's groomed fingernails, Vinny looked down at his own. His cuticles and hands were permanently blackened, and his stained clothes were stiff from the polish.

When Vinny had finished, Mr. Adams closed the newspaper and put it down on his lap. "How well do you know the layout of the city?" he asked.

"Real well, sir," Vinny answered, not sure why the man asked such a question and why he lied his response.

"I own a hat factory over on Thirty-ninth and Eighth. If you're ever looking for a job, stop by. Your enthusiasm would set a fine example for my employees. Bring your friend too." He tilted his head in Tony's direction.

"Thanks," they both chimed in.

Mr. Adams stood up and flipped Vinny two coins from his pocket before leaving.

Vinny opened his hand. "Wow, he just gave me a dime tip." His glee came to a disturbing halt as he reluctantly placed them in the bucket. "I don't think it's fair Sal Cigar takes all our tips," he grumbled. "You'd think that after all these months, he'd at least let us keep half."

"We use his stuff...and he pays us," Tony reminded him.

"It doesn't seem right," Vinny objected. "Tomorrow we get paid. The next day I'm going to go to Mr. Adam's factory like he said and get a job." He crossed his arms over his chest. "Are you in?"

"We'll have to tell Sal Cigar we're quitting."

"I'll take care of it," Vinny said, but he figured their boss would get the idea when they never showed up again.

Dressed in his Sunday best—shirt, tie, and a cap loftily propped upon his head—the cleaner line of work was much more appealing to Vinny. His first assignment was a delivery to Macy's department store on 34th Street and Broadway. The cumbersome boxes tied together and teetering from his hands constricted the flow of blood and numbed his fingers, but he eagerly zigzagged through the blocks before he realized he was going in the wrong direction. Turning around, he sprinted feverishly forward with the boxes jostling against his legs. This was his first encounter with a department store, and after delivering the boxes through a side entrance, the fashionably decorated windows lured him inside.

Roaming the floor and scanning the cases, Vinny was awestruck by the array of goods on display. One item in particular dazzled his eyes and stopped him in his tracks. He marveled at the shiny silver pocket watch that loomed below the glass. It was even more spectacular than the one Tony had from his grandfather. He vowed to own one exactly like it one day as its delicate hands suddenly alerted him to the hour. Bolting back to work, he ran through the open door.

Checking off numbers on a clipboard and without looking up, Mr. Adams questioned, "What took you so long?"

"They were backed up with deliveries, and I had to wait," Vinny said.

He chuckled a low, throaty sound. "I thought you made off with the goods."

Vinny turned away and wiped his brow, grateful that his boss had a sense of humor.

———◆•◆———

It was only ten o'clock in the morning, and Vinny looked up at the vast canopy of blue overhead, wondering how much hotter the day could get. Lugging the hatboxes during the fall, winter, and spring months had been bearable, but Vinny found the scorching summer's sun exhausting. One of his deliveries was to a building on Fifth Avenue where a uniformed doorman ushered him inside and directed him to take the elevator to the sixth floor.

A middle-aged woman wearing a sleeveless, green dress opened the door. She clapped her hands together.

"Oh, wonderful, my hats are here," she said. "Come in a minute while I get you a little something."

Entering the spacious apartment, Vinny looked around the finely decorated rooms, figuring she was probably the richest person in the world.

"I didn't think they'd come so quickly," she said, rummaging through her purse on the side table in the foyer. Turning around, she handed Vinny a quarter.

"Thank you, lady," he said.

She smiled. "It's awfully hot out there. Can I get you a glass of water?"

"Sure." He took off his cap and swiped his forehead with the back of his hand. "You're my fifth delivery this morning."

"Seems to me like you're a hard worker."

"I help support my family," he said proudly.

She raised her eyebrows. "That's a lot of responsibility for a young boy."

"I don't mind."

She walked into the kitchen and returned with a tall glass filled with water. "Would it be too personal if I ask you how much money you make?"

"A dollar a week, plus tips." He smiled broadly.

"My husband owns a warehouse where they distribute books for publishers. Would you like me to put in a good word for you? I'm sure he'll pay you more than you're making now."

"That'd be great," he said, wondering why she was being so nice to him. "I have a friend who's a real hard worker. Do you think you could tell your husband about him too?"

"It shouldn't be a problem," she said. "By the way, what's your name?"

"Vinny, and my friend's name is Tony."

She walked over to the desk and wrote on a piece of paper. Returning, she handed it to him and said, "This is the address, and my husband's name is Mr. Gordon. Go there on Monday...I'll let him know you're both coming."

"Thank you so much," he sputtered, barely able to contain his excitement. He ran down the stairs, and when he reached the street, he threw his fist in the air and whooped loudly.

———— ◆●◆ ————

Bright and early Monday morning, Vinny and Tony went to the warehouse and asked the red-headed woman seated behind the desk in the office to see Mr. Gordon. She escorted them into another room where they were greeted with a hearty handshake by a bald man with thick glasses who said that he had been expecting them. The allure of hauling hats vanished with Mr. Gordon's offer of a more lucrative position in his warehouse, sorting and boxing books for two dollars a week—each.

———— ◆●◆ ————

Vinny and Tony were satisfied with their new job since money lined their pockets and the books stimulated their curious minds. Frequently they borrowed several, and at the end of the day, they retreated to the clubhouse they had set up in an abandoned building near the 34th Street pier and sifted through their contents as if they were detectives unraveling a case. A dictionary rested atop the column of books rising from the floor with pages that formed stories and stories that formed worlds. Sitting on an old mattress with their backs propped against the wall, they conquered book after book, unwittingly becoming well versed in the English language.

Catherina and Gabriella had started their education, but the various books Vinny brought home accelerated their reading abilities. Dolls and toys were unaffordable luxuries, whereas books were available and became their playmates. Eagerly, they reread their favorite stories, reenacting the scenes they had committed to memory, and at every opportunity, Victoria joined in the theatrics. They learned to love the written word, which took them to places otherwise unimaginable, otherwise untouchable.

Vinny and Tony labored with the goals of men and with the enduring energy of children, a combination that churned them into hustlers. Unintentionally outperforming most of the other employees, they were often selected to work overtime.

One week Vinny worked so many extra hours he brought home five dollars. At dinner, Lorenzo stood up from his chair and saluted him with a glass of wine in his hand. "You've made an adult's wages. You've become a man today, Vincenzo." Pouring him a glass, he added, "This will keep you strong and healthy."

Thereafter, every evening Papa gave him a glass of wine, and Vinny's pride swelled with every fruitful sip. However, his financial windfall did not change Mama's position, for he still received an allowance of a quarter a week.

Vinny squirreled away most of his money, but when the Ringling Brothers Circus came to town, he and Tony splurged.

Walking into the big top with three rings bustling with activity, they weaved their way through the crowd to find a seat that would afford them the best view. Vinny was fascinated by the clowns in their outlandish costumes, his heart palpitated at the fearless high-wire acts soaring through the air, and he was amazed by the fierce animals trained to perform specific stunts at their master's commands. He left with a sense of what money could provide—entertainment, excitement, and escape.

———— ◆•◆ ————

The summer sun had finally set, and a welcomed breeze wafted through Vinny's window as he and Kenny drove back from a day of deliveries in Brooklyn. He liked when he was picked to help out a driver; it made the day go a heck of a lot faster. By far, Kenny was Vinny's favorite. He was younger and more talkative than the others, and over the last two years, they had become friends. Again, Vinny was listening attentively as Kenny explained in detail the mechanics of the vehicle and how to properly operate the pedals. Studying his actions with keen precision, Vinny hankered to experience the power and the freedom of the road. City streets had been transformed into rows of chugging machines, comfortably steering people for miles in every direction, and during breaks from work, Vinny would sometimes sit behind the wheel of a truck where he envisioned he was driving a Model T Ford.

Unexpectedly, Kenny pulled off the road into a clearing and grinned mischievously at him. "You want to take a turn at the wheel?" he asked.

Vinny thought he had heard him wrong. "Are you serious?"

"Be my guest. I think you can handle it," he said as his lanky body slid out the door.

Immediately scooting over, Vinny ran his hands over the steering wheel, feeling a rush of exhilaration and as if he were ten feet tall.

Kenny hopped in on the passenger side. "You remember what I taught you?" he said, sounding suddenly serious.

Vinny nodded while keeping his eyes focused directly ahead. He took a deep breath and put the truck in gear. Pressing down on the gas pedal with his right foot, he underestimated the tension of the clutch and released it too quickly, causing the truck to lurch forward. He slammed his foot on the brake, and Kenny grabbed the dashboard to brace himself.

"Whoa, a little less gas and a little slower on the clutch," Kenny said.

"Sorry."

"Try again."

This time, Vinny slowly eased the pedals, and the truck smoothly inched ahead.

Kenny patted his shoulder. "You're on your way, kid."

By the time they left, Vinny was certain he could manage on his own. "Can I drive back?"

Kenny laughed out loud. "A few more times, and you'll be driving like a pro," he said.

———◆◆———

When Vinny turned fifteen years old, he came up with the idea to alter his immigration papers to make him one year older so he could obtain a driver's license. He applied for a job with a meat vendor, promoting himself as a qualified candidate. His height and maturity were assets to his scheme, and he was hired on the spot to deliver their products to the five boroughs. Maneuvering the trucks with competence and confidence, he was thrilled to have reached his goal. His days stretched into the evenings, and many nights he arrived home after his family had gone to sleep—a metal plate sitting on the back of the stove kept his dinner warm.

———————◆•◆———————

Driving a truck for over a year, Vinny spent his time behind the wheel dreaming up schemes to earn more cash. Brainstorming with Tony, who had worked his way up to foreman at the publishing warehouse, they came to the conclusion that the only way to make decent money was to work for themselves. They decided to speak to the one person they knew from the neighborhood who could help them.

Given the nickname because he had his finger on the pulse of Hell's Kitchen, Philly the Mayor was a man of many contacts and brokered properties for a living. A rotund character with a raspy voice and pocked-marked face, he had little luck with the ladies, but the men looked to him for the lucrative deals he was able to procure.

Running into him on the street one day, Vinny said, "Hey, Philly, I've been looking for you. You're never in your office, where've you been hiding?"

Taking the cigarette out of his mouth with one hand, he extended his other. "How's everything? I haven't seen you around either."

"Yeah, I've been working day and night."

"Aren't we all?"

"Listen, Tony and I are looking to lease a piece of land, a parking lot maybe. You know of anything around?"

"Your timing is perfect, kid, something just came up. There's a lot next to the transportation terminal…great location…reasonable size. The owner's getting old and wants out."

Vinny's eyes lit up. "How much is he asking?"

"He's willing to negotiate an agreement in exchange for a percentage of the parking fees. No money down, just fifty percent of your take. What do you say?"

"Level with me, do you think it's a good deal?"

"I have plenty of guys who'd jump at this opportunity."

"Get the papers ready," Vinny said.

———◆•◆———

Two days later, Vinny and Tony met Philly at his office, and they signed on the dotted line. Wasting no time, they painted signs and nailed them to poles on street corners to solicit business.

Their resourcefulness and enthusiasm paid off, and before long, they had saved enough money to purchase a used truck of their own on installment. Most truckers considered it a nuisance to pick up merchandise from the busy Hudson River piers due to the long lines and endless delays. Vinny's patience and winsome personality worked to their benefit and resulted in solid business connections and friendships. Learning accounting from his father, who earned a living as a bookkeeper, Tony kept their finances in order.

Within a few months, word of mouth gave them more jobs than they could handle. Outgrowing the limitations of one vehicle, they acquired another, utilizing one set of license plates for both to save on the cost. Tony's younger brother, Giuseppe, tended to the lot, while Vinny and Tony drove the trucks. Renting a small building adjacent to the parking lot, they were able to warehouse merchandise for a fee until it was needed in the stores. Their business was growing and their profits rising.

———————— •◆• ————————

In 1917 President Woodrow Wilson called for a declaration of war against Germany, and America joined the allies in World War I. Talk of the conflict dominated the country. Advertisements that embraced the patriotic theme and aimed at the heart bombarded newsstands, and posters were plastered in every window. Fighting a force so foreign, no nationality was an exception to the cause that was promoted expertly and emphatically around the country. Everyone, every business, and every manufacturing company was geared to a nationwide endeavor of supplying the doughboys—men who selflessly served overseas—and Vinny and Tony were eager to join in the effort.

The Selective Service System held three registrations for military service. Vinny had missed the last draft, and Tony, who was a year younger, was also underage. Both old enough to be effective contributors at home, they dutifully volunteered as drivers for the Ambulance Corps. Several mornings a week, they rose a few hours earlier to transport wounded soldiers returning from combat and to respond to emergency calls throughout the area.

Factories were churning out supplies for the war—their employees laboring faster than bees making honey. The merchandise needed to be delivered, and Vinny and Tony were behind the wheel of their trucks by 7:00 a.m., inadvertently capitalizing on the moment and, as an added bonus, the ladies.

As more and more men left for the service, women took over the previously male-dominated jobs with the same patriotic fervor as the men registering for the draft. They were out of the home and into the factories and learning new skills, giving them a feeling of self-confidence they had never felt before. As much as they enjoyed the solidarity of uniting in the war effort, they also missed male companionship, and their choices were limited—there were either young boys or older men available to satisfy their yearnings.

Vinny and Tony were at an age when their hormones were raging and their interest in women was piquing. They looked mature, were handsome and personable, and were taking enormous pleasure in the bevy of female attention, ensuring them their pick of the litter. They were growing up fast and becoming men in more ways than one.

CHAPTER 20

At fifteen years old, Catherina was employed at a clothing factory in the garment district of Manhattan. Laboring in an overcrowded room where wires and pipes formed a grid of gloominess upon the cracked concrete walls, she worked sixty hours a week hunched over a wooden table, cutting patterns from unending bolts of stark-colored material. Her fingers were tightened into a clawed position around large, weighty scissors, and the muscles in her right hand bulged from pumping the cumbersome tool. She stood hour after hour, while some sat on hard, wooden chairs tapping a pedal with their feet in rhythm to the grinding of the sewing machines. Others sat stitching the finer details around long, narrow tables where spools of thread lined the middle and stood like soldiers. Dressed respectably, she was clad in layer upon layer of restrictive garments that flowed to the floor, solely exposing her face and hands. In the summer months, her only defense against the looming heat was to pin her hair on top of her head.

The constant ache in her back and hand never subsided, but Catherina considered herself fortunate because the owner ran his workplace with humanity and fairness. Philip Schultz gave his employees breaks and paid them for every hour they worked, not the standard four-day salary for a six-day workweek. Everyone knew his adherence to code was triggered by the horrendous fire that had erupted seven years earlier at the Triangle Shirtwaist Factory, incinerating almost one hundred and fifty workers—some jumping to their deaths desperate to escape. He promised his employees that all necessary precautions were taken to insure such a catastrophe would not be duplicated at his establishment, and he expected them to follow his rules.

Catherina had immediately stood out from the rest of Philip's workers. She took her job seriously and had a knack for spotting the slightest imperfections. Her maturity and intelligence transcended her youth and even some of the elderly workers looked up to her for direction. Bilingual and hardworking, she was a tremendous asset to Philip, and he recognized her competency. Within five months, he had promoted her to supervisor, a job she promptly proved she was capable of fulfilling.

———◆•◆———

Newspapers highlighted the progression of the women's rights movement, and daily, Catherina read the engrossing articles. She could not comprehend discrimination against any human for race, religion, or gender, and she developed a keen interest in the struggle.

"Maggie, there's a rally this Sunday, why don't you come?" Catherina asked her coworker and friend.

Maggie glanced up at her from the sewing machine. Her long, blonde hair was pulled back into a ponytail, and the light bulb hanging overhead illuminated her porcelain skin. "I'm not sure I want to get involved," she said hesitantly.

"It's quite an event. You'd be amazed how many women attend—from mothers to secretaries to socialites. The first time I went, I was so moved."

Their conversation was interrupted by Ethel, a dour-looking woman in her sixties who was stitching sleeves together at an adjacent machine. "Why are you stirring the pot?" she asked. "Who are you to stand up against our government?"

"The government needs to make changes. Men and women should have equal rights," Catherina said.

"All you're doing is making trouble," the woman scoffed. Letting out a dramatic huff, she grinded her machine to a start and went back to her business.

"You have a right to your opinion," Catherina said, brushing off her coworker's comment, "and so do I." She turned back to Maggie. "Why don't you see for yourself what it's all about?"

Maggie looked reluctant. "Maybe next time."

———◆•◆———

On Sunday afternoon, Catherina was handing out flyers on a street corner, advocating women's rights. She spotted Philip walking in her direction, and she smiled politely in return.

"Good afternoon, Catherina," he said as he approached her.

"Good day, Mr. Schultz."

"Please, there's no need for such formality outside of work—call me Philip. I'm surprised to see you here. I didn't realize the extent of your commitment to the movement."

She handed him a flyer. "One day women will have the right to vote. One day everyone will understand we all have the same heart that beats."

Philip arched his brows and tilted his head. "That's quite a compelling argument."

"It's true."

"Catherina, will you have lunch with me tomorrow?" he asked her out of the blue.

"Yes," she said, blushing slightly.

"Tomorrow then," he said. Adjusting the newspaper under his arm, he nodded politely and left.

———◆•◆———

Walking to the luncheonette together the next day, Catherina found herself hustling to keep up with Philip's lofty stride. Glancing at him sideways, she noticed that his hair, which was always combed back with tonic, shone golden in the daylight.

A hefty, gum-chewing waitress greeted them as they entered and led them to a booth. "What can I get you to drink?" she asked brusquely, placing two menus in front of them.

"Coca Cola for me, Mary," Philip said.

Catherina glanced up at the girl and smiled. Mary was one of the regulars, and she served her customers with a seasoned indifference. "Coffee for me, please."

Philip pulled his wire-rimmed spectacles out of the breast pocket of his shirt and wrapped them around the back of his ears. Opening the menu, he scanned the page. "Have you had the tuna on rye?" he asked, looking up. "I get it every time I come here, and I tell myself that the next time I'll get something different, but I can't seem to bring myself to do it."

"Sounds good, I'll have the same," she said.

Returning with their drinks, the waitress took their order.

"Philip, I've always wanted to know…what made you open a clothing factory?" Catherina asked when they were alone.

He looked at her and smiled slightly. "My father started the business almost twenty years ago. When I was a child, my parents had escaped the turmoil festering within Germany to seek solace in democracy, and my father opened with just two employees." He raised his eyebrows. "Of course, it's grown quite a bit since then. I've had the good fortune to attend New York University, so America and its opportunities have very sentimental value to me. When the president declared war against Germany, I virtually reorganized my factory overnight to assembling garments for the soldiers." He paused. "How did you get involved in the cause?" he asked her.

Catherina had always held Philip in high regard. He was dignified with a stateliness and formality in his manner and appearance, although his breeding did not intimidate her. "If there's to be true democracy, there needs to be changes. Why, it's an American right to vote, denied only to criminals, lunatics, *and* women," she said, having no qualms about voicing her beliefs. Letting out a deep breath, she gave him an exasperated look. "How ridiculous is that?"

The handlebar mustache wedged beneath his prominent nose shadowed his subdued smile. "To tell you the truth, as a male, I don't have the same passion for the issue," he said, sounding apologetic. He took a bag of tobacco from his pocket and filled his pipe.

"Maybe you would if you heard more from a women's perspective. Why don't you come with me next Sunday afternoon? There's a rally in Times Square. Mrs. Belmont herself is scheduled to speak. I've had the opportunity to meet her at smaller gatherings and she's an eloquent and knowledgeable spokeswoman and one who could open up a mind."

He stared at her intently. "You're very persuasive," he said. "How could I resist?"

———◆•◆———

Mrs. Belmont, the grand dame of New York society, made it fashionable to champion for women's rights. The feisty matron mounted the soapbox on the busy street with dignity and confidence. Catherina was filled with emotion as she listened to her well-versed, persuasive speech, which stimulated overall enthusiasm. Hundreds cheered and spontaneously tossed yellow daisies through the air, sparking a fire of unity despite those who attempted to smolder the impassioned crusade with counterdemonstrations. The song "Tipperary" harmoniously erupted from the depths of their struggle, signifying they were raging a battle for equality, and Catherina resolutely sang along.

As the icon maneuvered throughout the assembly, shaking hands and drinking in the adulation, she greeted Catherina with open arms, "Thank you, young lady, for all your help. You've proven to be invaluable."

"I feel the same way, Mrs. Belmont," Philip said.

Turning in Philip's direction, she asked, "And who's this fine gentleman, Catherina?"

"I'm Philip Schultz," he said, extending his hand. "It's an honor, Mrs. Belmont."

Clasping his hand between hers, she said gaily, "It's very nice to see we have a few men on our side." She turned back to Catherina. "I'm having a tea after this, dear, please join us. We can talk more about the cause over some warm biscuits."

"That's very kind of you."

"It was a pleasure to meet you, madam," Philip said, tipping his hat in Mrs. Belmont's direction. His eyes met Catherina's, and for a moment he held her gaze. "Good day, ladies, I must be on my way."

———◆•◆———

Daily, Philip stopped by Catherina's station, and gradually they developed an amiable familiarity. Occasionally accepting his invitation to lunch or dinner, Philip always behaved impeccably, and she was comfortable in his presence. The formula for their attraction was their contrasting pedigrees, and they were never at a loss for conversation. Even though Philip was fourteen years older, Catherina was falling in love with him, more for his brains than for his brawn.

Late one afternoon as Philip was making his rounds, he said, "Catherina, Mrs. Belmont's right. You're invaluable. I really can't thank you enough."

"This is so important for the soldiers," she said.

"Will you be joining me for dinner tonight?"

"Why don't you come home with me for a change? My mother always makes plenty, and my family's been asking to meet you. She's a wonderful cook...but I'm a little biased," she added with a grin.

"I'll be back with my coat."

———◆•◆———

Catherina was both anxious and excited for Philip to meet her family, and she could feel her heart beating faster as they walked into her home. Taking hold of

Philip's hand, she led him into the parlor. "This is Philip, my boss," she announced to her family sitting around the table. Bending over, she kissed Victoria on the cheek. "I've been bragging about your cooking, Mama, and I've asked Philip to supper." Going over to Lorenzo's chair, she kissed him on top of his head.

"Nice to meet you, sir," Philip said to Lorenzo.

"I hope you brought along an appetite," Lorenzo said. "Take his coat, Catherina."

"We're almost finished, but there's still plenty. Philip, you can sit there," Victoria said, motioning to the empty seat at the table.

Philip and Catherina shrugged off their coats, and she took them into the kitchen, hanging them on the hooks behind the door.

"Santo, get an extra chair from the bedroom," Lorenzo said.

Catherina grabbed a plate from the cabinet and sat down next to Philip in the chair Santo brought over. She pointed to her family and introduced them one by one. "This is my Uncle Dominick and Aunt Genevieve, their sons Nicholas and Roberto, my brothers, Vinny and Santo, and my sisters, Gabriella, Rosa, and Louisa."

Catherina knew Philip had lost his parents and had no siblings of his own, and during dinner, she noticed that he seemed to be enjoying the banter that filled the room. She also noticed that the more time they spent together, the harder it was getting for them to say good-bye.

———◆◦◆———

It still took Catherina by surprise when one month later Philip asked her to dinner and then he asked her to be

179

his bride. With her mouth open wide in surprise, she held out her hand, and he slipped his symbol of love onto her finger.

CHAPTER 21

Collectively, the family was bringing in sufficient income to provide for their needs, and Victoria was able to forego assembling piecework. She was thankful for the additional time with the younger children, Santo, Rosa, and Louisa, knowing time was a precious gift that could be taken away like a thief in the night.

Having lost Gennaro to tuberculosis, Victoria had discovered firsthand the interminable heartbreak of sending a son away and fervently praying he would come back healthy. She felt an overwhelming compassion for mothers whose sons were serving in the war. Knitting woolen socks and blankets for the soldiers gave Victoria back some peace. She also donated some of the books Vinny had brought home to supply reading material for the troops. She even had the children collect fruit pits, which she brought to the Red Cross to be burned to supply charcoal for gas mask filters.

One of the restrictions of the president's wartime program was Heatless Mondays to conserve energy. Tuesday mornings before anyone else was awake, Victoria descended the three flights of stairs carrying two buckets to retrieve coal from the backyard bin—the stove needed rekindling after a day of neglect.

Today she felt especially fatigued; her head was throbbing, and her legs were swollen. It had been unseasonably cool, and the chill went right through her brittle bones, making her shiver. She slept restlessly all night after rereading the letter Mama had written to them last year telling them Papa had died. Again, Victoria found herself wishing that they had been forewarned he was ill; maybe they would have had the chance to say good-bye. She and Dominick had agreed they would do whatever it took to return to Italy in the summer to spend time with their mother. Unfortunately, three months later they received a letter from an aunt informing them Angelina had passed away. Victoria surmised her mother must have died from a broken heart because, when she let it, she could feel the debilitating pain of hers breaking too.

With the heavy load clutched in her hand, she was struck by a wave of dizziness and collapsed to the ground—the coal scattering around her like leaves that had fallen from a tree.

———◆◆———

Entering the kitchen, Vinny saw that the stove was cold and the usual aroma of freshly brewed coffee was missing along with his mother. He had been noticing her recent bouts of pain that tightened her features, yet she had insisted it was nothing serious when he voiced his concern. With a sinking feeling in the pit of his stomach, he vaulted down the stairs and through the alley and found her motionless on the ground. Stopping dead in his tracks, he clasped his hand to his mouth as he gasped and dropped to his knees. "Mama, Mama, wake up," he repeated as he lightly tapped her cheek.

There was no response.

Suddenly, his adrenalin soared, and he scooped her into his arms and carried her up to the apartment. Gently placing her on the bed, his siblings gathered around— their unblinking eyes waiting for an explanation.

Wrapping her arms around Rosa and Louisa, Catherina pulled them close. "What happened, Vinny?" she asked.

He carefully covered his mother with the blanket. "I found her on the ground out back."

"Is she going to be okay?" Gabriella said hesitantly as she sat down on the bedside and gently touched Victoria's hand. "She's so cold." She looked up at Vinny, giving him a tragic look. "Shouldn't we get a doctor?"

Vinny leaned over and lightly placed his quivering fingertips on his mother's neck, searching for a pulse. Tears streamed down his face as he choked out the words, "I think she's gone."

"Santo, go get Papa at work," Catherina shouted. "And just tell him Mama's not well."

Fear pulsated through Lorenzo's veins as he rushed home with Santo following behind and leaving a trail of tears in his wake. Lorenzo flung open the front door and scaled the steps two at a time—trepidation spurring his pace. Horrified, he discovered his children sobbing over their mother's spiritless body. Falling to his knees beside her bed, he frantically embraced her. "Victoria, don't go. I need you...the children need you," he begged. Trembling, he shook his head and sobbed. "You're my world...my life...my beloved Victoria."

In the parlor, a simple, pine coffin rested upon a basin filled with blocks of ice. A vase of white lilies and several candles illuminated its dear contents. Victoria was laid to rest in the pink lace gown Catherina had made for her to wear at her wedding to Philip, which was just two months away. The pale dusting powder on her face casted an unearthly aura on her translucent skin. Her stiff hands rested on the same treasured Bible she had carried from her homeland, and rosary beads were entwined around her calloused fingers. Lorenzo believed they were vulnerable to superstitions that had survived centuries and generously sprinkled salt around her body and at the entrance of their home to protect them from ornery spirits.

For four endless days, Lorenzo and the children, along with Dominick, Genevieve, and their sons, Nicholas and Roberto, remained at the apartment while a procession of friends, neighbors, and coworkers paid their respects to the bereaved family, bringing gifts of food, wine, and money. The mourners, all dressed in black, lamented loudly, and the atmosphere was latent with sorrow—a sobering reminder of the fragility of life.

Somber and withdrawn, the question that ruminated over and over in Lorenzo's mind was impugning his faith. *Why would God take someone so young when an older man willingly stood before him?*

A horse-drawn wagon, followed by the forlorn, carried Victoria's coffin to mass as the tolling of the church bells echoed, creating an eerie, fading melody throughout the streets. Morosely trailing behind, Lorenzo's eyes remained transfixed on the casket as his heart lay shattered by Victoria's side. The Bible he had placed in her hands had sustained her in life, and in death he hoped it would guide her into heaven where she would peacefully dream for all of eternity.

In the weeks following the death of his wife, Lorenzo navigated each day in a bewildered state, struggling to keep up his stamina for his six children. His body and soul ached for Victoria, and the anguish had a way of distorting daily activities into insurmountable tasks. He could not fathom how he would ever overcome the pain because it would have meant he would have to get used to living with the loss.

Lorenzo did not know what he would have done without his older children, and he was grateful that they kept the family functioning. He admired their strength, feeling guilty they carried so much of the responsibility, but they handled it courageously. Lorenzo felt Victoria had deserved most of the credit. Instead of growing up with the image of a God of retribution, she instilled the image of a loving God, and it had made all the difference. Her religious beliefs encompassed the philosophy that there was a reason for everything and their faith would carry them through even the most trying of times.

———◆◆———

At only thirty-three years old, his mother's passing was a tragedy, but it was also a milestone for Vinny. As the oldest sibling, he felt as if it were his passage into adulthood at the age of eighteen. Relying on the example his mother had set, he realized it was she who had given him the strength he now felt. The snippets of her past prompted him to enjoy each moment, and he promised himself to live each day as though it were his last. In his eyes, he did not lose his mother, for he still felt her presence all around him.

CHAPTER 22

Thoughts of her wedding constantly made Catherina smile; unfortunately, two months before the blissful day, her exhilaration had turned to devastation when her mother suddenly died. As the oldest daughter, it was natural for Catherina to follow in Victoria's footsteps and become the matriarch of the family. The more she missed her mother, the more she submerged herself into the maternal role. She had helped rear her siblings since they were born, and now she was the one they looked up to for stability.

Catherina continued to work for Philip during the days and came home in the evenings to lend a hand with the chores and the children. The routine was the same; the difference was that she had to do it with a hollowed hole in her heart. Gabriella had volunteered to quit her job at a luncheonette so someone could take care of their home and be there for Santo, Rosa, and Louisa. However, Catherina was always the one they wanted to tuck them in at night.

Catherina appreciated that Philip gave her the distance she needed to mourn the loss of her mother. She knew her mood was as solemn as the dark clothes she wore, but she was torn and confused. *Should I go through with our plans so soon after Mama's passing? Can I juggle a new marriage and give the children the attention they need? Do I truly love Philip, or am I in love with who he is?*

———— ◆•◆ ————

Sunday supper's usual commotion had taken on a somber pace as thoughts of Victoria humbled the tone of the room. Everyone made an effort not to stir fragile emotions, replacing the spontaneity with carefully chosen words.

As Catherina studied Philip from across the table, she could feel her doubts resting heavily upon her shoulders.

When he looked up, their eyes met. There was an unmistakable tenderness to them, she thought, a tenderness that was meant only for her.

"When we marry, Catherina, you'll have more time with your family." He scanned the table. "You'll never have to work again."

She stared at him oddly, wondering why he chose to broach this subject in a room full of family, but his words struck a chord she had not heard before, compounding her ambivalence. Work gave her independence and friendships that she was unsure she was ready or willing to forego. "I think it's too soon for us to marry after all that's happened," she simply said.

Lorenzo put down his fork and gave her a soulful look. "Sweetheart, your mother's wish would be to see you happy. She wouldn't have wanted you to put your life on hold because hers had been taken too soon."

Catherina smiled at her father. She knew it had taken him time to warm up to Philip. It had nothing to do with his age; after all, Lorenzo was fifteen years older than her mother, but he had voiced his concern that she was marrying someone from another country so different from their own.

"Postponing the date won't change what has happened to Mama," Vinny added.

Catherina listened contemplatively as they conveyed their encouraging sentiments, and Gabriella continued with touching reasoning, "Remember how thrilled

Mama was when you handed her the box...and her surprise when she saw the pink dress you made for her to wear to your wedding? It brought tears to her eyes. She hung it on a hook in her room where she could see it every day. She couldn't wait to wear it. I know she'll be there in spirit."

Hesitantly, Catherina gave into the nudging of their support. "I suppose you're all right." She looked at Philip. "We'll go through with our plans."

"It's settled then," he said as he hoisted his glass in the air.

On Monday before the wedding, Maggie approached Catherina after work. "We need to talk," she said, sounding as despondent as she looked.

"About what?"

"Not here," she insisted. "Let's go next door."

Catherina's mind was racing as she silently followed Maggie out of the building and into the coffee shop. As they sat down in a booth, a petite waitress with short, curly hair immediately came over. "What can I get you ladies?" she asked cheerfully, pushing up the red-framed glasses on her nose.

"Just two coffees," Maggie said, barely glancing up at the girl. Maggie looked at Catherina. "Saturday night I was at Mulligan's with Caroline—my sister, Caroline, not the secretary that works in the office. Anyway, Philip was there with a bunch of guys, but he didn't see me walk in, and he was too drunk to notice where I sat. Unfortunately, we could hear everything he was saying." She let out a puff of air through her nostrils. "He was so loud, everyone could hear what he was saying.

He was bragging to his friends in this cocky voice and slurring his words. In the years working for this...I don't know...refined gentleman?" She looked at Catherina who nodded in agreement. "I would've never believed he could sound like that."

The waitress returned with their coffees and placed them on the table. She took a pad and pencil out of her apron.

"Could you give us a few minutes?" Maggie said dismissively.

Catherina straightened her back. "I knew he was there," she said in Philip's defense as soon as the girl left. "As he put it, he was out to celebrate the end of his bachelorhood with some of his friends."

"Well, he must've had too much to drink. He blatantly boasted that he would never allow his future wife... *you*...to spend so much time with her younger siblings. He actually thrust his finger in the air and said it was, and I quote, 'her old man's responsibility, and if he can't handle it, then they should be put in an orphanage.' What kind of man says that? He also said the only child he intends to foster is one of his own...and only one...he made *that* point clear. He said it's absolutely absurd that you want four."

"When I told him that, he never disagreed," she said, thoroughly confused.

"That's not what he was saying last night."

Eyeing Maggie suspiciously, Catherina shook her head. "That's impossible, it's so unlike Philip. I've never seen him drunk or heard him say a bad word about anyone."

"Wait, it gets worse." She looked at Catherina sympathetically. "I hate to have to tell you this."

"What? Just tell me."

"I wasn't sure if I should, but honestly, I would want someone to tell me if it were the other way around." Maggie took a deep breath and exhaled slowly. "He said...he was going to have a hard time getting rid of..." She nervously gnawed at her thumbnail. "Jane...he called her."

Catherina dropped her head into her hands. "Are you positive you heard him right?" she asked, looking up.

Maggie's eyes grew wide, and she slapped her hand against the edge of the table. "Philip made a fool out of himself. Don't let him make a fool out of you too, Catherina. I heard it with my own ears. We're friends, why would I lie to you?"

"I can't believe it." Catherina's body was shaking, but she tried to keep her thoughts steady. *When did he have time for another? Could I've been so blind?*

"How will you be able to live with or love a man so callous and controlling?" Maggie threw her hands in the air. "Why, it's against all your principles."

Catherina recoiled from the ugliness. She was still grieving from the loss of her mother, and to make matters worse, she was now confronted with the dishonesty of the man with whom she had planned to marry. "Oh, Maggie, what'll I do?" she moaned, the deceit was exacerbating her anguish.

Before Maggie had an answer, Catherina jumped up and stormed out of the shop, inwardly cursing Philip's existence. Stomping home, she made a life-changing decision. Not ready to face her family, she feverishly paced the sidewalk in front of her apartment building, waiting for him to arrive. When she saw him turning the corner, she hurried in his direction, trembling.

"You left work without saying good-bye," he said, leaning in for a kiss.

She pushed him away. "How was your night on Saturday?" she asked.

"What are you talking about?"

She struggled to hold back her anger. "I was told about the things you said."

"Catherina, I drank too much. I don't even know what I said."

"Let me refresh your memory then. Something about not letting me spend time with my family…about putting my brother and sisters in an orphanage…about not wanting more than one child. What the hell was that all about?"

"Let me explain."

"Explain," she countered. "How do you explain that?"

"I told you, I drank too much."

"That's your excuse? Who are you, anyway?" She pounded his chest with clenched fists and howled with frustration, "You're a liar—that's who you are!"

Grabbing hold of her wrists, he looked at her remorsefully. "Catherina…I love you," he said lamely.

Her eyes frosted over in icy detachment. "You love me—what about *Jane?*"

Letting her go, he stepped back, and his countenance waned white. "I'm sure this means nothing to you, but I'm sorry…I was going to tell her it's over. She means nothing to me."

"You were *going* to tell her it's over? Don't bother. I'm telling *you* it's over." Her face flushed with humiliation and rage. "This isn't going to work."

"After everything I've done for you," he said. The veins in his neck bulged. "I can give you anything you want."

Catherina could not believe what she was hearing. "What I want is for you to go away." With the anger of a woman scorned, she shoved him, and he stumbled into the street. "You only get to break my heart once," she said. She gave him one last contemptuous glare, turned away, and walked out of his life forever.

CHAPTER 23

Gabriella had blossomed into a precocious child. If she felt like singing, she belted out a song. If she had a question, she would ask. Sometimes others did not appreciate the uninhibited girl, but it did not bother Gabriella. Retreating into her own world, she would draw what she observed, finding splendor in the simplest things. She would work on a sketch for days until it was perfect, structuring her life with graceful lines and definition.

Often Lorenzo would affectionately muse while most looked at the world as either black or white, Gabriella was capable of adding the finer shades of gray. She would giggle and roll her eyes at her father, but she secretly loved the attention.

As a teenager, Gabriella wondered if everyone had a talent, one thing that determined their uniqueness, one thing that made them extraordinary—she called it their *uno*. Her mother had told her that it was the first word she uttered as a baby. Such a simple word, but it personified Gabriella.

Offering to stay home with the younger children, Gabriella had quit her job as a waitress after Victoria died. She missed working at the luncheonette and the interaction with the people who had become the engaging diversions in her ordinary life. It took time to become accustomed to the mundane routine, yet she approached the responsibility with dedication and affection, developing a maturity born from the throes of despair.

Gabriella had been busy in the apartment all morning, scrubbing clothes on the washboard and pushing the heavy iron back and forth in the stuffy kitchen. She looked forward to getting out into the fresh air to do her errands while Santo, Rosa, and Louisa were at school.

It was a magnificent day, the sky was a bright blue, and the nuance of springtime was budding in the air. Gabriella thought that even the most downtrodden would feel uplifted by its perfection. Walking through the streets with the warmth of the sun on her smiling face and a slight breeze blowing through her golden-brown hair, she felt unusually carefree. The bakery was her last stop that flawless afternoon. Papa had asked her to pick up something special for Rosa and Louisa's birthday.

On rare occasions Gabriella had gone to the bakery with her mother, but it had been many months since she was there. She waltzed into the shop with a spring in her step as she hummed one of her favorite songs. Besieged by the intoxicating aroma of freshly baked goods, she sighed as her tongue circled her lips.

The owner stood mesmerized as if he were looking at Gabriella for the first time, even though he had seen her before. "I'm sorry for your loss," Vito said.

"Thank you. It was so sudden," she said. "We miss her very much."

"If there's anything I can do..." His voice trailed off as if to let Gabriella fill in the rest. "Are you still working at the luncheonette?" he finally asked.

"No, now I care for the children. In fact, today's the twins' ninth birthday." She scanned the case. "Hmm, everything looks delicious. What do you suggest?" she asked, looking up at him.

"The chocolate layer cake is always a hit," he said, gazing back at her.

"I don't know. Rosa doesn't really like chocolate. Do you have anything vanilla or maybe strawberry? They both love strawberries and whipped cream."

"What's your favorite?" he asked.

"Definitely chocolate, but—"

An elderly gentleman who was leaning his elbow on the counter good-naturedly interrupted, "Can you please make up your mind, young lady. I'm getting older by the minute."

Gabriella flushed with embarrassment and looked up at the clock on the wall. "The children will be getting home from school. I should go," she said. "I'll take the strawberry."

Placing the cake in a box and securing it with string, Vito handed it to Gabriella.

"Thanks," she said, placing the coins on the counter.

Before Vito had a chance to say good-bye, Gabriella was out the door, but he was in her thoughts for the rest of the day.

———◆◆———

Louisa and Rosa arrived home from school overexcited by the attention they had received from their teacher and friends. Their brother, Santo, had dawdled behind, obviously irritated by their merriment.

The girls strolled into the parlor looking for Gabriella and realized they were alone. Spying the jar of cigars next to Papa's chair, Louisa reached in and took out two. With a wicked grin straddling her face, she handed one to Rosa. In an isolated moment of camaraderie, the sisters danced around playfully and imitated their father with exaggerated movements. They loved watching him puff on his cigar in the evenings—the curls of smoke hovering above him in a gauzy cloud. Their brandish display made them chuckle at each other's silliness.

Rosa was used to Louisa taking everything to the next level, adding that extra tinge of exhilaration when all consequences are ignored. She watched her sister brazenly strike a match on the floor and light the broad tip of her cigar while deeply inhaling. Her lungs rejected the foreign substance, and her body repeatedly jerked forward, spewing the pungent fumes. Hearing footsteps ascending the stairs, Rosa hastily stuffed her cigar under the cushion of Papa's chair, and catching her breath, Louisa did the same. They scrambled into the kitchen as Santo opened the door.

Afraid her brother would smell the odor of the stogie, Rosa begged, "Santo come outside and play with us." She grabbed him by the arm, dragging him onto the landing. "We need you to hold the jump rope—I want to show you what I learned."

He looked at her disinterestedly.

"It's our birthday," Louisa reminded him, closing the door behind them.

"How could I forget? It's all you two have been talking about," he said.

"Come on, please," they said in synchronized whining.

Santo pursed his lips and frowned. "All right, all right, just until Gabriella gets home."

Following him outside, Rosa assumed they were off the hook and heaved a restrained sigh of relief.

Skipping rope in the street below, they all looked up in unison at the smoke billowing from their parlor windows.

"What were you two doing in there?" Santo demanded.

Louisa's eyes brimmed wide with panic. "Rosa lit one of Papa's cigars."

"I did not, you liar!" Rosa shouted, jerking her neck in Louisa's direction.

"Yes you did...when we heard Santo coming, you stuffed it under the cushion of the chair," she stammered through her tears, working herself into her usual hysterics.

"Don't move till I get back," Santo ordered, dashing into the building.

Trying to ignore Louisa's dramatics, Rosa kept her eyes fixated on the door as a succession of Hail Mary's raced through her mind.

Coughing and wheezing, Santo stumbled out onto the front stoop and sat down on the steps. Holding both hands to his heaving chest, he slowly shook his head back and forth in somber disbelief.

———◆●◆———

Returning home, Gabriella was still in her sprightly mood as she mulled over her conversation with Vito. She visualized the way he looked—his ruffled hair, the tone of his skin, the contours of his face. She memorized the details with artistic precision, looking forward to transferring them onto paper. Spotting the large group of people staring aghast at the flames darting from their apartment, her eyes flew open, instantly snapping her out of her sweet daydream. The muscles in her arms went limp, and her groceries scattered onto the sidewalk. Her legs weighted with dread, she pressed onward. Catching sight of Rosa and Louisa clinging to Santo, she prayed they were unharmed.

"Oh, my God! Is everyone okay?" Gabriella fell to her knees in front of her sisters, scanning them from head to toe.

The elderly woman standing next to them said gravely, "The firemen are on their way."

Gabriella suddenly remembered the small, wooden box that held the few sentimental items they had from their mother and the tin filled with cash. Jumping up, she ran into the building and thundered up the stairs in a fervent attempt to rescue what little they had left.

Her eyes watered as she squinted through the thickening haze and gasped for air. Frantically, she grabbed anything she could salvage, flinging clothes and linens out the kitchen window into the alley below. Overcome by smoke, she crawled along the floor and searched for her way out, gripping tightly onto the box that held the memories of her mother and the tin that contained the worth of the family's hard work. She staggered outside and watched from the street in silent horror as the firemen competed with the angry flames, singeing off pieces of Gabriella's heart.

◆●◆

Lorenzo, Vinny, and Catherina returned from work to the charred remnants of their apartment now soaked from the drenching of the fire hoses.

Gabriella hugged herself to control the trembling as she wept, "This would've never happened if I'd been home. They could've been hurt…they could've died. I'm so sorry."

Lorenzo embraced her and said, "You couldn't have known your sisters would have done something so careless. They're safe, and that's all that matters."

Gabriella admired the way her father handled the devastating incident, with prudence and dignity. Lorenzo's love for them was so much more prevalent than the loss of their possessions. He was able to dust off the ashes and pragmatically move forward, telling her everyone is capable of making mistakes.

There were many vacant apartments in the neighborhood because the poverty level was below even a tenement's affordability. Fortunately, they had the means to rent a larger one on the same block with two bedrooms and a bathroom off the kitchen. Together with what Gabriella had recovered and the graciousness of neighbors and relatives, they moved in that night. They would make do with the few pieces of worn furniture and the beds that came along with the apartment; however, the neglected rooms clearly needed to be scoured. Lorenzo, with a bucket in hand, ordered Rosa and Louisa to scrub the walls and floor of their new home. All thoughts of a birthday celebration had gone up in smoke.

———◆◆———

Gabriella was wracked with guilt and escaped to the front stoop to sort through her feelings of blame. The night air was chilly, and she draped the cloak she held in her hands over her shoulders and sat down. She looked up. The blackened sky intermittently illuminated with flashes of lightning, but her tears never stopped coming as she thought about Louisa. Her sister had had her good days, but for the most part, she was a handful and forever trying their patience. There were times when her moods were extreme and her behavior was unpredictable, and today was definitely one of those days.

Gabriella spotted Vito turning the corner and holding a cake box in his hand. Clutching the delicate lace handkerchief her father had thoughtfully given her from the treasured box she saved, she placed it on her lap and quickly wiped her tears with her sleeve. His steps hastened when he noticed her, and she took several deep breaths to calm herself down.

Coming to a stop on the sidewalk in front of her, Vito looked both confused and concerned. "Gabriella, what's the matter…and why are you sitting *here*? I thought you lived over there," he said, pointing across the street.

She was unable to stop the tears from flooding her eyes again.

He squatted beside her and placed a consoling arm around her shoulders. "You can tell me." His voice grew somber.

Gabriella found herself disclosing the details of what had happened since she had left the bakery that afternoon. "Thank goodness no one was hurt…I couldn't have lived with myself." She was shaking her head back and forth.

"What your sisters did was simply a childhood antic. You shouldn't feel responsible," he said.

She looked at him appreciatively.

"I certainly caused my share of trouble as a kid," he told her. "When I was nine, my younger brother and I were caught stealing pocketfuls of candy. The owner of the shop dragged us home by the collar and told our parents." Vito stared straight ahead as if lost in the memory. "I thought my father was going to kill us. As soon as the man left, he pulled the belt right off his pants…I can still hear that swooshing sound. I think I still have the scars. He made us apologize, and as a punishment, we worked there every day after school for months. Humph, don't you know the guy checked our pockets every day before we left." He laughed. Picking the cake box off the step, he placed it on her lap. "Maybe a slice of chocolate cake will put the smile back on your face."

Gabriella chuckled for the first time in hours.

CHAPTER 24

Ever since Victoria had died, Santo realized if he kept moving he did not miss his mother as much. He believed she was the only person who had understood him, made excuses for him, and loved him unconditionally. Having five siblings, he had grown up vying for her attention, but Victoria had been pulled in many directions. Using his sisters as the brunt of his guile, he always made sure his pranks would regain her recognition. Harboring a variety of schemes up his sleeve, he smiled to himself remembering one he had been particularly fond of and one he had considered a sure bet. Sprinkling a jar of roaches under his sisters' blankets, his gleeful reward came from their screams of repulsion. Before discipline could be dispensed, he would pretend to wheeze as a decoy—his mother immediately scurrying for the tonic and foregoing his mischief. When his irritated siblings would complain about his behavior, his mother had dismissed them, saying, "He's not right." Santo now wondered if she had been referring to his troubles with breathing or the ones that had been wreaking havoc with his mind.

Santo found it almost impossible to sit still in school and concentrate on his work, and he had no interest in completing his assignments. When under a teacher's scrutiny, his thoughts were scrambled, and his words tumbled awkwardly, causing him to stammer in short, disjointed sentences. To hide his insecurities, he opted to be funny, and his classmates would laugh, perpetuating his nonsense. Never understanding when enough was already too much, Santo's impromptu disturbances became a challenge for his teachers. Regularly testing the limits of their patience, their dour reactions often bred scolding and belittlement, provoking him further into rebellion.

———◆•◆———

By sixth grade, his teacher, Miss Finch, conceded that it was easier to let one waver than let fifty falter and left it to Principal Graham to administer Santo's punishment. As Mr. Graham whacked Santo's hands with a ruler, he would reprimand him for his behavior, but it still did not discourage his unruliness. Santo believed nothing could hurt as much as the day his mother had died. Waves of malcontent skewed his reasoning, and he continued to channel his energy disruptively as anger bedeviled his soul with defiance. Eventually, he plotted a carefully calculated scheme that he thought would ensure his dismissal from school.

For several days, he collected rocks in his pockets and concealed them on top of the water box perched high above the toilet. When he had accumulated an adequate supply, he piled them in the bottom of the bowl. Tying a string around a brick, he fastened it to the pull chain, and its weight caused the tank to continually fill. The overflow flooded the bathroom and seeped into the hallway.

It took exactly eleven minutes for Mr. Graham to come barreling into Santo's classroom. "Have any of your students recently been given permission to go to the bathroom?" he asked Miss Finch.

The teacher exhaled a frustrated huff and looked grimly at Santo. "Santo Carnavale," she moaned.

———————◆◆◆———————

When Lorenzo came home from work, Santo was waiting for him in the kitchen with a note from Mr. Graham clenched in his hand. Solemnly, he handed it to his father.

Eyeing him skeptically, Lorenzo took the paper and read slowly. "It says here that your principal wants me to meet him after school tomorrow," he said, looking up. "How can I leave work early?" He grimaced. "What's this about, Santo?"

"I don't know," he said. "He just said you should come."

———————◆◆◆———————

Santo arrived at school the next morning and an unfriendly look came over Mr. Graham's bearded face as he approached him.

"Sit quietly on the bench outside my office until your father comes," he said.

Santo was perplexed. "You want me to sit there all day?"

"That is precisely what I want." Mr. Graham handed him several sheets of paper and a pencil. "You will write one thousand times: 'I am sorry for causing so much trouble for my teacher,'" he said sternly before leaving him alone.

Already bored, Santo wondered how he was going to sit still the whole day without going crazy. He wondered what Mr. Graham would say to his father and how his father would react. He wondered if what he had done was such a good idea, but he had to admit to himself that part of him was relieved that today might be his last day of school.

Opening the door of his office, Mr. Graham peered at the blank paper on Santo's lap. "This is why your father's coming today." His hand flew up in the air. "Next time I come out here, I want to see those pages filled." He slammed the door shut.

Santo thought that he would never be able to write anything ten times, never mind one thousand, and decided not to write a single word.

———◆●◆———

Lorenzo came walking down the hall soon after the dismissal bell rang.

"Hi, Papa," Santo mumbled as he approached.

Lorenzo looked at him wearily and tapped on the principal's door.

"Come in," Mr. Graham's voice echoed from inside. He immediately stood up from behind his desk as Lorenzo walked over and extended his hand.

"Mr. Carnavale, I presume," he said, returning the gesture. "I'm Mr. Graham." He pointed to the chair across from him. "Please have a seat."

Santo stood quietly behind his father, who glanced back at him with a mixture of confusion and disappointment on his face before he sat down.

Mr. Graham folded his arms across his chest and leaned back in his chair. "I've sent notes home with Santo several times before, but it seems they don't get delivered." He glanced at Santo and frowned. "If you didn't come this time, Mr. Carnavale, Santo was told that a police officer would pay a visit to your home. The truth is, we can no longer tolerate your son's insubordination. Perhaps a parochial school could manage a boy of his temperament."

For a few moments, Lorenzo sat silently as if trying to process what the man had just said. "What did my son do?" he finally asked.

"He deliberately used rocks to cause a toilet to overflow. The hallway was flooded by the time it was discovered, causing damage to the building." He ran his hand through his thinning hair. "Mr. Carnavale, as I said, this is certainly not the first time we've experienced behavioral problems with your son. Santo is disruptive and disobedient in the classroom. It is simply inexcusable."

"His mother died several years ago, and it hasn't been the same. Won't you reconsider, sir? One more chance is all he needs."

Mr. Graham looked pitifully at him. "We're very sorry about your wife," he said, "but your son ran out of chances a long time ago." He stood up abruptly and walked over to Santo, taking the paper from his hand. "I gave Santo an assignment when he came to school this morning, and this is what he's completed." He handed the blank pages to Lorenzo, shaking his head disgustedly. "My decision is final."

———◆•◆———

Once outside the school building, Lorenzo pinched Santo's earlobe between his fingers and growled, "Santo Augustine, how could you do such a thing? An education is a privilege and a necessity. You're far too old for such foolishness. You're capable of so much more. You should use your intelligence instead of wasting it on shenanigans. What do I do with you now?"

"Vinny stopped going to school at my age," he reminded him.

Lorenzo glared at him. "That was a mistake," he said. "Your mother wanted it to be different for you. I wanted it to be different for you." He stomped away in a huff.

Santo trailed behind, secretly ecstatic that his education abruptly ended.

When they arrived home, Lorenzo's face remained unsympathetic and hard. "You've gone too far this time," he said. "Don't think this is going to be easy. I'm going to talk to your brother, and tomorrow, you'll begin spending your days working inside the concrete walls of his warehouse, loading and unloading the trucks. Believe me, you'll wish you were back at school. Now get out of my sight."

———◆•◆———

The constant physical labor was exactly what Santo needed to alleviate his restless energy, but it did not soothe his restless mind. Using its potency to calm his anxieties, he pilfered bottles of the bootleg liquor from cartons—a pattern that evolved out of grief and insecurity. In the midst of Prohibition, Santo became an alcoholic before he reached puberty.

CHAPTER 25

Each evening, Louisa would upstage her sister and entertain the family over dinner while reenacting the events of their day at school as if they were choreographed scenes from a play.

Tonight, Rosa was feeling uncharacteristically excited about what had occurred during class and was eager to be the one to tell the day's outrageous tale. "Johnny caught a mouse at school—" she began.

"He put it in the teacher's desk before class," Louisa interrupted. "She had no idea. When she opened her drawer, you should've heard her." She put both hands to her face and screamed, duplicating the teacher's reaction. "It was so loud, the principal came running into our classroom."

Rosa was seething, fed up with her sister's conspicuous need to monopolize every conversation. Contrary to her usual complacency, she flicked her fork, sending a meatball sailing across the table, which smacked Louisa squarely on the forehead—the sauce splattering in her hair, the meatball plopping down onto her lap.

Louisa shot Rosa a searing look, which could have split her in two. Plunging her fingers into her plate and grabbing a mound of spaghetti, she leaped up to retaliate.

Lorenzo's face turned beet red, and his temples throbbed with disdain. "That's enough!" he demanded, hurling his knife over Louisa's head.

She stopped dead in her tracks, and everyone at the table jarred to attention as it struck with a foreboding crack, its blade embedded in the opposite wall.

"This is inexcusable," he said. "It's a sin to waste food."

Diverting her anger, Louisa pitched the fistful of spaghetti at Papa as her siblings cringed at her utter defiance.

"Louisa, go to your room!" he gruffly bellowed, swiping the pasta off his shoulder and onto his plate. "Don't come out until I figure out your punishment."

The tension in the kitchen hung awkwardly as they all silently hid their amusement, knowing full well Papa did not see the humor in the episode.

———◆◆———

Rarely did Lorenzo lose his temper, but when he did, it was certain that Rosa and Louisa were involved. The truth was that he found it exhausting when dealing with their skirmishes and blatant disrespect. Drained by his daughters' belligerence, he slumped in his chair with a surrendering sigh and lit a cigar. With every inhale, he attempted to exhale his exasperation, unable to reconcile the obstinacy of two people raised in an otherwise harmonious household. It seemed what made one happy made the other miserable, and keeping peace between them now that they were teenagers was becoming almost impossible; reminding them they were sisters and should try to get along was downright futile. Lorenzo felt flustered and incapable when faced with the insurmountable challenges his youngest daughters created.

Meanwhile, Louisa was stewing that Rosa was the one who had started the trouble, yet she was the one who was sent to her room. She decided she was not going to let her sister get the best of her and lay awake, turning it over in her mind.

She impatiently waited for everyone else to fall asleep so she could exact her revenge. Slipping out from under the covers without waking Rosa, she tiptoed around the bed where Catherina and Gabriella slept and snuck into the kitchen to retrieve her weapon of choice. Returning to the bedroom with scissors in hand, she crept over to Rosa and maliciously snipped the silky strands that fanned the pillow. Smirking at her own deviousness, Louisa slid back into bed, thoroughly satisfied.

The next morning Lorenzo heard a bloodcurdling scream and jumped up from the kitchen table, spilling his morning coffee on his pants. Bursting into the girl's room, he hollered. "What's going on in here?"

Staring at the clumps of hair scattered about her pillow, Rosa held her head as if trying to keep it from exploding. "My hair! My hair! What happened to my hair?"

Lorenzo took one look at Rosa and glowered at Louisa. "Did you do this?"

Rosa grabbed Louisa by the arms. "It was you! I know it was you!"

Sitting upright in their bed, Catherina and Gabriella looked on in horror while Vinny and Santo stood dumbfounded in the doorway.

"Louisa, answer me!" Lorenzo ordered through clenched teeth, wondering what on earth made her do such things.

She kept her lips pinched.

"Catherina, get the scissors. It's time your sister was taught a lesson."

Without a justifiable rebuttal, Louisa stoically stood as long curls spiraled down, gathering solemnly around her feet, a closely cropped cut left in their place. Catherina did her best to even out Rosa's lopsided locks as Louisa visibly gloated.

Shaking his head in disgust, Lorenzo sternly stated, "This'd better put an end to your nonsense. Louisa, from now on you'll sleep with Catherina. Rosa, you sleep with Gabriella. *Capisca.*" He thrust his finger in the air to make sure they got the message. "I should have done this a long time ago," he added, and then he turned around and left.

The discord between Rosa and Louisa was greater than the space of the rooms; consequently, not a look or a word passed between them. They were growing up in a generation Lorenzo was finding difficult to understand and a challenge to accept.

———◆•◆———

In the years following the end of the war, a new breed of youngsters emerged from the ashes. The 1920s signified the beginning of modern America, and teenagers were distancing themselves from their parents' old world customs. They craved excitement and boldly asserted their individuality. Life and its concerns were masked by idealism, freeing them to ride the wave of change that was sweeping through the country, threatening its purity and stability in the eyes of the older generation.

As it was for all teenagers, Rosa and Louisa's social scene was an intricate part of their lives. The highlight of their summer was attending the Friday night dances held in the park where teens would twirl to the sounds of the big bands and bop to the rhythm of jazz blaring from an Edison phonograph. They were ordered by Lorenzo to go together or not at all—an annoyance without an alternative. Their association ended the minute they were out of their father's sight. Louisa's flirtatious smile and swaggering confidence turned many boys' heads, while Rosa was content to spend her time distancing herself from the ostentatious pageantry of her twin sister.

———◆•◆———

One night a group of street hoods sauntered into the park, and all eyes diverted in their direction. One of the boys captured Louisa's attention as he slouched against a tree. The firm muscles in his broad shoulders supported his lofty stance. He had arresting good looks and a well-proportioned body. His white shirt was unbuttoned halfway, exposing his bare chest, and its short sleeves were taut around his upper arms.

As Louisa held onto the folds of her calf length skirt, her movements became more exaggerated as she danced. When the song ended, she brazenly paraded past him with a hip-swinging strut and gave him a cursory glance before her eyes flicked away. To her satisfaction, he stamped out his cigarette and grabbed her by the arm, swirling her into the rhythm. They spent the next several songs dancing with each other—Louisa reveling in the limelight and relishing the scrutiny of gossiping spectators.

Rosa was clearly perturbed and marched over to Louisa with a huff in her step. "It's time to leave," she announced.

Ignoring Rosa, Louisa kept her gaze glued to her dance partner. She truly believed her sister was incapable of having a good time. God forbid she would ever miss a curfew.

"I don't care what you do, I'm leaving," Rosa said, walking away.

Louisa begrudgingly decided to follow her to avoid crossing their father. His patience had worn thin, and she was aware that she was the main cause of his agitation. She decided not to ruin her chance of seeing this gorgeous guy again, and she shrugged her disappointment. "I've got to go," she said.

"I work at the pharmacy on Ninth and Twenty-Eighth...why don't you stop by sometime?" he suggested, winking her a good-bye. His voice was smooth and inviting.

"Maybe I'll see you there tomorrow," she said before reluctantly walking away.

"Hey, what's your name?" he called out after her.

She looked over her shoulder and simply gave him a smile.

———◆•◆———

Once home, Rosa sarcastically mocked Louisa, "You're as foul as the rubbish you danced with tonight. Everyone was watching—everybody was talking about you."

Infatuation was crowding out logic in Louisa's stubborn mind. "Let them talk," she said.

"You're an ass. You know damn well who he hangs out with—but that—that's what makes it even more appealing for you, doesn't it?" She wore a familiar look of distaste on her face.

"I couldn't care less."

"What if Papa finds out?" Rosa said with the hint of a threat rolling off her tongue.

Louisa stared her up and down and snickered. "You wouldn't dare."

———————◆•◆———————

Saturday afternoon Louisa went to the pharmacy. She had rehearsed the scene in her head until it was flawless. With titillating precision, she poised herself upon a stool and waited for him to notice that she was there.

Spotting her, he immediately walked over and met her on the other side of the counter. "You didn't tell me your name yesterday." He grinned. "So what is it?" he asked, lifting his chin just a tinge.

She crossed her arms in front of her. "I'm not sure I want to tell you."

"Well, I'm Marco," he offered along with a menu. "Whatever you want."

"I'll have an egg cream, please," she said, without taking it from his hand.

"That happens to be my specialty."

She watched him attentively as he mixed the chocolate syrup with milk and seltzer.

He precisely placed the frothy drink in front of her and slid forward on his elbows. "And what do you do for fun, mystery girl, besides dance?"

Louisa tucked her chin length hair behind her ears and expertly pursed her full lips around the straw rising from the froth. Slowly, she drew in the sweet liquid. Batting her eyelashes, she casually purred, "It depends on who I'm with." She basked in the pleasure that she thought she could see his heart beating faster. "I've never seen you at a dance before," she said.

"I've never had a reason to go," he said with a smile that lit up his face. "I'll be right back, don't go anywhere." He turned away to serve another customer.

Louisa liked the way Marco's body moved with purpose behind the counter, and she liked the way the corners of his mouth turned up every time he looked her way.

"Sorry, it's busy today," he said when he returned. "Will you be there Friday...at the park?"

"Yes."

"Maybe you could leave your friend home this time?"

She chuckled. "Oh, we're not friends. Unfortunately, that was my sister...the saint of the family," she said, rolling her eyes. "I'd love to, but my father would never let me go alone. Can you believe we're twins?"

"Really? You don't even look like sisters."

"Most of the time, I wish we weren't. I've learned to ignore her." She took the last slurp of her drink and slid off the stool. "By the way, my name's Louisa," she said.

"Louisa," he called after her as she walked toward the door, "I'll see you at the park."

From that point on, Louisa spent Friday nights dancing with Marco and other nights with him exploring the habits of an unfamiliar world.

———— ◆•► ————

When sleep descended upon the household, Louisa occasionally slipped out of bed and climbed through the kitchen window, having earlier placed her clothes on the fire escape. Gripping the pile under her arm, she deftly maneuvered down the vertical, metal ladder, cringing as it rattled. Changing in the alley, she scurried to meet with Marco and his friends in the park. She desperately wanted to fit in and unflinchingly acclimated herself to their vices, but she definitely overindulged.

Louisa's ruse was regrettably uncovered when she stumbled through the window in the middle of the night and landed with a loud thud, jolting the family from their beds. Lorenzo raced into the kitchen and found her sprawled face up on the floor.

Amused by her own bravado, she flippantly giggled until she realized she was not alone. Bleary-eyed, she faintly made out the silhouette of her father kneeling beside her and wincing from the stench of alcohol and smoke emanating from her breath, although she was thankful he could not smell the pills she had swallowed.

Lorenzo mumbled an array of impassioned Italian swearwords as he tried to lift her leaden limbs off the ground.

Louisa gagged, and Catherina scrambled for a pot, but it was too late. Her body jerked forward as she retched the contents of her stomach onto the floor.

Grimacing, Catherina cleaned up the raunchy repercussions of Louisa's self-indulgent evening and put her to bed.

Louisa was forbidden to socialize with friends for a month, but she concealed her chagrin, aware her escapades had warranted the punishment. The family kept a watchful eye on her, and she tactfully played along, acting obedient and repentant. Eventually regaining her freedom, her rendezvous with Marco became more discreet and shorter, buying time until she graduated high school.

CHAPTER 26

Americans were embracing the opportunities and reaping the benefits from the country's postwar economic growth, and it was a cause for celebration. The decade was being hailed as the Roaring Twenties, and the mentality of the youth was changing with the times. The rising workforce was the children of immigrants who had been raised in America and who were much more comfortable within its borders than their parents. More and more of them owned automobiles, and the mobility opened their worlds—making the possibilities endless. They had extra cash in their pockets, and they were feeling their oats, they even dressed as if they were living the dream. They had grown up in the land of the free, and to them, it meant free spirited.

Prohibition had been the government's strategy to cure a floundering economy. Removing the stench of alcohol from the breath of the nation and all the evils associated with drinking, they used psychology to convince people to conform. Promising a reduction in crime, a reduction in taxes, and a reduction in poverty, they predicted Prohibition was the magic formula that would solve all of the country's problems, but it was faltering with a vengeance.

The unrestrained immoral decadence of the twenties was enhanced by bathtub gin and beer—the allure of the bottle was its forbiddance. The government had taken away the medicine that had dulled the ache of the war and Americans defiantly violated the mandate, retaliation against a law they considered to be ridiculous. Prohibition was also a gift to racketeers as bootlegged alcohol and illegal bars flourished. Their tightly controlled infrastructure raked in cash, and their profits skyrocketed. Government enforcers were spread too thin and were grafted, insuring matters were overlooked.

Nightclubs, ragtime, jazz, and partying were the rage. Women flocked to the speakeasies, asserting their equality by imbibing in hard liquor alongside their male counterparts. Flaunting their newfound independence, they bared their arms, shortened their dresses, wore makeup, and smoked cigarettes, and men benefited from their promiscuity. During the week, their business demanded Vinny and Tony's undivided attention, but the weekends were for frivolity. Saturday nights they indulged in drink and basked in a plentitude of coquettish women.

They dressed like they felt—suave and successful—donning suits, ties, and fedoras. The cigar precisely positioned between their fingers was a fashion accessory that added to their appeal, and they were like catnip to women. They were handsome and had money to spend, and when there was money to spend, life could only get better.

The city had swanky clubs and speakeasies catering to contemporary clientele or modest establishments frequented by immigrants and locals. Crossing the Hudson River to New Jersey offered Vinny and Tony a different variety of clubs to explore. New Jersey girls had a mystique all their own, and unescorted ladies filled the lounges and clubs, making the excursion that much more enticing. Testaments to Vinny and Tony's flirtatious talents were the luscious additions that were ever-present on their arms.

After a night of club jumping and partying, they floated back to New York on the ferry. Their bodies were still pulsating from the rhythm of the music, their minds were still muddled from the booze, and their lips still bared traces of lipstick as they became lost in the thought of how it got there. Daylight was beginning to streak between the buildings as they shuffled back home.

———◆•◆———

The dog days of summer provided no escape from the incessant heat trapped in the cavernous streets of the city. After an exhausting day of driving trucks and lifting cartons, Vinny just wanted to cool down in the river. When Tony told him they had a job delivering furniture to a newly constructed hotel on Long Island's South Shore, he got an idea. "Let's go together after work on Friday and drop off the load early Saturday. We'll spend the weekend," he suggested as they were locking up for the night.

"We can hit Glitter Alley." Tony raised his eyebrows. "I hear it's a hotspot for clubs and single women."

Vinny briefly grinned at the thought. "Before we do anything, I just want to go in the ocean," he said, wiping his forehead with his sleeve. "It's so hot...I don't think there's been a damn breeze in weeks."

"I'm sure swimming in the ocean will beat swimming in the river," Tony said excitedly.

———◆•◆———

Their vacation began as soon as they climbed into the truck late Friday afternoon. Uncorking a bottle of whiskey, Vinny took a slug and decreed, "Here's to a good weekend."

Handing over the bottle to Tony, he took a generous swig and swallowed in agreement. They continued their thirsty exchange on their drive to Long Island. Compelled by the effects of the potent moonshine, they were feeling carefree and loudly singing their favorite tunes off-key as they careened through the narrow lanes of the dark country roads.

"Look out!" Vinny suddenly yelled.

Tony hit the brakes to avoid a deer, and the truck fishtailed, slamming directly into a large willow tree. Violently thrust forward, his head collided with the steering wheel as Vinny's struck the dashboard.

———◆•◆———

Vinny awoke dazed and confused to the morning's sun blazing through the windshield. His body drenched in sweat and his thoughts disoriented, he urgently shook his friend. "Tony, you okay? Wake up."

Tony stirred, "Yeah, I think so," he moaned.

Nauseous and unsteady, Vinny pulled the handle of the door and toppled out of the truck. Lying immobilized on the ground, he groaned, "Geez, what the hell happened?"

"There was a deer on the road...I guess I hit the tree instead," Tony grunted.

Battling his discomfort, Vinny mustered the energy to stand up and staggered over to the front of the truck. "Jesus, it's pretty banged up. Check it out."

Fumbling to get out, Tony joined him to survey the damage. "Hopefully it's still drivable. Let's see if it starts," he muttered as he slid back into the driver's seat. Adjusting the throttle lever, he flipped the ignition switch on. When the engine spurted to life, they both let out a resounding sigh of relief.

Vinny got back into the truck and rubbed his forehead. "My head's killing me."

Tony scrutinized his face. "You're starting to bruise."

"You don't look too good either," he said, noticing the scrape along Tony's chin.

"That's it." Tony shook his head briskly. "We'll never do that again."

Vinny nodded agreeably. "Yeah, next time we'll hold off on the booze until we get there."

———◆◆◆———

It was Saturday afternoon by the time Vinny and Tony unloaded the furniture. The Victorian hotel in all its glory had panoramic views. Wide, covered porches wrapped its exterior where guests relaxed to the soothing sounds of the surf and savored the cool ocean breezes. Equally magnificent homes lined the beach. This was the age of opulence, and for the affluent, ornate mansions were the vogue.

A refreshing dip was exactly what they needed to shake off the effects of the previous night. This was the first time they were going to swim in an ocean, and they approached it with heightened anticipation. The sand gave way to each step that hastened as the heat scolded their bare feet. Bolting to the water, they plunged head first into the invigorating surf. Dodging and diving into the waves was revitalizing, and they played with the earnestness of a child given a new toy.

Vinny caught sight of two girls strolling down the beach. The shorter one was attractive, but the taller one was absolutely stunning. She had long, mocha-colored hair and ruby lips, and her expressive eyes peeked out from beneath her wide-brimmed, straw hat. Her bathing suit exposed the smooth contour of her shoulders and her trim thighs.

Positioning themselves gracefully in the sand, the girls flamboyantly puffed their cigarettes and pretended not to look at them; however, their whispers and giggles were making it obvious they were fawning for attention. The tall girl flicked her cigarette and leaned back on her elbows, posing like forbidden fruit in the sand—her tempting smile a testament to its sweetness.

As Vinny watched her, it was as if time had stopped, but he moved in her direction, and Tony sprung from the surf just as eager to make their acquaintance.

The tall girl spoke first. "Hello, I've never seen you two around here." Her Southern drawl was slow and sexy.

"We're from the city," Vinny said. "We came for the weekend."

"New York City?" the other girl questioned, emphasizing the middle word.

"Yes," he said, grinning broadly. "I'm Vinny." He pointed to his friend. "This is Tony."

"I'm Sarah, and this is my little sister, Julia," the tall girl said.

"Oh, Sarah, stop," Julia protested, sounding annoyed. She looked at Vinny and Tony. "We're only fourteen months apart, yet she thinks she's so much older."

"Vinny has that problem too." Tony laughed. "We're a year apart, but sometimes he acts like he's my father."

Vinny brushed off his friend's comment with an irritated smirk. "Where do you live?" he asked the girls.

"Right over there," Sarah said, pointing with a flourish of her delicate hand to their immense home rising from the dunes. "We live in Georgia most of the year, but mother can't take the heat and humidity of the southern summers so we come here. Father is the president of a bank and meets us for the month of August. He just arrived last night." She angled her hat to block the sun from her eyes and squinted up at Vinny. "What happened to your forehead?"

"We had a little accident on our way out here, nothing serious," he said.

"And what is it that you boys do in the city?" Julia asked in perfect rhythm to her batting lashes.

Vinny took it as his cue to sit down, and Tony followed his lead.

"We *own* a warehouse and trucking company," Tony said, exaggerating.

Further trying to impress the girls, Vinny said, "We store and deliver everything from booze to general merchandise to the latest fashions for department stores."

"Do you know anyone famous?" Julia asked.

Vinny spun ingenious fabrications of their affiliations with formidable mobsters, and Tony readily corroborated. Adding to their mystique were the bruises that accented their faces, making it all seem so mysterious and dangerous.

The sun had lowered in the sky, and a breeze kicked up the sand. Julia stood up and brushed herself off as if she was about to leave, and Vinny felt a surge of disappointment.

"It's getting late," she said. "Would you like to come to our home for a party this evening? My parents are having a small gathering for their anniversary."

"What time?" Tony asked.

"Cocktails at eight," Sarah said from over her shoulder as they walked away.

Holding back the delirium erupting inside, Vinny watched the girls disappear into the sea grass that led up to their home.

Lingering long after the girls departed, Vinny and Tony slinked back to their vehicle. Driving to a public bathhouse to shower and dress, they took extra care with their appearance. Parting their hair in the middle, they slicked it back with tonic until it shone like patent leather. Their pinstripe suits were pressed, and their shoes were polished, and they were ready to have a good time.

Concealing their truck in a clearing off the road not far from Sarah and Julia's home, they walked through the gated entrance and up the immense, circular driveway surrounding an illuminated, statuesque fountain. Beds of lavish blooms bordered the manicured lawns. Refined women in the latest flapper fashions complete with bell-shaped hats and men in custom-tailored tuxedos, ascots, and top hats emerged from the newest model roadsters to attend the soiree.

"Good evening," the uniformed butler greeted them when they reached the doorway. "May I have your names, gentlemen?"

"Vinny and Tony," Vinny said.

"Your full names are needed, sir," he said tersely.

"Vinny Montanaro and Tony Rubino," he clarified, wiping his sweaty palms on the sides of his jacket.

The inhospitable man looked up at them from his paper and suspiciously glared at their faces. "Your names are not on the list. I suggest you gentlemen leave immediately without incidence," he said.

Vinny glanced at Tony, realizing the hues from their bruises had deepened and their regular suits were improper attire. He shifted nervously under the man's unflinching scrutiny. "Sarah and Julia personally invited us," he said, trying to sound casual.

"I can have you escorted off the property if that would make it easier."

"Oh, I'm so glad you're here," Sarah seductively panted as she emerged from inside the hallway. Looking directly at Vinny, she waved them inside with her white-gloved hand. "They're with me, Charles."

Sarah was dressed in a lavender, silk gown. Dangling earrings matched the layers of pearls that accentuated her long, supple neck. Her hair was transformed into a mass of curls entwined with miniature pink roses. Vinny was enchanted by her beauty, and the fragrance of her heady perfume was intoxicating.

"Follow me," she said. "I need another drink."

Vinny felt his knees go weak beneath the softness of her voice.

Sarah led them through the domed, marble entry foyer with its mosaic columns infused with intricate designs. The rooms were artfully arranged with overstuffed furniture, exquisite centerpieces of blue hydrangeas and white lilies were centered on lace table napery, and tapestry curtains draped the enormous windows. Crystal chandeliers sent sparkles of starlight onto the ornate rugs that littered the floors. Portraits of ancestors and paintings of landscapes adorned the walls. Vinny thought of the pictures in his home—one of the Virgin Mary and some of Gabriella's drawings. Realizing his mouth was agape, he quickly pinched his lips together.

Servants balancing platters of hors d'oeuvres were circulating throughout the rooms, and a waiter carrying a tray filled with flutes of bubbling champagne offered them a glass. Vinny snatched two, and handing one to Sarah, he proceeded to consume his in one gulp, hoping it would calm his uneasiness. This affair was not what he had expected. Apparently, their new friends had a different perception of a small gathering since more than a hundred guests were clustered in groups or milled about the rooms. Thoughts of leaving ran through Vinny's mind, and he searched Tony's eyes for an answer, but his friend just shrugged his shoulders, obviously devoid of an excuse to leave.

Oblivious to their tension, Sarah cooed, "Let's go outside and find Julia."

They followed her through a maze of guests and out the intricately carved French doors. The patio was framed with urns overflowing with exotic blooms and hundreds of candles illuminated its perimeter. A full moon cast a glow over the ocean, adding to the ambiance. Limber couples swung to the trendy music of a jazz band—a dozen tuxedoed musicians expertly blowing popular tunes from their brass horns.

Sarah scanned the veranda. "She's out here somewhere," she said in a raised voice to Tony, while pulling Vinny onto the dance floor.

Vinny fancied himself a good dancer, and Sarah felt like butter in his hands as he whirled her around, performing the latest moves. His confidence was restored with every step, and his smile never dimmed.

When the song ended, Sarah grabbed Vinny's hand. "I want to introduce you to my parents," she said, leading him over to one of the elegantly dressed couples standing on the edge of the dance floor. The woman looked twice the width of her husband despite the mask of her flowing, black gown.

"Mother, Father, this is Vinny...one of the fellows I told you that we met on the beach today. He's a businessman from New York City who owns a warehousing and trucking company." Shifting her gaze to Vinny, she said, "These are my parents, Theodore and Margaret Ashton."

Vinny's mouth was dry, and he could feel his chest pounding.

Mr. Ashton extended his hand, and Vinny gave it an enthusiastic shake. "It's a pleasure, sir."

"We were certainly intrigued by your skilled dance partner, dear," Mrs. Ashton said to Sarah, while looking in Vinny's direction. "Very nice to meet you." She gave him a cordial nod.

"What brings you to Long Island?" Mr. Ashton sounded more polite than interested.

"My partner and I have business here," Vinny answered. "Your home is beautiful. Thank you for having us."

The band began to play another song, and Sarah interrupted. "We'll talk later," she said, tugging Vinny away. "This is one of my favorites."

Barmen continuously poured the illicit alcohol, and they drank the evening away at a rate that kept pace with the flow. Enjoying its liberating effects, Sarah and Vinny left the party to stroll the beach alone. With her high-heeled shoes suspended gracefully in her hand and a flute of champagne in the other, she mischievously danced around him to the fading music of the band. Every cell of his body was aching in her direction as she provoked him with her sultry looks and suggestive moves. Embracing her, he covered the pout of her delicate mouth with a kiss. Their lips never parted, and the night heedlessly slipped by before the sun mounted the horizon.

———◆•◆———

"Oh my, it's morning already," Sarah rattled. Jumping up, she tugged Vinny to his feet. "We have to get back."

Hurrying down the beach, they found Tony and Julia comfortably sprawled on lounge chairs, sound asleep.

"Julia, wake up," Sarah said, nudging her sister's shoulder.

She opened her eyes to daybreak. "Father's going to be furious."

Sarah glanced up at the veranda. "There're still people here. Hopefully, they didn't miss us." Looking at Vinny, she quickly said, "Meet us on the beach at one."

"We'll be waiting," he assured her.

The girls hastily walked away, and Vinny and Tony took a roundabout route through the gardens to their truck.

"I need some more sleep," Tony said, resting his head on the back of the driver's seat and stretching his legs out on the dashboard.

"Yeah," Vinny muttered, yet he was already lost in the midst of a dream.

Watching the tide roll in, they waited for hours that afternoon; unfortunately, the girls never arrived. Vinny desperately tried to rationalize Sarah's absence—she was out of his league, and for an evening, he had lived a fool's paradise. Silently, they drove back to Manhattan, but for Vinny, it was with a broken heart.

CHAPTER 27

Santo developed a penchant for gambling that accelerated throughout his teens. If he could, he would have bet on two roaches crossing the floor if someone would take the wager. He followed the horse races on the radio as if following his destiny. As the week unwound, his adrenaline soared, anticipating Saturday afternoon at Aqueduct Race Track. Believing his path to success rested on the back of a horse, he befriended jockeys and owners, shrewdly eliciting inside information on odds. He began taking bets from his coworkers at the warehouse and the patrons at Bedford's Speakeasy, where men justified betting as a means to pay the bills while drinking to forget how much they had lost and why there would never be enough.

This side business was initially profitable for Santo, but he had a run of bad luck. Unable to cover the bets, the losses emptied his pockets and refilled his glass with humiliation.

Threatened with the promise of a broken leg by a few of his unsympathetic customers, he went to his brother again. "Vin, I need a loan. I'll get it back to you as soon as I can…I promise…I'm done."

"I've heard that before," Vinny said. "How much is this one going to cost me?"

Santo hung his head. "Can you spare a couple hundred?" he mumbled.

Vinny sighed heavily. He pulled a roll of bills out of his pocket and peeled off a few, handing them over to

Santo. "When are you going to stop? It's not the money—you know that. Who threatened you now? I've seen guys beaten to within an inch of their lives for less than this. I don't want to have to wash my hands of you, but I'm telling you this is it. And I'm docking your pay."

Santo glanced up at his brother. "Thanks," he said. Shoving the money into his pocket, he walked away figuring out whose bets he would cover.

———◆•◆———

Craving the activity and the excitement of the track, Santo decided to leave his job at Vinny's warehouse to work at the stables, mucking stalls and walking the horses. He worked in the days, bet in the evenings, and paid two dollars a week to have a bed in the stable barracks overnight—his life revolved within its perimeters, and his face became a familiar sight.

Santo realized quickly that riding a horse was certainly better than cleaning up after them, and he eventually coaxed one of the jockeys into teaching him how to ride. Agility and fearlessness were his assets, and when he mounted a horse for the first time, it was as easy as slipping on a glove. It was not long before he was given the opportunity by a trainer to exercise his horses. Santo was short and slight, and he felt that becoming a jockey seemed to be within his reach.

After months of apprenticing, he gained the practical and physical experience he needed to ride in a race, and he asked his family to come to his début. When he filed onto the field with the other riders and spotted his father and siblings in the grandstand cheering him on, he felt as though he were perched on top of the world.

The more Santo rode, the more confidence he gained, and the more races he won. His inherent ability also won him the recognition of his peers as well as that of the spectators. He finally felt he had found his niche in the world.

———◆•◆———

Santo was feeling especially pleased with himself that foggy spring night as he left the locker room. There had been intermittent periods of heavy rain over the last several days, and the track had been particularly sloppy. He won his first race and placed in another, and neither horse he was riding was considered a mudder.

As he was walking toward the barracks, an imposing man wearing a hat and a raincoat appeared out of the shadows. "Hey, kid, you wanna make some extra cash?" he offered with an edge to his voice. "Hold back Moonlight Madness in the third on Saturday. You'll get a big bonus after it's done." He winked at Santo. "I'm sure you've heard the name Patsy McFadden. Trust me, your lack of cooperation is ill advised." Pointing to him as if he were brandishing a gun, he strolled away.

The consequences were well known for those jockeys who did not abide by the mob's instructions, and Santo did as he was told. He was generously compensated to hold back a percentage of his starts to increase odds and was intermittently given the opportunity to be the first to cross the finish line. Santo willingly became entangled in their web of power and manipulation.

———◆•◆———

Purely by chance, Santo spotted a petite, slender girl in a yellow sundress with hair the color of milk chocolate standing near the paddock entrance. Plodding past her on his way to the starting gate, he looked down from his mount and smiled. "I'm a sure bet," he said.

She grinned back at him with a hint of amusement in her eyes, and her vision guided him victoriously to the finish line where he waved her down to invite her into the rousing hub of the winner's circle.

"You won," she said as Santo dismounted his horse.

"I told you that I would. Did you take my advice?"

She held up two tickets in her hand. "Yes, I did," she said.

"How about we celebrate over dinner?" He took off his hat and combed back his thick, curly hair with his fingers. "My name's Santo Carnavale," he said.

"I know. I looked you up in the program. Mine's Emily Benton."

"What do you say, Emily? Do we have a date? It won't take me long to get ready."

"It seems to me that you're a sure bet," she said. "I'll tell my friends to leave without me, and I'll wait for you in the stands."

Santo showered quickly, and he was glad his white shirt and suit were relatively clean. Dressing, he used his sock to give his shoes a good-luck spit shine. He had won both the race and the company of a pretty girl, and he was looking forward to seeing what other pleasures the evening had in store for him.

Over the last hour, the rain started to fall steadily. When Santo and Emily exited the cab in front of the speakeasy he had heard about, he shielded her with his jacket as they ran to the back door. Slowly knocking the obligatory five times to gain entry, they walked down the marble stairway and approached the maître d' behind the desk. "A table for two," Santo said.

"I'm sorry, sir, we're booked for the evening," the balding man replied apologetically. "Next time, please call ahead. We require reservations."

Knowing there were other means to get his way, Santo walked away mumbling to himself, "We'll see about that." As he was ascending the stairs to the exit, he purposefully slipped and tumbled down.

"Santo!" Emily yelled from the middle of the stairway.

Instantly, the maître d' was at Santo's side. "Are you all right, Sir? Let me help you up," he said nervously.

Santo moaned as if he was in severe pain. He looked up and, to his advantage, a crowd had gathered around him. Making sure he was heard, he loudly scoffed, "You should be more careful to mop the stairs when it rains. I could've killed myself."

Helping Santo to his feet, the man glanced uneasily at the onlookers. "Please calm down, sir," he said. "Let me take you to a table right away. It just so happens we've had a cancellation, and one of the best is available. Dinner is on the house."

That's more like it, Santo thought. Adjusting his coat, he winked at Emily behind the man's back as they followed him to a quiet table in the corner.

The maître d' pulled out a chair for Emily, and she sat down. When he snapped his fingers, a waiter came right over.

"I'll have a whiskey...maybe it'll ease the pain," Santo said sarcastically. "And a bottle of your best champagne for the lady. We're celebrating." He looked at her, and she nodded.

"Right away, sir," the waiter said, walking away.

"You fell on purpose, didn't you?" Emily asked in a hushed tone. She sounded both confused and amused.

"Let's keep that our little secret," he said, raising his eyebrows and smiling.

She eyed him inquisitively. "Are you really hurt?"

"There's an art to everything."

She shook her head, looking bewildered.

"What do you do, Emily?"

Still shaking her head, she said, "I work for Feldman's. It's a boutique on the upper east side."

"I've never been in that area of the city."

The waiter returned and placed a whiskey in front of Santo, who immediately took a swig. Popping the cork off the champagne, the man filled Emily's flute and placed the bottle in a bucket of ice.

"I'll have another," Santo said dismissively, holding up his glass. "Make it a double this time." Turning his attention back to Emily, he asked, "Where do you live?"

"Ninety First and Fifth," she said. She took a sip of her drink.

"Nice," he commented, bobbing his head up and down. "Do you live with your parents?" He brushed the ashes that had fallen from his cigar off the tablecloth.

"I live with my Aunt Millie. My parents are stage actors and travel the country with various shows and stay with us when they're in the city. I've lived with my aunt for as long as I can remember. She's quite a character." Emily giggled. "You should meet her one day, you'd like her. You both seem to have the same sense of the ridiculous."

The waiter returned and placed another drink in front of Santo, removing his empty glass.

"We'll have two of your best steaks and another bottle of champagne," Santo instructed.

"This is plenty for me," Emily protested, raising her hand in the air.

"Bring it anyway. Winning makes me thirsty," he rationalized, taking a gulp of his drink.

"How would you like your steaks cooked?" the man asked.

"Rare, please," Emily answered, looking up at him.

"I'd like mine well done."

"I'll put your order right in," he said, walking away.

"So, Emily, what did you mean by 'the same sense of the ridiculous'?" He poured himself a glass of champagne.

"She's eccentric, to say the least."

"You think I'm eccentric?" he asked.

"After your performance on the stairs, I'd say so," she admitted. "Unless you want to call it crazy."

He smiled. "Tell me more about this aunt of yours."

"My uncle was an actor and died the year before I was born, leaving my aunt well off. She spends her money as nonchalantly as her attitude. When I was growing up, she took me to the best restaurants. Hmm...I don't think we've ever missed the opening of a play. She's the one who got me interested in fashion, although we have totally different tastes in clothing. She prefers flowery caftans to dresses and doesn't care what people think or say about her. When I was a little girl, we would dress outlandishly on my birthdays, and she would take me to the finest tearooms in the city. People would stare at us as if we were insane. We had a lot of fun...she's still a lot of fun."

"The next time we go out, maybe I can meet her," he said.

"You're being very presumptuous." She chuckled.

———◆◆———

For their second date, Santo decided to meet Emily at Nino's Restaurant before the Broadway show she had suggested. Having never been to a play before, he was wondering how much the tickets would cost and if he had enough cash for dinner too.

Arriving an hour late, he spotted Emily sitting alone on a chair in the foyer. "Sorry, I was held up," he said as he approached her. The expression on her face conveyed her displeasure, and he suddenly wished he had been more conscious of the time.

She looked at her watch and stood up. "Forget dinner. We'll have just enough time to get to the play," she said.

———————•◆•———————

Santo continued to imbibe with belts from a flask throughout the play he and Emily were attending. When his stash depleted, his euphoric high started to fade. Unimpressed with the lengthy performance, he rudely began to drone sonorous snores.

"Santo, wake up!" Emily whispered.

He fidgeted in his chair.

"You're still snoring," she grunted, while nudging him with her elbow.

He gave her a blurry glance and closed his eyes again.

His loud, insulting noises prompted the main actress to stop the show in its midst.

"I'll not continue until that vulgar man is removed from the theater," she balked. Her eyes raged with disdain as she pointed in Santo's direction.

Everyone in the audience glared at him with equal contempt, including Emily before she slinked out of her seat. Stumbling out of his chair, he tried to catch up to her as she briskly walked out of the theater, followed by the rustle of belittling whispers.

Once outside on the sidewalk, Emily came to a dead stop, turned around on her heel, and glowered at him. "What's wrong with you? I've never been so embarrassed in my life! You behaved like a horse's ass."

"I'm sorry, Emily."

"I don't need this. Don't ever call me again," she roared as she stomped away.

Blistered by her criticism, Santo silently stood on the sidewalk, thinking where he would go for his next drink.

———◆◆———

Santo believed alcohol numbed the turmoil that festered deep within, but he was oblivious to the fact that he was on a downward spiral. If he were riding in a race, he would limit his intake, but off the track, his behavior was becoming increasingly erratic, and his friends were distancing themselves from his malcontent. He drank more to foster his confidence, which drove his mood to outrageous limits, augmenting the bedlam he created. The disturbances he made were not malicious; nonetheless, they were a disruption and a nuisance.

On a self-righteous bender, Santo walked out to the stables with a bottle of whiskey in his hand. Craving the company of another being that would listen to him without prejudice, he draped his arms over a stall door and spoke to the horse as if it understood. "No one cares," he announced. "You work your whole life and...it...it doesn't...matter. I'm the best damn jockey to ever race this track." He continued to bitterly purge his troubles to the captive audience in the middle of the night. "Ah...what's the use? They can all go to hell. I don't need anybody, not even Emily." Christening the wall with his empty bottle, he slurred his incense for the animal's cruel confinement. "They keep you locked up in here...for what? Run free." He began opening the doors to the row of stalls, letting several of the costly racehorses loose.

Santo should have been fired for endangering their safety, although he unshakably denied any involvement in the infraction when he was interrogated by track officials.

Knowing they would be keeping a wary eye on him, Santo tried to stay out of trouble, but he was like a loaded gun in the hands of a child, and his willpower diminished. Before one of the biggest races of the season, he arrived intoxicated and overzealous. With the clang of the starting bell, he whipped his mount, and it shot from the gate with timely swiftness. Losing control, he toppled from the horse, and it stumbled, causing others to become entangled in the chaos and severely injured. His privilege as a jockey was revoked by the track officials upon hearing the doctor's diagnosis of intoxication, and he was banned from the premises.

Santo self-perpetuated his own recklessness but deluded himself into believing he was the victim. Knowing they would never turn him away, he crawled back to his brother for work and appeared on his father's doorstep for a bed. Rather than admit the truth, he simply told them that he had had his fill of horseracing, but the dismay on their faces was evident as the excuses tumbled from his mouth.

CHAPTER 28

Gabriella wondered how something so awful could give rise to something so wonderful. The course of love's fate began with a chance encounter that memorable night of the fire over six years ago. Vito's comfort and concern was the harbinger of their future together and the setting that had changed her life. Now that she was a married woman, the desire to have a child was at the forefront of her mind.

The newlywed couple had moved into an apartment on the first floor of the same tenement occupied by Gabriella's family. When they gathered upstairs at Lorenzo's table for Sunday supper, they counted on Vito to bring the dessert from the bakery. Stashing the pastries in the hallway, he would usually arrive late and seemingly empty-handed.

"Did you bring the cannoli?" Gabriella would inevitably ask when he walked through the door.

"Oh, no," he said with a contrived frown and hitting his palm to his forehead. "I forgot."

"Again, Vito, how could you?" she groaned, playing along with her husband's charade.

"It's like forgetting to serve the wine," Vinny cracked.

"And God forbid we forget the wine," Catherina said sarcastically, while deliberately eyeing Santo.

At the conclusion of dinner and continuing their game, everyone exaggerated their cravings by exhaling moans of displeasure and complaining that they wanted something sweet.

Gabriella looked over at Louisa who seemed agitated and who was not finding any of their silly antics amusing, while Papa was clearly enjoying his children's banter. Standing up, she went into the kitchen to retrieve the pot of espresso. She placed it on the table along with a bowl of grapes and a chunk of provolone cheese and winked at her husband. "This will have to do," she said, sighing heavily.

"Okay, Vito, we know you brought them," Rosa announced, rolling her eyes.

"Really, this time I forgot," he said, continuing the farce.

Rising from the table, Rosa opened the door and picked up the box of confections on the landing. Plopping it down in front of Vito, she quipped, "Then I guess these just magically appeared."

Cheerful applause erupted at the sight of the brown box, and the contrast in the mood caused more laughter to ensue.

Gabriella worked at the bakery in the mornings with her husband, did her chores in the afternoon alone, and kept her job at a neighborhood speakeasy several nights a week to supplement their income. Charlie's place was somewhat of an institution in the neighborhood, and Gabriella had started working for him a few years before she married Vito. Charlie O'Keefe was a sweet, lively man who greeted everyone who entered his saloon with hospitality.

At the onset of Prohibition seven years before, his saloon had been disassembled and reconstructed piece by piece, reopening as a speakeasy in the cellar of its current location. Charlie himself had made the sturdy oak bar trimmed with a brass footrest that formed a semicircle into the middle of the room. Behind it, varying shapes of bottles and glasses were placed in neat rows on counters in front of mirrors reflecting the blithe faces of patrons imbibing in their libations. Colorful posters of actresses and actors promoting the latest picture shows brightened the dull, cement walls.

The speakeasy was concealed in a vacant storefront, and thick curtains covered the windows. A burly bodyguard manned the inconspicuous entrance, which remained bolted while he scrutinized guests through an eye level trap door. Regulars from the neighborhood and those invited were ushered through the dark foyer and descended a narrow stairwell leading to the warmth of its cocoon and an ongoing party.

Charlie kept his prices fair and his liquor unadulterated, and everybody, including Gabriella, considered him a friend. Unfortunately, his wife had passed away many years before, and he had no children of his own. His world was his saloon—his small group of employees was his family, and the patrons were his friends. He created a harmonious atmosphere, and they all enjoyed the company of the effervescent man. Music from a phonograph continuously played melodies, and Charlie's lilting Irish brogue lead the chorus and encouraged patrons to harmonize along. Everyone dressed in their best to bluff the drudgeries of life, and Charlie's place made it temporarily bearable.

It was no secret to anyone that Charlie's business operated under the protection of his childhood buddy, the well-known gangster, Patsy McFadden. Gabriella had heard many stories about McFadden, and although she had never met him personally, she had certainly met his employees. At first she was leery when having to interact with the intimidating men, but like everyone else, they soon became friends. In addition to supplying Charlie's booze, McFadden's lackeys took their cut to insure cops on the beat turned their backs on deliveries and the comings and goings of clientele. Prohibition had backfired and sired a whole new industry of illegal money making, and the government was incapable of enforcing the noble experiment.

———————◆◆◆———————

Gabriella had not been feeling well for weeks; fatigue and nausea gnawed at her with persistent irritation throughout her busy day. She purposely stopped by to see Catherina on her way back from Charlie's one evening after a particularly exhausting shift.

Lying sprawled on the sofa, she smoothed her hand over her stomach and yawned. "Catherina, I don't know what's wrong with me. I'm so queasy all the time, and I could fall asleep at the drop of a hat."

"You do look a little pale." She shrugged her shoulders. "You must be coming down with something."

The desire to have a child was at the forefront of Gabriella's mind. "But I've been feeling like this for weeks—"

Catherina eyes lit up. "Do you think maybe you're pregnant?"

"Wouldn't that be wonderful," she said, delighted her sister had the same thought.

———————◆◆◆———————

Gabriella confirmed her suspicion with the doctor the next day and was barely able to contain her pleasure until Vito came home. Calling Charlie to ask him for the night off, she admitted she had just found out that she was pregnant and wanted to be home to tell Vito the minute he walked through the door. While she prepared a special dinner, she could only imagine her husband's happiness.

◆◆◆

While Gabriella worked late at the speakeasy, Vito often played cards in the backrooms of neighborhood shops. The men sat around drinking, smoking, and chewing tobacco they repeatedly spat into spittoons— their language as filthy as their vile habits. Vito's bakery paid the bills, but baking the bread did not thrill him as much as winning the dough. No longer was gambling a distraction; it was his scheme to acquire extra money so Gabriella could quit her job at the speakeasy. The thought of men ogling her enraged him, and the thought of losing her made him crazy.

The euphoric highs Vito felt when he won compensated for the stinging lows he experienced when he lost; however, his losses were outweighing his gains. A streak of bad luck threw him into a state of impetuous desperation. Lately, he had been losing the daily proceeds from the store and resorted to borrowing from a loan shark to support his compulsive habit. His troubles had peaked that day when several unsympathetic men in dark suits came into the bakery to collect on a loan, and he could not deliver.

The hairs on the back of Vito's neck stood straight up, and a shiver ran down his spiritless spine. Pain seized the muscles in his chest as he whimpered, "I'll have the money in a few days. I'm going through a little dry spell." They dragged him from behind the counter and forced him to his knees. "Just give me till Monday," he begged.

Disgusted by his petty groveling, the intolerant trio deliberately poured the thick, sticky contents of a barrel of molasses over the counter. The ringleader of the group emphatically warned, "The next time we drop by, we're not going to be so charitable."

Further reinforcing the man's point, his two sidekicks threw the empty vat in Vito's direction and knocked him over. Too frightened to move, he kept his eyes tightly shut and waited until he heard their sinister steps stamp out the door.

———◆•◆———

It had been a harrowing day for Vito. It took him hours to clean up his shop, and all the while, he fretted over how he was going to pay off his debt and how much longer he could keep his money problems from his wife.

He opened the door to their apartment to a carefully set table, candles flickering, and the sound of Gabriella humming in the bedroom. Thoughts of a romantic interlude were the last thing on his mind as he padded into the room to find her sitting on the bed and brushing her wavy hair. "What's going on?"

Gabriella looked downright giddy as she handed him a package wrapped in brown paper and meticulously decorated with random sketches of baby bottles and booties.

Vito reluctantly ripped open the gift and found a small baby blanket. "What's this?" he asked.

"This was my blanket when I was a baby—I've been saving it just for this occasion." She stood up and hugged him. "Vito, I found out today. We're going to have a baby, and it's due before Christmas."

He took several steps back and tossed the blanket on the bed. Pulling his eyebrows together, he scolded, "How could you have been so careless with your dates? I'm not happy about this—not at all."

Gabriella's face dropped, and she placed both hands on her stomach. Her voice turned instantly somber. "I thought you'd be pleased," she said.

"We agreed to wait." His body tensed, and he clenched his fists at his sides. "You need to go to one of those doctors—you need to make this go away," he said as he punched the wall and stormed out of the apartment. His disappointment resounded as he stomped down the stairs.

Vito decided this day could not have been any worse. Worried and confused, he walked the streets trying to calm down and put everything into perspective. *How will I repay my debts? What am I going to do now that a baby is on the way?* Regretting his outburst toward Gabriella, he knew he had overreacted, and eventually his anger turned into angst.

In an attempt to remedy the situation, he returned home and found Gabriella eating dinner alone.

She looked up at him, and her eyes were red and puffy. Immediately rising, she turned and walked in the direction of the bedroom.

He pulled her into his arms, but her body felt unyielding. Kissing her on the forehead, he said, "I'm sorry. It's been one of those days when nothing goes right, and the news of a baby really threw me off guard."

"But…what you said." She hesitated. "It was so hurtful…so cruel…so unexpected." She searched his eyes as if hoping for a more convincing explanation, but he averted her gaze.

"I know I was wrong. I'll do anything to make it up to you."

"Then tell me you honestly want this baby." Her voice choked on the plea.

"I want this baby as much as I want you," he reassured her, forcing a smile.

"That's what I wanted to hear," she said, sounding as though she accepted his apology, but he could see the hurt lingering in her eyes.

Under pressure to pay off his debt, Vito went to see Charlie on Gabriella's day off. He knew the old man held a soft spot for his wife, and it was unlikely that he would badger him with questions. Taking Charlie on the side, he said, "I hate like hell to ask you this, but the bakery's been slow. I need some cash to get me through. I swear I'll pay you back as soon as business picks up." He swallowed hard. "I'd ask Gabriella's brother, but I don't want her to know."

Charlie gave him an apathetic nod. "How much?" he asked.

"Three hundred should do it."

"Wait here," he said and walked to the back room. Returning, he counted out the twenties into Vito's hand. "I'm doing this for Gabriella," he said as if he knew Vito had shrouded the truth.

Shifting uncomfortably back and forth on his feet, Vito stammered, "I'd rather we keep this between the two of us. I don't want her to worry in her condition."

"Of course," Charlie weakly agreed.

Vito believed it was time for the cards to turn in his favor and would soon be able to repay the loan.

Unfortunately, luck was not on his side, and he became more agitated and ornery with each unexpected loss.

———◆•◆———

To keep her distance from her moody husband, Gabriella rarely helped Vito at the bakery, but she continued to work for Charlie in the months leading up to the birth of their child. Even when their baby was born, the momentous event did not soothe Vito's gloom, but she refused to let him ruin one of the best days of her life.

Coddling their newborn in the bed of the hospital room, Gabriella's eyes were bright with awe as she stared at their daughter. "What do you want to name her?" she said after her family had left. "You heard—everyone was asking."

Vito stared out the window. The waning light of the sun streaked through the dusty glass and onto his sullen face. "You decide," he disinterestedly muttered.

"Then I think we'll call her Sophia. I always liked that name...and it's odd...she reminds me of a Sophia, like it was always meant to be her name." A warm smile spread across her face. "Is that okay with you?" she asked, glancing up at her husband.

He turned around slowly, avoiding her gaze. "I told you to name her whatever you want," he said.

Gabriella felt her chest constrict as she despondently realized she was going to be making more decisions on her own. What should have been a joyous time for both of them was becoming a tiring journey of one.

One month after Sophia was born, Gabriella told Vito she was ready to return to work for Charlie a few nights a week. Vito's financial situation had not improved, and he had no choice but to agree with his wife. On the evenings when she worked, one of her sisters gladly watched the baby upstairs so Vito could sleep since his days at the bakery began well before dawn and seldom ended before dusk. However, his woeful quandaries made it impossible for him to rest, and his reckless nights of gambling crept into the mornings. The more he wagered, the more he lost, and the more bitter and self-absorbed he became. Unshaven and hung over, he slithered into the bakery, wallowing in self-pity and passing off yesterday's leftovers as the day's creations.

Vito was never home anymore, and by now, Gabriella was convinced another had turned his head. She searched his clothes and his eyes for evidence, but she continually came up empty. Whenever she questioned his whereabouts, his temper would flare, and their conversations would degenerate into heated quarrels. Sadly, she had lost the battle so many times she eventually stopped fighting with Vito and existed in a state of oppressive melancholy, forgetting what it was like to be content.

When Gabriella was a child, she had decided everyone was born with a blank palette and color was added as their journey through life progressed. It was the twists and turns and ups and downs that determined the amount and array of colors one accumulated. As the painting filled with the darker tones of despair, it began to overshadow the brighter hues of happiness. Sinking deeper into a downward spiral, Gabriella felt as if she was at a pivotal point of no return and confronted her temperamental husband with an impulsive burst of courage. "Who's the other woman, Vito?" she demanded when he walked through the door several hours late.

She spotted the flash of fury in his eyes, and immediately she regretted opening her mouth, she regretted the words that escaped from her lips, and she regretted asking a question when the answer could be something she did not want to hear. As she saw the anger swell inside him, she took a step back and held her hand in front of her face, steeling herself for what she thought might come next.

Using the back of his arm, he knocked her to the floor.

Snatching a pile of her drawings from the bureau and holding them over her, he ripped them into shreds—the bits of paper fluttering around her and crushing her spirit piece by piece.

Sophia started to cry in her crib.

"No," Gabriella begged, looking over at their daughter.

Grabbing a tuft of Gabriella's hair, Vito pulled her head back. "So you think there's another woman?" he said, forcing out a phony laugh. "Another woman is the last thing on my mind." Releasing her dismissively, he stalked out of the apartment.

As Gabriella lay on the floor amidst the ruins of her sketches, her horror gave way to astonishment. The harshness of his words left her in a wasteland of confusion.

———◆◆◆———

Vito had no patience for their toddler, and Gabriella found herself tiptoeing around him on the rare occasions he was home. One wrong word, one wrong move, would turn his apathetic mood into a powerful storm. He developed a pattern of striking her only where her clothes could conceal his cruelty, always following with pleas of forgiveness. He attributed his conduct to jealousy and profusely promised it would never happen again. The culmination of his hypocritical apology was sex, but for Gabriella it did not compensate for the emotional turmoil and estrangement. She wanted him to love her despite the fact she had become terrified by his touch and bounced in and out of the contradiction. As his hands slipped through her silky hair, her mind remained tangled inside her head, trying to make sense of her husband's erratic behavior.

Gabriella was ashamed her marriage had fallen into such a hopeless state of disrepair, so she managed to pull off a plausible performance around her family. If she betrayed her husband by telling them, she feared the repercussions of his rage. She felt as if her canvas had turned completely black and wondered when and if the color would ever return.

———◆•◆———

When Gabriella arrived at work, she felt tense and withdrawn, but as the evening progressed, the distraction made her feel more cheerful and outgoing. As she was winding down to go home, her somber mood would resurface, and she teetered on a seesaw of inconsistency, knowing Charlie observed the disparity.

"What's going on, Gabriella?" Charlie asked her one night. "You don't seem like yourself lately. Is Sophia okay?"

"Yes, of course," she quickly responded. She took a rag from the sink and began wiping the bar to avoid his gaze. "I appreciate your concern, but everything's fine." Even she could hear the bleakness in her tone.

"Look, you know I think of you like a daughter. I hate seeing you this way."

Gabriella desperately wanted to purge the secret trapped in the vestiges of her soul, but this one was too hideous. Deciding to give Charlie an abridged version of her problems, she omitted the corporal suffering she was enduring. "It's just that Vito and I aren't getting along," she said dejectedly. "We don't talk anymore... all we do is fight and blame." She tried to keep her voice from cracking. "I don't know what's bothering him, but he's changed."

Charlie listened while eyeing her dubiously.

"We'll work it out," she said, swallowing the bitter truth that filled her mouth, but she could tell by the grimace on Charlie's face that he tasted its acidity.

<hr>

One busy evening, Gabriella's shoulder ached, causing the tray to wobble upon her palm. While serving her customers, she could feel the pain tightening the features on her face and tried her best not to wince.

"Gabriella, you seem tired. Why don't you go and rest on the cot?" Charlie suggested. "We're not busy now. Ellie can handle it."

Ellie, a short, stocky waitress in her fifties, obviously overheard what Charlie had said and walked over. "Go ahead. I'll call you if I need you."

Gabriella gave her coworkers a grateful nod and went to the back room. While sitting on the edge of the cot and holding a block of ice wrapped in a dishrag to her shoulder, Charlie unexpectedly walked through the door. Startled, she quickly lifted the edge of her blouse with her other hand, but not before Charlie had a glimpse of the purple mass of Vito's wrath.

"Did he do that to you?" he roared insistently in a tone she had never heard him use before.

She put her head down, wondering how she would explain the madness that was happening in her life.

"I can't stand around and allow him to get away with this," he said.

She looked up at him, unable to keep the tears from flowing. "Please, Charlie, I promise I'll take care of it."

Gruffly, he removed his glasses. "For your husband's sake, you better, or I will," he said as he left her alone.

———◆•◆———

Inside, Charlie was fuming as he grappled with the brute's immorality. Knowing Gabriella was being abused, he was unable to sit idly by and decided to take it upon himself to have Vito taught a well-deserved lesson.

Phoning McFadden, Charlie eased into the conversation by saying, "Patsy, we go back a long way. We've known each other since we were kids, right?"

"What's on your mind, Charlie?"

"You know I wouldn't ask you for a favor unless I thought it was important. One of my waitresses...Gabriella...a sweet girl...well...her husband's been slapping her around."

"I understand. My sister was slapped around by her husband, and she paid for her silence with her life."

Charlie had heard the stories about what happened to McFadden's sister and was horrified, thinking of Gabriella.

"Let me tell you, that cowardly bastard paid for his mistakes with his death," McFadden added.

"I think that might be a little extreme at this point."

"I get it. Where can we find him?"

"He owns the bakery on the corner of Tenth and 31st. His name's Vito Carrone. Thanks, Patsy," he said before he hung up.

———◆◆———

On his way home from work, Vito was accosted and dragged into an alley by three menacing strangers who beat him ruthlessly. Leaving his face unscathed, they left painful reminders of their message over the rest of his body. While he lay moaning in a fetal position, his assailants gave him one last kick in the groin and warned him to keep his hands to himself. He could only surmise Gabriella's brothers arranged to have him taught a painful lesson and temporarily restrained his fists.

———◆◆———

Saint Patrick's Day fell on a Saturday and the speakeasy was crowded with customers indulging in the merriment. Charlie was particularly animated behind the bar, telling jokes to the captive audience in his usual jovial flair. Gabriella enjoyed Charlie's lightheartedness and spontaneity, and he was always surprising her with new material to entertain the customers. His stance was always the same—thumbs hooked through the armholes of his woolen vest, and his eyes peeking over the horn-rimmed glasses clamped to the foot of his tipped nose. In the middle of his engaging display of theatrics, he collapsed to the ground, seemingly part of his contrived routine. Still laughing, Gabriella glanced behind the bar and found him clutching his chest, his frightened eyes bulging from their bloodshot sockets.

"Charlie, Charlie what's wrong?" Gabriella fell to her knees beside him.

He struggled to take a breath.

"Someone get help!" she yelled.

Charlie grabbed her arm and pulled her closer. She strained to listen as he mumbled, "Papers…safe," before his heart stopped beating.

———◆•◆———

Although Charlie had no blood relatives, the funeral parlor was filled with friends and employees. When McFadden walked into the room to pay his respects, the two men that were with him remained at the back—their arms crossed below their chests, their trained eyes scanning the bereaved.

Representing Charlie's family, Gabriella politely shook McFadden's hand.

"Thank you for coming," she said.

"I'm Patsy McFadden. Charlie and I were kids together. We had a lot of laughs growing up. He was certainly top shelf."

His sincere words and pleasant manner did not mesh with McFadden's nefarious reputation. Gabriella imagined he would be much taller, but they gazed at the same height, and when he grinned, his lips disappeared and the cleft in his chin became more pronounced. He could have been any man except for the meticulous silk suit that flanked his stout frame and the garish ring that gilded his pinky finger.

"I'm Gabriella. I worked for Charlie."

"He spoke fondly of you."

She was surprised by his remark. "He was more like a father to me than a boss. I'll miss his stories and even his singing." She rolled her eyes and smiled through the tears. "He'll be missed terribly by everyone," she said. "It's a shame the bar has to close."

"You never know," he said, leaving Gabriella wondering what he had meant.

———————◆◆———————

Gabriella was grief-stricken by the loss of Charlie, and his last words had made no sense until after the funeral. In the safe, she found his last will and testament and a letter personally addressed to her, revealing his bequest—ownership of the bar and property. He wrote that it was his gift to the woman who had replaced the loneliness in his life and who had shown him the love and respect of a daughter. She was honored and touched by the enormity of his generosity. Charlie had unknowingly passed her the key that opened the door to her independence.

———————◆◆———————

Vito kept his distance from the bar and Gabriella's family. He was brooding like an insolent child and inanely harassed her for running an illegal establishment, but she knew damn well he despised that she was able to manage a prosperous business. He would accuse her of neglecting their daughter, yet Sophia was Gabriella's first priority, and she lovingly attended to her every day. She learned to ignore her husband's unfounded, belligerent criticisms; however, she was still held down by the strong arm of his resentment.

Incapable of paying his gambling debts, Vito was forced to close the bakery. When Gabriella came home from work that evening, she found him stewing at the height of his abhorrence.

"You're never home! I want you here where you belong," he ranted. He threw her down to the ground and kicked her in the back.

"Please—Vito—please!" She heaved herself to her feet, but the punch that struck the side of her head knocked her back down. Reeling from the pain, she screamed, and it echoed throughout the building.

Hearing the sound of footsteps pounding down the stairs, Vito pointed his finger at her. "You keep your mouth shut," he warned.

Bursting through the door, Santo tackled Vito to the ground and repeatedly punched him in the face.

Vinny charged into the room and pried his brother off of Vito. "Stop before you kill him. He's not worth the rap!" he shouted.

Grabbing Vito by his shirt, Vinny jerked him to his feet. "I pray this is the first time you touched my sister!" he said furiously. "I promise you, you no-good bastard, it'll be the last." Throwing him out the opened door, he added, "Get the hell out of here. If you ever return, it will be for your own funeral."

CHAPTER 29

More and more customers were asking Vinny and Tony to hold their goods until they were needed on the shelves. The merchandise from the larger department stores piled high before the holiday season's onset, and the small building they were leasing was becoming overcrowded with cartons. They had employed a few of the kids from the neighborhood, including Vinny's cousins, Nicholas and Roberto, to help with their expanding business, but they were clearly outgrowing their modest facility.

Making the decision together, they went to see Philly the mayor again and explained their situation.

"There's a warehouse available on Twenty-Seventh Street between Eleventh and Twelfth, although it's much larger than what you need," he informed them.

"How much are we talking about?" Vinny asked.

Philly threw up his hands and frowned. "It's way out of your league. 'Bout twice what you're lookin' to spend."

Vinny hesitated. "I'd like to see it anyway," he said.

"What's the point?" Tony said incredulously.

Vinny shrugged. "It doesn't cost anything to look."

———◆◆———

Walking through the windowless, brick-and-cement, three-story structure, Tony looked disgusted. "It's like a cave in here—it's so cold and damp. And the floors are caked in dried blood...and what's this?" he balked, scraping his foot back and forth across the floor.

"Well, for years it was used as a slaughterhouse," Philly said. "They used salt to absorb the blood. It can be easily cleaned up."

Overlooking the putrefied stench of death that inundated the air and the work needed to scrape the grime from its floors, Vinny envisioned the possibilities. It was ideal for loading and unloading merchandise. Trucks could back into the many bay doors that ran along the streets, and railroad tracks recessed four feet below the center of the first floor provided easy access for shipments to be transferred to and from rail cars. "You know, Philly, this could work," he said.

Tony shook his head doubtfully and grimaced. "Are you crazy? Not only did I see a rat the size of a cat, this place is a lot bigger than what we talked about," he pointed out.

"But it's close to the piers, and with the extra space, we can take in more goods and make more money. We'll pay it off in no time." Vinny turned to Philly and said, "We'll take it."

"Where the hell are we going to get the cash?" Tony asked.

"I've got a plan," Vinny said, raising his eyebrows.

Vinny and Tony pooled every penny they had and borrowed from everyone, including sisters, brothers and friends, cutting them in on a percentage of the profits in proportion to their investments. They eventually amassed an amount just short of the asking price;

however, Vinny came up with another solution to make up the difference.

They guaranteed Philly his commission plus a handsome bonus when they got on their feet. Dressed in their finest, Vinny, Tony, and Philly went to the bank that held the deed on the building with a briefcase filled with cash. Philly explained to Mr. Parker, the banker handling the deal, that they were delivering payment for the property minus his broker's commission—his alleged fee exactly the amount they were short.

They signed the papers and walked out with the deed clutched in Tony's hand and Vinny's arm draped around Philly. This was the beginning of New York Warehouse and Trucking Company, a business that occupied an entire city block. Vinny and Tony were in their midtwenties and owned a piece of America. That day, they felt they could conquer the world, and that evening, they celebrated as if they had. They toasted with each glass and accepted the congratulations from friends and family with every shot.

———◆•◆———

Something else happened at the bank that momentous day—Tony recognized Sarah's father and pointed him out to Vinny. When Vinny mentioned that the gentlemen looked familiar, Mr. Parker told them that he was the bank president, Theodore Ashton. Casually soliciting more information, Vinny discovered that Mr. Ashton had been transferred to New York from Georgia and lived on Park Avenue.

Vinny was dumbfounded. Sarah lived right here in the city. It had been three years since he had seen her, and he wondered if she was married. He had replayed that night on the beach hundreds of times. Their romantic encounter blissfully began but had ended with dramatic disappointment. Vinny had had many women and relished the moments with each one of them, yet Sarah had left him under her spell. Picturing her living in an elegant apartment on Park Avenue, it reminded him that she was still beyond his reach—for now.

———◆•◆———

It seemed as though everyone had his hand out, and Vinny and Tony learned how to put theirs in their pockets to stay in business. Success came with a price as political corruption was rampant and bribery of police, judges, and public officials was obligatory. Gangsters also ruled the streets and made it difficult to sustain a competitive edge. Street hoods had joined the ranks of mobs whose members were ruthless, armed, and experts in intimidation. Survival was contingent on whom Vinny and Tony befriended, whom they avoided, and whom they paid off, diplomatically skirting confrontation.

It hit Vinny with stunning awareness when one of their employees was gunned down in cold blood right in front of the warehouse. Unfortunately, the word on the street was that Billy's physique and appearance had resembled someone who was marked, and he was mistakenly wasted to settle the score. The effrontery of organized crime was now taken in stride. Nine out of ten commandments were broken every day, and nine out of ten businesses failed under their pressure.

Protection had become a staple in Hell's Kitchen as vital as food and shelter. Nationalities were territorial and formed bands, pitting themselves against other nationalities. The streets indicated definitive boundary lines, and New York Warehouse and Trucking Company was on the border of the West Side Mob's jurisdiction—an Irish gang of mobsters who controlled the neighborhood and who were ruled by the notorious Patsy McFadden. Men were *made* members of the honored society and given nicknames. It was looked upon as a compliment, a sign of acceptance and trust to receive a label. Despite the fact that Vinny and Tony were Italian, they were given the mark of distinction and dubbed "the fair-haired kids of 27th Street." They had mastered the game with the finesse of experts, knowing when to refrain from asking questions when it was recommended they employ a particular person, to discreetly storing and distributing their contraband. They played by the mob's rigid rules in order to be under McFadden's umbrella of protection and stay in business.

New York Warehouse and Trucking Company was becoming a real presence, benefiting from McFadden's benevolence, but everyone knew McFadden never helped anyone without damn good reason.

CHAPTER 30

One rainy evening as the last of the winter snow funneled along the edges of the streets in slushy streams, a local storeowner named Blackie was looking for something to remove the chill from his bones and someone to possibly warm his bed.

Admitted into a local speakeasy, he ambled down the stairway into a welcoming room filled with people—some were involved in spirited conversation, while others sat alone swallowing away the time. A haze of smoke was suspended in the air, and familiar tunes sounded from the phonograph.

Scanning the room, Blackie's spotted a striking woman sitting relaxed at the bar. Instantly, he liked everything about her. Her long, mahogany hair perfectly complemented her soothing, copper eyes, and the warmth of her smile seemed to radiate through his body.

Without looking at anyone else, he sat down on the stool next to her. Removing his cap, he placed it on the edge of the bar and smiled at her.

She glanced at him warily.

"I don't know about you, but I'm glad this winter is just about over," he commented, stuffing his hands into the pockets of his coat to ward off the chill.

"I've never seen so much snow, but I think we've seen the last flakes of the winter," she said.

"My name's Frank Fanello, but my friend's call me Blackie," he said. "It looks like you could use a refill.

May I buy you a drink?" His manners were so polite that it left little room for a refusal.

She looked at the empty glass in front of her and hesitated. "I'm Catherina," she said, glancing at him sideways.

"Catherina," Blackie repeated, letting the word slowly roll off his tongue while nodding his head in obvious approval. "That's a nice name."

A slight smile played across her lips.

Turning to the woman standing behind the bar, Blackie said, "I'll have a scotch, and the lady here will have a…" He looked at Catherina for an answer.

"She knows what I drink. This is my sister, Gabriella," she said. "She owns the place."

"Really." He sounded thoroughly impressed. "Nice to meet you," he said, tipping his head in Gabriella's direction. "I'm Blackie."

"Would you like your scotch on the rocks?" she asked.

"Yes," he said.

"I'll be right back with your drinks."

"Is it only you and Gabriella, or do you have any sisters or brothers at home?" he asked.

"We have twin sisters and two brothers."

Blackie reflected back to his own childhood. Born in Lazzaro, a fishing port located in the southernmost part of Italy's mainland, he was the sole child of an abusive father and an alcoholic mother. When he was eight years old, his maternal grandparents took him along when they immigrated to Hudson, a small town adjacent to the Hudson River, and he had lived there up until last year. "I always wondered what it would be like to have brothers and sisters," he commented.

"It was a lot of work for my parents, but I'm glad I have my siblings."

Gabriella returned and placed their drinks in front of them. "What happened to your hand?" she asked Blackie.

Obviously appalled by her bluntness, Catherina narrowed her eyes and shot her sister a disbelieving glare. "Gabriella," she objected.

"I was just curious," she said.

"It's rude."

Watching the sisters' interaction, Blackie thought that his real past was something he not only wanted to hide but to forget. Back when he lived in Hudson, his former employer had been the foreboding character Patsy McFadden. Prohibition had turned out to be a profitable gift to McFadden and his factions. Resourcefully smuggling booze and brewing beer, his empire spread throughout New York State, and his notoriety soared. McFadden exuded power and intimidation, and Blackie felt lucky to have been working for his organization and to know him personally. Some of the local shop owners in Hudson had set up illegal distilleries, selling homemade hooch from the back of their stores. Under McFadden's jurisdiction, Blackie and his cohorts used threats of violence to extort payments from shopkeepers to keep quiet about their activities and protect them from the authorities.

Blackie looked down at his hand, remembering the day his luck had taken a wrong turn. It was bitterly cold, and he had decided Carl was their last call. He and his cronies entered the butcher shop to collect on their share, and before Blackie knew what was happening, Carl reached under the counter and retrieved a shotgun. Firing at him with rapid, calculated movements, he blew the gun out of Blackie's right hand and severed four of his fingers in the process.

After a two-month stay in the hospital, he spent two years in prison where his fellow inmates referred to him as Four Fingers Frank behind his back. Rumors had spread throughout the prison about his association with McFadden. Wanting to be left alone, Blackie donned a formidable air of defiance no one dared to test. The stories about him were unsubstantiated since he was unapproachable. His sentence had coincidentally coincided with his famed boss, who was indicted for extortion but whose stay was short-lived due to the expertise of his well-compensated lawyers. While they were imprisoned, there was not even a nod of recognition between the two men, and Blackie knew McFadden respected him for his solemn allegiance.

Upon his release, Blackie met with McFadden, feeling as if his usefulness to the organization had run its course. He was a trusted member of the family—it was the weak ones, McFadden had reminded him, which he never let go.

Blackie moved to Hell's Kitchen, using the money he had stashed from his ill-gotten gains to survive until he decided on a legitimate business. Eventually taking over a small grocery store, he slept in the back of the shop, working its front every waking hour.

———◆•◆———

"It's okay," Blackie said to Catherina. "I don't mind answering Gabriella's question. I was a fisherman before I moved to the city. This," he held up his maimed hand, "was the handiwork of a shark." He spontaneously fabricated his story as he spoke. "It was some fight. Three, maybe four hours into the catch, I thought he was tiring, and I took a chance at untangling the line.

All of a sudden, he shot out of the water in full view and came down right in front of me. The surge knocked me backward, and the line was wrapped around my four fingers." He held up his hand again. "The salt water was blinding, and the weight of the animal on the line plunging back into the water took my fingers with it." His tale sounded so convincing, he almost believed it himself. "I moved to New York when my days as a fisherman ended. Now I have a grocery store on Ninth."

"That's quite a story," Gabriella said, looking at Catherina with raised eyebrows. "I'd love to stay and hear more, but I have customers to serve."

"So how did your sister come to own this place?" Blackie asked when Gabriella had left.

Catherina shifted on her stool and turned toward him. "How much time do you have?" She laughed. "You think you've got a story."

He grinned. "I've got all night," he said, taking a sip of his drink.

The evening sailed by, and Gabriella informed the patrons it was last call.

Catherina instinctively slid off her stool to help her sister clean up. "Thanks for the drinks," she said.

"It was my pleasure. Thanks for the company." Blackie swigged the last of his scotch. "Good night," he said as he walked away.

On their walk home, the sisters talked about the handsome man who had unexpectedly sauntered into the bar.

"You were smitten with him. I haven't seen that look on your face in a long time," Gabriella teased. "In fact, I *never* saw that look on your face."

Blushing, Catherina shrugged off the insinuation. "I was not," she said, although she secretly hoped to see Blackie again. It was certainly not the first time she had been offered a drink, but it was rare she had accepted. After that dreadful altercation with Philip so long ago, she still had qualms about men—his duplicity had left her wary and unwilling. She never returned to her job at Philip's factory and swore never to let another man stand between her and her family again. Her search for employment had ended at Green's coat factory, and she was thankful, this time, the proprietor was an elderly, married man. It was a rare Saturday evening and six hectic years since Philip had betrayed her before another man made her heart flutter. Blackie was tall and rugged with pitch-black hair and eyes the color of coal. She found him fascinating and entertaining, and it seemed like ages since she had been this excited about a man.

———◆◆◆———

Catherina's frequent visits to her sister's bar were now laced with new meaning. She repeatedly glanced at the doorway willing Blackie to appear, but her expectations diminished as the weeks progressed. Just when she had talked herself out of the notion, she heard his voice.

"Hello, Catherina," he said.

Her body tensed, and she took a deep breath. Turning around, she saw him standing on the other side of the bar. "Blackie," she said, his name slipped through her smile.

He smiled back mischievously. "Did you miss me?" he asked.

"As a matter of fact, I didn't…expect to see you…that is," she said, stumbling through the lie.

Gabriella came over with a scotch and placed it on the bar in front of him. "Hello, Blackie."

He looked at her appreciatively. "You remembered what I drink," he said, as he eased his way onto a stool.

"I remember what everyone drinks. It's part of my job," she said, walking away to serve other customers.

Blackie turned his attention to Catherina. "Do you have time to join me for a drink?"

"Go ahead," Gabriella said from over her shoulder, "you don't even need to be back here tonight."

Catherina poured herself a glass of red wine and walked around the bar.

As she sat down next to Blackie, he looked her in the eyes. "Tonight, why don't you tell me your story?" he said.

"I'm afraid it's not as interesting as my sister's."

"Let me be the judge of that," he urged.

She picked up her glass with both hands and rested her elbows on the bar. Taking a sip, she said, "Well…I work at a coat factory for the most delightful gentleman, Sam Green. I live at home with my family, who can be very entertaining and sometimes draining." She giggled in the throes of the thought. "Gabriella and her daughter live in the apartment downstairs." Thinking how dull her life seemed at that moment and wondering what else she should share, she stopped.

"What about your parents?"

She paused. "My father's still alive, but my mother passed away right before the war ended. She would've been happy to know the soldiers came home."

"I'm sorry," he said.

"Thanks."

"Come on, there must be more. Anyone special in your life?"

"I was engaged once, but it turned out to be a mistake."

"I can't imagine why someone would let you go," he said seriously.

"I was the one who let go," she admitted.

Catherina surprised herself as she told Blackie the details of her previous relationship with Philip. It was the first time she had confided in another man, and it was the first time it did not hurt.

———◆◆———

Blackie studied Catherina as he listened to her story. *What a fool this guy must have been to let her go,* he thought. When he had first met her, he had toyed with the idea of asking her for a date, but intuition had curbed his desires since she did not seem ready to accept more than a drink. Listening to her now, he knew he had to break down a wall to reach Catherina's heart, and he looked forward to the challenge of wooing this unassumingly beautiful woman.

———◆◆———

In the months that followed, Blackie did his best to make Philip seem like a mere blip in Catherina's past. Although Blackie was still legally married to another, he did not want to dwell on his mistakes, and Lillian had definitely been a mistake.

Blackie had met Lillian one afternoon while she was strolling the shops in Hudson, and he asked her to join him for lunch. She lured him in with her searching blue eyes and her petite, curvaceous body, and to his delight, he found out quickly that she was also quite skillful at fulfilling his needs. Unfortunately, it soon became apparent that her sole ambition was to marry him, and she let it be known. Blackie was not a drinker or a gambler, his vice was women, but he did not want to be tied down, so he ignored her overt suggestions. It was difficult for Blackie to justify marriage since it had bound his parents together, eating away at their souls with sadistic rationale. But Lillian got his attention when she told him that she was expecting, and he caved to her wishes. Soon after the ring was on her finger, she said she had lost the baby. Surmising it had all been a lie, he realized he should have known better than to have married her so hastily. During the two years Blackie was in prison, Lillian's need for companionship and attention forced her into the arms of others. He had friends on the outside, and word got back to him of her infidelities. Moving to Hell's Kitchen had put distance between him and his cheating wife. To him, she was nothing but a whore.

Falling in love with Catherina had taken Blackie by surprise, and he felt he was ready to put his womanizing ways behind him if she would agree to be his wife. Even though he was still married to Lillian, the thought of bigamy had conveniently eluded his mind.

———◆•◆———

One night Blackie decided to throw caution to the wind and announced to the barroom filled with patrons, "I'm deliriously in love with this gorgeous woman sitting by my side, and I'd like very much to marry her. If she refuses, I'll have to take my life right here, and you'll all be the witnesses."

Catherina's cheeks flushed, and she nervously giggled. "I'll fetch you a knife so you can make good on your threat," she said, standing up.

Blackie was not about to back down and followed her into the kitchen. Catching up to her, he turned her around and pulled her into his arms. "I'm serious, Catherina. Will you marry me?" He looked at her tenderly. "I know we haven't known each other very long, but it didn't take me long to know that I want to spend the rest of my life with you."

"It's too soon," she said, sighing heavily. "I told you, I almost went down that road once before, and it didn't work out."

"The reason you've waited all these years is staring you in the face...you've found a better man. I'd never hurt you. You mean the world to me." He could feel her shaking and held her tighter.

"I'm afraid," she whispered.

He pushed up her chin. "I know," he said, kissing her.

Eventually, the word *yes* escaped from her lips.

———— ◆●◆ ————

Blackie had grown up in an atmosphere where spiritual guidance was nonexistent. Catherina was the antithesis. She drank in faith and breathed out joy, infecting everyone around her. By the time the priest blessed the couple at the altar, Blackie was so filled with serenity that he was convinced something immortal filled Saint Raphael's church.

At their reception, which was held at Gabriella's bar, he toasted his wife, danced expressively, and broke out into song, finding himself participating in traditions he had never fathomed and realizing it was the people who surrounded him that made it possible.

They moved into an apartment in the building adjacent to Catherina's family, and for the first time in his life, Blackie felt he had found a real home at last in Catherina. He was aware her family was special; they embraced him with exuberance, making him feel as though he belonged. He admired the way they looked out for one another, cared for one another, and drew strength from one another. Having grown up with an austere father, Blackie was developing a close bond with Lorenzo and was learning what it was like to be treated like a son.

CHAPTER 31

Although they were the youngest of the siblings, Rosa and Louisa were the only ones to complete their high school education. To celebrate her sisters' accomplishment, Catherina offered to host a special dinner in her new apartment. She began cooking several days before the party, and after the family had arrived, they did not stop eating and drinking for hours between the singing and dancing.

Lorenzo took two small boxes out of each of his pants' pockets. Handing them to his daughters, his face beamed. "I'm so proud of you," he exclaimed. "An education opens doors in this city where closed doors lead back to the streets." He put his right hand on his chest, and his eyes shone with tears. "It was your mother's dream for you...for all of you. I know she's here with us."

Opening her gift, Rosa hugged and kissed her father for the thoughtful gold cross and chain.

Louisa mimicked her sister's gratitude but was bored and restless, thinking that there were other places she would rather be.

———◆◆———

The next day Rosa woke early, put on her favorite blue dress, and secured her ponytail with a ribbon to match. She had worked most weekends and the past few summers at Gabriella's bar, and she was thinking how different it would be to work with a stranger. She felt both eager and anxious as she went in search of her first full-time job.

Passing a law office three blocks away, she stared at the help wanted sign in the window, mustering the nerve to go inside. Taking a deep breath, she straightened her back and walked through the door, prepared to greet the person on the other side with an air of efficiency and confidence.

"Can I help you?" a man asked, looking up from his desk.

She walked over and firmly shook his hand. "Hello, my name is Rosa Carnavale, and I'm here about the job. Is it still available?"

He nodded his head. "Yes."

"Are you the person with whom I should speak?"

He nodded again. "I'm Brian Sinclair. Do you have any experience, Miss Carnavale?" he asked, leaning back in his chair.

Rosa's knees were shaking, but she tried to keep her voice from quivering. "I finished high school at the top of my class in typing and stenography. I'm fluent in both English and Italian." She continued to rattle off her qualifications. "I'm very organized and conscientious, and if you'd like, I can begin immediately."

"I need someone to answer the phone, type, and file," he pointed out. "Right now, I'm the only one here. My father just retired, and unfortunately for me, our secretary retired too. So I do need someone right away. I could use someone fluent in Italian." He hesitated. "I think you'll do fine…just fine."

Brian stood up. He was a tall and lean with a ruddy complexion; twinkling, blue eyes; and a full head of blond hair. Definitely Irish, Rosa surmised. She found her concentration was fluctuating between studying the outline of Brian's face and listening to the lilt of his voice.

"Can you start tomorrow?" he asked.

Almost missing the point that he was offering her the position, she finally said, "Certainly...thank you...what time?"

"I'm here by eight."

"I'll see you then," she said. "Good day, Mr. Sinclair." When she turned to leave, a broad smile stretched across her face.

"A very good day, Miss Carnavale," he countered.

As soon as Lorenzo walked in from work, Rosa excitedly told him that she had found a job with a lawyer named Brian Sinclair. Lorenzo said he had heard bits of praise from people in the neighborhood regarding the young man. He had a reputation of being lenient with cases of hardship, and Lorenzo was thankful she would be working for such an honorable man.

Knowing she did not possess the same dedication or enthusiasm as Rosa, Louisa had trouble finding employment. She would have been just as happy to keep working at Gabriella's bar, but her sister insisted it would be ridiculous; after all, a high school graduate could find a better paying job.

Louisa was relieved when she was offered a position as an operator at the phone company, but she found it daunting to be courteous to customers ten hours a day.

She had no interest in socializing with her coworkers, and she knew she was not particularly well liked. All Louisa cared about, thought about, and wanted was Marco.

———◆◆►———

One steamy night when Marco and Louisa arrived at the park, Johnny, who was usually the jokester of their group, looked agitated and paced back and forth on the fringe of their circle of friends. As they approached, he grabbed Marco's arm and said, "We've been all over the place—the streets are dry. Let's go to the pharmacy and get some pills." There was no hint of humor in his voice.

"I don't think so," Marco said, pulling his arm free.

"Come on, buddy, we can do this," Johnny said, sounding desperate.

Louisa had been feeling anxious all day and was looking forward to something to calm her uneasiness. "Do it for me, Marco," she said.

Marco grinned at her and shrugged his shoulders. "Let's check it out first," he said. Still holding Louisa's hand, they walked in the direction of the pharmacy, and the six others followed behind like ravenous rodents in search of their next meal.

As they turned the corner, Marco looked up at the apartment above the store. "The lights are off," he said to Louisa. "My boss must've gone to bed." He turned around. "It's a go," he told the others from over his shoulder.

Marco nimbly picked the lock on the back door, and they quietly entered the darkened store. Reaching under the counter, he grabbed the key and unlocked the glass-fronted case that secured the potent remedies. He emptied several pills from various jars into the palms of his friends' hands and carefully replaced the glass containers.

As they scurried out the door, Marco's employer blocked their way with a club cocked in his hand. Milton's deep-set eyes glowered at them from beneath his unruly eyebrows. "Drop everything," he demanded.

One by one, they dropped the pills in front of the armed man and took off.

A look of disappointment immediately registered on Milton's face when he saw Marco. "I thought you were better than this," he said, "but obviously you're just another one who's fallen through the cracks." He shook his head. "Never show your face around here again."

Marco stuffed his hands in his pockets and skulked away, privately regretting his decision. In the six months that he had worked for Milton, he had actually grown to like the man. Although his boss towered over most by a foot or more, his size was his only intimidation, for he was genuinely a goodhearted person. He thought about how Milton had offered him a job when he needed one and was angry with himself for giving in so easily to his friends.

———◆◆◆———

Marco started spending his days looking for work and spending his evenings searching for solace in Louisa's arms. His tarnished reputation preceded him, and he was unsuccessful finding employment. Bored and disgruntled, he wandered home early one afternoon and found his mother in bed with a man. An empty bottle and a pile of bills stood out on the nightstand, slapping Marco in the face.

When Marco was a young boy, his father had walked out on his mother and never returned, leaving them alone and destitute. He grew up indigent. Their shabby apartment had no heat or hot water, and they survived on slivers of sustenance. As far back as Marco could remember, he had fended for himself. His mother slept the days away, and in place of her husband, an empty bottle lay by her side. In the evenings, she left Marco alone and told him that she worked the night shift at the hospital laundry, but at that moment, he realized she worked on the corners shedding her clothes and selling her soul.

Marco hurdled over his mother, howling obscenities and violently attacking the naked man. He wrapped his fingers around the stranger's throat—the veins in his arms pulsating with vengeance.

Shielding her nudity with the bed sheet, his mother leaped up. "Marco. What are you doing? Stop!"

The flustered john pried Marco off and tossed him from the bed. Grabbing his clothes and money and without a word, the man scrambled from the ill-fated scene.

Marco leaned back against the wall as visions exploded in his head, and it all began to make sense. They triggered childhood memories he had suppressed, but now they were stinging his subconscious with scorching offensiveness and vindication. He turned on his mother with the rancor of a snake spewing venom. "You're disgusting— you're a lying slut!"

Her lower lip quivered, and tears sprung from her eyes. "Marco, you don't understand," she cried.

He jumped up. "What's to understand?" he wailed, snatching the bottle off the nightstand and throwing it at her. "Damn you! I bet it was you who chased my father away. He knew exactly what the hell you were. I remember now—the men, the never ending fighting, the *lies!*" his voice exploded. "It was you who destroyed our family."

"That's not true! Your father was never around. He made excuses not to come home. He'd be gone for days at a time!"

"It's was because of you!"

"No, you're wrong. In the beginning, I did it for companionship, and then it became a necessity...a way to put food on the table. I'm sorry...I'm so sorry." Her voice was a penitent whine.

"Where is he? Where's my father? Is he still alive?"

"It was so long ago when he left...I've never heard from him again."

"You make me sick," he snarled. "All these years you've kept this from me."

She looked down, dropping her head in her hand. "I had no other choice," she choked. "I did it for you."

"Go to hell," he spat, and he stormed out of the apartment with the intention of never going back again.

———— ◆•◆ ————

The streets became Marco's home; he slept in the alleyways and scavenged for food. He felt alone and confused as he tried to combat the intractable feelings gnawing at his insides. As a child, the neglect he had endured and the inconsistencies he had subconsciously felt repeatedly assaulted his memory. He had feebly attempted to banish thoughts of other men, shielding himself behind a mask of masculinity, but the thoughts he had repressed his whole life were now filtering through with clarity and decisiveness, culminating in resentment for women and yearning for male companionship. There was no escape from the turmoil raging within him—the repercussion was a disturbing mixture of shame and relief. He realized that his romantic connection to females, especially Louisa, was an unconscious deception, and the desire to unleash his true self became as strong as his animosity for his mother.

———◆◆◆———

Marco spent less and less time with Louisa and acted distant when they were together. She would approach him, hoping for a sign of warmth or acceptance, but she was crushed when he shunned her advances. Gradually, her self-esteem began to crumble as the intimacy they once shared dissipated without reason.

The day that Marco pushed her away, calling her "a pain in the ass" and "crazy" was the day Louisa's world came crashing down, and she fell into a state of hopeless desperation. It felt as if a piece of her heart had snapped off, leaving her incomplete, humiliated. Getting through her days was draining. Her mind raced through the endless hours and collapsed exhausted at its unproductive end.

Distracted and incapable of doing her job, she was fired from the phone company, demoralizing her further. In the mornings she left the apartment for work with everyone else, but she would return soon after to conceal her inadequacies from her family and wallow alone in her grief.

———◆◆◆———

Running late, Rosa dashed out the door one harried morning, overlooking the files she had organized the evening before. Deciding to go home on her lunch hour, she entered what should have been an empty apartment. She heard crying coming from the bedroom and slowly cracked the door open, not so surprised at what she saw. Amidst the ruins of the disheveled room, Louisa sat on the floor clutching her knees to her chest and sobbing into her folded arms.

Rosa crouched down beside her. "Louisa, what's wrong?" she asked. She tenderly rubbed her back, while anticipating the worst.

Drowning in her tears, Louisa purged, "Marco hates me...I've lost my job...I hate myself." Her voice cracked in alarming distress.

Rosa instantly flashed back to what had happened on her way home from work last week. Walking past a dingy alley, she caught sight of two men in an intimate embrace. The amber street lamp illuminated their silhouettes, and she recognized one as Marco's. She quickly fled, praying he did not notice her, but unfortunately, he flew after her like a jackal. Forcefully grabbing her arm, he jerked her about-face. In place of his usual cocky expression was one filled with toxic superiority. Terrified, she cowered beneath his vicious glare, and his words made her shiver. "If you tell anyone, I'll kill you," he snarled. He held on to her tightly for a moment to make sure she got the message and then flung her away like a piece of trash.

Marco's hostile words echoed through Rosa's mind as she listened to her sister vent her anguish. "I saw something shocking that I think you should know about," she blurted it out before she lost her nerve, "I saw Marco hugging a man in an alley."

Louisa looked up; her eyes were bloodshot and swollen. "What's that supposed to mean?"

"I think you know what it means." Rosa's tone was filled with insinuation.

"You liar!" Louisa roared, shoving her away.

Rosa caught herself from falling sideways. The space between them was now compounded by disbelief.

"You and your perfect life—your perfect job! You think you're so smart. You never liked him."

"I knew you'd say that," Rosa said. In a burst of grave frustration, she took hold of Louisa's shoulders and yanked her close. Locking eyes, she added, "He threatened to kill me if I told anyone—you have to believe me."

———◆●◆———

The realization hit Louisa like a tornado, spinning her into a realm of infuriation twisting perilously with retaliation. She leaped up and ran. Grabbing a knife from the kitchen drawer and slipping it into the sleeve of her blouse, she charged out of the apartment. Her tears turned to blind rage as she raced through the streets and found Marco in the park. "You're a queer. That's why you're ignoring me?" she hissed in gasping spurts of fire.

Seemingly unperturbed, he coolly responded, "You're crazy. This...you and me...was a fling. I'm moving on, baby." He grabbed the closest girl next to him around the waist and kissed her hard on the lips, acting as if he was thoroughly enjoying himself.

———◆●◆———

Out of breath, Rosa spotted her irate sister wielding a knife in Marco's direction. She felt as though she was suspended in slow motion as she watched Louisa lunge forward, thrusting the knife into Marco's chest—the thud of its blade piercingly conclusive.

"No, Louisa!" Rosa screamed. "No!"

At the sight of Marco's ashen face and motionless body, the group recoiled and scattered into the streets. Louisa's hands and dress splattered with blood, she collapsed onto Marco, plunging the knife deeper into the finality of death.

Rosa stood frozen, embedded in the moment before the horror could register. She stumbled toward Louisa, tripping through the nightmare. "Let's get out of here," she pleaded, while forcibly yanking her sister's arm. "Hurry, we have to go!"

Louisa would not budge.

Within minutes, police sirens erupted with unnerving consequence.

Handcuffed and taken to the station for questioning, Louisa was incoherent and unable to speak. She sat slumped in the chair with her hands limp in her lap, her glassy stare devoid of detail. Rosa called Louisa's name repeatedly, but her sister was lost in an unreachable place buried deep within herself.

Rosa frantically sputtered Brian's number to the police officer, and he handed her the phone.

She began to sob when Brian said, "Hello."

"I'm so glad...you're there. I'm at the...police station...Louisa...she..." Rosa was hysterical.

"I can't understand you. Calm down," he urged.

She took a few deep breaths. "I'm at the police station with Louisa. She's been arrested."

"I'm on my way," he shouted.

Brian dropped the phone and sprinted the five blocks to the precinct. Arriving within minutes, his face was flushed with perspiration and concern. He took over compassionately and knowledgeably, arranging for Louisa to be transported to Bellevue Hospital for psychiatric evaluation.

―――――◆•◆―――――

In a tiny appendage of a darkened hallway, Louisa sat isolated from humanity in her dreary room, the bars on the window symbolic of her mental imprisonment. The muted walls chipped with paint as her mind drained of thought, and invisible straps of constraint bound her limbs. She was led like a helpless child to a metal-spring cot to sleep away her nights and awakened in the mornings to slumber through her days. Each time the family visited, their expectations for her recuperation dwindled. They talked aimlessly about the happenings in the neighborhood and in their lives as if she were part of the conversation, as if she understood. Sadly, Louisa remained oblivious to their presence, condemned to an unforgiving world of solitude.

After months of unresponsiveness, her case was dismissed on the grounds of insanity, and she was permanently committed to the sanatorium.

―――――◆•◆―――――

Lorenzo asked Rosa to go with him that cold, cloudy Saturday afternoon to meet with Louisa's doctor and hear the latest update on her condition. Rosa still blamed herself for what had happened to her sister, even though her father reminded her that Louisa had created her own misfortune.

A nurse led them down the hallway to Doctor Bailey's office.

"Good afternoon," the doctor said as they walked through the door. He came out from behind his desk wearing a white lab coat and a stethoscope draped over his neck.

"Hello, doctor," Rosa said, hoping today would be the day they would hear some positive news.

Doctor Bailey shook Lorenzo's hand. "Thank you for coming," he said, looking at him thoughtfully. "Please have a seat." He gestured to the two chairs across from his desk and leaned against its edge. "As you know, Louisa's case has been very challenging, and the medications we've tried are not working." He paused. "I've asked you to come here today to discuss another option."

"What is it?" Lorenzo asked with a tinge of optimism in his voice.

"From what we have learned from speaking with you, Mr. Carnavale, and your other children, Louisa has exhibited both compulsive and depressive tendencies since she was a child. What we think has happened is that it has been compounded by the traumatic stress brought on by the incident, causing her profound breakdown. Electric shock is a radical treatment, but there's a possibility it may revive your daughter," he said consolingly. "We would pass electrical currents through her brain to jar it back to reality. It may take multiple treatments before we'll be able to determine if it'll have an effect."

Morosely, Lorenzo looked at Rosa. "What do you think we should do?"

"I'm not sure," she said, reaching for his hand and wondering how dangerous the procedure could be.

"There are risks involved, and we can't promise you it'll work," Doctor Bailey said as if reading her mind. "Although, we also believe that in Louisa's extreme case it's our only alternative."

"Papa, if there's a chance it will help her than maybe we should let the doctor do whatever needs to be done." She squeezed his hand, feeling as though they were in the throes of a never-ending nightmare.

"You don't have to make a decision right now. Go home and talk it over with your other children," Doctor Bailey said.

Lorenzo stared at him somberly. "Please, save my daughter. Do whatever you can to save her," he begged. Haunting tears streamed from his eyes.

Men in white coats strapped Louisa to the table, her limbs outstretched and tethered. They placed a rolled cloth between her teeth while a nurse immobilized her head with her hands. A doctor dampened her temples with a sponge and touched the prods against them as another nurse flipped the switch on the black box. Louisa's body involuntarily arched as the gripping current was sent jolting through her nerves, but her brain was unreceptive to its benefits. She was hanging on a dangerous precipice, and the violent bolts of energy released her over its edge, plunging her into its eternal cavity.

After six chilling weeks of torturous therapy, Louisa subsisted in a world of lethargic complacency, a stranger to her family and herself. She spent the rest of her days in a sanatorium, sequestered inside a tomb of repentance as if the sin on her soul could never be healed.

The family struggled to get through the hours as if they were days, to get through the months as if they were years. Together, they were making an effort to subdue the sadness that enveloped their lives—modest attempts at mending the bits and pieces of their broken hearts. They had lost Louisa to the clutches of an illness they could not understand and were unable to rescue Rosa from the penance of regret.

It was as though all their wasted years of estrangement had come to a head for Rosa. She grieved for the time lost to dissension and carried the burden of unleashing the unbearable truth. If only she could have stopped Louisa. She kept revisiting the past, and it was devouring her present.

Rosa took time off from work to nurture her sister, to grieve over the loss, to comprehend the reality. Faithfully, she went to bathe, dress, and feed Louisa, continually professing loving words that could not be reciprocated, could not be discerned. Strangely, it was the first time Rosa felt she had a twin—a bond that emerged from the depths of regret and responsibility.

The whole ordeal had dramatically changed Rosa. While Louisa lingered in a state of forsaken oblivion, Rosa was inflicted with an agony equally debilitating since she was conscious of the destruction, the degradation. The sight of her sister's listless body slouched in her chair relentlessly imprisoned Rosa's mind—it was difficult to see the light when sorrow blurred the way. She tried to make sense of it all and wallowed in guilt, chipping away at her spirit with an ice pick of remorse. In the confines of a confessional, the priest reminded her of the power of prayer and absolution; nonetheless, she waned with the battle. She had witnessed the preciousness of life slip away, defying reason, and found it unsettling to have faith in a God that had abandoned her sister.

Mourning the loss until she could mourn no more without forsaking her own sanity, Rosa slowly began to crawl along a path to recovery with her loved ones guiding her through the hills and valleys. Gradually, she began to latch onto the simple pleasures, stretching them into lifelines, tenaciously holding on.

———————•••———————

Getting back to work was just the remedy Rosa needed to bolster her rejuvenation. When she walked through the door, it opened Brian's smile.

He dropped what he was doing and went to her, giving her a warm hug. "I've missed you beyond belief," he admitted.

Rosa could feel his heartbeat over her own, pumping her with possibilities. She had realized the degree of Brian's affections since this all had happened. He had been a true friend, offering his expertise and support. He was so caring and concerned, although she had lacked the energy or time to respond. Her every thought had been of Louisa, and there was no room for anyone else. Now, as he held her in his arms, she was ready to accept that there was much more than friendship between them.

"You know I love you." He looked at her tenderly. "What else can I say? I don't want any pretenses here."

Rosa felt the same way, and her chest swelled from the absolute truth of it all. "I love you too."

The words they professed had been previously muted by circumstance, but now, their exchange gave new meaning to both their lives.

Brian was Rosa's anchor, and being with him every day was a blessing. She felt as though she was on a roller coaster of emotions, and he was the pendulum that kept her steady. He often stopped at the flower cart on the way to the office, purchasing a single rose and bestowing it upon her with the grandeur of a garden in full bloom. He spontaneously broke into song, making her giggle at his silly lyrics—the lines a rhythmical expression of his devotion.

Rosa knew her father respectfully appreciated all Brian had done for Louisa and for her. When Lorenzo told her that he wanted to thank the man who put a smile back on her face, she invited Brian to Sunday supper.

When Brian arrived, Lorenzo greeted him with a kiss on both cheeks. "I'm glad you could join us."

"Thank you, Mr. Carnavale. This is for you," he said, offering him a cigar. And ladies, these are for you." He gave a slight bow and handed a red rose to Catherina, Gabriella, and Rosa.

"I've brought up a jug of my special wine from the cellar for the occasion," Lorenzo said, grinning.

"I'm honored, sir."

"Dinner's served," Catherina announced, sitting down next to Blackie.

"Honey, it's time to eat," Gabriella called to Sophia who was busy stacking blocks in the parlor.

The toddler stood up, and her black ponytails bounced up and down as she ambled over. Attaching herself to her mother's side, she looked at Brian curiously.

"This is my daughter, Sophia," Gabriella said.

He crouched down to her eye level. "My name's Brian," he said. "I've heard all about you from your Aunt Rosa. She didn't tell me how pretty you are."

Sophia smiled shyly at him.

"Sit here," Rosa told Brian, pointing to the seat next to her.

Immediately, Sophia climbed into the chair on his other side.

"I think I might have some competition," Rosa whispered, leaning close to Brian.

He chuckled. "She's adorable. I think she looks a lot like her Aunt Rosa."

"I was never that cute," she said.

Santo uncorked the jug and generously poured the red liquid into his glass, the first gulps seemed to steady his trembling hands. Rosa shot him a stern look, a silent warning not to make a fool of himself yet again. Ignoring her completely, he continued to imbibe. The drink loosened his tongue, and during dinner, he served a repertoire of off-color jokes as they all digested their tastelessness.

Shaking his head in disgust, Vinny removed the glass from Santo, who abruptly sprung up to retrieve the drink. He blocked his inebriated brother with his forearm, causing him to stumble backward and tumble to the floor.

Sluggishly rising on his feet, Santo braced himself on his chair and cocked his free arm ready to strike.

Banging the table with his fist, Lorenzo interrupted his son's despicable display, making even the table jump. "Stop it, right now!"

Santo backed away, cowering to the sofa to snore off his tactlessness.

Thoroughly mortified, Rosa wanted to shake the sense back into her brother. "I apologize for him," she said. "He obviously had a little too much to drink." She raised her voice in annoyance so Santo could hear her resentment.

Easing the tension battering the room, Brian cheerfully said, "I'd love a second helping of macaroni, please."

Rosa felt the color return to her face as she gladly served him more.

———◆◆◆———

Brian became a regular at the dinner table and in their lives, even accompanying the family on their occasional Sunday picnics to the cemetery. Rosa had laughed when he told her that he thought it was a most peculiar custom, but he would do anything for her, even if it meant having lunch amongst the dead.

———◆◆◆———

Rosa would always remember the night Brian had asked her father for her hand in marriage. She was ecstatic when Lorenzo warmly embraced him and said he would be honored to have him as a son-in-law, but she had to giggle to herself when he jokingly added that he never imagined having an Irishman as part of the family. She decided never to tell Brian that she had overheard their conversation from the kitchen, and when he proposed, she feigned her surprise, but she did not have to feign her happiness.

Their magical wedding night was only the beginning of what Rosa dreamed would be a perfect life together.

Brian proved to be a wonderful husband, more than she could have ever hoped. They worked side by side at the law office and lived in Brian's brownstone apartment on the east side of Manhattan. Accustomed to living with so many people, Rosa felt that sharing a spacious apartment with one was a liberating experience, but at times, she found herself missing the chaos and liveliness of her family.

CHAPTER 32

Although Gabriella was physically free of her cowardly husband, she was still hurting from the emotional aftermath of Vito's misplaced aggressions. Sophia was Gabriella's pride and joy, and she deserved more than a mother weighted down by the gloom of the past. She felt her daughter, who was two years old, had seen and heard too much, but she prayed she was still young enough to forget. For the most part she was a contented child, but there were times when she moped around, and Gabriella wondered what she was thinking.

Gabriella was grateful that her family took extra lengths to fill in the hole left by Sophia's absentee father. When she snuggled with Lorenzo on his lap, he would secretly slip her a nickel, and she would smother him with thankful hugs and kisses. Never having a girl of their own, Gabriella knew Uncle Dominick and Aunt Genevieve felt a particular attachment to Sophia and enjoyed having her to themselves. Vinny, Catherina, and Rosa also gave Sophia special attention and affection, and they were always dropping by the bar to buoy Gabriella's spirits and to remind her she was not alone. Even Santo tried his best whenever he was around.

Despite everyone's admirable intentions, Gabriella still felt the color had not yet returned to her life and needed to find a way to brighten her world again. Divorce was against their religion, but maybe it would eliminate the unremitting torment that was eating away at her self-confidence and allowing her only minute moments of happiness.

———◆◆◆———

One day Gabriella decided to phone Brian at his law office, knowing Rosa was home with the flu.

"Brian Sinclair here," he said when he answered.

"Hi, Brian."

"Gabriella?"

"Yeah, it's me."

"Sometimes it is hard to distinguish between you and Catherina over the phone."

"We've heard that before," she said.

"Well, this is a pleasant surprise—a call from my new sister-in-law."

"The reason I'm calling is because I'd like to discuss something personal with you, and I need your advice… but I'd rather not do it on the phone. Can you stop by the bar sometime alone?"

"Tomorrow after court I'll come by…probably around two. Is that okay?"

"That'd be great. Can you just keep this between us?"

"Of course," he agreed. "Gabriella, is everything all right?"

"We'll talk tomorrow," she said instead of a good-bye.

———◆◆◆———

The next afternoon when Brian arrived, he immediately asked, "What did you want to talk to me about? You sounded so serious." There was a distinct look of concern on his face.

"Let's sit down first." Gabriella was glad the lunch crowd had dispersed and turned to her employee. "Edith, I'm going to take a few minutes," she said. She looked back at Brian. "Would you like something to eat or drink?"

"No thanks, I grabbed a sandwich at the courthouse."

She led him to a table and sat down, and he took the seat across from her.

"I'm having a very hard time making a decision, and I need your input," she began.

"Go on," he encouraged.

"I know Vito is out of my life, but I want to officially end our marriage. I don't know how my family is going to feel about a divorce, especially my father." She rubbed her temples to combat the headache that had been escalating all morning. "You know how he is...he's so religious, and I don't know how he'll react." Although she did not ask a question, she looked at him for an answer.

"You have every reason to go through with this. You're only twenty-four years old and have many years ahead of you," he said sympathetically. "You may meet someone else and—"

She put her hand up to cut him off. "Please, I'm not thinking about that."

"Well, I'm sure your family will understand your feelings," he said adamantly. "And the courts typically grant a divorce in cases of abuse and abandonment."

"Of which he's done both," she said, infusing her words with sarcasm. "It's funny...we took our time getting married...years, in fact. He was so busy with the bakery and taking care of his mother. While we were dating, I never saw that side of him. I thought we were in love…at least I was. I would've never imagined this could've happened to us. He was very good at hiding his dark side *and* his money problems. When we married, I was blindsided." Tears blurred her vision, and she blinked them away. "Look at me, here I am talking about divorce, and you just got married," she said, perking up. "I'm sorry. I'm really happy for you and my sister. You make a great couple."

He rested his hand on hers. "You'll be fine."

"How do I go about this? Can you help me?"

"I'm not well-versed in divorce litigation, but I have a friend in Yonkers who specializes in domestic relations law. Though I should warn you, it'll take a while for the process to move forward. After the papers are filed, there'll be a trial, and then there's at least a six-month waiting period to see if Vito can be located and if he has any objections before the judge will grant the decree. If he decides he wants custody of Sophia or to share custody of her, it becomes more involved. Personally, from what I've heard about him, I think the chances are very slim that he will. You'll also need witnesses to support your case."

She sighed. "This is an awful lot to digest."

"Gabriella, think about it. You have a good case. There should be no problem. If you'd like, in the meantime, I'll make that phone call for you."

"I'd appreciate it." Standing up, she gave him a hug. "It's certainly helps to have a brother-in-law who's a lawyer."

Gabriella's mind was whirling for the rest of the day over what she and Brian had discussed. She knew she had to broach the subject to her family, and when she got home that evening, she decided to be honest and straightforward.

"I know you've all made a tremendous effort to help me and Sophia, but I need to move on. I'm thinking about divorcing Vito." She looked at her father for his reaction. "I spoke to Brian about it, and he assured me there should be no problem considering the circumstances, unless Vito comes forward...which seems unlikely."

Lorenzo put down his cup of coffee and sat quietly, studying Gabriella. "You deserve to be free from that bastard. If this is what you need to make you feel better, then you have my blessing."

Tears rolled down her face. "Thanks, Papa. I needed to hear you say that."

Catherina looked at her compassionately. "You should do this for yourself," she said.

Gabriella took a napkin from the table and blotted her cheeks. "I'll need witnesses at the trial, and then there's a waiting period of about six months before it becomes official, and hopefully Vito stays far away," she said, while thinking to herself that if there was any justice in the world, he would never be found.

"Santo and I can testify on your behalf," Vinny offered. "I can't imagine anything that'd give me more pleasure."

Santo nodded his agreement.

———◆◆◆———

Gabriella's prayers were answered when Vito never showed at the trial or was heard from in the six months that followed. A small part of her still loved him, but a greater part of her hated him for what he had done, stripping her heart of any forgiveness.

Waiting for the decree to become official, she had marked each day off on her calendar, and in that time, she had come to terms with the finality of her marriage.

Several days before Gabriella was due to go to Yonkers to finalize the paperwork, she was relieved that Santo volunteered to take the day off and go with her for support. He even offered to borrow a truck from Vinny so they would not have to make the journey by train. Santo was not a demonstrative person, but it was times like these that made her remember how much he genuinely cared.

<hr />

As Santo and Gabriella drove in relative silence to Yonkers, she was feeling nauseous and relieved at the same time. She looked down at Sophia sleeping soundly on her lap and thought all she wanted was for her daughter to forget Vito, but Gabriella realized that she first had to do it herself.

When she finished signing the documents, a strange feeling of relief washed over her. The muscles in her body relaxed as the years flowed through the pen, leaving an albatross of sadness on the paper for no one else to decipher. A smile washed over her, the first one in a long time that had come so naturally.

"I feel like a new person," she admitted to Santo with a slight shrug of surprise as they climbed into the truck to leave. "I'm so glad that's over."

"Let's get something to eat and celebrate," he said, sounding sincerely happy for her. "We could both use a drink."

Squirming in her seat, Sophia moaned, "Mommy, I have to go to the bathroom."

Gabriella turned to face her daughter. "We're going to stop at the next restaurant. Right, Uncle Santo?" she asked him in an emphasized tone.

"There's one not far from here. I saw it on the way up," he said.

"Hurry, I really have to go."

Pulling over to the side of the road opposite the restaurant, he told them, "Go inside. I'll park and meet you."

Gabriella quickly got out and helped Sophia down. Taking hold of her daughter's hand, they hastily crossed the road as a truck suddenly came barreling over the hill—the sun's blinding ray's reflecting like lightning off its windshield.

The last words Gabriella heard was her brother screaming, "Get out of the way!" She instinctively shoved Sophia to the side of the road and was struck by the oncoming vehicle that killed her instantly.

———◆◆◆———

The family was inconsolable, especially Lorenzo. He sat day after day in the chair recently given to him by Gabriella, replacing the one that had been lost in the fire years ago. With his Bible draped open on his lap, he searched for solace in Scripture, but it was impossible to concentrate on the words that lined the pages when pictures of his beautiful daughter flooded his mind. Sifting through the years, he rehashed the muffled arguments coming from their apartment. *Why didn't I intervene? How did I not know what was really going on? I saw the sadness in her eyes, but I hoped they'd work out their differences on their own. If I had gone to her, would she have told me the truth? Would I be holding onto my daughter, instead of holding onto her memory?* Regret tore at his psyche.

———————◆•◆———————

One night after Catherina had tucked Sophia into bed, she was glad everyone was still there when she returned to the kitchen. Closing the door to the bedroom, she looked at her family thoughtfully. "I know Gabriella has only been gone for a few weeks, but I think it's time to make some decisions together," she said, holding back her tears. "Of course, Sophia will remain here with us."

"Brian and I would love to have her," Rosa interrupted, glancing at her husband.

Catherina sat down and looked at her sister appreciatively. "Since you and Brian moved across town, we don't see you as much. Sophia doesn't need any changes right now, and you're about to have a baby of your own. Staying here will give her stability. She also has Papa and Vinny and Santo next door...somebody's always around. I think the main question is, what do we do with the bar?"

"I'm too busy with the warehouse," Vinny said.

"We've got the store," Blackie shrugged.

Catherina studied Santo from across the table. As usual, he looked distant and disheveled, nursing another hangover, she assumed. She wished he could handle it, but running the bar would certainly be his demise. "Papa, what do you think?" she asked.

Lorenzo looked up at her; his face was a picture of pain. "We should sell it and put the money in the bank for Sophia's future."

There was a long silence as everyone thought about what he had just said, and one by one, they nodded their heads in solemn agreement.

———◆•◆———

Despite a concerted effort to mollify her sorrow, Sophia's anguished screams could often be heard in the night when her sleep was interrupted by the haunting nightmares of her mother's mangled body.

CHAPTER 33

Catherina and Blackie's days were now bustling between raising their niece and running their business, and Sophia slowly seemed to be adjusting to her new life and home. When Catherina became pregnant, she and Blackie were overjoyed for themselves, but they were also thrilled that Sophia would have a cousin to share in her life. Blackie adored Sophia, and Catherina had witnessed firsthand that he was a loving uncle and imagined he would be the same as a father. When their tiny infant gloriously appeared, she would never forget the look of gratitude in his eyes. He told her that Annabelle had captured his heart at first sight exactly the way she had when he first laid eyes on her.

———◆•◆———

One morning, while Blackie was out purchasing stock from the local vendors, Catherina was alone in their grocery store, and Annabelle was napping in the back room. Taking advantage of Aunt Genevieve's offer to watch Sophia during the day, Catherina had started bringing Annabelle to the store when she was less than a week old.

Two men burst through the door pointing guns and demanding their cash. Their eyes menacingly peered at her from behind the slits of the black woolen hats pulled over their heads. Her body trembled and her fingers fumbled as she awkwardly opened the register. "Please, please, don't hurt us," she whimpered. "Take it all, just leave us alone." She instantly regretted saying *us*, praying Annabelle did not stir.

Forcing Catherina to the ground, one of the thieves brusquely bound and gagged her as the other hastily dumped the contents of the drawer into a cloth bag. Leaving her immobilized on the floor, they flipped the sign on the window to *closed* and disappeared out the door.

Blackie entered the store and turned the sign over, thinking that it was odd he forgot to change it that morning. "Catherina, I'm back," he called out, assuming she was in the storage room. The banging from behind the counter drew his attention, and he rushed over to find her lying restrained on the ground. Her eyes bulged with terror and her words were unintelligible.

Immediately, he removed the rag stuffed in her mouth. "What happened?" he stammered, untying her with panicked urgency. "Are you hurt?"

Catherina gasped several breaths before she was able to speak. "Check on the baby," she begged.

He sprinted to the back and swiftly scooped Annabelle out of her carriage. Nestling her to his chest with sobering relief, he brought her to Catherina and placed the infant into the outstretched arms of his traumatized wife. Disheartened, he cradled them so tightly that Annabelle began to cry. Blackie was livid. Flashing back to his darker days, he was blindsided by remorse. Now that he was the victim, he understood their fright.

Three months later, the store was robbed again. Having purchased a gun of his own, this time Blackie was alone and prepared. As the thieves entered the store, he grabbed the weapon from under the counter and fired three deafening shots into the air. He snickered to himself as he watched the two men scurry out the door.

Hearing the gunfire, the owner of the adjacent store called the police. Blackie was booked for possession of an illegal weapon—he had refrained from obtaining a license due to his previous conviction.

"Guilty." The judge banged his gravel. "One year in the penitentiary with six months' probation," he ordered.

Shaking, Catherina sprang up from her seat and held on to the back of the bench in front of her for support. Mustering her courage, she pleaded, "Please, Your Honor, my husband was acting in self-defense."

"Your husband has a prior record, ma'am. I'm afraid there's no choice."

Catherina had agreed with Blackie when he had made the decision to acquire a gun, but she was unaware there was trouble in his past. Shrinking back, she wrapped her arms around her body, trying to hold herself together. She wondered what he could have possibly done, but she knew there was nothing more she could say.

Stone faced, Blackie was led from the courtroom in handcuffs like an animal being led to his cage, while Catherina was left to digest the unsavory truth—the past had caught up to him with a vengeance.

Blackie felt demoralized in prison. He had a legitimate business, a wife and child he deeply loved, a niece that completed his family, and a respectable life. *How am I going to explain this to Catherina? What good would it do to tell her the truth?* he fretted. *I can't lose her now.*

Anger festered like an open wound as he languished away in a cell, and his temper emerged from its cavity. Blackie snapped when one of the inmates swiped his tray off the cafeteria table and condescendingly referred to him as a "guinea bastard." Whatever forces were bound up inside of him were unleashed that night, and he attacked the unlucky antagonist until he was satisfied the man would never use the derogatory slur again.

Blackie paid dearly for his outburst. He was made an example to the other inmates and put in solitary confinement. A grotesque hole so cramped, he barely had room to sit. So hot, he thought he would suffocate. The sweat poured from his body, and for two weeks, he wore the same soiled clothes. Strands of light filtered through a tiny, barred opening and were the only indication another day had begun. Carved by the fingernails of past offenders, graffiti covered the walls—blaring words of doom he began to believe. The evenings fell like a mask of darkness, too black to watch which creature was crawling on his skin. He struggled to stay awake because the nightmares he had when he slept were worse than the one he was living.

Catherina had gone to see Blackie just once before he was denied any further visitation rights or parole. He had explained through the metal screening that separated them that he had owned a gun when he was a fisherman and did not mean to wound anyone that miserable night. Returning from having a few rounds of drinks with his buddies, he had merely intended to scare off the man he caught rummaging around on his boat. He swore it was the first and last time he had fired the weapon, and a day he clearly wanted to forget; therefore, he never mentioned it to Catherina before. He apologized for keeping it from her, but he asked her to understand. When a guard alerted them that their ten minutes were up, Blackie put his hand against the grating, and Catherina placed hers on the other side. In that last moment, he thought he saw a hint of forgiveness in her eyes.

Thereafter, their only communication was by letter where Blackie attempted to convey his affection on paper, while longing to hold Catherina in person. They thoughtfully tried not to exasperate the other's burden and sorrow by holding back the disturbing details of their difficult days.

———— •‣• ————

It was after the morning rush, and Catherina wheeled Annabelle's pram next to a chair by the window, taking a few minutes for herself. It was a blustery fall day, and she was relishing the warmth of the cup of tea she held in her hands as she sat down. Gazing out the store window, she thought about how much older she felt than her twenty-six years and about how much she missed her husband. She believed it was a series of unfortunate circumstances that had put Blackie behind bars, and she worried about his mental state. She would have described her husband as easygoing to anyone who asked her, so it was hard to understand that he had been put in solitary confinement for attacking another with the "voracity of a monster" as the warden had put it. There were so many questions she wanted answered, but she would wait until Blackie came home to ask.

Compounding her anguish, the responsibility of the store, Annabelle, and Sophia rested upon her shoulders, and she was dragging from the perpetual toil. She tried to hold back the tears as she thought about Gabriella and the beautiful little girl she had left behind, but she could not hold back the smile when she thought about Rosa cradling her newborn, Constance, across town.

Catching sight of Sam and Ida walking down the street suddenly lifted Catherina out of her melancholy mood. She had worked many years at Sam Green's coat factory before she married Blackie, and she had become extremely close to Sam and his wife, Ida. Catherina giggled to herself, thinking that they were the quintessential, quirky couple and a sight to behold. She saw Ida's hat coming down the street before she saw her. It had a plethora of colorful flowers and a plume of feathers that ostentatiously protruded from its top. The fur boa was the next thing that grabbed her attention. The pelt hung decoratively around Ida's neck and over an exquisite, handmade coat perfectly tailored to fit her plump frame. She was dressed as if she were going to the opera, complete with white gloves and a silver-chained evening bag. If Catherina did not know her, she would have thought that she was prim and proper; however, she had the good fortune to have discovered that she was full of piss and vinegar.

Sam was just as captivating. Taking two steps to Ida's one, his stubby legs moved briskly to keep pace with his lofty spouse. His face was a caricature, sporting a large, bulbous nose and chubby cheeks. Wisps of sparse, silver hair were parted on the side and its tonic-induced shine matched the glimmer in his eyes. Catherina thought by no means was he handsome, though there was nothing ugly about Sam, for his heart far outsized his stout, rotund body. She had often said that if you were lucky enough to work for Sam Green, you were lucky enough.

Sam and Ida did not live in the neighborhood, but they frequently stopped by the store to visit. Sam used the excuse that he missed his favorite employee, but Catherina knew Annabelle had become the main attraction.

They walked into the store like a breath of fresh air, and immediately, Ida picked Annabelle up out of her pram. "Hello, baby girl," she said.

Sam handed Catherina the package he was carrying. "There're two coats in there for the girls. Sophia told me that her favorite color is blue."

Catherina huffed. "You don't have to bring them something every time you visit."

He chuckled. "Don't tell your old boss what to do," he said, turning his attention to Annabelle.

Fussing over the baby, Ida said, "Catherina, you're not nursing anymore, why don't you let us watch Annabelle for a few days. With Blackie away, you could use the help."

Catherina appreciated that there was no judgment in her voice when she mentioned Blackie's name. "I couldn't possibly..." she said.

"Please, say yes. You know how much we adore her," Ida sincerely persisted. She looked at her husband. "Don't we, dear?"

"Why of course," Sam agreed. "It'll give us a chance to spoil her." His jowls jiggled when he laughed.

Catherina always found herself smiling when they were around. "How can I ever repay your kindness?" she said.

"Don't be silly—you're doing us a favor," Ida responded with genuine fervor. She cradled the cooing infant in her arms. "You needn't worry, she'll be fine."

"Are you sure?"

Sam and Ida were so enthralled with the baby that they did not hear her question.

———◆•◆———

The time Blackie spent in prison dragged on for Catherina. The Greens continued to occasionally take Annabelle, and sometimes even Sophia, for an overnight stay in their home, and Catherina was grateful for their thoughtfulness and generosity. She was now making extra money selling soups and sandwiches she prepared at home, but sleep was a rare luxury. It seemed she needed to work around the clock in order to keep up with her days.

———◆•◆———

After serving his sentence, Blackie was released from prison and unexpectedly strolled into the store, startling Catherina.

A rush of relief washed over her, and she dashed from behind the counter, shrieking with excitement, "Oh my God! Blackie, you're home!" Throwing her arms around her husband, she kissed every inch of his face and smothered him with affection. Her elation was short-lived for what followed was a sudden surge of grave concern.

Jail had aged Blackie. He was frail and gaunt, and at thirty-five, his hair was almost fully white, and a bristly, unkempt beard covered his gray complexion. "I'm back, and I promise I'll never leave you again," he said as he looked at her with sunken eyes that expressed how much he loved her. Softly caressing her cheek with his hand, he weakly whispered, "I'm sorry I put you through all this. I've missed you so much."

No longer did Catherina feel it was necessary to know the details of his past or to dwell on the mistakes he had made, she saw he had been punished enough. "I'm getting you something to eat," she insisted, walking over to the stove and dishing out a plate of pasta that could have fed a family of four.

------◆•◆------

Whenever Blackie sat down, Catherina put more food in front of him, and his stamina slowly returned, yet his personality fluctuated. At times, he was irritable and impatient, and other times he could be attentive and loving. He always showed composure when it came to Annabelle and Sophia, but Catherina treaded on unsteady waters, trying not to rock his boat. She attributed his outbursts to the strain of prison, and she was giving him time to recover from the emotional upheaval.

------◆•◆------

It was at the end of one of Blackie's more unsettling days, and Catherina was mopping the floor of the store after closing. Smoking his evening cigar, he flicked the ashes carelessly as he counted the proceeds from the day.

Catherina placed an ashtray next to him. "Could you use this, please?" She was feeling bone tired, and she resented his blatant disregard.

Knocking the ashtray off the table, he defiantly tapped his ashes on the ground. "Don't ever tell me what to do, damn it!" he roared with a coldness in his voice that gave Catherina a chill.

She glowered at him as if he were a stranger and firmly took a stand. "I don't deserve to be treated like this. I'm sick of being the brunt of whatever is bothering you." She was shaking her head back and forth now. "You've got to come back to me. You've got to come to terms with your past so we can have a future. I don't care what happened before you met me, but..." Her eyes filled with tears. "I don't know who you are anymore, and I'm having a hard time remembering who you were." Dropping the mop, she left the store in a huff with her baby and her niece.

As Catherina and Sophia pushed Annabelle home in her pram, Catherina prayed that the Blackie she had known and loved would miraculously return.

———◆◆►———

Their customers' continual requests for Catherina's homemade food and the extra money it provided gave Blackie the incentive to sell the grocery store and open a restaurant on Eleventh Avenue. His temperament seemed to mellow, and their problems seemed to wash away as they scrubbed, cleaned, and refurbished their new establishment.

The sunny storefront had dangling, dome-shaped lights interspersed on panels of a tin-patterned ceiling. Tables for two could easily be joined together to accommodate larger groups. Catherina sewed floral print tablecloths, curtains, and seat covers, and the cold, brick walls warmed under the cozy atmosphere. Customers hung up their hats and coats on one of the many hooks near the entrance and often told Catherina and Blackie it was as if they were walking into the comfort of a friend's home.

———— ◆•◆ ————

One afternoon, Patsy McFadden and his associates were conducting business in the neighborhood, and he instructed his driver to pull over to the local eatery for lunch. McFadden was diligent at keeping track of former members and was well aware that Blackie and Catherina were the proprietors. The other reason for his visit, McFadden kept to himself.

———— ◆•◆ ————

When McFadden strolled into the restaurant, Catherina instantly recognized the infamous gangster and his son, Patrick, from their pictures in the newspapers. As she eyed the young, red-haired man standing by McFadden's side, there was no basis for the eerie tinge of familiarity that fluttered through Catherina. She had read that they lived on an estate in Hudson and Patrick attended a private school. She assumed he was being groomed for the day he would take over his father's empire, and he lived a life of privilege unfamiliar to Catherina. "Do you know who that is? It's Patsy McFadden," she whispered to Blackie.

He raised his eyebrows as if he had no idea and greeted the group. "Good evening," he said.

A hefty, well-dressed man stepped forward. "We need a table for five."

"We have a full house at the moment, but I can set a table in the back room," Blackie offered. "It'll just take a few minutes," he added.

The man glanced over at McFadden who gave him a slight nod. "That'd be fine," he said to Blackie.

Catherina kept her nerves under wraps and took extra care preparing the dishes the intimidating party ordered.

They sumptuously fared on every morsel, and after dinner, McFadden raved to Catherina as she cleared the table. "That was the most delicious meal I've had in a while," he said, patting the bulge of his stomach.

She felt herself blush. "Thank you. I'll be right back with your espresso."

Catherina returned with the small pot and a platter of assorted fruits and pastries. As she filled their cups, she sensed McFadden's eyes following her and it made her feel uneasy.

"I apologize for staring at you," he said, "but you bear an uncanny resemblance to my sister who recently passed away."

"I'm sorry for your loss," she said.

"It's been difficult, though somehow seeing you now is like seeing her again." An unmistakable softness fell upon his seasoned face.

From that day forward, the restaurant became a regular hangout, profiting generously from the well-heeled men.

———•••———

Blackie looked forward to the fall when he and his cronies escaped to the mountains. The hunting shack where they converged was nothing more than a ramshackle cabin, but to them, it was better than the Plaza Hotel. It was a place to let down their guard and do all the things they liked to do best—hunting, card playing, and drinking—the proof of the alcohol enhancing the unforgettable events that transpired.

During the last rowdy card game, the drunken pack heard a car screech to a halt outside the door. Nunzio, a regular at the restaurant, kicked open the screen door and shouted in a belligerent tone, "Blackie, you bastard! Keep your hands off my wife!" His nostrils flared as he swayed back and forth on his stubby legs.

Blackie snickered to himself, thinking about Eleanor. He personally seated everyone that walked into the restaurant and took pleasure in the task. He especially enjoyed flirting with the female customers, although he could tell that their male companions were not always as pleased. He had to agree that Eleanor was attractive and wondered why she had married such a homely man. He also had to admit to himself that in the days before he had met Catherina, he would not have thought twice about bedding Nunzio's wife.

"I never touched her," he said.

"I see the way you look at her," he loudly slurred, "and the way she looks at you."

"Then maybe the problem's with your wife," Blackie said, laughing out loud.

"You think…this…this is funny?"

Annoyed, Blackie threw his cards down on the table and told Nunzio, "We'll settle this outside." Shoving the enraged man out the creaking door, he said to his friends from over his shoulder, "This won't take long."

Nunzio threw the first punch, and Blackie confidently retaliated with multiple blows. "Get the hell out of here before you get permanently hurt," he warned, turning his back on the cowering man. Hearing the rustling of bushes, he instantly whirled around and saw Nunzio crouched on his knees, pointing a shotgun in his direction. Before Blackie had time to react, Nunzio fired, blowing off Blackie's right leg from his knee down. He fell through the door—blood spouting from the mutilated stump. The men sprang from the table, and while some tore the shirts off their backs and used them as tourniquets, the rest tackled the fleeing Nunzio and beat him unmercifully.

They carried Blackie's convulsing body to the car and carefully laid him on the backseat. He floated in and out of consciousness as they drove with breakneck speed to the hospital, while several men stayed behind to deal with Nunzio.

Driving his car to a cliff, they sat Nunzio's listless body behind the wheel, put the car in gear, and pushed it off the precipice, avenging Blackie's ruthless attack. The car tumbled over the rocks and landed like a boulder into the rushing waters. As they watched the coursing current drag the capsized wreck downstream, they spat three times in unison as a final farewell.

———◆●◆———

The disturbing incident was explained to hospital personnel and family as a hunting accident, and those involved conspired to take the truth to their graves. Blackie remained in the hospital for almost two months before he was sent home to convalesce. Bored and impatient, he eventually returned to work at the restaurant using a wooden prosthesis and crutch, refusing to let his injury intrude on his life. However, it was not long before he had another challenge to resolve.

Blackie was glad he was alone in the kitchen when he opened the unfamiliar envelope that arrived in the mail that chilly November day. Lillian had written that she read the article in the newspaper about his hunting accident, yet she was not as shocked by his injury as she was to find out he had taken another wife. She threatened to sue him for bigamy unless she was legally divorced and generously compensated.

Blackie was angry with Lillian, but he was furious with himself. He was foolish to believe he was free of her forever, but he knew exactly who to call to help him put an end to the marriage once and for all.

———◆•◆———

Immediately, Blackie contacted the lawyer that McFadden recommended, and it took less than a month before he had the final paperwork in his hands. He drove alone to Hudson to personally give Lillian the divorce papers and an envelope stuffed with cash. Pinning her against the wall with his crutch in the darkened hallway, he warned, "This is the first and final payment." The rancor in his voice made his point clear. He allowed that terrorizing flare in his eyes to return just long enough to remind Lillian why she should never contact him again. "Stay out of my life, you bitch." Dropping the envelope on the ground, he left.

CHAPTER 34

The many years as a cobblestone layer had inadvertently caught up with Lorenzo, and debilitating arthritis in his joints had forced him into retirement. His mind was strong, but his body was failing, and he resented the restriction. With nothing but time on his hands, he sat in his chair and often thought about his children. Vinny had a successful business, but the pride Lorenzo felt for him ran deeper than any possessions he could amass— he was smart, hardworking, and both a loving son and brother. Lorenzo knew Santo would never be like his brother, he just wished he would sober up. Catherina was a rock and reminded him the most of Victoria, especially the way she had embraced Sophia after Gabriella's death and loved the child like a daughter, even after Annabelle was born. Blackie certainly had had his share of bad luck, and Lorenzo admired the way Catherina stuck by him while he was in jail. He knew that his son-in-law respected him like a father, and he grew to love Blackie like a friend. He thought about Rosa and Brian and how well they got along. Lorenzo had always considered Brian to be a gentleman and appreciated that he was also a loving husband to Rosa and a doting father to Constance. Sophia, Annabelle, and Constance were welcomed bursts of energy that wisped through his life, and he relished every minute he spent with his granddaughters; however, his thoughts would inevitably turn to his daughters. Louisa's mental illness broke his heart, but Gabriella's tragic death made his body ache from head to toe. When he was alone, he watched the clock tick away the hours and count down the minutes as if waiting for the second when time would finally stand still.

Lorenzo's disquietude was unsettling for Vinny, and he loathed seeing him fade into the ravages of old age. Coming home one evening, he sat down on the sofa across from his father and looked at him thoughtfully. "How you doing, Papa?" he asked. "Did you and Santo have dinner?"

"Catherina brought us over some eggplant and macaroni. Santo's not home yet, and I already ate." Lorenzo tapped his pipe on the edge of the ashtray. "There's plenty in the icebox if you're hungry."

"I'll eat after I wash up, but I wanted to talk to you about something first," he said.

Lorenzo looked at him quizzically over the rim of his spectacles and rubbed his bristly beard.

"Lately, merchandise has been disappearing from the warehouse, and we need to hire a watchman. You'd be perfect for the job," Vinny told him.

"I'm too old, I'm almost sixty," he scoffed. He looked down at himself sitting in the chair. "You need somebody younger…somebody stronger."

Vinny held up a hand. "We need someone we can trust," he protested, wondering if there was one pivotal point at which a parent and child reversed rolls, or did the process occur over time like a rite of passage. "Tony and I spoke about this, and it was his idea to hire you." Handing Papa a khaki-colored shirt and pants, he said, "I expect you to be ready for work bright and early tomorrow." He noticed a flicker of enthusiasm widen the orbs of Papa's sunken eyes.

"Just until you find someone else," he conceded.

———————◆•◆———————

The next morning, Vinny awoke to find his father clean-shaven and dressed in his uniform.

"You're not official until you're wearing a badge," Vinny said when they were ready to leave.

His father stood up straighter as he pinned a shiny shield on his shirt. It was hard to tell which was glowing more, the badge or the smile on Papa's face.

"I put a chair by the entrance to the building. You'll need to make sure no one leaves with more than they should."

"I think I'll be able to handle that," he said, patting Vinny's shoulder as they walked out the door.

———————◆•◆———————

Lorenzo affably greeted the workers as they signed their time sheets and the truckers as they picked up and delivered their loads. Immediately noticing a marked improvement in his father's mood, Vinny felt satisfied he had accomplished what he had set out to do and reveled in the pleasure of having him nearby. He had lost his mother many years ago and felt compelled to spend as much time with his father, knowing any day could be his last.

———————◆•◆———————

Vinny and Tony were caught up in the ostentatious lifestyle of the younger generation and splurged on two brand new Fords for cash. The first thing Vinny thought about as he drove his black sedan off the lot was that he wanted Papa to be the first take a ride—out of respect.

Vinny parked in front of their apartment building and got out of the car. Looking up to the third-story window, he could see Papa dozing in his chair. He leaned gallantly on the side of the polished automobile with his foot poised on the footboard, his fedora tilted to one side, a cigar protruding from his lips, and his hand pumping the horn.

Lorenzo was jarred awake when he heard the incessant honking and peered out the window. His sagging face broadened with admiration, and the ends of his white handlebar mustache lifted as Vinny signaled for him to come down.

Walking out onto the front stoop, Lorenzo lifted his arms. "Where'd this come from?" he exclaimed.

"I just bought it—Tony bought one too."

Vinny swore he noticed a slight bounce to Papa's feeble gait as he descended the stairs.

"I'm so proud of you, son," he said, hugging and kissing Vinny on both cheeks.

"I wanted you to be the first to take a ride." He opened the passenger door and waved his father inside. "Where would you like to go? Your choice."

"Let's go by Saint Raphael's."

"Sure, Papa." He wondered why his father wanted to visit a church they went to every Sunday.

As they pulled up to the front of their parish, Lorenzo made the sign of the cross. "I don't need to go in," he commented when Vinny started to get out of the car. "Let's go by the Protestant church on Thirty-Eighth."

Vinny eyed him inquisitively but followed his instructions.

Lorenzo made another sign of the cross as they stopped in front of the building, and this time, Vinny did not attempt to get out.

"There's a synagogue one block over," Papa said, pointing out the window. "Let's go there next."

Vinny could no longer restrain himself and threw his hands up in the air. "I give up. What're you doing?"

"I figured I'd ask the God of several religions to bless and protect my eldest son," he said, patting him on his knee.

From the corners of his eyes, Vinny watched his father tuck a piece of garlic under the seat. "Now, what are you doing?" he asked.

Lorenzo grinned. "Just in case," he said.

On the way home, Vinny told him, "There's something else I want you to see."

He pulled up to a building on 34th Street and turned to his father. "You know I'm happy living at home, but I can't stay there forever. Tony and I've been thinking about this for a while, and we've rented an apartment here." He lifted his chin toward the building. "I want you to be the first to see this too." Vinny braced himself for his father's reaction; however, he remained quiet. Getting out, he walked around the car and opened Lorenzo's door. "It has an elevator—we're on the fifth floor."

His father looked up at him. "I guess it's time," he said. There was a distinct sadness upon his face.

Walking into the apartment, Lorenzo removed his rosary beads from his pocket and hung them on a hook on the back of the door.

Vinny smiled to himself. "It has two nice-sized bedrooms," he pointed out as he took his father for a tour. "The living room has a fireplace and two large windows."

When they entered the kitchen, Lorenzo placed a piece of garlic in a kitchen cabinet.

Vinny chuckled. "Not again."

"Just in case," he said. "Promise me that you'll show up for Sunday suppers." There was a mixture of pride and loss in his tone.

"Papa, I wouldn't miss them for the world."

———◆•◆———

Keeping their destination a surprise, Vinny planned a special outing for the family and told them to be ready Sunday after mass. Having asked them to bring only a change of clothes, he shook his head in amazement as they traipsed down the stairs, carrying pots and pans and trays of food. It was an endearing moment for Vinny, yet the ride turned into complete and total chaos as they chugged along.

Holding Constance, Rosa sat in the front seat between Vinny and Brian. In the back, Lorenzo, Santo, Catherina, and Blackie had Sophia and Annabelle straddled on their laps. There was a pyramid of people and food teetering and jostling precariously with every bump on the antiquated roads that led out to Coney Island. They were laughing and singing when, all of a sudden, they hit a hollow in the road. The pan of macaroni balanced on Sophia's legs flew into the air, scattering like raindrops.

Startled, Vinny cringed amongst the red, starchy debris. Taking a deep breath, he nonchalantly picked a piece of pasta off his lap and popped it into his mouth. "Thanks, I was getting hungry," he wisecracked, shrugging off the bedlam that had just taken place, and once again, the laughter erupted.

They arrived at Coney Island without any further incidence and with plenty of food still intact.

It was a day of firsts for everyone. It was the first time they had picnicked on the beach and waded in the ocean. It was the first time they rode a roller coaster and other thrilling rides that made their stomachs churn. It was the first time they played games of chance and won cheap prizes. It was the first time they spent the day smiling together since Gabriella had died, but it was definitely the last time Vinny allowed them to bring food into his car.

Vinny was fortunate to be living the good life, yet bad times were about to hit America hard as the 1920s were coming to an end.

CHAPTER 35

Even though lotteries were abolished in the United States, the Irish Sweepstakes was launched as a gambling scheme to raise money to build hospitals in Ireland. The prospect of making a few dollars by spending pennies on a wish was catching on with alarming interest as jobs were becoming scarce and there seemed to be no other way to make a dime. The status of the popular black market item had reached worldwide distribution, while America's unemployment rate was reaching epidemic proportions.

Tickets were transported from Ireland and inconspicuously delivered to the piers in Manhattan to be circulated throughout the city by runners for the West Side Mob. If there was illegal money to be made, it was certain McFadden's name was connected. The rackets he had his hands in were as diverse as the minions he ruled and the states he covered. While working at Vinny's warehouse, Santo also became a lackey for Joe the Baron, one of McFadden's more adept protégés. McFadden had personally instructed that Santo be given another chance, and everyone knew better than to question his intentions.

———◆●◆———

The last few years had been a succession of misfortunes and tragedy for Santo. Before he could get up, another knocked him down, until the only way he could get up was with a drink in his hand. He had been rejected by Emily and destroyed his livelihood as a jockey. Witnessing the harrowing death of his sister, Gabriella, the vision played over and over in his mind like a record skipping ruthlessly on a phonograph. His temper flared easily, and his actions were unpredictable—his personality was a mixture of alcohol and unsettledness that spilled from his runaway tongue with flagrant indiscretion.

Joe the Baron warned Santo more than once, "Straighten out, kid, and keep your mouth shut, or you'll no longer be considered part of the organization or the living. I've got my eye on you." His voice was hard and thick with consequence.

"Sure, boss," Santo grumbled, but he had difficulty heeding advice. While his brother, Vinny, had learned to respect the mentality of the mob and shake a hand instead of pointing a finger, Santo was undaunted by their strict protocol.

———◆●◆———

Santo longed for the turn of the New Year. He decided it would be the end of the setbacks that had beleaguered his world, and his luck would change. Vowing it would be the final sendoff to his wanton habits and strife, he defined New Year's Eve as his last hurrah. Tomorrow he would begin to fight off the demons wreaking havoc in his life.

He and his scant band of cronies set out to paint the town red, and they agreed to hold their celebration at the famed Cotton Club in Harlem, one of McFadden's prized acquisitions. It was the place to hear the best black jazz bands of the era and sample the finest liquor—its clientele ran the gamut from fearless mobsters to famous celebrities. As part of McFadden's organization, Santo would be granted entry into the coveted nightclub.

Santo began drinking well before he met up with his friends and was ossified by the time they arrived at the club. As they were being escorted to their seats, Santo stumbled into a table, spilling its contents onto the well-dressed patrons.

The women were appalled that their evening gowns had been splattered. "Look what you've done!" they admonished.

The men became hostile, and Santo caught a left hook to his cheek that knocked out several teeth—blood trickling from his mouth.

"Someone get this drunken bastard out of here," they roared. The band played louder to drown out the noise of the ruckus unfolding as a bevy of goons swiftly converged on Santo's group and tossed them like trash into the street.

Head cocked in mock indignation, Santo blatantly bragged in a raucous slur, "Do you know who the hell I am? I work for McFadden! You can't treat me this way."

Two broad-shouldered bouncers blocked the entrance when he obnoxiously tried to muscle his way back inside.

Repeatedly poking his finger in the chest of one, Santo blabbed, "Let me tell you…I'll make damn sure… the boss hears about this."

The men snickered at the idiocy of his barefaced arrogance and pushed him into the street, this time face down.

At a table tucked into a darkened corner, McFadden's consigliere and a party of his powerful guests had watched the scene unravel. Informed of the incident that had erupted outside, the trusted advisor to the boss signaled for a phone. Word had gotten back to McFadden before Santo was able to lift his head.

Several days later, McFadden and his entourage stopped in for lunch at Catherina and Blackie's restaurant. Respectfully taking Blackie on the side, McFadden relayed the unfortunate circumstance. "Your brother-in-law has become an intolerable burden to the organization," he said. "In deference to our friendship, I'm forewarning you that I've no other choice but to permanently remedy the situation."

Blackie knew exactly what he had in mind. "Isn't there another way to handle this? Please, let me try to talk to him," he pleaded.

"You don't know the half of it what he's done, and you don't want to." McFadden emphatically pointed his finger in the air. "I've given him one too many chances already."

All the color in Blackie's face drained down to his toes as he comprehended the inevitable. Nothing he could say would change the firm and ruthless mind of Patsy McFadden. When trust was compromised, there was no room for sentiment. It was as simple as that.

Blackie had seen a lot of himself in Santo. Recounting his own mistakes, he had repeatedly tried to steer him off his destructive path, but the results were always the same. Santo would nod his head in acknowledgement; however, the minute he walked away, any advice was left at the door. Santo had stubbornly decided to move in his own direction; consequently, at the age of twenty, he was never seen or heard from again. Blackie knew it was wiser to keep the atrocious truth to himself—McFadden had ordered his henchmen to inter his brother-in-law at the bottom of the East River.

———————◆•◆———————

At first his family thought Santo had gone on another bender. In the past, there had been long periods of time when Santo did not call or come home, and when he did, it typically was with his hand out. Lorenzo despised that his son's road to destruction was paved by addiction, and over the years, he painfully watched as Santo was lured deeper by the demons of dependency.

When Santo had been missing for several weeks, the police questioned neighbors, coworkers, employees, and patrons at his local hangouts, but there were no clues to be found. By now, Lorenzo had realized something was terribly wrong and thought that it was possible that maybe, this time, his son had crossed the wrong people. Knowing all too well the type of characters Santo associated with, Vinny had surmised what had happened to him, while Catherina and Rosa prayed that he was mistaken. They all loved and missed Santo, and they shared the hope that he was alive somewhere.

The weeks turned into months, and Santo's file joined a stack of unsolved cases, leaving the family in a state of unmitigated despair.

CHAPTER 36

The 1920s long boom had taken stock prices to historical peaks, and people kept buying on margin, further inflating their value. Stocks could be purchased for a minimal down payment and the balance financed by brokers' loans. Toward the end of the decade, the market started to slump. Overextended investors sold stocks at distressed prices to pay back outstanding loans, causing a selloff that snowballed out of control. Banks unsuccessfully tried to collect on the loans made to stock market investors whose holdings were now worth little or nothing. Word spread, and depositors rushed to withdraw their savings, and banks began failing by the hundreds—the Depression hit with a momentum that knocked millions into the depths of poverty and oppression.

------◆•◆------

Sarah's father was mortgaged to the hilt, and he had everything in the stock market, buying more and more on margin. When the market crashed and the banking system collapsed, he lost his job and everything he owned. Losing his summer home on Long Island and having to sell his valuable possessions, they moved into a two-bedroom apartment in Manhattan far from the affluent community where they had once belonged. It was all too much for him to handle. Theodore Ashton's suicide was reported on the front page of the newspaper Vinny was reading.

Vinny was horrified. Someone who had so much had now thrown his life away, leaving his family alone and penniless. He pondered the scenario, feeling blessed that he had been spared such overwhelming financial misfortune, but he found it hard to accept the finality of Mr. Ashton's decision.

───────◆•◆───────

Vinny wanted to pay his respects. He wanted to see Sarah again. When he arrived at the funeral parlor, he had expected a large crowd, but it was surprisingly empty. The adage,"When times are good, everyone wants to be your friend, and when times are bad, everyone runs"came to his mind. He spotted Sarah courteously listening to an elderly couple. Her arms were crossed below her chest as if attempting to stifle her anguish, although the look on her face exposed her broken heart.

Handing his overcoat and fedora to an undertaker, Vinny walked up to Sarah and waited his turn. Her sorrowful expression and red, puffy eyes did not mask her exceptional beauty as she returned a faint smile to Vinny's sympathetic nod.

Vinny kissed her on both cheeks. "I'm sorry for your loss," he sincerely said, pulling her into a warm embrace. Her body felt fragile in his arms as he breathed in the flowery scent of her hair and fought the desire to keep her close.

"Thank you for coming," she said through her tears. "How are you? It's been ages."

"Too long," he said, meaning it. "I'm fine."

"How did you hear about my father?" Her tone was numb.

"I read about it in the paper."

"It's so humiliating." She wiped her face with her fingers and tucked her smooth, shoulder-length hair behind her ears. "I still can't believe what he did. I don't know how I'll ever get over it," she said, shaking her head slightly. Her southern drawl was barely audible, obviously dulled from the years of living in the north.

"If there's anything I can do." He took a box of matches out of his pocket and scribbled down his phone number. "Please, call me anytime," he offered. "I mean it." Kissing her lightly on the cheek, he felt the softness of her skin against his lips and reluctantly left.

———◆◆———

As the depression unfolded, men deserted their families to avoid watching hunger bloat the bellies of their offspring and malnutrition muddle their minds. Food stamps were instituted by the government to help women and children who were left abandoned. Gratefully accepting the assistance, they scrimped by on the barest of essentials and squirreled away the remainder, worrying it would only get worse.

During these hard times, many spent their last pennies on alcohol, trying to forget their problems and the ones that beset the country. A staggering amount of people were forgoing basic needs to drink away their troubles; therefore, bootlegged liquor was the most demanded commodity. The preferable mode of transportation was by rail car since the probability of inspection by authorities was less likely. New York Warehouse and Trucking Company was in a prime location, and the railroad track that ran through the center of the ground floor made loading and unloading convenient and discreet. There was a labyrinth of obscure rooms in the capacious building to hide the booze until it was hauled by trucks to clandestine destinations.

The poor needed to eat, and the government stepped in as conditions approached famine. Vinny and Tony were contracted by the government to pick up food from the piers and deliver it to the many private and municipal charities that fed millions of starving people waiting on lines that wrapped around city blocks—the grumbling sounds from their hollowed stomachs rattled like engines running on their final fumes.

The loans for the trucks they bought on installment were obliterated when the bank faulted and closed its doors. Their warehouse held goods for businesses that vanished into thin air and left their merchandise behind.

Vinny and Tony were fortunate to be weathering the devastating economic downpour that had left the majorities out of work, destitute, and hungry. They managed to live in relative comfort, but they grappled with the poverty and degradation surrounding them.

———————— ◆◆◆ ————————

In the months following her father's funeral, Sarah was overwrought with loneliness. The circle of friends that were present at every party, every function, and every gala affair vanished along with her family's fortune. She wondered how she going to support herself, and how she was going to live alone. She wondered how she was going to make it in an unfamiliar world in which she never had tread. She needed a way out of her predicament and out of her gloom and spent her days and nights consumed by the thought. Convinced all she had left to offer was her femininity, she elected to use it, having one particular prospect in mind.

Vinny had been such a gentleman to come to the funeral. His manners were impeccable, and the physical attraction was still apparent. Steeling herself against her nagging conscience, she decided to use him as her scapegoat and came up with a plan.

Impulsively removing the matchbox from the desk drawer, she picked up the phone. Her long fingernail circled the dial as she rapidly spun the numbers before she could lose her nerve.

"Hello?" Vinny answered.

"Hi, Vinny, it's Sarah."

Her voice seemed to catch him off guard. "How've you been?" he questioned.

"Not so good."

"I'm sorry to hear that."

"The truth is, I need a job. I hate to ask you this…I was wondering if you knew anyone who's looking for help? I can type, take stenography, file, answer the phone…I'll do anything at this point."

"Not right now, but I'll certainly check around," he offered. "Give me a few days. Why don't we meet at Delfino's on Thursday around seven? It's on Forty-Second between Eighth and Ninth. We can discuss this further. Is that okay?"

"Yes, it'll be nice to see you again."

"Then Thursday it is."

"Vinny, I really appreciate your help," she said, smiling to herself before hanging up the phone.

———◆◆———

Lingering over a spaghetti dinner, Vinny studied Sarah's face and felt the lines of time reconnect between them. "You haven't changed a bit," he commented.

"Thanks, but the years haven't been very kind to me." She winced.

He grinned. "Not from where I'm sitting."

She averted his gaze as she picked over her pasta.

"I've always wondered why you and Julia never came back to the beach that day…" His voice trailed off.

She seemed lost in the memory, and it took her a few moments before she said, "My father was furious that we stayed out all night…he forbade us to leave the house."

"I thought it was something I did."

She looked up at him and shook her head insistently. "It wasn't that at all. I wanted to see you again."

Vinny felt all those years of doubt melt away. "That's too bad," is all he could think of to say. "By the way, how's Julia?"

"She's been married for over two years now. She moved to London with her husband when he accepted a position at an engineering firm, and I haven't seen them since. She's expecting a baby any day…that's why she wasn't at the funeral. I wish she could've been there." She sounded disheartened. "I hear from her occasionally, but with both our parents gone, I feel so alone. I miss her terribly."

Vinny had read in the paper that Theodore Ashton was a widower, but he was hesitant to ask Sarah what had happened to her mother.

She looked at him as if she were reading his mind. "My mother had a heart attack the winter after you and I met. My father took it very hard and was never the same." Her face was cloaked in sadness, and her voice was somber.

He reached over and caressed her hand.

"Why don't we change the subject?" she said, taking a deep breath and blotting her eyes with a napkin. "Do you keep in touch with Tony?"

"We're still in business together. I see him every day." He laughed. "We even live together."

"Is he serious with anyone?"

"Nah, he's having too much fun to settle down."

"What about you? Haven't you found the right girl yet?"

He raised his eyebrows. "You never know," he said. "I'd like you to come to dinner with me tomorrow…to my sister's restaurant. It's the best food in town."

"Two nights in a row, I wouldn't want you to get sick of me."

"That's impossible," he said with a smile as broad as his shoulders. "Besides, I'm waiting to hear back from someone who might have a job for you."

———◆•◆———

It was the first time Vinny had called ahead to fill Catherina in about a female companion—he wanted everything to be just right. Vinny cherished Rosa and Louisa, but as the oldest siblings, he and Catherina were especially close. They had held the family together when tragedy had struck multiple times with a vengeance. The unimaginable had claimed the lives of their mother; their brothers, Gennaro and Santo; and their sister, Gabriella; and had stripped their youngest sister, Louisa, of her dignity, leaving her incapacitated. Their bounds of grief seemed to lessen as they learned the true meaning of survival from each other.

"I'm bringing someone special with me to dinner tonight," Vinny informed Catherina when she answered the phone.

"Someone special?" she repeated.

"The girl I told you about...Sarah...her father committed suicide... it was in the papers, and they lost everything in the crash."

"Yes, that was so tragic."

"Save my favorite table by the window."

Catherina chuckled slightly.

"What's so funny?"

"You just sound so serious."

"This means a lot to me. Sarah's been through so much."

"I can only imagine."

"I told her that it was the best food in town," he continued.

"Thanks, the flattery will get you everywhere," Catherina said. "I'm looking forward to meeting her. What time?"

"Around eight."

"Ciao."

———————◆•◆———————

Catherina set the table Vinny requested, adding a vase of daisies to the ambiance.

Sitting down for a moment, she remembered that raw, rainy evening when Blackie had sauntered into Gabriella's bar and asked her if she wanted a drink. She thought how mysteriously they connected, and how miraculously they never parted. She was amazed at how much she still loved him even after all the heartache they had endured. Life had made Blackie tough, and for him, losing a leg was like losing a tooth and did not cripple his dogged spirit and wry sense of humor. He had a knack for making her laugh and keeping her wondering what mischief he would create next. Before Vinny and Sarah arrived, Catherina also remembered to caution her husband to be on his best behavior.

———— •••• ————

Walking into the kitchen, Vinny kissed Catherina on the cheek. "Blackie told us to come back here."

"This must be Sarah," she said, wiping her hands on her apron. On the phone, Vinny had made it sound as if Sarah was penniless. However, her clothes and demeanor depicted someone of wealth and class, and Catherina was taken aback. "I've heard so much about you."

Sarah glanced at Vinny with a coltish grin. "All good, I trust," she said coyly, shaking Catherina's hand.

Catherina assumed Sarah would be fragile and timid following the suicide of her father. Instead, she spoke with an air of haughtiness as her throaty voice exhaled the smoke from her filter-tipped cigarette.

"Hey, something smells great in here," Vinny said, lifting the cover and peeking into one of the pots on the stove.

"I made your favorite," Catherina said.

"I can't wait." He looked at Sarah. "You're in for a treat."

"Well, go sit down," she said, noticing her brother did not take his eyes off Sarah.

Catherina did her best to make the night perfect for Vinny. The streetlight cast a romantic glow on their candlelit table, and she could see her brother basking in the reflection of Sarah's radiance. She was pretty; that was undeniable, but Catherina hoped she was not clinging to her brother for the wrong reasons. Vinny had obviously already warmed to her wiles.

Throughout dinner, Catherina and Blackie periodically stopped by and chatted with the flirtatious couple as they brought them their food and drinks. They refrained from asking Sarah questions about her family, aware of the tragedy of her father's passing.

The few patrons that were there had trickled out by the time Catherina brought a dish of biscotti and espresso to her brother's table and sat down. Blackie joined them with a bottle of *grappa* and four petite glasses. Catherina affectionately studied her husband as he sat down—his full head of white hair, his strong jaw, his broad chest. Blackie had certainly mellowed with life, although life did not mellow his good looks. Pouring everyone a drink, Blackie lit a cigar and flashed Catherina one of his mischievous grins. She watched him suspiciously as he subtly removed the prosthesis from his leg and leaned it against his chair.

"Sarah, you don't mind if I make myself comfortable?" Blackie said.

She turned her head toward him. Out of the corner of her eye, she spotted the partial leg with a shoe attached and gasped. Flinching backward, she spilled the glass of sticky liquor, soiling her blue, velvet dress. "You've ruined my dress!" she said. She obviously did not appreciate being the brunt of Blackie's prank, and her temper erupted. "Are you some kind of lunatic, scaring me like that?"

Seemingly amused by her snooty reaction, Blackie snickered. "It's not that bad," he said with a shrug of his shoulders while handing her his napkin. "It was just a joke."

Catherina covered her face with her hands in exasperation. "Sarah, I'm so sorry. My husband has a strange sense of humor."

Sarah shot Blackie a bemused, dismissive look and threw the napkin down on the table. Emphatically, she grabbed her coat off the hook as she stalked out of the restaurant in a self-righteous snit.

Letting out a deep sigh, Vinny looked at Blackie as he stood up. "Couldn't you have gotten to know her better before pulling such a stupid stunt?" He turned to Catherina. "Thanks for the dinner. For the most part, it was a wonderful evening," he said and walked briskly out the door, following in Sarah's wake.

Catherina was not surprised by Sarah's ridiculous reaction and had secretly enjoyed seeing her get riled.

When she looked at Blackie, he recoiled as if bracing himself for her dour reaction, but instead, she raised her glass to him and leaned in for a kiss.

———————— ◆◆◆ ————————

As Sarah stomped down the street, she thought to herself that she could not have planned it any better.

Vinny called after her, "Sarah, stop. Sarah. Let me explain."

She ignored him until he outpaced her and blocked her path.

"Please, listen. I should've warned you about my crazy brother-in-law. He's really a harmless character."

"Are you kidding me? He's an idiot."

"You can't let his foolishness come between us. It was destiny that I found you again, and this time…" His voice grew deep and deliberate. "I'm not going to let you slip through my fingers."

Sarah had Vinny right where she wanted him and preyed on his vulnerability. "Why don't you take me back to your apartment for a nightcap and a more befitting apology?" she suggested.

As Vinny poured them a drink, Sarah slowly unbuttoned her dress and let it slither to the floor. She tousled her hair and edged closer to him, softly grazing his body with her silk slip. "I'm ready for my apology now," she said. The seduction was swift and effortless, and he pulled her into his arms. Her body went limp, and her insides quivered as he lifted her onto the couch.

In a sensuous whisper and in morning's early light, she told him what she thought he wanted to hear, "I feel so safe lying here in your arms." She looked up at him, and he pulled her closer. "I was thinking how happy I am at this very moment, and that I wish I never had to leave."

"You don't have to," he said, kissing her warmly.

And she never did.

———◆•◆———

It was an unusually busy day at the warehouse, and Vinny and Tony were helping unload the trucks when Tony lost his footing. Falling backward, he struck his head with a ghastly thud on the concrete floor.

Vinny turned and found him lying flat on his back, streams of wine trickling through the damaged carton. "Are you okay?" he yelled. "What the hell happened?"

"I'm fine, I'm fine. I just tripped." Rising on all fours, he swayed as he stood and fainted into Vinny's arms. His breathing was shallow and his skin was clammy.

Easing him to the floor, Vinny felt a warm, wet sensation on his hands, and when he looked down, he panicked when he saw they were covered in blood. The gash on the back of Tony's head was bleeding profusely, and Vinny bellowed, "Somebody call for an ambulance! Tony's hurt!"

———•••———

Vinny road along with Tony as he was rushed to the emergency room at Saint Vincent's hospital. His head was shaved, and while the doctor was stitching his wound, he vomited over the side of the gurney.

"What's today's date?" the doctor questioned, rubbing his fingers across the stubble on his chin.

"Thursday?" Tony was clearly confused.

"What's your name?"

"Huh?" He looked around the room searching for clues.

He shined a light into his glassy eyes. "Mr. Rubino, you have a concussion and symptoms of amnesia. We're going to keep you overnight for observation."

"That's not necessary," he balked. "I'm going home."

"And where do you live?" the doctor said cynically.

When Tony could not answer, Vinny knew his friend needed to stay.

———•••———

Tony's true love literally walked into his life when she walked into his hospital room. The girl standing before him had piercing, ebony eyes and thick, rippling hair.

"Hi, my name's Marie, and I'm your nurse this evening. I'm here to change your bandages and administer your medication," the woman announced.

She handed him a glass of water and a pill. "This will help you with the pain, but we would like you to stay awake for the next few hours so we can monitor your symptoms."

Instantly, Tony became numb to the throbbing pain in his head—his mind was fixated on the slender woman who stood amiably over him. "Do you have anything stronger than water?" he devilishly teased.

Marie chuckled. "So how did this happen?" she asked, standing over him as she skillfully redressed his wound.

"I have no idea," he said, "but one thing I'll never forget is your face."

She cleared her throat. "Apparently, your wit hasn't disappeared along with your memory. Maybe it would be wiser to save the flattery for your wife."

"I don't have a wife," he retorted. "I think *that* I would remember." His smile widened. "Would you care to fill the position?"

She looked down at him as if he were crazy.

"I'll gladly arrange for a priest to come up and perform the ceremony right now."

"Your persistence is very charming, Mr. Rubino," she said, wrapping a bandage around his head.

Suddenly remembering his name, he blurted, "Please call me Tony—why, we're almost married."

She laughed. "Maybe you should concentrate on getting better."

"I don't ever want to get better if it means leaving this hospital and never seeing you again."

The banter continued until Marie was out of the room, but over the next two days, she made up a myriad of excuses to stop in to see Tony, and he counted the minutes between her visits. They talked about anything and everything, and their exchanges were playful. She was born in America, yet coincidentally, their families emigrated from the same region of Italy, which gave them more fodder for conversation.

When Marie handed him the release form to sign, Tony adamantly said, "I won't sign this paper until you write down your phone number."

"The hospital frowns on employees fraternizing with patients."

"I think it's too late for that. We've been flirting for days."

"Flirting? I wasn't flirting, I was just doing my job," she feebly objected.

"It's your choice—your phone number or I stay." He held out the pen.

She rolled her eyes and grabbed it out of his hand. "You're impossible," she said, writing down her number.

Tony called the first night he got home and every night thereafter. He courted Marie with flowers and romance, and they were so well suited, they could finish each other's sentences.

———◆◆———

Vinny was impatient to meet the woman that kept his friend out every night and singing in the shower every morning, but it seemed Tony was hoarding this girl all to himself. Finally having had his fill of Vinny's cajoling, Tony agreed to go on a double date to celebrate their birthdays. It was something they did together every September since they were born a year and a day apart.

Meeting at the restaurant, they made their introductions and sat down.

After the white-jacketed waiter poured them all a glass of champagne from the bottle they ordered, Vinny took a dollar from his pocket and handed it across the table to Tony, who reached into his pocket and handed him a dollar in return.

"Happy Birthday," Vinny announced, lifting his glass in the air.

"You, too. I couldn't have asked for a better friend."

"To friends. *Salute!*"

They clinked glasses.

"What's this all about?" Sarah asked.

Tony grinned. "It's kind of a ritual we've had for years. Instead of giving each other a gift, we exchange a dollar. It reminds us of the first dollar we made together," he explained. "I guess it keeps us humble."

Sarah and Marie looked at one another and smiled.

"How sentimental," Marie said, kissing Tony on the cheek.

He turned toward her. "You didn't know you were dating such a sentimental guy." Pulling her head to his, he tenderly kissed her lips.

"Get a room," Vinny said.

Blushing, Marie rose from the table. "The only room I'm going to now is the ladies' room."

As soon as Marie was out of earshot, Vinny said, "This one's a keeper."

Sarah kept her voice low. "She's lovely."

"You'd be crazy to let this one go," Vinny added. "She's a looker."

Sarah elbowed Vinny. "Hey, keep your eyes where they belong."

"Yeah, she's a good girl," Tony agreed. "I'm a lucky guy."

———◆•◆———

Three short months later, Tony asked Marie to marry him. For a wedding gift, he bought his new wife a house in the suburbs of New Jersey. In the summer months, its garage became a spacious dining room where relatives and friends gathered to eat, play cards, and escape for a few hours from the congested city. The small Cape Cod surrounded by a picket fence was everything they had ever wished for. The American dream had come true for Tony and Marie and was perfected by the birth of their baby boy nine months later.

Vinny was delighted for Tony and Marie, but he also felt a twinge of envy. He was not envious in a spiteful way, yet he wanted the same. He adored children and felt an overwhelming tenderness toward his nieces, inciting a powerful paternal craving that he was unable to shake. On Sundays he looked forward to family dinners so he could spend time with the girls; however, they were a constant reminder of what was missing in his own life.

Never arriving empty-handed, he brought whatever merchandise had fallen off the back of a truck that particular week. From the street below, he could see Sophia, Annabelle, and Constance's noses pressed against the parlor window in anticipation of his arrival as though they were waiting for Santa Claus. By far, his nieces' most treasured gift from him was a Zenith radio. Gathering in the parlor in the evenings, they listened to the news of the day, the latest songs, and fantastic stories with vivid plots that would unfold daily, exposing them to the wonders and activities of the outside world.

In the early 1930s, the country was hungering for change. President Franklin D. Roosevelt's New Deal was the medicine that was curing a depressed and paralyzed nation and restoring faith in the future. In living rooms across the country, the sound of a pin dropping could be heard as millions gathered around radios to listen to their redeemer. He was the breeze that lifted the people's spirits, marketing his policies with radio's captivating style. During his fireside chats, Roosevelt had outlined his programs for reform that mended a broken nation and put food back on the tables and families back on their feet.

With the repeal of Prohibition and the positive effects of the New Deal, the nation began prospering. Newspapers fell to the wayside as people became fixated on the tabloids. They doused their headlines and covers with the mindless gossip of the rich and famous and filled the pages with stories of their glamorous lifestyles. The masses were given a glimpse of how the upper class behaved, what they were wearing, and how they spent their money, influencing the mindset and culture of a country.

As the doors of speakeasies closed, a glut of chic restaurants opened in their place. Vinny knew Sarah desperately wanted to be a part of the Café Society, and he willingly indulged her. Money was made to spend, and Vinny spent it as fast as he made it. Custom suits became staples in his wardrobe. His dignified appearance and Sarah's catlike confidence and style gained them entrance into the cocoon of high society. Beginning with elegant dinners at the best restaurants and ending up swinging to the music of the big bands, their social scene was a whirlwind of activity, bordering on the sublime. After a night on the town, they would stumble home in the wee hours of the morning, and while Vinny worked,

Sarah would recuperate just in time to do it again. She told him that she felt like a kept woman, and she seemed perfectly content in the position.

———◆◆———

The night air was filled with autumn's chill and Sarah snuggled close to Vinny in bed. "Why don't we take a vacation? I'm not looking forward to the cold weather," she grumbled. "How would you feel about going someplace warm? You could certainly use a rest."

Vinny looked at her intrigued. "What did you have in mind?"

"Well, I'd love to go to Miami Beach. It's the talk of the town," she chortled, tightening her arms around him.

"I'm not sure I can get away. We're really busy with the holidays coming, and Tony's been preoccupied with his new baby."

She rolled on top of him and kissed him hard. "I'd do anything to go," she said temptingly.

He raised his eyebrows. "Anything?"

Sarah was extremely adept at getting Vinny to do what she wanted.

Consequently, he made the arrangements before the week's end.

———◆◆———

Vinny gave Sarah a sizeable sum to spend on new outfits, and she effortlessly spent every penny. She fastidiously packed her new wardrobe in trunks, which were delivered to their stateroom before they arrived.

The spacious quarters were a far cry from the steerage compartments Vinny vaguely remembered. The elegant ocean liner that sailed away from the New York harbor exuded luxury and class. Vinny and Sarah drank cocktails on lounge chairs by the pools starting at noon, feasted in the marbled dining rooms, and danced till dawn in the massive ballroom festooned with gilded fountains.

Vinny thought he had seen it all, but when they disembarked in Miami, it embodied decadence and extravagance and was the epitome of modern-day America. The tropical art deco resort area had hotels and restaurants that catered to celebrities, and Vinny was immediately caught up in the excitement and the festivities. At the casinos, he was itching to spend the huge wad of cash that was burning a hole in his pocket as skimpily clad cocktail waitresses served complementary imported whiskey and Cuban cigars as part of the game. Standing at his side, Sarah rooted him on as he played poker and craps where a single ante climbed higher than a round trip fare. For a fleeting moment, Vinny thought he was in his element, but the stakes were too high, and he lost more than he should have. On the streets of Hell's Kitchen, he had witnessed firsthand what losing more than one had could do to a man, and he left Miami a little wiser and ready to settle down.

———◆●◆———

As the ocean liner cruised down the Hudson River toward the pier, Vinny was filled with emotion as he remembered gazing upon the city for the first time as a young boy almost thirty years ago. He thought about how much of his life had passed and how far he had come. He turned to Sarah and looked at her contemplatively. Taking her hands in his, he drew them to his lips and kissed them tenderly.

"What's wrong?" she asked.

"Maybe you should be asking me what's right."

"What are you talking about?"

"I realize how much I love you and want you to be a permanent part of my life. I want you to be my wife. I want us to be together forever."

"We are together," she said.

"Sarah, I want to start a family with you."

"I never wanted to have children," she said insistently, "and I still don't. Marriage isn't important to me."

"I think you'd make a wonderful mother."

She shook her head in disagreement. "I see how much you love your nieces and how much you adore Tony's little boy. He's lucky to have you as his godfather. I probably should have told you this before we got this far, but when my parents died, that's when I knew I never wanted to have children of my own. I'd never want them to suffer that kind of pain...that loss. I'm being honest with you. It was a decision I made a long time ago, and I've never looked back."

"Maybe in time your feelings will change, and maybe they won't, but if there's a choice between you and a child, then I choose you. I want to marry you, no matter what."

She looked at him skeptically. "You mean that... really?"

He brushed the back his hand down the side of her face and gave her a soulful look. "Really."

Falling into his arms, she said, "Of course, I'll marry you."

CHAPTER 37

It was a Sunday morning and Catherina was up early to make breakfast and get the children ready for church. She dreaded waking the girls, thinking about the ensuing dramatics. How could she coax them this time when she knew the twisted climax of their day would be their monthly excursion to the mental hospital and then to the cemetery?

As the girls deliberately dawdled over breakfast with the intention of missing mass, Annabelle whined her dispassion, "Why do we have to go to the hospital to visit Aunt Louisa? That place scares me. She doesn't even know who we are."

"And spending the rest of our Sunday with the dead," Sophia grimaced.

Annabelle was the most outspoken. "Family outings are supposed to be fun. Why are you torturing us?" Her tears appeared just at the right moment to top off her performance, and Sophia's somber face would make any mother wince at their melancholy.

Catherina would ultimately become frustrated with the uncooperative girls.

Her youngest sister's descent into oblivion preyed on her mind every day, and she hoped their presence somehow brought comfort to Louisa. Their family had been plagued with many deaths, and going to the cemetery gave Catherina solace and the connection she needed. Vinny was her saving grace. He would always find a way to make light of their draining visits when he arrived, and the girls loved being with their favorite uncle. "Let's get you girls dressed before Uncle Vinny comes. Maybe he'll bring a surprise for you," she said.

Lorenzo seemed especially tired the night before, and Catherina let her father sleep later than usual on this overcast morning. She knew age was creeping up on him with unstoppable cruelty, and she was glad she had insisted that he move in with them.

Glancing at the clock above the sink, Blackie suggested, "Catherina, you should wake your father. He wouldn't want to miss mass."

She knocked lightly on Lorenzo's door and let herself in. As she approached his bedside, there was an eerie stillness in the air. With his eyes open and a contented look upon his face, his head was tilted toward the picture of Victoria on the nightstand. Catherina lightly nudged him, but his cool, lifeless body did not respond.

She clasped her hand over her mouth to muffle the sob that escaped from her heart. Hesitantly, she sat down beside him and gently lowered his lids. She gazed upon the father she treasured—a man who had given so much of himself to his family. His passing would leave a tremendous void in her life. To Catherina, he was not just her stepfather; he was truly her Papa.

"What's taking so long?" Blackie asked as he hobbled into the room.

She turned her head to look at him, but her tears blurred her vision.

"Catherina, I'm so sorry," he whispered, coming closer. "He was the best." He softly kissed her on the head and squeezed her shoulder in support. "Why don't I take the girls to mass? They don't need to see their grandfather being carried away."

She nodded appreciatively. "I'd like to be alone with him."

When Blackie left, Catherina thought of her biological father for the first time in many years. After her mother had died and Catherina read her journal, she wondered how different their lives would have been if Victoria had stayed in Italy with Salvatore. Catherina barely remembered him and felt nothing for him, no innate attachment, just a consummate sadness for what her mother had endured. She was grateful Victoria had met Lorenzo and felt blessed they grew up with him as their father. "Thank you for loving my mother," she whispered. "Thank you for loving us."

When Vinny arrived, he immediately phoned Rosa and then the parish priest, sharing the sorrow between his tears.

Catherina looked up as Rosa walked into the bedroom.

"I knew this was coming." Rosa wept as tears streamed from her eyes.

"I think we all did," Catherina agreed, grabbing her hand.

Brian, holding Constance in his arms, followed behind. "I'm sorry," he said to everyone. "He was such a good man."

"I think he went peacefully," Catherina said solemnly. They grieved over Lorenzo's body, reminiscing and expressing their farewells until Father Lombardo arrived. In preparation for his soul to enter heaven, the priest anointed his forehead while reciting poignant words from the Bible. The undertakers placed a cloth over Lorenzo's stiff body, hoisted him onto a canvas stretcher, and carried him away. Catherina and Rosa nestled closer into their brother's broad embrace to shield themselves from the disturbing sight. In the midst of the gloom, Constance began to cry.

Rosa looked over at her child. "I wish Constance had the chance to get to know her grandfather."

"He was never the same after Mama's death," Vinny reflected.

Catherina looked at him pensively. "Lately he's been calling me Victoria," she told him. "The years apart did not dull his love for her. It almost seemed as if her memory was overwhelming his aging mind."

"It could've been a sign," Rosa rationalized. Brian handed her a tissue, and she blew her nose. "Maybe she was calling him...maybe now they're together," she said.

Somehow the thought made Catherina feel better.

CHAPTER 38

During Lorenzo's funeral, Sarah stood by Vinny's side, but she seemed detached from the grief. She had not shed a tear for Lorenzo or for Vinny, and he was disappointed to think she could be so unaffected. His father's death was making him feel contemplative and concerned. The stunning realization of the brevity of life consumed him with an unfulfilled urgency. Maybe it was selfish, but the love of a child was something he wanted to experience. *Who would be standing at my deathbed if I don't have children? Who would miss me when I'm gone?* He had secretly hoped marriage would have softened Sarah's resolve, and he could convince her to have a child; however, she was unyielding. Now he was left with a nagging void in his life that he was finding harder to disregard.

———◆•◆———

It was their second anniversary. The dinner reservation had been arranged at Sarah's favorite restaurant, and Vinny headed to Macy's after work to purchase a suitable gift. When he walked into the store, he headed straight for the jewelry department, but instead of buying a necklace that he had in mind for Sarah, he impulsively purchased a silver pocket watch for himself. Immediately taking it out of the box, he cupped it in his hand, appreciating its significance more than its beauty. He slipped the memory into his pocket, finally fulfilling a childhood promise he had made to himself.

Department stores employed models to walk the floors wearing the latest fashions. When Vinny spotted a girl in a floor-length fur coat, he knew it would be the ideal present for Sarah, but he wanted to see other styles.

The perky model led him to the collection of coats where she tried on all of his selections. As she enveloped her body in the luxurious furs, she sashayed and swirled, performing a show in front of her captive audience. There was only one problem—the coats were not the object of Vinny's attention. The woman that paraded before him had poise and grace and innocent charm. Her creamy white complexion was merely the backdrop to eyes that glistened like prisms. She was enchanting, and he was enamored.

"Is there one in particular you prefer, sir?" she asked.

"I'll take that one," Vinny decided, pointing to the red fox. "It's for my wife. Today's our anniversary."

"That's the first one I was wearing. You could've saved yourself a lot of time." She giggled.

"What's your name?" he asked, following her to the register.

"Ava," she said, looking back over her shoulder, "Ava Meyer."

"Well, Miss Meyer, it wasn't just the coats I was admiring. It is Miss, isn't it?"

"Yes," she said. She smiled at him on the edge of uneasiness and turned back around.

Placing the coat in a garment bag, she sighed. "This is one of my favorites. Your wife is a very lucky woman."

Vinny almost forgot for whom he was buying the fur, and when he reluctantly left the counter, he did it empty handed.

"You forgot your coat," Ava called out, holding it outstretched in her delicate arms.

The first thought that came to Vinny was to tell her to keep it. Suddenly, he was aware that his heart was beating.

"Thank you," he said and left the store, although he did not go home. Instead, he stopped at Pete's Bar for a drink. As he puffed on a cigar, his head was telling him that he should go home to Sarah, but something indisputable was leading him in a different direction. Blurring the lines of logic with liquor, he was on his third drink when he glanced at his watch and panic replaced his pensiveness.

Vinny jumped up and quickly paid his tab, wondering how he was going to come up with a plausible explanation for missing their dinner reservation. Outside, he decided to walk home, undaunted by the chilling rain. By the time he reached his apartment, he had devised a feasible excuse. The expensive fur coat spared under the garment bag was his peace offering.

As he opened the door to their apartment, he dodged the vase of flowers he had sent to Sarah earlier that day.

"We missed our dinner reservation! Where've you been?" Her voice was filled with fury, and her eyes were wide with rage. "I've been dressed for hours."

Vinny instantly noticed that she looked stunning in the strapless satin dress that outlined her flawless figure.

"Where the hell were you...not even a damn phone call? I tried calling the warehouse, but no one answered—I thought you were dead!" Now she was throwing the pillows from the sofa in his direction.

Vinny knew Sarah would be angry; however, he did not expect to find her in such an exasperated state. Holding up his arm to block his face, he bleated, "I'm sorry."

"Sorry isn't good enough!" she screamed and proceeded to barrage him with a string of profanities.

Sarah was the most educated, sophisticated, and polished woman Vinny had ever known and just some of the qualities that made her unique. Yet he had grown used to her dramatics when she was agitated—a side she reserved exclusively for him. Even for Sarah, this tantrum seemed extreme; nonetheless, Vinny let her continue until her verbal tirade played out.

When he tried to embrace her, she pushed him away, propelling him against the wall. "I know it's our anniversary, but there was an emergency at the warehouse. Sit down and listen to me for a minute." His tone was serious, and she dropped back in the depths of a chair, eyeing him sanctimoniously.

The lies continued to tumble from his mouth. "A main pipe burst and flooded the basement, damaging merchandise. I was caught up in the chaos of salvaging goods and didn't have a second to call." His soggy state was a testimony to his story.

"You really expect me to believe that?"

"I'd never miss our anniversary or any night I could spend with you. Really it was a mess—still is—but all I thought about was you."

Her face somewhat softened, and her shoulders relaxed.

"Happy anniversary," he said, handing her the coat.

Removing the fur from the bag, she slipped into its luxury, and all was forgiven.

Time seemed to stand still, but a month had passed, and Vinny could not get Ava out of his mind. There was something genuine about her, something he had trouble labeling. He wondered why he felt this way, especially about someone he barely knew. After all, he had a woman that he loved waiting for him at home, and when he was with Sarah, he could not have asked for a more attractive and engaging companion. Obsessing over the dilemma, Vinny decided he had to see Ava again—maybe it would eliminate the mystery, the allure.

———◆•◆———

Vinny called Sarah from work, feigning a business obligation. He explained that he would be home right after dinner and promised to take her somewhere special the following night. When she said good-bye, he could picture her pouting on the other end of the line.

Taking a chance that Ava would be there again on a Thursday, Vinny gravitated back to Macy's before it closed, and waited for her to emerge.

"Hello," she said, looking surprised to see him. "Did your wife like the coat?"

"My anniversary didn't go as I planned. I hope tonight goes better."

She seemed confused, obviously unaware where this was going.

"Would you join me for a drink?" he asked. "My name's Vinny."

"Hmm, I don't think your wife would approve," she said, frowning.

"It's awfully cold out. Just one drink to warm up," he said, trying to sound casual. "This is a perfectly harmless invitation. I was passing by and saw you come out. I'd like to thank you for being so patient with me. Pete's

Bar is right across the street." He tilted his head in its direction.

She rubbed her hands together. "I guess one drink couldn't hurt."

<hr />

Watching Ava from behind as they made their way to a table, Vinny noticed that she had a slight wiggle when she walked. When she removed the scarf from her head, he also noticed the waves of her auburn hair glistened like silk under the dim of the light.

A waitress came over when they sat down. Vinny ordered a dry martini, and Ava ordered a rum and coke.

As Ava took off her gloves and shimmied out of her coat, Vinny moved the small vase of red carnations to the edge of the table to get an unobstructed view. He smiled when she looked up and met his gaze.

"You know where I work. What do you do?" she asked.

He told her about his warehouse, and after the waitress had returned with their drinks, he continued to tell her about how he and Tony became friends.

"It's amazing that you've known him since childhood," she commented when he had finished. "And imagine, you met on the ship coming over."

"Where you born in America?" Vinny questioned.

"Well, my parents came from Germany, though my sister and I were born here. My father taught Morse code and invested every spare penny he made in the stock market...he lost everything. Now, his aging mind slips in and out of sensibility, and he's no longer capable of much. My mother lost her sight ten years ago from diabetes. I live with them." She took a sip of her drink.

"Are you sure you want me to continue?" she asked. A slight smile played across her lips.

"Of course," he prompted.

"What else would you like to know?"

"Tell me about your sister."

"Iris...she's two years older than me and away at college on a scholarship." Ava said.

"Do you plan to go to college too?"

"No, I work at Macy's and take care of my parents. Iris helps when she comes home, and my father's sister, Rena, lives down the block. She comes by every day to cook for us. She's this short, skinny woman, but she comes in like a storm and takes over, making meals and a mess in the process. She leaves a trail of cigarette ashes wherever she goes." Ava chuckled. "She can be a little grumpy at times. I think she invents things to complain about...it's quite comical. She's a handful, but I don't know what I would do without my aunt. She definitely breaks up their day."

"That's some responsibility."

"Modeling pays the bills, but sometimes I feel like I'm eighteen going on eighty."

Almost two decades stood between them; however, their difference in age seemed immaterial, and Vinny found himself wanting to know everything about this hauntingly beautiful woman. "How do you do it?" he asked.

"Thank goodness for Rodney. I've known him since childhood, and we've been dating for several years. He's the only bright spot in my life right now. On the days when I want the world to end, he gives me a reason to live."

"Ava, you're an attractive, intelligent woman and have everything to live for." He was having trouble believing what she had just implied. "Why, you're absolutely gorgeous."

She looked at him appreciatively. "I'm sorry I sound so glum. I know everyone has their crosses to bear."

"That's for sure," he agreed, thinking that Ava carried more than her share.

The time slipped by effortlessly. Vinny reluctantly paid the tab and helped Ava on with her coat. Outside, they were assaulted by snow and sleet, and he quickly hailed a cab. Opening the door, he waved her inside. "Thank you for your company. I thoroughly enjoyed myself." Handing the driver more than enough fare, he said, "Take the lady wherever she'd like to go."

When he closed the door, he stared at her through the frosted window. He stood anchored on the sidewalk with his hands thrust deep in the pockets of his overcoat. Snowflakes accumulated on the rim of his hat, while his thoughts teemed with infatuation. He had asked Ava for a drink to get her out of his head, but she seemed to have seeped her way into his heart. As the cab slowly pulled away, he wanted to stop the car, he wanted to scoop her into his arms, he wanted to never let her go, but all he could feel was the distance between them grow farther.

———◆•◆———

Seeing Ava again was a dreadful mistake, and Vinny had to force himself to stay away. Her image kept popping into his head ever since he had met her, rendering him distracted. He fought the desire to see her again with sound reasoning but subsequently lost the battle. Three days later, he went to Macy's around noon and found her at the register.

He waited until the customers had cleared and walked over to the counter. "Hello, Ava."

———◆•◆———

Vinny was the last person Ava had expected to see, but the only person she thought about. His honey-colored hair reflected the hues in his hazel eyes, and his broad grin revealed unforgettable dimples. "Well, hello. How are you?" she asked.

"I miss you," is all he said.

"Please don't, Vinny. You're married."

"I know." He sounded serious. "Is it possible you could just join me for lunch?"

That indescribable feeling that churned in Ava's stomach when she was with him was back. If his circumstances were different, she would have gone with him in an instant, but she knew the risk of spending time with him. "You're making this very difficult for me," she said. "I like you, you're a nice guy, but you have to stop coming here."

"Look at it this way. We're just two people who enjoy each other's company." He shrugged his shoulders. "We're both in relationships. What harm could it do?"

She studied him carefully, and several beats of silence cast a spell between them. She glanced down at her watch, noting the time of her surrender. "I can take my lunch in ten minutes," she conceded, having a feeling her life would never be the same again.

———◆•◆———

Their luncheon dates progressed from once a week to three times a week. Ava found herself repeatedly glancing at her watch in the mornings, willing it to reach noon. In the beginning, she had deluded herself into believing it was an innocent friendship, but with every meal, she became more and more engrossed. She knew Vinny was unavailable and chose to disregard the obstacle, and now her heart was the obstacle that kept her from changing her mind. Soon their lunches had nothing to do with food. Instead of reserving a table at a restaurant, Vinny was reserving a room at a hotel.

———◆•◆———

On spontaneous whims, Vinny whisked Ava out of the confines of the cluttered city, surprising her with romantic interludes. To celebrate her December birthday, he spirited her away to a winter wonderland for an afternoon of stolen moments.

When they arrived at the lake, he told her, "Don't get out of the car until I call you."

She watched him through the windows as he walked around the back of the car. Flakes of snow softly floated down around him as if in slow motion. When he opened the trunk, the hood obscured her view, but she could hear him rummaging around.

"Okay, you can come out now," he said, sounding downright giddy.

Ava shook her head and smiled at the sight of his flashy raccoon hat and devilish grin. From behind his coat, he pulled out a matching hat and two pairs of shiny, new ice skates.

"You don't expect me to put on that silly hat," she laughingly protested.

"I guarantee you won't catch a cold in this one," he said.

He led her to a fallen tree, and she sat down on the trunk. Surrounding branches crystallized in ice shimmered above him. He took off her wool beret and replaced it with the one he brought.

"Do I look as ridiculous as you?" she asked.

He eyed her from head to toe. "You're gorgeous, no matter what you wear."

She giggled as she struggled to slip her foot into the arch of the stiff boot. Feeling the sensation of pebbles tickling her toes, she turned the skate upside down, and a pearl bracelet slipped out onto the crust of the frozen snow.

Vinny picked it up, and it dangled from his fingertips. "This is for you," he said.

"I can't accept such a generous gift," she insisted.

"*A caval donato non si guarda in bocca.*"

"What does that mean?" she asked.

"My mother always said, 'Don't look a gift horse in the mouth.'"

Ava fell into his arms, and when he kissed her, she felt like the luckiest girl in the world.

Lovingly fastening the bracelet to her wrist and the skates to her feet, Vinny escorted Ava onto the ice. He orchestrated her around the frozen arena, slipping and sliding with the whirl of the wind whipping at their backs, nudging them closer. By afternoon's end, they were blissfully gliding in a world they had created unto themselves.

———◆•◆———

Two months later Ava realized she was pregnant and panic replaced her bliss. The crushing reality pinned her to a stonewall, gripping her with the inevitable consequence of her imprudent behavior. Hounded by the psychological humiliation, she made a disturbing decision—one she would never share with another human soul.

Morosely, she dragged herself up the stairs to the discreet apartment in the back alley and rang the bell. She was almost relieved when no one answered and forced herself to press the button again. A nurse wearing a blood-splattered apron opened the door and looked knowingly at her. "There's a sign-in sheet on the table. Wait here, and we'll be with you momentarily," she said brusquely, before disappearing into a room off of the small hallway.

Ava scribbled a fictitious name and sat down in a chair in what appeared to be a parlor. The curtains were drawn, and it was dimly lit, but she could see that the furniture was worn and the walls needed painting. She thought it smelled like death—musty and raw—or was it just her imagination? It made her feel dizzy and faint. Hesitantly awaiting her turn, erratic thoughts pounded her head. *How can I go through with the procedure? How would I be able to raise a child and take care of my parents? How could I destroy the child of the man I love?* The strain was fracturing her resolve, and when she heard the high-pitched cries of a woman, she darted out the door in a cold sweat and burst into tears of confusion.

———◆•◆———

The next day as Ava walked to the restaurant to meet Vinny, the wind kicked up, and she wrapped her scarf over her head and buttoned her coat. She was glad she wore her long sleeve turtleneck sweater, but she wished she had chosen her brown flats instead of the heels. With every step, she became more convinced that she was making the right decision. She knew Vinny's religion and vows to Sarah were beliefs he could not overlook— he had been honest with her from the start. She berated herself again. *I should've said no to him right from the beginning. I let him sweep me off my feet. I was weak and stupid. Did I ever seriously think he would leave his wife?* She spotted him waiting outside and smoking a cigar.

He leaned in to give her a kiss. "Hi, beautiful," he said.

She let herself, for the last time, taste the tobacco on his lips and fill her lungs with his musky scent. Stepping back, she looked at him for a moment and could tell he immediately sensed something was wrong.

He furrowed his brows. "You look upset," he said.

"I can't do this anymore. This affair has to end." Her mouth felt dry and pasty, and her voice was cold and final. "The only reason I came tonight was to tell you in person."

"You don't mean that." He shook his head in disbelief.

"You know how I feel about you, but Rodney promised to marry me." She lied. "With you, there would never be such a promise." She paused, swallowing to keep her throat from closing. "You look surprised. Did you think I gave up everything for you?"

He ran his hand through his hair. "You know my situation, Ava," he said.

She willed the tears pooling in her eyes to dissipate. "This shocks you? What'd you expect?" Using the strength of her conviction to camouflage the hurt, her face was expressionless, and her performance brilliant. "I can't...I mean I won't be a mistress for the rest of my life. Let's face it. We both have compromised our morals to be together. The dishonesty is tearing me apart. I've agreed to marry Rodney," she said firmly. "Don't call me again, and don't come by the store." She watched him crumble in the wake of her words as her heart simultaneously shattered inside her chest. His eyes grew so wide, she thought she could see right through to his wounded soul, and she turned around before he saw the same. "I'm sorry," she whispered to herself as she walked away.

"Don't do this, Ava. I love you," he called out.

The sheer tenderness in his voice unnerved her, but she kept her stride, reeling at the impasse and leaving him laden with memories of a love doomed by words of promise to the wrong woman. Vinny could give Ava anything she needed, except the one thing she wanted—a husband.

———◆◆———

The only person Ava felt she could share the honest, painful details of her predicament with was her sister, Iris, when she came home for the holidays.

As soon as Iris walked through the door, she dropped her suitcase, and Ava embraced her, silently absorbing the comfort and familiarity.

"I've missed you so much," Ava said.

"I can't tell you how much I've missed you too." Iris looked around. "Where are mom and dad?"

"Sleeping...where else would they be at eleven o'clock?" she said, rolling her eyes.

"Sorry. My train was delayed because of the weather." Iris hung her pocketbook on the doorknob and took off her coat, throwing it over a chair.

"They told me to tell you that they'll see you in the morning."

Iris yawned. "Not too early I hope."

"Lately, they're up with the sun," Ava said, knowing it all too well. "Why don't you put your things in the bedroom and we'll talk? I have something to tell you."

Iris placed her suitcase and pocketbook on the floor of the bedroom they shared and plopped back on the bed. "It's so good to be home," she said, stretching out.

"You look different…older. College agrees with you," Ava said, studying her sister. "Your hair got so long."

"I thought you could trim it for me over break," she said, sitting up and gathering it back into a ponytail.

"Sure. I could use one too."

"So tell me. What's up with you? I knew something was wrong the minute I walked in. You look like you've seen a ghost."

Ava sat down next to her, unable to stop her tears from flowing. "Oh, Iris, I'm pregnant."

"What! You're joking…Rodney?" she blurted, obviously taken by surprise. "I can't believe it."

Ava shook her head. "No, it's not Rodney's."

"Whose is it then?" Iris looked dumbfounded.

"I've been seeing someone for a while…Rodney had no idea."

"Who?" Iris asked, handing her a tissue from the box on the nightstand.

She wiped her face. "His name's Vinny…we met at the store."

"Why didn't you ever tell me about him?"

"Well, there's a problem."

"Problem?" Iris repeated. "What kind of problem?"

"It's sort of complicated…he's married. I knew it from the beginning."

Iris threw her hands in the air. "You were sleeping with a married man! What were you thinking, Ava?"

Defending herself, she said, "It wasn't like that. It started out as a friendship, but we fell in love...and somehow it got out of hand."

"Is he leaving his wife?"

"No," she said flatly. "I know it may seem crazy, but he's Catholic, and divorce is not an option."

"What!" Iris shouted, "and sleeping with another woman is acceptable? You've got to be kidding."

"Keep your voice down," Ava said, glancing in the direction of their parents' bedroom.

Iris took a deep breath and lowered her tone. "Does he expect you to raise this child alone?"

"I didn't tell him that I was pregnant. I told him that I was going to marry Rodney."

"Are you?"

"He asked me, and I thought about it, but I had to turn him down. He sensed the growing distance between us, and I think he proposed out of desperation. Rodney's my best friend, but I don't love him *that* way. I never even slept with him," she admitted.

Iris stood up and took a pack of cigarettes and matches out of her pocketbook. Lighting one, she took a deep drag and exhaled slowly. "Let me get this straight," she said, pacing back and forth. "You lied to your best friend *and* the father of your child. This is so unlike you—it's insane. You owe Rodney the truth, and you have to tell Vinny that it's his baby."

"I can't. I don't want this child to be the reason for breaking up his marriage. I don't want to force him to leave his wife, and it would crush Rodney to know I slept with another man." She closed her eyes and shook her head. "I know I won't be able to keep it from him for too long."

"How do you think you're going to do this on your own? It seems so unfair. Vinny should help you, or is money a problem?"

"No, he owns a warehouse on Twenty-Seventh Street down by the pier and makes a good living. I told you, I don't want him to know."

Iris stared at her sister blankly. "What are you going to do?"

She smoothed her hand over her stomach. "I have no idea."

———◆•◆———

Iris pondered the unfairness of it all and risked losing her sister's trust when she stormed into Vinny's warehouse the next day. Approaching the first person she spotted, she abruptly asked, "Does Vinny work here?"

The young, blonde-headed man eyed her suspiciously. "Is there anything I can help you with?"

"Are you Vinny?"

"No, I'm Tim."

"This is a private matter," she said. "I need to talk to Vinny."

He lifted his chin in the direction of the room behind her. "He's in the office," he said.

Opening the door, Iris glared at the person sitting behind the desk. "Are you Vinny?"

"Yes...and you are?"

She could see how her sister found him attractive, but she had pictured someone younger. "Iris, Ava's sister," she said.

"Is she all right?" he asked, obviously concerned.

Iris courageously confronted him with the simple truth. "Ava's pregnant with your child."

"That can't be," he said incredulously. "Isn't she marrying Rodney?" He looked confused.

"No, she's in love with you." She watched his face soften and the edges of his mouth turn up. "She couldn't handle the guilt of breaking up your marriage, and she's planning to raise the baby alone." She pointed her finger in his direction. "It's your child, too, and you should help support it," she said, bracing herself for an altercation.

"I can't believe we're having a baby," he marveled.

Catching Iris off guard, Vinny jumped to his feet and kissed her with a loud smack on the cheek. He vanished out the door before she could finish her lecture.

———◆◆◆———

Vinny hopped into his car and raced through the streets en route to Macy's, feeling both ecstatic and overwhelmed. He was going to be a father, and he was hoping Ava would give him a second chance. Wanting to savor the present, he pushed thoughts of Sarah aside. He parked in front of the 35th Street entrance and bolted through the door, scanning the floor for Ava. Composing himself, he nonchalantly walked toward her and smugly remarked, "That's a beautiful coat you're wearing. I'd like to see some more styles."

"I'll gladly get you another salesgirl," she said. She turned to walk away.

"I guess I could inform your boss that you're being uncooperative," he threatened.

Inside, Ava was seething, and she closed her eyes for a moment to keep from screaming. Rankled with indignation, she led him to the racks of coats where he sat down to watch her try on his selections.

"Why don't you show me your favorite? It might hasten the sale," he suggested.

As Ava put on a black sable coat, Vinny took out a cigar and struck a match on the bottom of his shoe, lighting its broad tip.

Irritated, she looked at him. "There's no smoking in the store," she said curtly.

"It's customary for a man who is about to be a father to have a cigar."

I can't believe he's buying another fur for his pregnant wife. Trying to control her fury and the bile rising in her throat, Ava stoically ignored his comment. "Should I continue or will the one I'm wearing suffice?" she impatiently asked.

Standing up, Vinny slowly walked around her while examining the coat. "It's certainly the perfect fit for the mother of my child and the woman who's made me the happiest man in the world," he said.

Ava tore the fur off her back and headed for the register. He was being offensively bold, and she wanted him to leave at once. She kept her head down to conceal the tears welling in her eyes as she placed it in a garment bag. She had to stop herself from throwing it at him. "I'm sure your wife will be thrilled," she said, handing it over. Picking up the bills he placed on the counter, she quickly turned around and walked toward the register to ring up the sale. Watching him from the corners of her eyes, she noticed he had removed the coat from its cover, and he was now walking behind the counter.

"It's for you," he whispered in her ear as he draped the fur over her shoulders. His voice was soft and genuine, and she could feel his warm breath on the back of her neck. "I know you're having our child."

Ava was stunned. "How?"

"Your sister came to see me."

"I'm going to kill her."

"No, don't be mad. She did the right thing." He caressed her slightly from behind. "Why would you keep this from me?"

Slowly, she turned around to face him, but she avoided looking directly into his eyes. "We both know the answer to that," she said.

"Ava, you know how much I love you. I'll take care of you and our baby forever. I'll buy you a house in the suburbs big enough to bring your parents and hire a nurse to help you with the baby and their care. I'll buy you anything you want."

Ava was exhausted and vulnerable, and she would have followed Vinny to the ends of the earth with just one word of tenderness, but his promises seemed endless. At that moment, it all seemed too good to be true—and it was.

He gently cupped her face in his hands and remorsefully told her the one exception that made her wince. "I can't divorce Sarah. You know that. I'll spend every spare minute with you and the baby. I swear, somehow I'll make this work."

Ava actually caught herself entertaining the preposterous arrangement Vinny was proposing. No matter how she played it in her mind, the truth was that she was miserable without him and desperately wanted him to be a part of their lives. Devoid of reason and words, she slid his hand from her face to her stomach, giving him her answer.

———•••———

Vinny was true to his word and moved Ava and her parents to the house he bought in New Jersey. Materially, he gave her everything she could ever want, but he would disappear for days, leaving on a whim and returning with gifts in lieu of explanations. She felt lonely and despondent over his absences, and at times, she wanted to throttle Vinny. He made her feel like a princess except she had to share her prince, and the jealousy was tearing her apart. *How could he expect me to go on like this?* she obsessed. But the minute he walked through the door and gave her that Cheshire cat grin, all doubt and angst would suddenly fade away. When he was around, she felt as if she was the most important person in his life.

Vinny was living in a whirlwind of this unconventional arrangement. He thought he had it all, and when Ava gave birth to Clare, it far surpassed the joy he had imagined. He treasured every moment he spent with them, wishing that there were twice as many hours in a day. On weekdays, he stayed in the city with Sarah and took her to dinner at night. On weekends, he drove out to New Jersey to the family he created there. He led a double life, flip-flopping between two different worlds, between two different women he loved for two very different reasons. He dazzled them with lavish gifts, spending generous amounts of money to make up for the time they were apart, and they voluntarily teetered on a scale, balancing the two contrasting sides of Vinny's personality—contented family man and convivial enthusiast.

Unable to find the words to explain the bizarre circumstances that had become his life, Vinny had decided to keep it from his family, but it was bothering him more and more now that Clare had entered the world. He wanted them to share in his happiness, and he wanted his child to know her roots.

Tony and Marie had never judged Vinny's lifestyle, and he appreciated their discretion, but when he asked for their opinion, he also appreciated their candor. They told him that they were fond of both Sarah and Ava, but they admitted they were bewildered by his arrangement from the start and encouraged him to be honest with his family.

Taking their advice, Vinny chose to tell Catherina first and stopped by the restaurant the next night. It was closed, but he could see her setting tables through the window, and he tapped on the door.

She looked up, and her face brightened. She walked over and unlocked the door. "What are you doing here? Do you want something to eat?" she asked, kissing him on the cheek.

"No thanks, I didn't come to eat. Do you have a few minutes to talk?"

She looked at him oddly. "Sure," she said, pointing to the table next to them. "How about here." She tucked a few strands of stray hair into her bun as she sat down. "I think I'm getting too old for this business."

Vinny smiled at her, noticing more gray streaking through her hair. "Where's Blackie?"

"He took the girls home to get them ready for bed. You just missed them."

"How are my adorable nieces?" he asked.

"Sophia's become a big help around here after school," she said. "At nine, she's already started waiting tables. She has some memory. She gets that from

Gabriella. And Annabelle…I've never seen a six-year-old so talkative, she doesn't stop. Thank God the customers find her amusing." Catherina chuckled in the throes of the thought. "Rosa and Brian had dinner plans for their anniversary on Saturday, so Constance slept over. You would think she and Annabelle were twins, they look so much alike…more so as they get older. Oh, by the way, Rosa told me to say hello when I see you and that we don't get together enough. She's right, you know. She said she tries calling you, but you're never around. She reminded me that the last time you came to Sunday supper was what…two months ago? The girls miss their Uncle Vinny. Where've you been hiding?"

"That's what I'm here about. My life's been kind of crazy lately."

"Really, do tell," she said, raising her eyebrows.

"Where do I start?" he said. "I met someone. Her name's Ava."

Catherina's jaw dropped. "What happened to you and Sarah?

"I'm still with Sarah."

"Then who's Ava?"

"Someone I met at Macy's. She's a model."

Catherina rubbed her forehead and sighed. "Start from the beginning," she said.

Vinny decided to tell her everything from the moment he had met Ava, up until the point where she gave birth to their baby girl. As he spoke, he heard how absurd it all sounded, and he watched his sister's eyes grow wider with each disheartening detail.

After he had finished, Catherina remained quiet, obviously processing what he had told her. "Why did you wait until now to tell me all this?" she finally asked. "I'm just finding out I have a niece. Does anyone else in the family know?"

Vinny shook his head. "No," he said. He realized why he had avoided telling her before—the look of disappointment that shrouded her face made his stomach turn. "I guess it's because I knew it would be hard for anyone to understand." He drew a deep breath and shifted uncomfortably in his seat. "I'm sorry. I should have told you sooner. Now that you know, what do you think?"

"What do I think? I think you're crazy."

"Besides that?" he asked.

"Sarah knows about the baby, and Ava knows about Sarah." She let out an exasperated sigh, and her eyes grew wide and raw. "I know it can't go on this way. There're too many people getting hurt." She sat silent for a moment. "Let's think about this," she said more calmly. "You love both women, but that doesn't matter anymore. This isn't about you, Vinny. You have a child who needs you. You know I've grown to care for Sarah, even love her, but she was never right for you. She seldom came to our dinners…she never seemed to have a sense of family. You've always wanted a family, and now, Ava's given you that. From what you've told me, she sounds like a wonderful mother."

He rested his chin in the palm of his hand as he spoke. "It seemed so easy in the beginning. How did I ever think I could pull it off?"

"As your sister and someone who loves you more than anything, I want you to be happy, and I think being with your child is where you belong. Don't you want her to know her family, her cousins? Isn't that how we've lived our lives? How we were raised?" She reached out and touched his hand.

"You're right…I feel like an ass. Clare shouldn't have to grow up to discover that her father cheated her out of time."

Catherina looked at him soulfully.

"I know what I have to do," he said.

———— •◆• ————

Vinny left Catherina and made a brief stop at the next bar. He ordered a scotch to soothe his nerves and another to summon his courage before he went home to face Sarah.

She was sitting at the kitchen table in her white nightgown and reading a magazine. "Oh, I'm glad you're finally home. I was just thinking about going to bed," she said, looking up. She pushed her chair back and started to rise. "Care to join me?"

Vinny had never refused that smile before. "We need to talk," he said.

Searching his eyes, she lowered herself back into the chair.

Sitting down next to her, he gently caressed her hand. "I think we both knew this day was coming," he said. He watched her smile crumble and the color drain from her face. "You know I love you, I always will, but we're not right for each other anymore."

Sarah's head dropped, and a tear dripped onto the magazine.

Vinny wanted to hold her, to make her feel better, but he knew it would not make it all right.

"I can't believe you're doing this to me," she said, sounding more hurt than surprised. She looked up at him. "I let you have everything you wanted. You have your child. I gave you your space."

"It's not enough...this isn't where I should be." He decided to be brutally honest. "Half my life is over, and I don't want to be a part-time father and husband anymore. I've been living a lie." He corrected himself.

"We've been living a lie." He let her hand slip through his as he stood up.

She was crying so hard, she fought to catch her breath. "Don't do this, not now," she heaved.

He had to be strong. "I'll make sure all my clothes are out of here by the weekend. Everything else is yours. You can stay as long as you want. The rent will be paid… whatever you need," he said solemnly and walked straight out the door.

------◆●◆------

Sarah was flabbergasted. In the beginning, it was she who had used Vinny for her own self-serving agenda, yet in the end, she had been beaten at her own game. She had consciously dismissed his infidelity and filled the void with companions of her own, but none of them came close to summoning the passion in her like Vinny. She never truly believed he would leave her; however, his candid admission finally tightened the noose that precariously hung around her neck, and its grasp was suffocating. The person who turned out to be the man of her dreams had walked out of her life and into the life he had dreamed for himself.

When Sarah succumbed to death several years later, it was not only from the cancer that had ravaged her body, but from the terminal heartbreak of losing Vinny, for she knew he had found true love in his family.

------◆●◆------

Shortly after Sarah had passed away, Vinny and Ava were married in a civil ceremony at City Hall, and by then, they were the proud parents of two beautiful daughters, Clare and Ann. Two years later when their son, James, was born, the cycle of life was complete for Vinny—the immediate affirmation the lineage would continue. He felt a profound sense of optimism that his son would grow to be a better person than he and prayed that, one day, James would look into his father's eyes and see a worthy man.

———◆•◆———

You gain strength, courage, and confidence by every experience in which you really stop to look fear in the face.

—Eleanor Roosevelt

EPILOGUE
New York, 1991

The momentous day passed swiftly, yet I had listened to a lifetime. The sun was descending toward the horizon—its rays casting an illuminated pathway upon the glistening water, the Statue of Liberty rising at the threshold of its far-reaching corridor. Her steadfast spirit contrasted the subdued mood of the weary visitors boarding the ferries back to Manhattan.

As if I had not heard enough, my father patted me down when I began to rise. "Clare, there's more to the story that I need to share," he said.

I slowly sat back, searching his eyes for a hint of what more he could possibly have left to unveil.

He started his unsettling disclosure with the visit he had received from a lawyer ten years ago. The impeccably groomed gentleman prefaced his message with the adage, "Confession is good for the soul even after the soul has been claimed."

Everyone knew that Patsy McFadden; his wife; and their son, Patrick, were killed in a devastating fire that consumed their home—it was an incident that had headlined the news. Unbeknownst to the world was the fact that Patrick was actually Gennaro Montanaro, a child too young and too ill to remember he had another family, or remember he had another name. To him, he had been born a McFadden and remained one until the day he tragically died.

McFadden's wife, Francis, had been quarantined for tuberculosis at the same sanatorium in Saranac Lake, New York, where Gennaro had been admitted. She fell desperately in love with the pleasant, curly-haired child who had an uncanny resemblance to the son she had lost to the dreaded disease. She begged her husband to use his persuasion to arrange for Gennaro's adoption if they both recovered. McFadden would have promised his sick wife the world to help foster her health, and he always made good on his promises. Money can buy silence of any degree, and Doctor Stern was persuaded to cooperate for his sister's sake. McFadden's funding and control over the facility made it possible for him to pull off the ruse and impossible for the staff not to go along with the immoral conspiracy. In return for taking away their brother, McFadden anonymously touched each of Gennaro's siblings' lives—his twisted way of atoning for the sin of severing a family.

The lawyer went on to explain the connections with shocking revelation. It had not been a coincidence that my father, Vincenzo Montanaro, an Italian immigrant from Hell's Kitchen, had been protected by McFadden's legions and financially thrived under the sway of their influence. Gabriella had been willed the bar as a bequest from Charlie, but McFadden was the actual owner and the generous benefactor. McFadden also made sure her husband, Vito, would never return. Catherina and Blackie's restaurant was frequented by McFadden's entourages, which brought them a profusion of business. Rosa had married Brian, a gifted lawyer whose heart got in the way of making money, but he prospered from the wealthy clients McFadden had steered his way. Louisa had been transferred to a private facility in Connecticut and was cared for with dignity until the day she died. The family was told the government approved Louisa's beneficent assignment since it would aid doctors in the study of her paralyzing mental condition, but McFadden had been the anonymous donor. McFadden had tried the hardest with Santo. Orchestrating the events that gave rise to his success as a jockey, which he reduced to ruins with his habitual inebriation, McFadden provided him with an unheard of second chance working under Joe the Baron.

McFadden had his hands enmeshed in the shadiest of schemes, but to him, drugs were unconscionable and a game he would not play. While selling lottery tickets, Santo crossed even the morals of a mob by using McFadden's name to purchase heroin and marijuana from suppliers in Staten Island and deal it on the streets of Manhattan. Santo was the black sheep that had darkened the family, and McFadden made sure he never saw the light of day again.

———◆◆◆———

In one afternoon, my father had handed me the wisdom of a lifetime. With the insight harvested by his years, he put the past in perspective and shared lessons of courage, love, and forgiveness that would have otherwise taken years for me to cultivate. He revealed the stories that he wanted me to pass down so the lives he spoke about would be remembered, knowing once they are forgotten, they no longer exist. Family was the most important part of his long life and gave him the foundation that forged his days on earth. He looked to the future with appreciation instead of apprehension, because "every day you're alive is a beautiful day."

I had heard many of these stories throughout the years from family members, and sometimes there were several accounts of the same incident. Now I felt overwhelmed with the truth and the details—all of their journeys so much more difficult than I could have ever fathomed, so much more arduous than my own. I knew faith had helped my father throughout his life, and especially through the sorrow of my mother's death twelve years ago. I knew I had received a gift far greater than one I could have ever conceived of giving—a gift I would carry with prudence and someday pass to my children.

Just when I thought I could process no more, the part he saved for last left me speechless. Patsy McFadden's last will and testament stipulated that if Gennaro died before he was married or had a family of his own, his inheritance would go to his surviving siblings along with an explanation. Catherina and Rosa had passed away, and my father was left alone to deal with the unspeakable truth. Considering it blood money, he had never let it soil his fingers. The bequest was so astronomical that it had taken him years to come to terms with where it had come from, and the clarity to make the decision as to where it should go. His eyes glazed over when he asked me to fulfill his dream of building a children's hospital in Hell's Kitchen that would never turn away the needy— Gennaro's memory had given him the idea. He likened his request to cleaning dirty laundry.

My father's wisdom had left an imprint on my mind, and his love had left an imprint on my heart. I was both inspired and exhausted from the journey we had just taken through his life, and I imagined he was also. The horn resolutely resounded, reminding us that it was time to go—the last ferry was about to leave. As I gently attempted to help my father up, his eyes were closed, his spirit was gone, as if each story had taken part of his soul and carried it up to heaven, leaving his legacy behind.

Made in the USA
San Bernardino, CA
12 July 2017